# LORD of LIES

## AMY SANDAS

Copyright © 2017 by Amy Sandas
Cover and internal design © 2017 by Sourcebooks, Inc.
Cover art by Gregg Gulbronson

Published by Sourcebooks Casablanca, an imprint of Sourcebooks,
Inc.
P.O. Box 4410, Naperville, Illinois 60567-4410
(630) 961-3900
Fax: (630) 961-2168
www.sourcebooks.com

Printed and bound in Canada.
MBP 10 9 8 7 6 5 4 3 2 1

*This series is dedicated to my sisters.*
*A.K.A.*
*Obviously.*

# *One*

PORTIA CHADWICK WAS TERRIFIED. AND FURIOUS.

And *terrified*.

Perched on the edge of her seat in the racing carriage, her legs braced for action, Portia clenched fistfuls of her skirts in a vain attempt to contain her panic.

Not twenty minutes ago, her sister Lily had been abducted right off the street in front of their great-aunt's house in Mayfair. They had just arrived home after an evening out when the assailant had come out of nowhere, knocking their driver to the ground with one blow and hauling Lily off her feet. Portia had scrambled from the carriage just in time to see her sister being tossed into a waiting vehicle that took off as soon as the kidnapper climbed in after her.

Portia's immediate instinct had been to chase after the carriage with her skirts lifted to her knees. If her great-aunt hadn't shouted after her with the uncharacteristically rational observation that she had no chance of outrunning a racing carriage, Portia would still be sprinting down the street.

Angelique had insisted there was another way.

And now here they were, driving at breakneck speed to the East End to search the streets for a boy wearing a red cap.

It was ludicrous! Angelique had clearly lost her mind this time.

Portia's gaze darted toward the elderly lady. Despite the perilous nature of their current plight, the Dowager Countess of Chelmsworth appeared shockingly unperturbed. "We should have contacted the authorities," Portia argued once more, fear making her combative.

"The authorities will do nothing but write up a report. Word of this will spread like a disease through the gossip mills," Angelique replied. A heavy French accent still colored her words, though she'd lived in England for decades. "We need to save your sister, and quickly, but the authorities will be more harm than help."

Portia wasn't sure she agreed, but she had accepted Angelique's lead on impulse and now had no choice but to follow it through.

She hated feeling so ineffectual, so bloody useless.

If only she had gotten out of the carriage first, then *she* would have been abducted instead of Lily. She would give anything to be in her sister's place right now. At twenty, Lily was more than a year older than Portia, but she was far too gentle and trusting to fare well in the hands of a ruthless kidnapper.

And Portia had no doubt her sister's abductor was quite ruthless. The kidnapping had to be the work of

Mason Hale, who had been sending threatening letters to their oldest sister, Emma. The same man who had accosted Lily just two nights ago, demanding repayment of a loan their father had incurred before his untimely death.

But Hale had given them until the end of tomorrow to come up with his money. Why would he kidnap one of them now? It made no sense.

Unless it was not Hale after all…

Portia's throat closed up in fierce rejection of the thought. It had to be Hale.

"How in hell is a boy in a red cap going to help us?" Portia pressed again, desperately needing assurance that they were not on a fool's errand as they raced toward a corner of London's East End where no gently bred lady should ever consider visiting.

"The boy knows how to get in touch with a man who can help us," Angelique answered. "Trust me, darling. It is our very best chance to save your sister."

Portia's stomach twisted.

"What kind of man?" she asked. "Who is he? How do you know he will help us?"

"He is known to do many things…for the proper incentive," Angelique replied evasively.

"Incentive?" Portia's anxiety spiked. "But we have little money."

"We have enough to bluff, *ma petite*. Now stop arguing." The elderly lady leaned forward to peer out the window. "We are almost there. Keep your eyes alert for the boy. Remember to look for a red cap."

Portia shivered—from fear, anxiety, and the effort it took to suppress the urgent need to take action. Her heart was wedged firmly in her throat, and her jaw ached from clenching her teeth against the desire to shout her sister's name as loudly as she could into the night on the insane hope that Lily might somehow hear her and know they were doing all they could to get her back.

She was desperate to be moving, running, talking. *Something* to produce progress. While they rolled through the narrow, twisting lanes, Lily was being taken farther away from them.

Instead of bolting out of the carriage and scouring the streets uselessly, Portia focused all of her energy on scanning the streets through the window. Streetlamps were sparse, casting deep shadows through which anonymous figures moved about. It was near midnight, and the East End was rife with activity.

Questionable activity.

The carriage slowed as they wound their way along the dark lanes. Portia saw various characters moving about in the night—men, women, and far more children than she would have expected, but not a single red cap.

And then, as they turned another corner—there!

A boy strolled casually with a chimney sweep's broom. One hand was stuffed deep in the pocket of his oversize woolen trousers, a red cap sitting jauntily on his head.

"Is that him?" Portia asked, a flash of hope making her chest tight.

Her great-aunt leaned across Portia to peer out the window. "Let us hope so." She knocked on the roof, signaling for the carriage to stop. A moment later, Charles appeared in the doorway. A heavy bruise had already formed above his temple where he had been struck by Lily's attacker.

"Go fetch that boy there," Angelique said.

"Yes, m'lady."

While the loyal servant did as requested, the ladies waited in tense silence. Several moments later, the carriage door opened again.

"Wot do you fancy pieces want?"

The boy in the red cap peered in through the open door while Charles stood stiffly behind his shoulder. The lad's young face was smeared with soot, making it hard to discern his age. But judging by his size, Portia guessed him to be about eleven or twelve. A bit old for a chimney sweep.

He stood warily scanning the interior of the carriage, expertly assessing what danger they might represent. He dismissed Angelique quickly enough, but took a few extra seconds studying Portia. When he gave her a jaunty little grin and tipped the brim of his hat, Portia realized with a touch of shock that the child was flirting with her.

Angelique leaned forward from the shadows, bringing her face near to the boy's. Her age lines looked deeper in the uncertain light, but her dark eyes were piercing and direct. If Portia hadn't known better, she would have been intimidated by the sudden intensity within her great-aunt's stare.

"We are looking for Nightshade." Angelique spoke in a dramatic whisper, though there was no one beyond Portia and the boy near enough to hear her.

The child snorted and eyed Angelique as though she was daft. Portia worried again about having followed her great-aunt's suggestion so readily. The dowager countess was generally just a harmless eccentric, but so far she had led them on a search for a boy in a red cap, and now she was asking for a poisonous herb.

"I ain't no apothecary," the boy said.

Angelique flashed a coin in the palm of her gloved hand. "You know whom I seek, boy. We haven't the time for games and subterfuge."

A shadow of respect crossed the boy's face, and he reached to take the coin, testing it between his teeth before shrugging his shoulders. "Can't take you to 'im. Not how it works. I deliver a message, an' his man'll contact you."

"No, please," Portia said, drawing the boy's eyes back to her. "We don't have time for messages." She finally had some hope her great-aunt had not led them astray, and she was not going to let the opportunity slide away. "You must take us to this man directly. Immediately."

The boy narrowed his sharp gaze and flashed another grin. "Fer another coin an' a kiss, I may change me mind."

Angelique made a sound that could have been a scoff or a chuckle or something in between. But she reached back into her purse. "Here is your coin." She waved a hand toward Portia. "Give him a kiss so we can move this along."

The coin quickly disappeared into the child's pocket before he swept his hat off his head and turned his face to Portia. Feeling more than a little silly, Portia leaned forward to briefly brush her lips across the child's cheek.

He gave a quick whoop then smashed his hat back on his head.

Turning to Charles, who still stood beside him, he said, "Head down the street a ways, then swing right after the butcher's place. Keep going till you pass the park. There'll be a row of houses that all look the same. Go to the one nearest the broken streetlamp. That's where you'll find Nightshade's man." He looked back to Portia and Angelique. "And I'd be grateful if you don't tell him it was me who sent ya. He'd have me hide fer not following the rules." The boy tossed a jaunty wink at Portia. "I like me hide."

The boy was ridiculously charming, and Portia smiled despite her anxiety. "Thank you. We do appreciate your help."

The boy tipped the brim of his cap then backed away. Charles quickly closed the carriage door, and a minute later they were off again.

Portia stared across the carriage at her great-aunt with a dose of newfound respect. "Who is Nightshade?"

The lady's expression was vague as she replied, "No one knows, *ma petite cherie*."

"What do you mean?"

"He never meets his clients face-to-face." The old lady gestured toward the window. "There is a strict process to getting in touch with the man. We are fortunate your kiss is so highly regarded," she added with a sly glance.

Portia resisted the urge to roll her eyes. *Among young boys maybe*. "Can this Nightshade be trusted?"

"He would not have gained the reputation he has if he were untrustworthy or incompetent. They say his insistence on remaining anonymous allows him to move through any environment undetected; that he is capable of infiltrating even the most elite social groups."

Portia leaned forward, captivated by the idea such a man existed. "How do you know of him?"

"Word gets around when there is someone willing to do what others cannot. Or will not." Angelique paused and looked down at the ring on her left hand. "A few years ago, I hired him to help me with a certain personal matter. If anyone can find Lily, it is Nightshade."

Portia fell silent, hoping her great-aunt was right.

After several minutes, the carriage reached the area the boy had mentioned. It was a more residential neighborhood, and both sides of the street were lined with brick row houses two stories high with narrow fronts and identical entrances. Portia peered through the window, straining to locate the broken streetlamp that would mark the correct house.

There. The moment she saw it, the carriage pulled to the side of the street. Charles must have seen it as well.

Portia took her great-aunt's arm in silence as they made their way up the walk to the dark front door. She swept her gaze in all directions, trying to pierce the night surrounding them, alert for any threat. The shadows were deep in front of the house, and no number marked the address. Two small windows bracketed the door, but no light shone from them. Portia tipped her head to look at the windows on the upper level. All was dark.

Blast. What if no one was home?

Angelique lifted the tarnished brass knocker and issued a loud, echoing announcement of their presence.

Silence followed. And then a soft noise.

The door opened unexpectedly on well-oiled hinges, revealing a petite man in his later years with a smallish head and iron-gray hair worn back in an old-fashioned queue. Despite the man's diminutive height, he somehow managed to look down at them along the length of a hawklike nose.

"Wot?"

His one word, uttered with none of the graces assigned to even a poorly trained butler, threw Portia off. She stiffened in affront, then prepared to respond to the discourteous greeting with a bit of insolence herself.

Angelique saved her the trouble as she pushed through the door, past the little man who was helpless to stop her, and into the hall, saying as she went, "We have a matter of vital importance that requires Nightshade's immediate attention." She swung around to cast the little man a narrow-eyed look. "Where shall we wait?"

"Don't know who yer talking 'bout."

"Yes, you do. Now fetch your master, or I will seek him out myself."

Portia was infinitely impressed. Who knew the woman who barely remembered to put on her shoes before leaving the house could display such an air of unquestionable command?

The little man pinched his face into a sour expression as he glanced toward the door then back to Angelique as though debating the benefits of tossing them both back onto the street. He cast a critical gaze over their appearances, seeming to take mental note of the quality of their clothing. Then he snorted and turned to amble into the shadows at the back of the hall.

Angelique released a pent-up breath, her previous arrogance falling away like a discarded cloak. She turned to Portia. "Come. Let us find somewhere comfortable to wait."

The front hall was dark and narrow. Stairs rose up along the left side, and three doors opened to the right. The hall itself contained nothing but a small table set near the door. Portia wandered toward the first door to peek into the room beyond.

It was a small parlor.

"This way," she said as she strode into the room.

The room was also quite dark. Only the faint glow of distant city lights filtered through the window, but it was enough to see the outline of the furniture and a small candelabrum set on a table near the sofa. Angelique took a seat in an armchair while Portia went directly to the cold fireplace, looking for something to light the candles.

It felt good to finally have something to do even if it was as mundane a task as lighting candles. It kept her thoughts from flying in all sorts of wild directions. Once the candles were lit, she found herself unable to sit still. Though she tried several times to take a seat, she inevitably jumped to her feet again in a matter of moments as fretful energy continued to rush unheeded through her body.

Rather than perpetrating a pointless battle against the urge to move, she took to pacing the tiny room.

# Two

IT FELT LIKE THEY WAITED FOR HOURS IN THE DIMLY lit parlor for Nightshade's man. Angelique sat quietly, her eyelids dropping in the semidarkness. Portia almost envied the old woman her drowsiness as her disquiet steadily grew. The longer they sat unattended, the harder it was going to be to track Lily down.

Portia wondered if perhaps the rude little butler had simply gone to bed rather than informing his master of his guests. After making her hundredth turn at the fireplace, she took off toward the door at the opposite end of the room with purposeful strides, determined to go in search of someone herself.

Just as she neared the door, however, a figure appeared in the dark frame. The man made such a sudden and silent appearance Portia was nearly startled from her skin. As it was, she was under the force of such fierce momentum, she barely managed to stop herself from colliding with the man by bracing her hand hard on the doorframe.

She looked at the newcomer sharply. Her worry

and impatience coalesced into anger now that he had finally appeared.

He was a rather nondescript man in his later years, perhaps in his fifties, with light hair that was going to gray, a pale, almost sickly complexion, a beard that had grown a bit bushy, and small, wire-rimmed spectacles. He was dressed in a brown suit with matching waistcoat and stood with sloped shoulders, his hands stuffed into the front pockets of his coat.

Seemingly unconcerned with their near collision, he looked down at her from almost a foot above her with an expression that could only be classified as annoyed.

The longer she stood there staring up at him, the more annoyed he became, evidenced by the lowering of his untamed brows and the pursing of his thin mouth. And yet he was the one who had kept them waiting while her sister was dragged off to who knows where.

She pushed off from the doorframe and planted her hands on her hips.

"It is about time. Do you have any idea how long we have been waiting?"

The thick eyebrows shot up, reaching far above the top rim of his spectacles. "You have been waiting less than fifteen minutes," he replied in an entirely unhurried tone. "Do you have any idea what time of night it is?"

"I would say it is nearing one o'clock in the morning, which should signify that our issue is of such importance it cannot wait until a more reasonable hour, which should in turn have pressed you to a more hasty response."

The man made a sound in the back of his throat—a

sort of abbreviated snort—then stared, saying nothing more. His lips pressed into such a tight line they lost all hint of color, and his eyes narrowed to a squint behind his spectacles.

"Portia, come sit. Allow the poor man into the room so we may conduct our business."

Portia realized then that her challenging stance essentially blocked the doorway, keeping the new-comer stranded on the threshold. Executing a little snort of her own, Portia turned with a whip of her skirts and strode to where her great-aunt was pushing herself a bit straighter in the armchair. Rather than sitting—which she knew wouldn't last long anyway—Portia took position beside the chair and waited for Nightshade's man to step forward and take control of the situation.

*Taking control* was not how Portia would describe the man's next actions.

After a slow glance at Angelique, he strolled into the room, keeping his hands in his pockets. He walked past the lit candelabra, his brows shooting upward again, as if the fact that they had lit the room was more of an affront than their untimely visit.

Portia studied him, irritated and curious.

*This* was the go-between for the highly skilled and ruthless Nightshade? He looked more like someone's daft uncle or a confused schoolteacher.

"Mr. Honeycutt," Angelique said, "we met once before, a few years ago—"

"Of course, Lady Chelmsworth," Honeycutt inter-rupted without turning to face them as he wandered to the window overlooking the front street. "I recall our introduction. I assume tonight brings you here on another matter."

Portia bristled at the impatience obvious in his tone. The man was sorely lacking in manners.

"Indeed. This is my great-niece, Miss Chadwick," Angelique replied, waving an elegant hand toward Portia. "Her sister has been abducted tonight. Taken off the street and carried away. We need Nightshade to recover her."

Portia watched Mr. Honeycutt carefully, expecting some sort of reaction to the news of a young lady being kidnapped in such a way. But he gave no acknowledgment at all, just continued to stare out the window with his shoulders slouched and his chin tucked to his chest.

Portia couldn't stand any more of it.

"Mr. Honeycutt," she began in a sharp tone, but just as she spoke, he turned around again and pinned her with a stare that stopped the rest of her words.

Something in his manner, his gaze, his sudden focus managed to suck the dissent right out of her. Somewhere deep within the ugly brown coat and sloped posture she detected a strong thread of competence. She rolled her lips in between her teeth in a way she hadn't done since she was young and her mother had chastised her for her naughtiness…which was often.

After waiting long enough to be assured she would not be interrupting any further, Honeycutt shifted his attention back to Angelique. "Have you any idea who may have perpetrated the abduction or why?"

Angelique looked to Portia, giving her a nod.

During their drive across London, Portia had

confessed to Angelique the truth about the mysterious loan and Hale's recent threats. The Chadwicks had initially decided to keep the full nature of their dire circumstances from the lady's knowledge rather than risk the possibility it might influence her decision to sponsor the younger sisters for the Season.

Portia straightened her spine and looked the man directly in the face. She realized it was vital he have all the information available if this Nightshade were to have any luck in tracking down where Lily had been taken, but it didn't make it any easier to admit her family's secrets to a stranger.

"Since my father's death several months ago, my oldest sister, Emma, began receiving notes from someone named Mason Hale regarding an unpaid loan. Last night, my sister Lily—the one who was just abducted—was personally threatened by Hale. He stated we had two days to repay him in full, with interest. He indicated he would have his money, one way or another." She paused, looking for some indication that Honeycutt was listening. He provided no reaction at all. "Hale gave us until tomorrow to get the money to him. We had a plan to come up with the amount, but something must have changed. Hale must have decided not to wait. Lily was the first to exit the carriage when we arrived home this evening. Before we knew what was happening, our driver was knocked unconscious, and my sister was tossed over the shoulder of a very large man who stuffed her into a carriage across the street. They were gone in a matter of moments."

Honeycutt was silent and unmoving for several minutes.

"Does anyone else have any cause to take your sister? Vengeance, lust, greed?"

"Not that I know of," Portia replied, less certain than she would have liked.

A sick rush of guilt settled in her stomach. She and Lily had not been talking as much as they used to. Portia had been so ill-humored since she had begun her debut Season, she had not been very attentive to her sister.

"Do you know of Mason Hale? Where to find him?" Portia asked when Honeycutt remained silent longer than she was comfortable with.

He narrowed his gaze in irritation again, and Portia stiffened. If he wasn't so bloody tight-lipped, she wouldn't be forced to press him.

"I will address the issue with my employer," Honeycutt finally replied.

The man turned his gaze to Angelique again. "As you may recall, his services require a partial payment up front. The urgency of the matter will demand a substantial fee, my lady."

The dowager countess grunted in acceptance and reached into her reticule for a small sack of coins. She handed them to Portia, their eyes meeting briefly as she did so. The old lady lived on a limited allowance from the present earl, and Portia certainly had no money.

This was the bluff her great-aunt had mentioned earlier.

Portia brought the sack of coins to Mr. Honeycutt, looking him directly in the eye as she came to stand before him.

"That is all I have on my person at the moment, Mr. Honeycutt," Angelique explained. "I did not waste time going for more funds but came directly here, you understand. I can promise the full fee once my niece is returned safely home."

Honeycutt glanced down at the small purse in Portia's hand, making no move to take it from her.

Portia's anxiety grew unbearable.

He had to accept it. Nightshade was their only option at this point. Precious time slid away with every second Honeycutt took to respond. Lily's image flashed through Portia's mind. Her sweet and gentle sister needed someone to take action.

*Now.*

Portia stepped toward Honeycutt, her anger over his obvious reticence forcing her hand. On impulse, she grasped his wrist and yanked his hand out of his pocket. Before he could resist, she pressed the purse into his large palm. Holding it there with both of her hands, she looked up into his face, forcing him to meet her eyes.

"You have to accept," she said through a tight throat. "Nightshade has to find my sister. There is no other option."

He glared at her with narrowed eyes.

Portia, full of fear and stubborn determination, refused to back down. She could feel the tension in his body...but it was more than annoyance, she realized. He possessed a sort of physical readiness she hadn't noticed before, when his slow movements and careless posture had suggested a distinct lack of interest. His hand, enclosed in both of hers, felt stronger, more capable than she had expected. Standing close enough that she had to tip her head back to look into his face, she sensed something powerful emanating from him.

Something that forced a subtle shiver to course through her body.

She peered into his eyes. They were shadowed by his bushy brows and distorted by the glass of his spectacles, but she swore she saw something significant there. She tipped her head to the side and a frown creased her forehead as she focused her gaze—trying to discern just what it was that had caught her attention.

But then he curled his hand into a fist, claiming the purse before abruptly turning to walk away.

"I will get a message to my employer. I offer no guarantee." Honeycutt paused in the doorway. "Return home. Word of the investigation will be sent to you there."

"We will wait here for news," Portia replied.

"Impossible. There is no telling how long it will take for my employer to discover your sister's fate. It could be several hours. Or days."

Portia thought of going back to the house and awaiting word. She thought of Emma returning and having to be advised of Lily's abduction.

No. She could not go home without some solid results...even if she had to go out into the night and get them herself.

She folded her arms across her chest and squared her shoulders. "We will wait here."

Honeycutt stopped in the threshold to glare back at her over his sloped shoulder. "You cannot."

"We will," she insisted with an insolent lift of her eyebrows, "unless you intend to cause a scene by physically forcing two screaming females from your home." She smiled with false sweetness. "I received the impression you prefer to keep these dealings more discreet."

For a brief second, the man seemed at a loss on how to handle Portia's insistence. Then he gave a short grunt. "Do not expect any hospitality," he muttered.

And then he was gone.

# Three

PORTIA STOOD THERE, APPREHENSION COMING BACK TO
the fore now that she and Angelique were alone again.
The few minutes since Honeycutt had left the room
passed like hours. She glanced back toward her great-
aunt, whose eyes had grown heavy as her chin bobbed
repeatedly toward her chest. The elderly lady would
be asleep within minutes.

Portia made a swift decision. Picking up her skirts,
she crossed the room in long strides, then paused at
the door, peering into the hall. Everything was dark
and silent.

Creeping forward, she strained her ears to hear any
indication of where Honeycutt had gone. Had he left
the house, gone to Nightshade already?

The floorboards just above her gave a telltale creak.

It was the height of impropriety to consider sneaking through a stranger's home. Yet Portia did not
think twice as she made her way toward the narrow
stairs leading up to the second floor. There was far
too much at stake to worry about proper manners.
Going excruciatingly slowly, she incorporated into her

movements all of the little tricks she had developed as a child.

Portia had been only twelve when her mother had fallen ill. Emma, at eighteen, had cared for their mother almost night and day. Except for the rare occasion when they were allowed into their mother's bedroom for a few whispered words and a brief touch of her hand, she and Lily had been ordered to stay away.

Even then, Portia had hated taking orders. She had found a way to sneak in and out of her mother's bedroom during those times Emma or the maids went to fetch something, or in the middle of the night as everyone else slept. She had claimed a corner behind the heavy fall of the drapes where she would sit for hours sometimes, listening to her mother's shallow breath or Emma's murmured words of comfort and assurance.

After their mother's death, their father spiraled into grief at the loss of his wife. His behavior grew more and more erratic and suspicious. Since Emma refused to be forthcoming about the changes in their father, likely trying to protect her younger sisters, Portia took matters into her own hands.

She further developed her skills in moving about undetected as she spied on her father's late-night activities. Somehow, discovering his growing obsession with gambling and drink—seeing it firsthand as he stayed up until dawn, insisting Emma help him practice his card-playing skills—made her feel less insecure than when her head was filled with visions of the unknown.

Stupid, really. As an adult, she understood why Emma had tried to shield her and Lily from much of what went on with their parents. Knowing about something could not stop it from happening.

Only action could do that. She had been unable to help her parents, but she sure as hell wasn't going to sit back and do nothing while Lily was in danger.

Patience was not something Portia normally possessed, but she had learned to harness the elusive virtue over years of practice and could employ it when it mattered. Incorporating an intense awareness for every minute bit of influence her body had on her environment, she placed one foot in front of the other up the stairs. Keeping her back angled toward the wall, Portia shifted her gaze back and forth between the space in front of her and the darkness behind her, ever watchful for movement in the shadows to warn her someone was coming.

At the top of the stairs, Portia peered down a narrow hallway, dark but for the light from one room seeping through the crack of a door barely left open. Portia crept forward, undeterred. Angelique seemed to trust this Nightshade character and his associates, but Portia was not so easily convinced.

Nearing the lit room, Portia heard the low murmur of two distinct voices. But she could not make out what they said. The hallway was long and narrow and not at all conducive to hiding. There was not even a table to crouch behind.

A scowl crept across her brow. Of course, Honeycutt would be unaccommodating in this as well.

Creeping forward, she got as close as she could, stopping in a deep shadow just beyond the pale beam of light extending across the floor. Pressing her back flat against the wall, she eased her breath into a slow, deep, and silent rhythm as she had trained herself to do long ago.

Then she listened.

"This don't sound like somethin' Hale would do." Portia recognized the guttural tone of the rude little butler's voice coming from just inside the door. "He ain't no kidnapper."

"He never was before, but you and I know people can be pushed to do almost anything under the right circumstances."

Portia tensed.

This last had been spoken by an unfamiliar voice. She had expected to hear Honeycutt, but this man spoke in a much lower tone, and his words revealed the barest hint of Cockney buried beneath the layers of finer intonation.

The butler murmured something in response, the words lost beneath the creak of a floorboard.

Breathing so slowly she could not even feel the air moving through her lungs, she waited. She had no idea what she would do if someone stepped into the hall and saw her skulking there. It was not in her nature to think so far ahead, preferring to rely on instinct and inspiration in such situations.

When, after a few minutes, no one came out of the room, she began to relax. She could still hear quite a bit of movement within, and her curiosity won out over caution. Twisting her upper body, she leaned forward until she could take just a quick peek through the crack in the door.

She saw the butler first. He stood with his back to

her, thank God, as he rifled through the drawers of a tallboy dresser.

Beyond the butler, Honeycutt was only partially visible where he sat on a bench turned three-quarters away from her in front of a large mirror propped atop a table.

Portia scanned the room for the other man she had heard speaking. She saw no one else in her limited view. It made her nervous, not being able to see where the third man may be. But then her gaze swung back to Honeycutt as he grasped the bottom hem of his coat and drew it up over his head—along with the waistcoat beneath, the shirt, and the neckcloth.

It all came off in one attached piece.

Portia was pondering the reason for such a strange design when her attention was forcefully snared by what had been revealed by the sudden disrobing.

Honeycutt was not a man in his later years.

His upper body was sharply defined by hard, lean muscle beneath smooth, tawny skin. As he lifted his arms to clear the garment from his head, the dim candlelight rippled over the contours of his shoulders and back. There was not a bit of extra bulk or flab. Just taut, agile strength.

"Wot'll you do, Mr. Turner?"

The butler's voice pulled Portia back from her momentary distraction. A strange heat bloomed just beneath the surface of her skin as she felt a wave of light-headedness, making her realize that she had stopped breathing. She spun around to press her shoulders to the wall again, grasping her skirts in her hands to draw them in so as not to be seen from inside the room.

She had forgotten herself for a few moments and had gotten frightfully close to tumbling right into the room. Chastising herself for such carelessness, she fought to regain control of her breath. But it was not so easy now that she had the surprising image of Honeycutt's strong masculine physique stamped indelibly in her mind.

"I'll pay Hale a visit," said the low voice with the subtle Cockney accent. "Find out if he knows anything about this girl. Even if he wasn't involved, Hale may have some information."

Honeycutt had talked with the intonation of the middle class. This man spoke in a way that brought up impressions of back-alley dealings and midnight capers. There was a depth to his voice, a thread of danger in the low tenor that made Portia's skin tingle with alarm.

*What did the sour little butler call him? Mr. Turner?*

An unexpected thought occurred to Portia, sending a wild tingle through her blood.

"Wot costume should I ready?"

*Costume?*

"Mr. Black, I think. And toss me the face cream, would you? I need to get this beard off."

There was a pause and the sound of some jars moving about on a shelf. Then a muttered "thank you" as she imagined the butler handing off the requested cream.

Fury welled hot in Portia's stomach. She had been right to be suspicious. What kind of scam were they running? Had Angelique unwittingly walked them into a fleecing? They had already given Honeycutt—or was it Turner?—a significant purse.

But no. They had been talking about Hale. There seemed to be some intention to investigate Lily's abduction.

*But what about this Nightshade? Why are they not contacting their supposed employer? Or is it possible…*

There were several more minutes of shuffling movement as Portia contemplated the situation with rising trepidation. Then there was the distinct sound of water being poured into a basin, followed by the splashes of vigorous washing.

"Wot if Hale don't know nuthin'?" the butler asked.

Portia tensed. It was a question she had not allowed herself to consider in any depth. The abduction *had* to be connected with Hale. There was no other logical possibility. No other lead to follow if that were the case.

"Then we made a pretty purse for an hour's worth of work."

Portia's intention to remain hidden in the hall immediately disintegrated. Pushing off from the wall, she burst into the little room. "Like hell you did."

The butler was nearest to the door, and he gave an obvious start at her sudden intrusion. Portia ignored his shocked glare. All of her attention focused on the man who sat in front of the mirror with a towel draped over his head as he dried his hair. She fixed her furious gaze on his broad shoulders, the fire in her blood rising exponentially.

"You have been hired to bring my sister home, and that is what you will do," she declared in a commanding tone she had borrowed from her formidable sister Emma. "Am I clear, Mr. Honeycutt? Or is it Mr. Turner? Or should I just call you *Nightshade?*"

The butler took a swift and menacing step toward her, placing himself between her and the exit. Portia did not acknowledge him, waiting instead for the other man to respond.

At first, Turner did nothing to acknowledge her presence, as though his strange toilet was often interrupted by angry young women. While she watched, waiting with her arms crossed indignantly over her chest, he finished drying his hair. The movements of his arms caused a fascinating bunching and releasing of the muscles across his shoulders and down his back. After a minute of this, as Portia's mouth went curiously dry, he stood from the bench and turned toward her.

Standing at full height, he grasped the ends of the towel with large hands to keep it shadowing his face like the hood of a cloak. He was still bared to the waist, and his woolen trousers rested low across lean hips. Portia's attention was immediately snared by the way muscles cut across his abdomen and angled past his hips in intriguing lines she hadn't known the human body possessed.

Her breath arrested quite forcefully on its way out of her lungs. Her knees locked, rooting her to the floor. And a frightening shiver skittered down her spine, while another entirely unfamiliar sensation rippled through her insides.

There was something inherently dangerous about the man before her. Though his posture gave no indication of a threat, it was there anyway. In the subtle tightening of those angular muscles across his chest and abdomen and the way she could feel him staring at her, though she couldn't see his face beneath the deep shadow created by the towel.

Portia swallowed hard and lifted her chin.

She could not back down. Lily needed her to follow this through. No matter how intimidating the circumstances, it could not be close to what her sister was likely enduring even now.

"Wot should I do with her?"

Portia tensed.

"Nothing," Honeycutt/Turner/Nightshade replied darkly, sending a shiver down Portia's spine. "I will handle her. Go ready the carriage."

The butler left the room, and Portia squared her shoulders, forcing herself to continue. "I am not leaving until you promise to do everything in your power to retrieve my sister."

"Then you delay me unnecessarily," he replied tersely. "I always do everything in my power." He turned and crossed to where a set of clothes had been laid out over a chair. With his back to her, he dropped the towel and bent to retrieve his clothing. She was so distracted by the sight of his woolen trousers tightening briefly over very firm masculine buttocks that she only just then noticed his new clothing was sewn together as one piece in the same manner as Honeycutt's costume.

In the moment before he drew the garment over his head, Portia noted his hair was not the pale blond and gray it had been as Honeycutt. It appeared much darker, with some caramel-colored streaks, though that impression could have been a trick of the candle-light reflecting on the damp, tousled locks.

He spoke with his back still to her. "If Hale is not behind your sister's abduction, what would you have me do? Young women disappear off the streets all the time and are most often never seen again."

Panic and pain lanced through her center, and her stomach churned queasily. She could not contemplate such a possibility. "I do not accept that."

"You may have to."

"It has to be Hale," she insisted. "It is the only thing that even partially makes sense."

He grunted at that but did not reply as he walked back to take a seat before the mirror. She noticed that he was very careful to keep his face averted. From where she stood, all she saw in the mirror was the empty space over his shoulder.

"Take the old lady home so I can do what you hired me to do."

Portia's mind whirled as a strange resistance settled deep in her bones. She stood stiffly, watching as he reached for the towel again and draped it around his shoulders. Then he expertly applied a black, greasy substance to his hair, which had started to dry in a riotous mess. The grease smoothed his hair back along his skull, completely eliminating any suggestion of lighter streaks. After washing his hands in the water basin, he began applying something to his face. His movements were swift and competent, as though he had performed these same actions a thousand times.

Portia watched in silent fascination. Sidling farther into the room, she tried to get a better view, wondering why he donned his disguise so openly in front of her.

By the time she got around to where she could see his face, however, she realized why he hadn't bothered to chase her off before beginning his ministrations.

He had become a different person.

Not quite as old as Honeycutt, this incarnation appeared perhaps thirty-five to forty, with black hair, a slightly swarthy skin tone, imposing black eyebrows, and a thin black mustache. Put together with the simple white shirt, navy-blue coat, and the basic neckcloth he had donned, he looked like a man of the upper middle class. A lawyer perhaps, or a banker.

She stared in amazement at how completely he had transformed from the forgettable Mr. Honeycutt to this strange man in a matter of minutes. And all while effectively preventing her from seeing anything of his true self—aside from his bare upper body and a firm backside, which she was not likely to forget anytime soon.

Her amazement shifted in an instant to admiration and then determination.

"I am going with you," she declared.

# Four

DELL TURNER—WHO OCCASIONALLY WENT BY THE
names Honeycutt, Black, Nightshade, and a host of
others—pretended not to hear her. The ridiculous
announcement did not deserve a response.

He crossed the room to an oversize bureau in the
corner and opened the top drawer to choose some
accessories to complete his guise. A watch fob, a pair
of leather gloves, a specially designed pistol that he slid
into the pocket of his coat. The knife already strapped
to his ankle rarely left his person. His line of work
tended to become dangerous on occasion.

He didn't expect any specific trouble from Hale,
but it was essential to be prepared for anything.

As he finished dressing, Dell recalled everything
he knew about Hale. Mason Hale had become a
celebrated pugilist from his very first fight at the age of
seventeen. His career had been lucrative, but Hale had
taken his last purse a few years ago. He now handled
the stakes for many of the blokes who used to bet on
him in the ring. And seemed to be doing quite well
with the business.

He also did not suffer fools lightly and never let a loan go past expiration, so the Chadwick woman's story fit.

To a point.

Dell had never known Mason Hale to resort to kidnapping. It was not his style. After leaving the ring, Hale had preferred to use his brain more than his brawn to make his way. Dell was curious what the man would have to say about the Chadwick girl's abduction—he fully intended to pay him a visit.

Once he got the pest out of his house.

"Did you hear me?" she asked behind him. "I am going with you to see Hale."

Dell took a steadying breath. It was not to cool his temper. Dell did not have a temper. One had to experience some degree of passion to be pushed into a loss of control. Dell Turner preferred to keep things strictly business. His life was work, and work was lucrative.

Still, he needed a moment before turning back to face Miss Chadwick.

When he had stepped into the doorway of his parlor and nearly collided with the young woman bristling with energy, something disconcerting had caught and held in his awareness. He had an ingrained skill for reading people within a split second of meeting them. Vital for survival when he had been a lad running the streets, it was an invaluable tool in his current profession. But never had he felt the kind of sharp tug he'd experienced then—and again now as he turned to see her standing stubbornly in front of the doorway, essentially blocking his exit.

He eyed her critically.

She was beautiful. A mass of very dark hair was piled atop her head in a slightly mussed arrangement that allowed for glossy curls to fall against her stunning cheekbones, pert jaw, and slim neck. Her eyebrows winged elegantly over her gaze, and her large gray eyes were frighteningly direct. For a man who relied on going mostly unobserved, her penchant for staring irked his composure.

Yes, she was beautiful. Striking, actually. And annoying to be sure, but he could manage annoying people easily enough by ignoring them.

Unfortunately, neither of those things explained the internal discomfort he experienced in the woman's presence. He forced aside his internal disquiet before answering. "You and the old lady are going home."

She narrowed her gaze, and Dell felt that irritating tug again. He stalked toward the door.

Which unfortunately brought him closer to her.

She tipped her chin back as he approached, and he realized anew how small she was. Petite and slim, she barely reached as high as his shoulder, yet she stood her ground.

"I want to know what Hale has to say, and I intend to be there for my sister."

"Your sister would be better served if you allowed me to do what you hired me for. Your presence will jeopardize the process."

Those winged sable eyebrows dipped low.

"You do not understand. Lily is very sensitive. She will be frightened."

"If you come with me, she could end up dead."

Horror flashed in her gaze, but her teeth clenched tight in resistance.

Dell did not explain his methods for getting things done, and he did not argue with clients. He did what he did because it was what needed to be done. It was the reason people came to him. He did not bother with unnecessary niceties.

"Look at yourself, Miss Chadwick," he began, irritation thick in his voice. "Hale will take one look at you in that pure-white dress and velvet-lined cloak and clam up. You do not belong where I am going. Your kind is not trusted. Rouse the woman snoring in my parlor and go home. I will send a message when I have news."

It looked as though she would argue some more. She wanted to. Proof of it was evident in the tension radiating from her compact feminine form, the bullish tilt of her chin, and the piercing nature of her stare. And yet she said nothing.

After a minute, she shifted her weight, and Dell assumed she was going to step aside to let him pass. Instead, she stepped toward him. Toe to toe, she tipped her head back and lifted her hand to tap his chest with an elegant finger.

Another fierce tug of discomfort.

"You will bring my sister back to me, Mr. Turner. Alive."

Dell looked down into her beautiful face, meeting her stark, gray gaze. "That is what you are paying me to do," he replied.

"Excellent. I will wait with my great-aunt in your parlor."

He struggled to hold back the sharp word that

pushed against the back of his teeth as the maddening woman turned to leave the room. He stood for a moment, listening to her light tread make its way down the hall then the stairs.

He aimed a mental kick at himself for getting so off track. Time was of vital importance in a kidnapping. He needed to move.

Shoving thoughts of the woman from his mind, he descended the stairs two at a time. Out on the street, Morley, the closest thing Dell had to an assistant, had already brought the carriage around and was perched in the driver's seat.

At least someone knew how to follow instructions.

As soon as Dell climbed into the carriage, they were off.

Gratefully, Hale was not far away, and within another fifteen minutes, the vehicle pulled to a stop in front of the two-story building nestled along a dark lane.

Dell had been here many times before, but as himself.

Mason Hale had been training him for years. The former prizefighter had not only taught Dell how to hold his own with his fists, but had also trained him in a variety of wrestling holds and escapes, throws and pins, and even some street-fighting techniques. All of which had come in handy over the years.

It was always a bit tricky when Dell encountered someone he knew personally while in the guise of one of his characters. There was a brief few minutes when he could not be sure if he would be recognized. To date, he had never been discovered. But there was always the chance of a first time.

Though the neighborhood was not the safest, Dell was not worried. He'd grown up running through dark alleys and gritty streets. But he was not Dell Turner right now. He was Mr. John Black, a solicitor to the middle class. And Mr. Black would be *very* anxious.

He slowly exited the carriage, casting nervous glances in all directions as he stepped to the street outside Hale's place of business. Mr. Black's work rarely brought him to these rougher areas of London. Luckily, the solicitor possessed just enough sense to be cautious when venturing so far outside what was familiar to him.

Dell glanced upward.

No lights shone from the windows on the upper level where Hale had his office and training space. The main level of the narrow building was also dark, except for one window that glowed with a pale light.

Making a show of tugging his coat into place and smoothing his waistcoat, Dell cast a quick look toward Morley, who sat holding the reins with a practiced air of distraction. The man would keep his eyes and ears perked for any trouble. Dell walked purposefully to the front door and knocked with the bold arrogance of a man who thought himself more clever and intimidating than he actually was. Anyone with any sort of streetwise awareness would take one look at Mr. Black and know right away that whatever he was doing, he was in over his head.

When no one answered his first round of knocks, Dell knocked again. Louder and longer.

Finally, there was a skittering of noise from within. Then some jostling of the doorknob preceded the opening of a narrow crack along the doorjamb. The

sharply angled face of Mr. Smythe, Hale's clerk and
general servant—a pale and nervous man of indeter-
minate age—pressed into the crack of the doorway.

"What do you want? Don't you know it's the
middle of the night?"

"I know that very well, sir, but it does not change
the fact that I must speak with Mr. Mason Hale immediately. I understand this is his residence as well as his
place of business?" Dell said the last with a proper
sneer of disgust.

"He ain't here."

Dell's instinct told him the man was not lying.

"And when do you expect him to return?"

"I've no idea. He could be gone hours or days. Hale
does what he pleases. Now, be off with ya."

Smythe leaned back to slam the door shut again. He
didn't make it that far. Dell gave a swift shove, which
sent the door and the servant flying back. Dell stepped
over the threshold, closing the door behind him as he
waited for Hale's man to finish whimpering and get
to his feet.

"Damn me," Smythe cried, both hands covering his
face, "I think you broke me nose."

Dell seriously doubted it.

"Are you aware of the business Hale conducted
earlier this evening?"

Apparently so, judging by the sudden panic in
Smythe's watering eyes and the way he braced for
flight. Before Smythe could bolt, Dell grasped him by
the shirt and spun him up against the wall, pinning the
smaller man with a minimal press of his forearm across
Smythe's chest.

"Where did he take the girl?"

"He didn't take her nowhere—hasn't seen her in weeks."

That confused Dell, but his gut told him there was a connection. He trusted his gut.

"He stole a young lady off a street in Mayfair a couple of hours ago. Where did he take her?"

The trembling man's eyes widened.

"You know what I am talking about," Dell insisted, ignoring the surge of disappointment he felt at discovering that Hale was involved in the abduction after all. He pressed his arm a bit more firmly to the man's chest, compressing his lungs, just short of cracking his ribs, as he leaned into him. "Where did he take her?"

"I...can't be sure," Smythe choked out, his eyes going buggy. "But earlier...I sent a message round to Pendragon's. Hale said it was urgent."

Dell released the clerk immediately, then reached down to grasp the man by the shoulders and haul him to his feet after Smythe crumpled to the ground. The little man coughed and sputtered for breath as Dell propped him against the wall.

"Thanks, mate," he said once he was assured the man had his feet. Then he stepped back to open the door. "No need to apprise Hale of our little conversation. He need never know of your disloyalty."

If Hale were to find out, the scrawny clerk would not fare well beneath the bare-knuckle fighter's fists.

But that was not Dell's problem.

Pendragon's Pleasure House was some distance away, located much closer to the nabobs it served. At worst, the Chadwick girl had been sold into an

overseas sex trade. She may already be aboard a ship
bound for a foreign shore. There were organiza-
tions that specialized in the sale of young women.
Mostly the women were tricked into thinking they
were being sent for gainful employment; others were
already prostitutes, who had displeased their pimps and
were traded for a profit. On occasion, a young woman
might be stolen off the street if she had a certain look
that was prized by the slavers.

Dell thought of the dark-haired young woman who
stubbornly awaited his return in his parlor. If her sister
looked like that one, she would likely fetch a hefty
price. And if she were a virgin…

Still, Dell doubted this was the Chadwick girl's
fate. Madam Pendragon was an extremely discerning
businesswoman, who was unlikely to engage in such a
high-risk venture.

He had been to Pendragon's Pleasure House multiple times. His line of work often required the information only a well-connected madam could provide.
Pendragon's position gave her access to her clients'
most guarded personal secrets. Her brothel was one of
the most elite in town and catered to the more specific
and deviant tastes of London's gentlemen.

He considered taking the time to change his
appearance.

Pendragon knew him as Robert French, a charming
and reckless young man who had gathered information
for Nightshade when he had assisted the madam with a
very sensitive matter a few years ago. A matter that was
difficult to repay by monetary means alone. As such,
she could occasionally be persuaded to provide French

with helpful information on various investigations, as long as it did not break any of the strict rules of discretion she maintained for her clients.

Pendragon would not be so forthcoming with Mr. Black, whom she had never met, but he could not afford to waste time in changing personas just now.

Dell needed an angle. And fast.

# Five

MORLEY DREW THE CARRIAGE TO A STOP ACROSS THE street from the common-enough brick building that housed the elite brothel. Dell looked out the window and saw a group of gentlemen staggering down the street a short distance away. Based on their fancy togs and ribald comments, their intended destination was not difficult to assume.

Perfect.

Dell exited his carriage in a sudden lurch then tripped over his own feet, nearly sprawling into the road. He righted himself just in time to save his face from the pavement. He stumbled and swayed his way to the brothel's front door. His coat was askew, and his eyes drooped blearily. Bursting through the front door, he collided with Pendragon's doorman, a beefy fellow who served well as an all-around keeper of the peace.

Slapping a sloppy grin on his face, Dell patted the man's shoulder as he righted himself.

"'Ello, good sir. I hope I've made it to the right place," he exclaimed jovially.

"That depends on what you seek."

Dell continued to sway precariously.

"Pleasure. Beauty." He waggled his eyebrows. "A lovely friend with whom to while away the hours."

"Have you a sponsor?"

"Sponsor? I've got plenty of coin," Dell replied, patting at his coat pocket, making sure the man heard the jingle of coins inside.

The doorman shook his head. "You must have a sponsor, or you go no farther."

Dell scrunched his face into an expression of exaggerated distress. "Well, damn me."

Perfectly timed, the fine-dressed gentlemen from the street pushed in through the door behind Dell, causing a momentary ruckus as they filtered through the foyer and into the drawing room beyond. They were all obviously familiar with the place and must have been known by the doorman as he nodded them through without concern.

As they passed, Dell flicked a quick and assessing glance at each of them, looking for one who would welcome his offer. He knew the one in an instant and acted without hesitation. As the man with ruddy ears and bloodshot eyes stepped past him, Dell gave him a friendly nudge of his shoulder.

"'Ello, my good man. It seems I'm in need of a sponsor. Be a mate, would ya?"

The gentleman was several years older than Dell, but about the same age as Mr. Black. He narrowed his eyes to look at him, though Dell doubted it helped him to see any better, considering he was about as drunk as Dell was pretending to be.

"Who the hell are you?"

"Name's Black, and I've got enough gold in my purse to buy us a good bottle of scotch once we get into that room." He pointed in the direction of the drawing room.

The other man lit up with a wide grin as he threw his arm around Dell's shoulders. "Well, all right then, consider yourself sponsored, Mr. Black. What shall we toast to?"

The doorman stepped forward. "You do understand the consequences if there is any trouble?" he asked solemnly of Mr. Black's new best mate.

"Of course I do," the gentleman replied breezily, waving off the doorman's concerns. "You've never had a problem with anyone else I've sponsored."

After another brief hesitation, the doorman stepped aside. "Of course, Your Grace. Enjoy your evening."

"Always do," the apparent duke replied as he propelled them both into the drawing room.

Robert French always asked to speak with Pendragon privately, bypassing the common areas. But Dell didn't want to speak with the mistress this evening. He needed a chatty girl with just enough information.

Stumbling into the dimly lit room with a goofy grin on his face, Dell glanced about.

Pendragon's drawing room was done up in Grecian-themed decor. A large, vividly painted mural covered one wall. It was a dreamy scene depicting several woodland nymphs being pleasured by the attentions of a randy satyr. The chandelier hanging from the center of the room was sparsely lit, providing just enough light to cast a golden glow through the multifaceted crystals that comprised its structure. Chaises and sofas

filled the space, with privacy curtains placed strategi-
cally about to create little arbors for couples to retire
to. Girls, dressed in frothy, Grecian-style creations that
revealed more flesh than they concealed, wandered
about with wine or sat cuddling with gentlemen. A
voluptuous woman danced provocatively on a makeshift stage in the center of the room, while another
woman stood nearby singing a seductive tune.

Dell had visited the brothel only once as a client,
when he had come looking for a girl, any girl. He
had been young and stupid, with a bag of shiny gold
and a sponsorship voucher from a very happy client
after completing a risky job as Nightshade. He had
thought he could lavish his newfound wealth on a
pretty woman. Instead, he had gotten two women
prettier than he could have hoped, a night of perfect
debauchery, a morning hangover he'd never forget,
and no money left in his purse.

It hadn't been worth it.

Whenever he got to the point where he desired a
woman's company, he went back to the theater dis-
trict. He knew plenty of women there who welcomed
his random visits. Women he called friends.

Such visits were few and far between. Nightshade's
work kept him very busy. He enjoyed being busy.

It took a little time to excuse himself from the
duke's company. Leaving behind the newly acquired
bottle of scotch helped. After bidding the duke good
evening, Dell executed a disgraceful bow that had him
dancing on his toes again to keep his feet, before he
swung around to stumble toward the stage.

Dell chose a seat in front of the dancer, tilting his

face up to watch her rolling movements in awe. He paused every now and then to scan the room and its occupants.

He knew which girl he wanted to talk to. He had encountered her a time or two as Robert French. She was a bubbly little thing with a penchant for giggling and gossip.

And she currently appeared to be unoccupied.

It took only another moment to catch her eye. She bounded over to him, her large breasts bouncing in time to her steps. Not wanting to disappoint her obvious effort to draw his gaze to her bosom, Dell ogled the generous globes, making sure to put an appropriately salacious expression on his face.

"Can I get you some wine?" the girl asked.

"Oh, sweetheart, I've had enough wine tonight. I'd rather have you. On my lap, if you please."

The girl giggled delightedly and took the seat he offered.

Dell took a few minutes to tickle her playfully and nip at her neck. Her skin tasted of cheap perfume, but she smelled clean beneath it.

"I can't believe I've never visited this delightful establishment before. I daresay I've been missing out on a lot of fun," he slurred amiably.

"Well, I'm delighted you dropped in." She squirmed suggestively in his lap. "What brought you to us?"

The precious girl had asked just the right question.

"Some blokes were talking about something special happening here tonight. I decided right then to leave the party I was at and see if I could discover what the fuss was about. Or was I at the pub? Damn me! I can't recall where I've been tonight. I'm lucky I found my way here."

"I think I'll count myself as lucky too," she purred sweetly, trying to reach for the buttons of his shirt.

Not wanting her to discover that the buttons didn't actually work, Dell grasped her hips and made a clumsy play of turning her back to him so he could gain better access to her breasts. He cupped her flesh in his hands, kneading enthusiastically, silently apologizing to the girl for having to put up with his "drunken" groping.

He pressed his lips to her ear. "I heard something about a fancy piece, virginal and all that."

The girl stiffened and replied evasively. "All us girls are for sale for the night, darling. None of us are virgins, but I promise you'll be happy for that." She arched her back and ground her buttocks against his groin.

Dell decided to take a stab in the dark. "Just as well, I suppose. I doubt I'd have the blunt to afford a virgin anyway."

The girl snorted on a laugh. "You're likely right about that. Only our most elite clients were given the opportunity. And it'd've cost you more than I'd charge you for a month of fun."

"Did I miss it, then?"

"I'm afraid so. I promise I can make it up to you," she suggested in a sultry tone.

Dell smiled with true satisfaction. So the Chadwick girl had not gone to the flesh traders. Not that a wealthy bloke with a fortune to spend on his pleasures would be much better.

He had about as much information as he would get as Mr. Black. He would be better off returning as Robert French to talk to Pendragon directly.

Dell sent his body into a sudden spasm as he choked on a deep cough.

The girl on his lap spun to look at him in alarm. "What the…"

Dell bulged his eyes and brought his hand to his mouth as he convulsed again.

"Oh no," the girl exclaimed as she jumped to her feet.

Dell immediately lunged from the sofa and ran from the room and out the front door. He made sure to stop and lean into the bushes to gag and cough for proper effect. No point in completely burning his bridges. There may someday be cause for Mr. Black to visit the brothel again. After giving a convincing show of emptying his stomach, he swayed to his feet and started strolling lazily down the sidewalk, as though he had completely forgotten where he'd just been.

Morley caught up to him with the carriage around the next corner.

As Dell settled back into the cushions, he prepared himself for the confrontation ahead. He would have to tell the irritating Chadwick girl what he had discovered. He knew it was bad news as well as good, but she was not likely to see anything beyond the fact that her sister was not in his company.

He grimaced at the thought of what awaited him back at the house.

# *Six*

PORTIA COULDN'T BELIEVE IT.

Lily had been sold. Like a horse at auction.

She stared at the man named Turner, who was also Nightshade, currently Mr. Black. She didn't say a word. Just stared.

He had come into the small parlor less than five minutes ago. The candles Portia had lit earlier had all burned low, casting the room into an eerie darkness. Portia had been pacing to the rhythm of her great-aunt's snores, her arms locked across her chest to keep from wringing her hands.

And then he had appeared in the doorway. Silent and alone.

Portia had stopped in her tracks, waiting for him to explain why her sister was not with him.

His explanation had been succinct.

Hale had taken Lily to a brothel, where it would seem she had been auctioned off to the highest bidder. A gentleman, assumedly.

Portia heard the words. She understood them. She just couldn't believe it.

She stared at the man, scrutinizing his unwavering gaze, looking for falsehood, waiting for him to take back what he had just said.

After a moment, he scowled. Heavily.

"Miss Chadwick. You've received a blow. I imagine you are at a loss."

"I am not at a loss," Portia disputed in a tone nearing shrill. The release of her voice also released her feet from where they had been rooted to the floor, and she resumed her pacing. But now, her steps were reckless, and her hands gestured wildly. "I am bloody furious. How in hell can such a thing happen? Sold. Like...like livestock! It is disgraceful. Disgusting."

She stopped at the top of her path, near the fireplace, and whirled around to pin the investigator with a sharp glare. "What sort of gentleman would participate in such behavior? Where would he take her? Damn it, Turner, if she is harmed by this man, I will have his head." The boiling fury inside her forced her back into movement, and her long, whipping strides brought her back across the room toward the doorway. "How do you intend to get her back?"

She stopped right in front of him. Her chest heaved, her gaze was hard and direct, and her jaw ached with how fiercely she clenched her teeth. She realized her stance was aggressive and unladylike and rude and any number of other things Emma would chastise her for.

She didn't give a damn.

He looked down at her with a narrowed gaze. His eyes, an indiscernible color in the unreliable light, met hers without reticence.

He did not answer her right away. Considering the amount of anger and fear building within her, his lack of immediate response should have sent Portia into another temperamental outburst. Oddly, it had the opposite effect.

She was suddenly struck by his overpowering calm. Despite her tirade—which would have had Lily blushing furiously and scowling in disapproval over the inappropriate language—he appeared unruffled. Completely in command.

Portia admired his coolness. She had never managed to cultivate such a level of self-possession.

She took a long breath, hoping to ease the tight constriction that had wrapped around her torso. "What will you do?" she asked again, thankful that her tone was much more reasonable this time.

He continued to eye her for a moment longer, as if assessing her state of mind and the likelihood of another outburst.

"I will change and return to the brothel to obtain more specific information."

He stopped and frowned. His lips firmed, drawing Portia's attention to his mouth.

Such a masculine mouth, all hard angles and unforgiving lines. For a brief moment, the subtle but deep sensuality inherent in its shape stole Portia's breath.

She looked back to his eyes, obscured beneath the weight of his brow. He was clearly warring with himself over how much to tell her.

He cleared his throat.

"You will return to Mayfair and await my report."

Portia was about to argue, but he stopped her with a hard look.

She shut her mouth but gave him a fierce glare to let him know she did not appreciate being silenced.

"If your sister should try to get a message to you, where would she send it?"

Portia imagined the helplessness of waiting at home for news. The last two hours had been bad enough while she paced the parlor. But at least here she felt as though she were involved in something, doing something. At home, she would be debilitated.

And then there was Emma.

Portia would have to explain Lily's disappearance to their older sister, and it would all become so much more real somehow. She closed her eyes as the burn of tears threatened.

"Miss Chadwick…"

"You are right," she interrupted, forcefully willing away the fear and heartache. She glanced over her shoulder at where her aunt still slept, oblivious to Turner's return. "We will go. You do what you have to do and send us word as soon as you know anything. Anything at all," she insisted, turning back to meet his gaze. "Do you know the address?"

He gave a nod.

They stared at each other for another breath or two, then he turned away to disappear into the darkness of the hall.

Portia stood there for a moment, listening to the subtle creak of the stairs as he went up to change his disguise. Something about the return of the silence—the odd, echoing pressure indicating a lack of distraction—slipped beneath the wall of anger and terror that had built over the last hours.

A sob caught in her throat.

Caught and held because Portia knew tears would not help Lily.

Instead, she breathed deep and long. She resisted the urge to curl up on the floor and indulge in a wrenching cry.

And after a few minutes she felt a little stronger. She pressed her fingers to her burning eyes then crossed to where Angelique slumped in an overstuffed chair to gently nudge her awake.

After Portia explained what Nightshade had discovered, the lady's aged face tightened with distress. "The man is correct. If given a chance, Lily will send word home. We must be there. *Viens avec moi.*"

The drive back to Mayfair was silent. Both women gazed out the window, consumed by thoughts of Lily. Portia could not imagine how frightened—how devastated—her gentle sister must feel. God, she hoped she was not being abused. But really, was such a hope realistic? Portia was not naive. She understood there were evils in the world. Her mother's illness and her father's descent into addiction and excessive drinking had shown her that.

But Lily had always been so different. Lily was gifted with an unrelenting ability to see the best in people. She trusted in goodness and honestly believed the world was a lovely place.

Portia wanted to scream at the injustice of her sister's abduction.

She wished again that she had been the one snatched off the street rather than her sister. She would have found a way to fight, maybe even escape. But Lily...

With gut-wrenching regret, Portia considered the possibility of her sister being lost to them.

No. She refused to accept it. Angelique had said Nightshade accomplished things no one else could. Portia had to believe he could save Lily.

The town house was dark and solemn when they returned.

Portia went immediately up to Emma's bedroom to see if her sister had returned from the gambling hell where she had gone in a desperate attempt to win enough money to pay off Hale. Emma had been working secretly as a bookkeeper for Bentley's, a gambling club, for weeks now to earn funds to keep Lily and Portia out in society long enough to snag husbands. When Hale's demand for repayment had grown more threatening, Emma had made the bold decision to attend Bentley's in disguise as a guest, hoping to win the funds necessary to pay their father's last debt.

Unlike their father, Emma was an exceptional card player, but there was enormous risk in a lady of quality attending a party at a notorious gentlemen's club. It was amazing to think it had been just tonight that Portia and Lily had worried for *Emma's* safety, lost in the midst of the gambling hell.

How quickly things changed.

Emma's room was empty. She had not yet returned.

Portia went back downstairs and saw light coming from the parlor. Angelique was there, fully alert and, though she tried to hide it, as worried as Portia.

Glancing at the clock, Portia was stunned to see it was only half past three in the morning. It felt like

an eon had passed. "I will send a note to Emma. She
would want to know what is happening."

Angelique hummed agreement as she walked to
the bellpull. "Shall I see if we can rouse anyone for
some tea?"

Portia gave a nod then made her way to the writing desk in the corner. Her feet felt unreasonably
heavy, her arms as well. All the rage that had fired her
through the long wait for Turner's return had sapped
her of strength.

Barely able to function, she stared at the blank
paper, trying to figure out an appropriate message. It
needed to communicate the urgency of the situation,
but she rejected the idea of stating plainly that Lily
had been kidnapped, without the opportunity to offer
more explanation. After several minutes of mental
fighting, she settled on a short message she knew
would strike Emma most effectively.

> *Something terrible has happened. We need you
> home immediately.*

Such a stark message would send most people into
a panic. But not the eldest Chadwick sister. Emma
managed crises with more poise and strength than a
seasoned general.

The message would bring her home. That was all
that mattered.

# Seven

A LARGE-MUSCLED MAN MADE HIS WAY ALONG THE twisting lanes near the London docks in Wapping. He moved swiftly despite his size, his focus fixed on his destination.

Mason Hale hadn't been to this area of London in years, but it hadn't changed much since the days of those back-alley fights. He'd hated the dank smell of the Thames then and hated it even more now. He had grown accustomed to some of the basic luxuries his fighting career had afforded him. The sooner he got away from the seedy lanes that reminded him of a more desperate time in his life, the better. He wanted to see this last bit of business done so he could finally get Molly away from the vices that had led her so far astray.

The Green Hen proved to be one of the more respectable of the inns lining the streets leading away from the docks. He was surprised Molly had chosen such a place for their meeting. Respectability was not a word he'd have associated with her. He hoped it confirmed she was intent upon changing her life for the better after all.

But Hale was no fool. Molly had spun more lies over the years than anyone he'd ever known. A liar and manipulator to be sure, but Hale had believed her to be a good mother to their daughter. At least in the beginning.

Lately, Hale had been seriously questioning the intelligence of leaving the babe with her mother. Then he'd think of what little he had to offer a small girl-child.

In truth, Claire would be better off without either of her parents.

But maybe that could change.

Molly had once been a sweet young woman with laughing blue eyes and a smile full of life. She could be that woman again if Hale could get her out of Covent Garden and away from the opium dens.

She had come by his office earlier that day demanding the money he'd promised to help her. True to her vindictive nature, she'd declared that he would never see his daughter again if he didn't get the money to her by dawn.

Hale didn't want to believe Molly would actually keep his child from him, but she had become someone he barely recognized. He couldn't take that chance. Though his means may not have been fully justified, Hale had gotten the money Molly demanded.

Hale's only concern had to be for Claire.

Light shone from the windows of the inn, and the mumbled sound of conversation could be heard from within as he neared the front door.

He entered the public room and scanned for Molly's pale-blond curls, straining his ears for the distinct sound of her trilling laugh. Despite the late hour, a few people sat about enjoying ale and the company of fellow travelers, but Molly wasn't one of them.

Hale tamped down the rise of panic that flared to life in his gut. Maybe she was in one of the private rooms. Of course. Claire would be asleep at this time. Molly had to be with her.

Hale made his way across the room to the bar at the far end. The guests stopped their conversations to eye him warily as he passed. He ignored them. Resting his elbows on the bar, he tried to give the impression to anyone who watched him that he was not there to cause trouble. People often noted his large-muscled build and assumed he was a brawler looking for a fight.

Hale never looked for fights these days. But they often found him anyway.

"What can I get for ya?" the barkeep asked with a puffed-out chest and narrowed gaze.

To set the man at ease, Hale ordered an ale, though even that short delay had his skin crawling with impatience. When the barkeep set the mug in front of him, Hale paid the man but didn't take a drink.

"I'm supposed to meet someone," he said. "A young woman with pale hair and blue eyes."

The man behind the bar nodded. "I know the one."

"Can you let her know I'm here?"

The barkeep shook his head, taking a step back as he squared his shoulders. Hale knew the stance. It was one of anticipated hostility. He'd seen it enough times in life to recognize it.

His insides clenched tight. Something was wrong. It was obvious in the barkeep's sudden defensive posture. Tension stiffened Hale's limbs and tightened the muscles across his torso. He stood straight and splayed his hands palms down on the bar as he met the barkeep's eyes. "Where is she?"

At that moment, a barmaid came out from the kitchen. Her gaze was down, and she practically ran into the barkeep before she stopped herself with a gasp and looked up to see the two burly men squaring off over the bar. She took a stumbling step back with a muffled whimper.

Hale didn't bother to assure her he had no intention of throwing any punches. His only thought was of Molly and his daughter.

"She left not two hours ago with a couple of blokes," the barkeep answered gruffly.

Hale's heart iced over even as his blood burned with fury.

"She left the inn?" he clarified, wanting to leave no room for misunderstanding.

"I saw her collect her bags myself, before she got into a carriage with two fancy gentlemen."

"Where did they go?"

This time it was the barmaid who answered, stepping forward bravely. "I heard them talking about a holiday in Bath."

Hale's mind was spinning in disbelief. She had left London?

How could she?

He had gotten her the money she wanted, and she had taken off with Claire anyway. Before he could see his baby girl one last time. Before he could stop her.

Feeling more pain than he had ever known in his

life, Hale turned away and stumbled out of the inn. Even the worst beatings of his youth had not hurt as bad as the wrenching agony that gripped him then from head to toe.

All he could see was the round little face of his daughter with her quiet, trusting gaze, surrounded by a halo of curls. He clung to the mental image, suddenly terrified it might slip away as easily as Molly had taken her from him.

Claire was gone.

And the light of the world had gone with her.

# *Eight*

"WE MUST BE PRACTICAL ABOUT THIS."

At the sound of Emma's firmly controlled voice interrupting the momentary silence, Portia stopped her pacing and turned toward her sister. Anticipation lit in her center. This was the response she had been waiting for.

Emma had arrived home a short time ago—and not alone. Her employer, Mr. Bentley, had arrived at her side. Emma's slightly disheveled appearance may have caused Portia to suspect her very proper sister of engaging in a bit of improper behavior tonight.

Of course, the idea of Emma doing anything of that sort was near ludicrous.

Portia had always known her oldest sister to be unfailingly capable. Sensible in everything, Emma possessed a sort of ingrained assuredness. She could manage any crisis, calculate a solution to any problem, and had always been there when either Lily or Portia needed a guiding hand.

And so her initial response to the news of Lily's abduction had been disconcerting. For a few moments,

Emma had appeared at a total loss. The tension and fear was obvious in the way Emma sat stiff and unmoving on the sofa. As was the self-blame.

But now, it seemed Emma had regained herself.

She lifted her shrewd gray eyes to meet Portia's then gave a pointed look toward Angelique as well, who had been sitting quiet and solemn in her chair before the fireplace.

"You have faith in this Nightshade?" Emma asked.

Portia thought of Turner and the competence he embodied in his strength of purpose and plain-speaking attitude.

She nodded readily. She trusted the stranger more than she trusted anyone outside her family.

Then Emma turned to Mr. Bentley, who had stated earlier during Portia's explanation that he knew of Nightshade and his work.

The tension between these two was fascinating in its intensity. The way the gambling-hell proprietor looked at Emma, with so much depth in his gaze, made Portia feel like an intruder upon an intimate scene. But Emma, typically so self-contained, had barely glanced at the man until now, which told Portia her sister either had less than zero interest in the man or she was feeling far more than she believed herself capable of concealing.

Portia suspected the latter.

At Emma's questioning look, Mr. Bentley gave a nod as well. "He is highly regarded and has been reported as accomplishing tasks no one else would dare to attempt."

Emma's expression did not change, but Portia saw

a shift in her sister. Emma's initial shock seemed to be wearing away, and her characteristic fortitude, which had gotten the Chadwicks through the last several years, lit fiercely in her eyes.

"Then I shall endeavor to trust in his abilities as well, which means Lily *will* be returned to us," Emma stated in a tone that allowed no room for dissent or doubt. "We must consider every contingency to protect Lily from whatever may follow after tonight."

"Yes," Portia agreed wholeheartedly. Finally, something to do beyond the endless pacing. "That is exactly what we must do."

"An excellent plan, my dear." Angelique also appeared relieved to have something to focus her thoughts on.

"I am afraid I must take my leave."

Portia looked at Mr. Bentley in surprise. She honestly hadn't expected him to stray far from Emma's side tonight, not with the intent way he had been focused on her sister. Emma looked up at his words, and Portia had to glance away from the strange and awkward intimacy that passed between her sister and the gambling-hell proprietor.

Something very interesting had occurred between these two this evening.

"I wish I could stay," he continued, "but there is something I must see to without delay."

"Of course, Mr. Bentley." Emma rose from where she had been sitting on the sofa. "I am sure you are anxious to return to your club. I imagine there is much you will have to do after last night's celebration. Please allow me to show you out."

Though they both said all the right things, Portia got a strong sense they wished they could be saying something else.

Mr. Bentley turned to Angelique and Portia. "If there should be anything I can do to assist your family, on this matter or any other, please do not hesitate to ask."

Angelique lifted her opera glasses from the folds of her skirts to study the gentleman through the viewer before replying in a silken tone, "Thank you, *monsieur*. Do not be a stranger."

As soon as Emma and Mr. Bentley quit the room, Angelique turned toward Portia and practically leaned out of her chair as she whispered in a voice far louder than it needed to be, "That man can grace my parlor any day. He is far more fun to look at than the drapes."

Portia pressed the back of her hand to her mouth in an attempt to restrain the urge to giggle. It seemed Angelique, at least, was rather taken with the man. Leave it to the old lady to shift the mood with such a salacious comment.

"Tell me you do not think he is handsome," Angelique insisted as she tucked her opera glasses back into the deep pocket of her skirt.

"I am not sure this is very proper conversation, Angelique."

The aged lady gave a snort and waved her slim hand in a dismissive gesture. "If a lady cannot discuss such things in the privacy of her own parlor, where can she?"

Portia had to admit there was no good argument against such logic.

When Emma reappeared, her usual determination had been relit in her eyes. She came forward to sit beside Portia. The three women looked around at each other for a moment, then Emma said, "There is no telling what Lily might have endured by the time she is returned to us. There is much to discuss if we are to properly manage whatever might come after this night."

"Where do we begin?" Portia asked, trying not to focus on the worst of her thoughts.

Emma took a heavy breath. "I thought we might start by taking a critical look at each of her suitors. Who might have the fortitude to withstand a scandal? Whose loyalty is most in question? And so on."

Portia nodded. It was as good a place as any to start.

As more hot tea was fetched and the minutes ticked away, it helped to feel they were accomplishing something as they waited for word from Nightshade.

Nearly an hour later, as she and Emma argued the character of one particular gentleman, Portia felt a silent shift in the room. A tingle passed over the back of her neck. She glanced away from Emma and lost her breath at the sight of Lily standing silently in the doorway.

"Lily!" she shouted before she jumped to her feet and rushed across the room to wrap her sister in a fierce embrace. Relief flooded her system as Lily hugged her back. Portia dreaded letting her sister go again, but she did and stepped back to allow Emma and Angelique to assure themselves that Lily was truly home.

"Tell me you are unhurt," Emma said sternly.

Lily's smile was small but genuine. "I am fine, Emma."

"Thank God."

Emma enclosed Lily in a firm embrace while Portia took note of several pertinent elements of Lily's appearance.

Her sister did not give the impression of being in any particular distress. She did not move with any hesitation or discomfort and did not appear to have suffered any injuries that Portia could see. Her clothing was pristine, her manner calm, though perhaps a bit awkward.

What struck Portia most was the fact that Lily's brunette hair was tied with a simple ribbon at her nape, the long tresses falling free to her hips. It bothered Portia to know she had suffered even that minor indignity, and she looked harder into Lily's face, hoping to be assured her sister had not endured worse.

It was then she noticed that for all Lily's smiling composure and apparent relief in being home, she seemed reluctant to meet Portia's gaze for longer than a brief moment at a time. Such avoidance did not sit well with Portia. Something was definitely off. She could feel it.

"Come sit, *ma petite*," Angelique suggested. "Have some tea. It may still be warm."

Portia managed to contain her curiosity only long enough to allow Lily to remove her cloak and take a seat beside her on the sofa. Once Lily had a cup of tea in her hands, Portia could wait no longer.

"Tell us what happened, Lily. You must. I have been frantic with worry all night and cannot wait another moment to learn how you managed to get home."

"Give her a few moments, Portia," Emma insisted. "She has likely been through quite an ordeal. We can be patient."

Portia really detested that word. "Maybe *you* can."

She tried to distract herself by soaking up the physical proof that Lily was home safe. She would never admit out loud that there had been moments through the night when she had feared it may not end so happily.

Angelique rose slowly from her chair. "I am off to bed, darlings."

Portia looked at the older lady in stunned surprise. "How can you leave now? We are finally going to learn what happened to Lily."

Angelique smiled. "When you have had as many adventures as I have, one becomes much like the last. You girls should talk. I find myself desperately desiring the comfort of my bed. *Bon soir.*"

"I will walk you up," Emma offered.

Portia groaned at the thought of further delay. Thank goodness Angelique waved Emma off.

"*Non*, you stay—I shall find my bedroom. I assume it is where I left it this morning."

And then it was just the three sisters in the parlor.

Portia sat beside Lily, holding one of her hands tightly in her own. "Now, let us get to it, shall we?" she blurted rather abruptly as she sat forward. "What in bloody hell happened? How did you escape the brothel?"

She was rewarded for her bluntness by Lily's shocked expression. "How do you know about that?"

"Angelique and I have been on a mission to find you all night," Portia explained.

"You have?"

Her sister's surprise irked Portia. "Of course. Did you think I would just watch you get carried away and not do anything to save you? It so happens Angelique knows of this mysterious man in the East End they call Nightshade. We hired him to help us. He tracked down Hale and learned the despicable monster had you auctioned off at a brothel," Portia explained. Lily's eyes widened even more. "But he lost you after that. Nightshade is even now still trying to learn what happened to you."

"You have to stop him," Lily interrupted, turning to lay a hand on Portia's arm.

"What? Why?" Portia asked, alarm and suspicion spiking. Why on earth would Lily want to halt Nightshade's investigation?

Emma leaned forward, entering the conversation. "Are you certain you are unharmed, Lily?"

She seemed to have noticed some of Lily's oddness as well.

Lily's eyes darted between them for a moment, giving Portia the sense she was choosing her words carefully before she replied.

"I cannot say I wasn't frightened. I was, terribly so. There was a woman at the brothel. I thought maybe she would help me. Instead, she gave me something to drink that made me feel quite strange."

Lily paused and looked down at the teacup in her hands, as though trying to remember. "I do not know much of what followed. It is all muddled and foggy in my head. I remember a room…with men. Laughter and talking. It wasn't until later, after the drug started to wear off, that I learned what had happened."

Portia suddenly felt terrible. She slid closer to Lily and put her arm around her shoulders. Here she was, growing suspect of her own sister, when Lily had obviously been through a horrendous experience.

"I am fine, really," Lily continued in a lighter tone. "One of the gentlemen recognized me. He knew I should not have been there, and he rescued me. His only request was that his identity remain entirely unknown. His reputation—his family— would suffer if anyone knew he had been present at such an establishment."

Lily looked pleadingly into Portia's eyes. "Please, Portia, you must stop any further investigation. I would not betray this gentleman after he saved me from what could have been a disastrous fate."

Portia struggled to understand. "But the information would be revealed only to us. We could keep it from becoming known any further."

"No. I would betray this man to no one. Not even you."

Lily's tone was firm in a way Portia had never heard before. Warning bells sounded again in her thoughts. She glanced to Emma for assistance.

"I think we must honor Lily's wishes, Portia," Emma said. "Can you send a message to this Nightshade to call off any further investigation?"

Portia frowned. Lily's insistence on protecting her rescuer's identity struck Portia as exceedingly odd. That she chose to keep this detail to herself made Portia uneasy and suspicious. She wished she could come up with a good argument for Lily to reveal the full truth, but found none at that moment.

"If that is what Lily wants, yes, I can contact him."

"Thank you." Lily's shoulders drooped a little in her obvious relief. "Now, I wonder if I might retire. I feel like I could sleep for a week."

"I think we could all use some sleep," Emma said as she rose to her feet, essentially signaling the conversation over. "Come, I will walk you up to your room."

Portia did not follow them right away. Something was not right. She could not let it go.

Before leaving the room with Lily, Emma turned back again. "Perhaps you should send off the note to Nightshade before you retire."

Portia had a better idea.

"Yes. I will do it right away," she replied. "Good night. Or should I say good morning?"

Portia smiled and glanced toward the front window where the brightening dawn was displayed.

Emma shifted her gaze between Portia and Lily. Her sigh was quiet but weighted. "I am so proud of how both of you handled the events of last night. I will never forgive myself for not being here."

Lily quickly tried to assure her. "You could not have known Hale would preempt his deadline."

Which reminded Portia of Emma's plan to win the money to repay the loan. "Speaking of…how did you fare last night?"

"I won more than enough to pay Hale," Emma replied with another sigh. "If he had just waited until tonight as he had indicated he would…"

"Please, Emma," Lily said, ever sensitive to the distress of others. "There is no changing what happened. I am home safe. Can we not put this all behind us and move forward?"

Portia planted her hands on her hips. "I agree. Once Hale is in custody, facing the full consequences of his crimes, we need never think of it again."

"No." Lily's denial came swiftly. "We shall not report Hale to the magistrate."

"You must be joking," Portia argued. "He deserves to be hanged for this. Kidnapping is a capital offense. He sold you to a brothel, Lily."

Her sister's eyes narrowed. "I know. I was there. What do you think will happen once the *ton* discovers this little tale? The minute we report this, everyone will know where I was tonight. There will be no coming back from that."

Portia hated the logic of her argument. She would much rather see the man responsible for Lily's trauma properly punished, but her sister was right. The lack of justice was infuriating.

"Please, Portia," Lily continued, "I do not fear Hale. He has his money and no further cause to threaten us. But I do not think I could bear it if this ignoble adventure were to become common knowledge. I am home. I am unharmed. Can we please let the rest of this go?"

"Of course, Lily." Emma entered the fray to support Lily once again, which essentially closed the discussion, much to Portia's frustration. "We can talk more about what we plan to do after we have had a chance to restore ourselves."

Both women turned to leave, but not before Emma issued another reminder about Nightshade. "Do not forget to send that note."

"Go on to bed," Portia replied. "I will take care of it."

And she would. Just not in the way Emma had instructed.

She waited until her sisters reached the second

floor, then she rushed across the front hall. She knew exactly where Emma kept a handful of pound notes in case the cash was needed in a hurry. Portia had come across the stash a couple of weeks ago when she had begun to snoop around for more information about their financial situation.

Portia took just a few notes from the desk drawer in the study, along with some loose coins, before she went back into the hall. Luckily, her cloak was still draped on the hook by the door where she had left it. Securing it quickly about her shoulders, she stuffed the money into the pocket, then slid silently from the house and strode down to the street.

Though it was morning, it was still quite early. Portia's impatience led her down the street for a while as she scanned for a hired hack. Not many people were about at that time as the gray sky of dusk gave way to a golden sunrise. Though Portia continually scanned her surroundings, taking note of those she passed, her mind was occupied with what she intended to say to Nightshade.

She had agreed not to allow Lily's so-called rescuer to be identified, and she would not go back on that promise, but there was more than one way to ease her suspicions.

After walking a few blocks at a swift pace, she managed to hail a passing hack. The driver looked as if he wished to refuse when she gave the address she had memorized earlier in the night—just in case—but the man accepted her fare nonetheless. Within minutes she was on her way back to the East End and Mr. Turner.

A smile curved her lips at the thought of how annoyed he would be to see her again.

# Nine

DELL WANTED NOTHING MORE THAN TO SLEEP. AFTER getting the Chadwick woman and the elderly dowager countess out of his house, he transformed himself into Robert French, a young man who dressed like a dandy and thought himself an accomplished Casanova. Then he returned to Pendragon's to see what he could learn. The brothel's business was still in full swing though morning approached, but Dell managed to obtain a few minutes of the madam's time.

Instinct warned him not to press the matter of the abducted Miss Chadwick too openly. He chose not to reveal who had hired Nightshade and gave the explanation that he was working on behalf of one of the gentlemen who had not managed the highest bid. He said the gentleman simply wished to know how to contact the girl once her duties were fulfilled with the man who had claimed her.

As expected, the madam was tight-lipped regarding the events that had occurred at her place earlier in the night. Though she could be persuaded to toss him bits of information on common enough things, anything that dealt specifically with her clients—especially one who belonged to the higher echelon of society—was irritatingly off limits.

Dell would have kept working on her if they hadn't been interrupted by the delivery of a note, indicating someone else desired an audience with her. Apparently, the newcomer was far more important than the dandified and streetwise Robert French. The madam did not hesitate to bring their interview to an end with a generous smile and a sensual brush of her hand down Dell's arm.

Since no one bothered to come and walk him out, Dell took the opportunity to duck into an unoccupied room near the stairs. He closed the door behind him, leaving a narrow crack through which to observe anyone who passed along the hallway where Pendragon conducted all of her more private business. He was rewarded by the sight of the madam passing by a few moments later to enter another room two doors down.

Dell was too far away to hear anything beyond the low murmur of voices. He remained silent and unmoving. Barely thirty minutes later, a dark-haired gentleman exited the same room. The man was not much older than Dell himself, but infinitely more affluent, as evidenced not only by the elegant cut of his coat, but also by his general bearing and manner.

There was nothing about the dark character to suggest he'd had anything to do with the events of the prior evening. There could have been any number of reasons unrelated to the Chadwick girl for the aristocratic gent to meet with the madam at the unusual morning hour, but Dell decided to follow him all the same.

Waiting a few minutes to ensure there was no other movement in the hall, he crept through the brothel and made it outside just as the dark-haired gentleman drove off. Dell quickly got to his own carriage and followed discreetly. As expected, the gentleman made his way to an elegant mansion in Mayfair.

Dell felt an instinctive urge to enter the house to see if the girl was there. But he had no evidence to connect this man to the kidnapping. It could have been coincidence that had the man at Pendragon's this morning. Besides, infiltrating a gentleman's home was not an easy task, and the consequences for being caught could be dire. He was not about to risk arrest on a bald hunch.

Still, he waited outside for a time to ensure no further movement before heading back to the East End with a plan to have his informants dig up what they could on the gentleman. A hunch may be all he had, but his hunches often led him in the right direction.

He was home for only a few short minutes—not even long enough to shed the guise of Robert French—before there was a sharp knock at the front door. Morley was still taking care of the carriage and horses so wasn't available to answer.

With a growl at being disturbed so blasted early in the day after being up all night, Dell lumbered from his study where he had been organizing a plan for his next steps in the Chadwick abduction. He opened the door just as the caller was about to knock again.

The disturbing slate-gray gaze of the precocious Miss Chadwick widened with a start before she lowered her arm.

Dell's immediate instinctive response was to slam the door shut. This woman triggered far too many distractions in his mind, as well as his body. She set him on edge, made him feel less in control.

He didn't slam the door because his next thought was the realization that such a reaction would only pique her curiosity even more. He would need to employ another tactic to get rid of her.

Altering his voice to the smooth, unassuming, lilting tones of Robert French, Dell asked, "Can I help you, miss?"

She tilted her head beneath the wide fall of her cloak hood, and her striking eyes narrowed dangerously. He was suddenly intensely aware of his appearance. French's look often drew interested gazes from bold young women. Women who understood his jaunty swagger and the overt sensuality in his movement and expression.

Dell felt Portia Chadwick's gaze like a stream of concentrated interest shooting straight to the center of his chest.

Then she smiled.

His body instantly reacted.

*What the hell?*

Dell straightened his spine and tried to look down his—or rather French's—nose at her. Not that he thought any kind of intimidation would work on the chit, but he needed some distraction from his unwelcome and wholly disturbing reaction.

"I believe you can," she answered before she boldly strode across the threshold.

At any other time and with anyone else, Dell would never have allowed a person to just enter his home in such a way. But his current physical sensitivity to this woman had him stepping back on instinct to avoid direct contact, which gave her just enough room to sweep the rest of the way into the house.

*Damn and blast.*

Closing the door with a hard click, he turned to face her and saw that she had already crossed the small hall to the parlor. Dell gritted his teeth so hard his jaw ached. Following her into the front room, he watched with a further tightening in his loins as she swept her voluminous cloak from her shoulders to toss it carelessly to the sofa.

She was still clothed in the same evening gown from the night before. Dell couldn't stop his gaze from dropping briefly down her narrow back to the suggestive curve of her hips and buttocks before she spun around again to face him.

"I do not believe it is proper manners to so rudely force your way into someone's home," he said almost plaintively. "Especially when they are not at home."

She laughed then, a full-bodied sound accompanied by a knowing flash in her eyes. She arched her winged black brows and placed her hands on her hips. "Do not bother with the theatrics. I know it is you, Mr. Turner," she declared.

How the hell had she known?

The first time anyone had ever seen through one of his disguises, and it had to be she.

Dell considered denying it, but figured the truth would likely get her out of there faster.

"Fine," he said in his natural voice, which carried more than a hint of his annoyance. "Mind telling me what the hell you are doing back here? I told you I would let you know when I learned something."

"And did you? Learn something?" she asked, her tone hopeful.

"Not yet," he replied stiffly, expecting her to press him further or demand he do more.

"Well, the situation has changed."

Dell narrowed his gaze. "How?"

"My sister returned home safely less than two hours ago."

It was not what he'd expected to hear. But it would do. "You have come to pay the remainder of my fee, then?"

She tipped her head, allowing the black ringlets falling from her coiffure to gently graze her collarbone. "Not exactly." Turning away, she strolled toward the front window.

"Then what? Exactly?" he asked, fighting the inexplicable desire to follow her across the room.

She glanced back over her shoulder with a challenging light in her gaze. "You were hired to find my sister and bring her home. Since she obviously managed to do that on her own, I have decided to give you another chance to earn your full fee."

Crossing his arms over his chest, Dell asked, "What would you have me do now?"

She shifted the direction of her gaze, glancing down to where her slim fingers fidgeted with the seam of the curtains. There was a hint of reluctance in her manner. But she was clearly determined.

She lifted her chin and once again met his gaze with a direct and stubborn look.

"Apparently, my sister was rescued from the brothel by a gentleman who recognized her and decided to do the honorable thing. She has indicated that she does not want his identity to become known. Out of some odd sense of loyalty, she wishes to protect the man."

There was a pause while she set her chin at a stubborn angle. He knew what she was going to ask of him before the words came from her mouth.

"While I promised I would not try to discover this gentleman's identity, I want you to keep watch on my sister for a while. Covertly, of course."

As a rule, Dell did not argue with his clients. He did what he was hired to do, and that was that. But something in this woman's obstinate conviction urged him to at least try to help her see reason.

"You want me spy on your sister?" he clarified.

"Yes," she replied.

Dell sighed. "You said she is home again and unharmed?"

She frowned and turned to face him. "So she says."

"Then what cause do you have for further investigation?"

"Because she is lying."

Dell eyed her skeptically.

"It is true. I always know when Lily is being deceptive." She walked to the window, where she stopped to stare out at the street. "It is not like her to keep secrets from me. Something is not right."

She pivoted in place and strode toward Dell as he stood leaning against the back of the sofa, his ankles crossed in front of him in a casual stance. His muscles tensed when she stopped all too close for his peace of mind to stare at him with her sharp, fixed gaze.

"I need to be certain she is not still in some sort of trouble. I must be assured she is safe."

Instinct urged him to refuse. One thing he had learned was that when people spied on loved ones, they often discovered things they were better off not knowing.

Still, there were only a couple of things he would never agree to do regardless of the profit. Outright murder was one. Harming a child was the other. Beyond those two rules, he was willing to do anything as long as it paid well. He had spied, stolen, threatened vile consequences to get what he needed, and infiltrated gangs and crime rings. He had used physical force to make a point and to save his own hide, and had occasionally been forced to do things he was not particularly proud of. But it was the purse that mattered, not the job. His success was based on his ability to remain passionless and detached. That philosophy had done well for Dell over the years.

There was no reason to change now.

"Once her well-being and security are confirmed, you will pay the remainder of the fee?" he asked.

Her eyes narrowed just slightly, triggering a subtle alarm in Dell's head.

"Of course," she replied in a flippant tone.

Dell scowled. The girl had better intend to pay him. He was about to say something to assure himself of that when she took a disconcerting step even *closer* to him. Her skirts brushed his shins as she tipped her head back to better look into his face.

Dell fought to retain his ground. She carried with her the subtle essence of warm vanilla mixed with something unidentifiable that made him think of moonlit summer skies. The scent went straight to his head.

"Are you always in disguise?" she asked.

"When I'm working."

Her smile then was a delightful quirk of her full lips that had Dell's mouth going suddenly dry.

"Why do I get the sense you are always working?"

He didn't reply.

"When do you get to be simply yourself?"

"We are done here," he stated as he straightened to his full height. He expected her to step back.

She didn't.

"Oh, please don't be that way," she said with laughter in her voice. "I am curious. I find what you do extremely fascinating."

"Well, I find you extremely annoying," he grumbled as he stepped around her and headed for the door.

"I hear that often," she replied ruefully as she followed him into the small foyer.

Dell ignored the way her self-deprecation caused a strange tug inside him. He strode to the front door and opened it. Looking back, he saw her standing there in his hall, her cloak draped over her arm. Her expression was open, and a tilt of her head brought his attention to her strong little chin.

When he continued to glare at her, she heaved a labored sigh and swept her cloak around her shoulders, lifting the hood to conceal her face. But of course, the woman would not leave so easily. Once again, she stopped in front of him before passing over the threshold.

Dell gritted his teeth.

Stupidly, he had placed himself right in the doorway where he had no room to step back from her. The fall of her cloak hit his boots as she narrowed her gaze on his face. Her focus traveled intently over his features. Her silvery gaze was unnerving.

Dell's main skill was in blending into his environments as though he belonged. He had spent years learning to become a part of whatever world he entered so he did not draw attention from those around him. His disguises worked well enough for the casual observer, but were not exactly designed to hold up under close and constant scrutiny.

His scalp began to itch beneath French's blond wig, and the clump of putty he had shaped into French's prominent nose started to feel heavy and awkward on his face. Again, her scent, warm and mysterious, distracted him. He tensed his stomach muscles and pulled his shoulders back as he tried to keep from breathing too deeply.

Aside from physically forcing her through the door, which would require he place his hands on her, he had no choice but to endure her rude inspection.

The longer it took, the tighter he wound up inside.

When she finally looked into his eyes, he felt her gaze like a steel-pointed spear.

And when she smiled, that spear drove down through his center, searing his insides.

"Fascinating," she whispered softly. Her voice was smooth and sultry.

Lust ignited, hardening his body with fierce and near-painful desire. "Are you finished?" he asked through tightly clenched teeth.

Her smile turned to a smirk as one corner curled up in a way that made him want to touch his tongue to it. "For now," she said. "You will watch over Lily? Ensure she is at no further risk?"

Dell already regretted it, but he gave a short nod. "Do not come back here, Miss Chadwick," he added sternly.

With another smile, she stepped out into the early morning light.

He remained in the doorway until she was safely back inside her hired hack. Then he closed the door with a muttered curse.

"I've lost my blasted mind."

# Ten

THE NEXT NIGHT, PORTIA STOOD BESIDE LILY IN THE Duchess of Beresford's drawing room.

The Chadwicks had agreed to go on with life as usual, hoping Lily's abduction did not become common knowledge. Emma advised pragmatically that until they had some reason to do otherwise, they would be best served to behave as though nothing had happened.

Lily, for the most part, had seemed more than willing to put her harrowing adventure behind her. In truth, Lily was possibly the most composed of the three sisters.

Which only concerned Portia more. Whenever Lily put on such a show of unruffled serenity, it was because she was experiencing internal turmoil about something and did not want to burden her sisters with whatever was upsetting her.

Portia considered forcing the issue by demanding Lily confess to whatever she was keeping secret, but a strong instinct urged against it. Such a tactic could

very well backfire, causing Lily to withdraw even further. For now, all Portia could do was trust in Turner's
ability to accomplish what she'd hired him for.

Thinking of the enigmatic man, Portia wondered if
he might be at the ball tonight. He was supposed to be
watching over Lily, and Lily was here now, so it was
not unreasonable to think he might be as well.

Excitement danced through her blood. She scanned
the growing crowd intently, wondering if she would
be able to identify him. It was one thing to arrive at
his home and detect the evidence of a disguise when
there was only one person to study.

But with a whole room of people…?

He could be anyone. That had been proven by the
transformations she had witnessed so far. The man
was skilled.

But Portia was clever. And determined.

She stared hard at the guests passing before her.

No. He would most likely find a stationary spot to
observe from a distance, getting a better view of the
room to observe Lily's movements in greater context,
as well as that of any gentleman who may seem to have
an inordinate amount of interest in her sister.

That is what Portia would do, anyway.

She extended the reach of her gaze. Scanning door-
ways and alcoves. Looking for someone who seemed
to blend in with the crowd yet remain apart from it.
After a few minutes, she felt the distinctive prickle
along her nerves associated with being watched.
Glancing aside at her sister, she noted Lily was indeed
studying her with an odd expression.

"Is there a problem?" Portia asked, wondering if

Lily was finally going to admit something of the secrets she was keeping.

"I do not know," her sister replied. "What has your thoughts so occupied?"

"Nothing. What has your thoughts so occupied?"

"Nothing," Lily replied in a breezy tone.

Portia did not believe her for a second. But she knew pressing Lily directly for information on what was really going on inside her sister's unfathomable mind was likely to be futile. "It feels different, somehow, don't you think?" she asked, wondering if a more roundabout route into her sister's thoughts might work. "I mean, now that Hale is no longer a threat, and Emma won enough to save us from the financial pit of ruin…for this Season at least."

That morning, Emma had received the original loan document signed by their father and Mason Hale. Sent by messenger, it had been marked PAID IN FULL.

Lily did not answer. Instead, she directed her gaze to where Emma stood by Angelique in the chaperones' corner.

Portia felt it wise to issue a warning. "I wouldn't stare too long if I were you. You may get turned to stone like she has been."

"Portia." Lily gave her a look of reproach, to which Portia responded with a shrug.

"Honestly, have you ever seen a harder expression anywhere?"

Both girls openly observed Emma as she stood against the wall, stoic and unmoving. Even her gaze was frozen, fixed doggedly forward. She had not been the same since the night of Bentley's masquerade and Lily's abduction.

More withdrawn and taciturn than usual, it seemed Emma still expected Lily and Portia to see out the remainder of the Season, even if she was no longer being militant about it. Though they no longer stood under threat from Hale, the Chadwicks were still in debt, with the only means of rectifying their situation being marriage to noble English gentlemen.

Portia hated the marriage market. The ladylike glances and coy giggles. The gentlemen with their most times covert, but occasionally bold, assessments of the present year's stock of debutantes. The super-ficiality of it all was disturbing.

She tried to keep her frustration from showing in her expression, but realized she likely failed miserably.

"At least she hasn't been pressuring me to make nice with all the eligible bachelors tonight," she mut-tered, trying to take a leaf from Lily's book and find something positive in the situation.

"And you are bored out of your mind, aren't you?" Lily observed.

"An understatement, I think," Portia admitted reluctantly. "I cannot wait for this bloody Season to be over."

If she had her way, she would never attend another event of the beau monde ever again.

Lily did not reply. Portia wished she would, even if it was to chastise her for her unpopular sentiment. Whenever she was in a wretched mood, it helped to have an outlet for her irritation, but it seemed Lily was not willing to oblige her with an argument.

With rather unfortunate timing, a merry group of gentlemen and young ladies happened to pass by just then.

Portia glared at them. How did they manage to look so bloody pleased to be there, giggling and flirting and sending coy glances at each other? Perhaps there was truly something wrong with her that she detested the frivolity in which everyone else seemed so willing to indulge.

She forced herself to glance away or risk offending someone with her dark expression. Her gaze swept past the row of terrace doors thrown open to allow fresh air into the growing stuffiness of the room, aching to escape out into the night. It was then that her attention snagged on an elderly gentleman positioned near the door.

There would have been no reason for his appearance to catch her notice if not for the fact that he was staring straight at her.

She experienced a sharp and sudden flare of awareness.

The second her eyes met his, he looked away. It was such a brief moment of eye contact, she likely would have dismissed it if something hadn't struck her as odd about the man.

He was quite old, with white hair and a feeble posture. He sat in a wheeled chair with a heavy rug placed over his legs. His shoulders were rounded and hunched forward with age, and he stared out over the room through a thick monocle that he held to his eye with a trembling hand. He was dressed in an elegant, though slightly old-fashioned style and appeared to be absentmindedly observing the movements of the guests around him, as though he wasn't entirely certain why he was there.

Portia could not figure out what it was about him that sparked her curiosity. But then, as she continued to study him, he swept another glance in her direction.

There was another brief moment of eye contact.

And another rush of intense awareness.

It was Turner.

She knew by the way he steadfastly refused to look her way again. And she knew by the inexplicable excitement tumbling through her like a waterfall.

"I am going to get some air," she announced to Lily, then without awaiting a reply, she started toward the nearest doors leading out to the terrace.

She wasn't exactly sure why she felt such a compulsion to approach him.

To prove to herself perhaps that she was as clever as he was. To have some evidence to support what she'd believed all her life: that she was meant for more than standing along the wall, waiting for an invitation to dance.

Somehow, Nightshade and his work had come to represent all she wanted for herself. She needed to be a part of it, even if it was just in knowing that although Turner was adept at fooling everyone else, she might be the exception.

He was positioned with his back to one of the open doors. He must have been dying from the heat of the heavy wool blanket covering his lap and likely needed the stiff breeze to keep from passing out.

Lest he glance her way again and suspect her approach, Portia slowed her pace. She forced herself to continue across the room at a sedate stroll, smiling at various acquaintances as she passed. Once she had slipped out onto the terrace some distance from where the white-haired gentleman sat, she kept to her casual pace along the length of the balcony, grateful there were not many other guests outside enjoying the night.

Seeing the wheeled chair through a set of doors ahead of her, she approached quietly from behind. She crept up to within a couple of feet of him before stopping in the doorframe and linking her hands in front of her in her best impression of a young lady casually claiming a bit of fresh air.

Forcing a bland expression to her face, she tried to think of something to say that would force Turner to reveal himself. She glanced at him from the corner of her eye and paused in a moment of uncertainty.

The man looked quite aged, with his sloped shoulders and curved spine. His face was turned away from her, but what she could see of his skin was pale and deeply lined. His hands rested in his lap. The fingers were curled with arthritis and covered in age spots.

Could she have been wrong?

Was she so anxious for some sort of excitement that she imagined the odd sense of familiarity in this old man's distant glance?

As she stared surreptitiously, she saw him move one of his hands, just enough for her to realize that despite their awkward positioning, they were not the hands of an old man. She narrowed her gaze. His shoulders, though hunched in an uncomfortable way, were broad. And the shape of his legs beneath the rug appeared to be anything but feeble.

It had to be him.

Excitement burgeoned in her chest.

But how to prove it?

"Lovely party," she said casually.

"Eh?" His response was quick and in character. He angled his head in a way that implied he was hard of hearing, yet she had spoken rather softly. His immediate reaction suggested he'd heard her just fine.

And he had known she was there.

Portia stepped closer to him and leaned over his shoulder. "I said it is a lovely party," she repeated loudly next to his ear. Taking advantage of the momentary proximity to observe him more closely, she noted a few interesting details.

First, there was a fine dusting of gray powder in an exact match to his hair on the shoulder of his coat. Also, his ear was actually quite handsomely shaped. Not that she had ever studied such a feature before, but in being forced to think about it, there had never been a man matching this one's advanced age who did not have some sagging about the earlobe and an overabundance of hair growing from the center.

This gentleman had neither.

Lastly, she was quite certain she caught a glimpse of something resembling glue just under the corner edge of his drooping white mustache.

"If you say so," he muttered. Then he gave a rough sort of grunting cough and turned away from her to hack revoltingly into a handkerchief he held to his face.

Portia suppressed her smile as she took a small step around to face him more directly.

He continued to avert his focus, holding the handkerchief over his mouth.

"Forgive me," she said sweetly, "you seem terribly familiar to me. I am certain we have been introduced, but I cannot recall your name."

She waited for his response. She could practically feel his annoyance surging through the false frailty of his body. He was likely considering what risk there might be in ignoring her completely. No doubt his mind was working through the possible ways he could be rid of her.

"Lord Seymour," he finally replied in a wavering tone.

"Oh, my parents knew some Seymours from Suffolk," she lied. "Would they be your family?"

"No," he grunted. "I hail from the north."

"I see. Distant branch, perhaps."

He gave another grunt.

There had to be some way to slip past his guard without exposing him to anyone else.

She stood there pretending to contentedly observe the party. After a moment, she had an idea. It was a bit drastic, but she was compelled to prove to herself and to him that she was correct. Either she verified her suspicion or made a total arse of herself.

In truth, she would probably accomplish both.

She issued a long and practiced sigh. "I hear the music has started up, and I think I see my partner for the first dance all the way across the room." She didn't actually have a promised partner, but it seemed a likely reason for her to depart the old man's company. "It was delightful speaking with you, Lord Seymour."

She stepped around his chair as she spoke, smiling

down at him. He made a point to be looking elsewhere, of course. This worked into her plan, since at
that moment, she intentionally caught her foot against
the wheel of his chair, which sent her tumbling forward. She executed a swift twisting of her body, and a
moment later, she was sprawled across his lap.

She wasn't sure how she had expected him to react
to her physical blunder, other than hoping he would
do something to reveal the strength and reflexes of a
much-younger man. She thought perhaps he would
reach out swiftly to stop her fall, or mutter something
in surprise that would give him away.

What actually happened was so much better.

She should have known someone of Nightshade's
skill would not be so easily shaken out of character.
Turner likely had infinite experience with handling
unexpected surprises. Her falling quite literally into his
lap proved to be no exception.

As the feeble old Lord Seymour, of course he
would have no way to stop a woman, even one as
petite as Portia, from falling rather roughly across his
legs. However, once she landed there, he was also
helpless against removing her, though he made a good
show of huffing incoherent words of indignation at
her supreme faux pas.

It gave her plenty of time to note the bright flash
of anger that flared beneath thick white brows as he
looked directly at her for the first time since the start
of their encounter. She realized with amazement that
his eyes were a lovely hazel color: deep gold with a
dark-blue ring around the outer edge and flecks of
brown and green throughout the rest. She also noted

that his legs were well formed and dense with muscle beneath her buttocks. His hand—which she doubted he even realized had fallen onto her knee—radiated heat. And the shape of his lips beneath his mustache was firm and sensual.

Then, there was the fact that Portia's entire body ignited with a thousand tiny sparks, instantly heating her blood and turning her thoughts inside out.

While they continued to stare at each other, neither of them willing to do what was necessary to right her again, others in their vicinity began to notice their predicament.

Portia was grateful for the sudden attention. It allowed her to play off the heated blush on her cheeks as being from embarrassment, when she knew it was due to something else entirely.

"I knew it was you," she whispered with a tight little smirk just before a conscientious bystander stepped forward to offer her a hand in rising to her feet.

Turner narrowed his gaze, and those masculine lips of his thinned with tension, but he said nothing.

She gave a wonderful performance, muttering her apologies and claiming to be notoriously clumsy. She brushed out her skirts as others stepped forward to ensure that she and her hapless counterpart were none the worse for the unfortunate accident.

As Portia leaned toward him again to offer her apologies, he met her gaze. The irritation she saw there nearly had her grinning, but she held herself back. "I am so very sorry, my lord. Please forgive my clumsiness. It shall not happen again."

He gave a rough grunt. "See that it doesn't."

She curtsied and walked away, biting her cheek to keep from grinning widely at the elation running through her.

She had done it. Not only had she confirmed Turner's identity, but *he* knew she knew, which made it all the more satisfying. And she had done it without revealing his disguise to anyone else.

It felt amazing to have accomplished something so tricky, and Turner's annoyance over her achievement was a delightful bonus.

Portia spent the rest of the evening stealthily observing the aged and surly Lord Seymour in an attempt to determine if he was directing his attention to any particular gentleman in the crowd. After a few hours, she had to admit that Turner was very good at his job. Though he always seemed to be in view of Lily, she had not been able to discern through expression or action if there was anyone else he might be watching.

When she saw a footman pushing his chair out into the hall and he failed to return, her interest in remaining at the party went right out the door with him.

# Eleven

DELL WAITED IN THE COMFORTABLE DARKNESS OF HIS carriage. He had long ago taken advantage of the vehicle's privacy to remove his white wig and mustache and had wiped away most of the makeup that had been caked on his face to suggest the aged skin of Lord Seymour.

The disguise was no longer needed, as he had no intention of interacting with anyone for the rest of the night. His next few hours would be strictly surveillance.

Watching Lily Chadwick all evening had revealed very little. The woman had proven to be somewhat difficult to read. She looked much like her younger sister in her general features, including her smaller stature and gray eyes. But her hair was lighter than Portia Chadwick's dark-sable tresses, and her figure more rounded around the bust and hips.

Not to mention, Lily Chadwick carried herself with a sort of serenity his impertinent client was simply incapable of. If he had not known the young lady had gone through a rather harrowing series of events just two nights prior, he never would have suspected she was anything other than completely composed and perfectly content.

That is, until he noticed her occasionally sweeping her gaze over the guests, clearly searching for someone. The gentleman who had rescued her, perhaps? Or was it that someone at the party posed a threat to her as Portia suspected?

It was possible, though without noticing anything revealing, or even curious, in Lily's interactions with the gentlemen present, there was nothing that made one of them stand out over the others.

Dell decided to come at the issue from another direction.

Through a narrow crack in the drawn curtains of the carriage, he finally observed the Chadwick sisters departing Beresford House with the Dowager Countess of Chelmsworth. Just the sight of the youngest Chadwick woman tightened his muscles with tension.

It had been a bold and foolish move on her part to force their interaction earlier. It irked him how easily she saw through his false personas.

One thing was certain: if she expected him to be able to do his job, she had to keep her distance.

If *he* expected to be able to do his job, he would need to get his reactions to the chit under control.

Damn her inexplicable allure. If she hadn't looked so bloody enticing in her ice-blue gown with green trimming, he would never have been caught staring at her, which had drawn her attention in the first place. He hadn't made such an amateur move since he had created Nightshade and all his guises.

Though he enjoyed placing blame squarely on

Portia Chadwick's lovely bare shoulders, he knew it was his own lack of self-possession that allowed the slip. He needed to get himself together. Sexual attraction—even that as compelling as he was experiencing for the dark-haired young woman—had no place in an investigation. No place in his life, to tell the truth.

Such things only complicated matters.

A much more casual approach in his sexual relations with the female gender had served him well for quite a while. There was no way he was going to indulge in the unexpected fire of need this particular woman caused. The sooner he convinced his body of that, the better.

He watched as the Chadwicks piled into their carriage and drove off. Glancing back to the house, he noticed he had not been the only one waiting for their departure.

As Lady Chelmsworth's carriage rolled away, another figure stepped through the Beresfords' front door: the same elegant gentleman who had visited Pendragon in the early morning hours after the auction, cutting French's interview with the madam short.

An interesting coincidence.

Dell had intended to follow the Chadwicks' carriage to ensure the ladies made it home without undue incident. But as the mysterious lord approached his own vehicle, Dell decided he might be just as well served to follow him.

He was not disappointed.

They did not go far before the gentleman's carriage turned onto the narrow lane that ran behind the town house that was currently the residence of the dowager countess and her three great-nieces. Dell knocked on the roof of his own vehicle, signaling Morley to stop more than a block away.

He would need a closer look.

Instructing Morley to wait, he drew his greatcoat closer about his frame and tucked his chin in the shadows of the large collar. The street was relatively quiet at this time of night, but the standing gas lamps had been lit, casting everything in a steady glow.

Dell strolled down the street in the opposite direction from where the gentleman's carriage had turned into the lane. Keeping to a sedate yet intentional pace, he continued around the corner and entered the mews from the opposite end. He clung to the shadows, creeping on silent feet as he made his way along the back wall of the Chelmsworth garden. The lord's carriage was up ahead, partially concealed beneath the fall of a large willow. Finding an agreeable spot behind some thick shrubbery, Dell leaned into the deep shadows and positioned himself for a long wait.

More than an hour passed before he heard someone coming from the garden inside the privacy wall.

A few moments later, a gate near the middle of the wall swung open, and a solitary figure stepped out. The figure was small in stature and was draped in the folds of a dark cloak with its hood pulled up. Only a narrow flounce of white skirts could be seen beneath the hem.

The garden gate closed quietly behind her, yet the woman did not continue forward. She stood against the wall, staring down the lane toward the partially concealed carriage. When she still did not move after several minutes, the carriage door opened, and the dark-haired gentleman stepped out.

Dell studied the hooded female carefully. He had been hired to determine whether or not Lily Chadwick was in danger. Clearly, she had ventured outside her great-aunt's home intentionally, but there could have been some means of coercion causing her to do so.

He noted how the woman turned to face the gentleman directly. There was no reluctance in her movements. In fact, the man's appearance outside the carriage seemed to bolster the woman's courage as she started toward him with swift and light strides.

She stopped again before actually reaching the gentleman's side, but when he lifted his hand to her, she continued forward without further hesitation and placed her hand in his. As she did so, the movement of her arm swept her cloak aside just enough for Dell to note that her gown matched that worn by Lily Chadwick earlier in the evening. As she stepped up into the carriage, the woman briefly glanced back down the alley toward Dell's position in the shadows, and he managed to catch a glimpse of her face.

It was, indeed, Lily Chadwick.

A few moments later, Dell lowered his chin to better conceal his face as the carriage rolled past him. Dell pushed off from the wall, intending to go back to his own carriage so he could follow the couple to their next destination.

However, before the vehicle completely cleared the mews, another figure stepped through the garden gate. The newcomer was similar in height and with a dark, voluminous cloak exactly like the one worn by Lily Chadwick.

Seeing the carriage turn out of sight, the second young lady gave a disappointed huff. "Blast," she muttered angrily.

Dell tensed.

Portia.

Her hood swung in his direction, though he knew he had made no noise to call her attention. She followed her gaze with a few steps. Then she halted, as though listening. She was still for so long, Dell wondered if she was all right.

"Turner. Are you out here?"

*Bloody hell.*

Dell stepped forward from his shadowed corner.

Her light gasp at his sudden appearance confirmed she had not seen him.

The woman was far too bold as she approached him in long strides. What if it wasn't him at all? It was on the tip of his tongue to start lecturing her for her carelessness and lack of concern for her own safety. Not only in approaching a shadowy character on a dark lane, but in traipsing about alone so late in the first place.

He knew before he spoke, however, that a sensible lecture would only end in a roll of her fascinating eyes or a snort of derision before she went along doing exactly what she wanted to do anyway.

It seemed the more effective option would be to show her just how dangerous such behavior could be.

As soon as she came to a stop, he grasped her upper arms in his hands and swung them both back into the dark corner behind the shrubbery. He pushed her up against the stone garden wall, stepping close enough to keep her in place, but still far enough for the fall of her cloak to swirl in the space between them.

She gasped then clutched at the front of his coat as she leaned to the side to scan down the lane. "What is it?" she asked breathlessly. "Are they coming back?"

Dell wanted to shake her. Instead, he growled in anger, "No, you bloody idiot. What in hell are you doing out here? Have you any idea what manner of trouble you could have found yourself in the midst of?"

Hadn't he decided a lecture would be pointless?

The woman was making him lose his mind.

"What? Do you mean like my sister climbing into a carriage in the middle of the night and riding off to who knows where with who knows whom?" she replied testily, angling her head back so she could look up into his face.

The act caused the hood of her cloak to fall back off her head. The light of the moon favored Dell with a clear view of her winged eyebrows arched over a bewitching gaze, her fine cheekbones, and lush little mouth. Even the woman's nose contributed to her stunning beauty.

His chest tightened, and desire pulsed through his blood, angling straight to his groin. Dammit, she was doing it again. Making him forget himself.

Luckily, she seemed far too irritated to notice anything untoward in his manner.

"Did I not hire you to keep her safe? What are you doing hiding in the bushes when my sister is out there?" she finished with a jerk of her arm.

Dell released her with a low grunt as he took a step back.

"You hired me to determine if she was still in any danger," he replied in clipped syllables. "That is what I am doing."

"But you just let her leave." The damnable woman was obviously intent upon arguing.

Dell was exasperated enough to oblige her. "I saw no evidence of coercion or threat. Your sister left willingly."

Her fine features were tense under the moonlight. "But why? It is so unlike her." She gasped in sudden surprise. "Was it the gentleman who rescued her from the brothel?"

"There is no evidence of that."

"But you suspect it is," she added confidently. "Who is he?"

Dell's sources had provided the gentleman's name and more, but before he could form a reply, she gave a swift shake of her head. "No, do not answer that. I promised Lily I would not try to discover his identity. Do you know where they were going?"

"I would have discovered their destination if I had been free to follow them."

Her expression changed then. The tense little scowl slid away. One brow lifted in an impertinent arch, while her lips tilted upward at the corners and her eyes flashed from a narrowed gaze.

He had thought her stunning before. In possession of a unique sort of confidence all her own, when challenged, she proved she could be downright bewitching.

"You are just miffed that I saw through your disguise earlier, aren't you?"

He could not risk anyone seeing through his camouflage. He hated to admit she was right—that her ability to recognize him annoyed the hell out of him—but he also needed to know for certain what had given him away.

"How did you know it was me?"

Her mouth curved into a wide smile. "It was in the way you looked at me."

Dell stiffened. Not *that* he had been looking, but *the way* he had been looking. That couldn't be. She couldn't possibly have detected his attraction to her. "I barely glanced at you."

She shrugged, and her cloak parted with the movement to reveal a significant portion of her figure still gowned in ice-blue silk. Dell had to drag his attention back to her face.

Damned distraction.

"But that glance was more than enough to detect the irritated sort of glower you like to give me. See! You are doing it right now." She tilted her head and planted her hands on her hips. "It gives me the distinct impression that you'd like to turn me over your knee."

*She did not just say that.*

Lust blazed through him at the image her words conjured, even though he knew she could have no idea what kind of suggestion she had just made. As he fought a primal urge to grasp hold of her and do just that, she grabbed him instead.

Her hands curled into the material of his coat, and she hauled him toward her until she was flat against the wall with his body pressed full-length to hers in a way he had been fighting the urge to do from the moment he'd met her.

He had been right to avoid such contact.

When she'd grabbed him, he had reacted automatically, sliding his arm around her waist. His instinct had been to shield her from whatever threat had spooked her.

However, the heat of her silk-clad body tugged his focus in an entirely unwanted direction. As did the wonderful female scent drifting from her skin, the barely perceptible flow of her breath against his throat, and the slide of her sable hair against his temple.

Her shape was small and feminine, but the energy contained within her slight form fairly buzzed with intensity.

With the blood suddenly rushing from his head, it took Dell an extra split second to hear what she had obviously already noted—the sound of someone humming.

The voice was a woman's and came from the garden. The fact that a seven-foot wall separated them from the unexpected intruder made it obvious their current position was entirely unnecessary. That knowledge should have inspired Dell to step back again.

He didn't.

Instead, he remained as he was—one forearm braced against the wall beside her shoulder and his other arm wrapped securely around her narrow waist beneath the fall of her cloak—listening to what sounded like someone taking a late-night stroll through the garden.

"Angelique."

Portia whispered the name so softly there was no way anyone but Dell could have heard. It was possible he hadn't heard it at all. It was entirely possible he simply felt the word as she breathed it silently against his ear while he stood with his head dipped low beside hers.

Dell had been in some extremely challenging circumstances in his career. But this—enduring the near embrace of this small woman—was almost more than he could handle.

Finally, the humming started to drift away. A few minutes later, it could be heard no more.

Neither of them moved. Then Dell felt the slightest shift in her weight. He straightened his spine and lifted his head at the same time that she tipped hers back to look him full in the face. Her mouth was a breath away from his.

"She has gone back inside."

"You should go in as well," Dell replied, the words suddenly thick in his throat.

"I will," she whispered as she uncurled her fingers from his coat to flatten her hands against his chest.

*Now* was the time to step back.

Miss Chadwick was as green as they came, despite her impulsive nature. She was heading for trouble a thousand different ways, and he had no intention of being there when she found it.

Why in hell didn't he step back?

"Do you think they are lovers?" she asked. The words, spoken in the lowered tone, took on a sultry quality.

That did it.

Dell retreated, withdrawing his arm from around her body and stepping back until no part of them remained in contact. "A reasonable assumption," he replied.

A deep furrow formed between her elegant eyebrows, and she shook her head. "Remarkable."

Dell had seen the reaction before. Many times. It amazed him how people could think they truly knew their loved ones. No one ever wanted to believe someone they cared about would lie to them. But everyone lied.

She peered intently into his eyes. "And you think he is the same gentleman who took her from the brothel?"

"It's just a hunch."

She was silent for a few moments…then a strange smile slid across her features.

Dell's stomach tightened again. There was danger in that smile.

"Does your hunch tell you where they might be going?" she asked slyly.

Dell did not answer; he obviously didn't need to.

"Well, let's go," she insisted. "Before we lose them."

"I will go. You will stay here."

"I want to come with you."

"We have been over this," he replied, not bothering to keep the exasperation from his voice.

"But that was in regard to visiting Hale," she argued.

Why couldn't the woman simply accept his dictate?

"This is different," she continued. "My sister is with the man, for God's sake. Surely, wherever they are going, I can go."

"You are not coming with me," he said with finality as he turned away and started down the lane with long strides.

"Damn, but you are a stubborn one," she muttered behind him.

He answered with a rough snort and kept walking. He was surprised she didn't follow, and grateful.

It wasn't until he was back in the carriage that he realized he had barely retained any of his disguise during his interaction with the Chadwick woman. He had never been so careless. He could only hope the night had been dark enough that she had not been able to detect much more than a general impression of his features.

Portia Chadwick already knew far too much about Nightshade. Any more, and Turner's livelihood would rest entirely in her elegant hands.

# Twelve

A COUPLE OF DAYS LATER, PORTIA SENT TURNER A note to inquire on his progress in determining if Lily remained in any danger. She would have loved to go back to Honeycutt's brownstone in person, confront him directly and demand an update on his investigation, but she couldn't find a proper opportunity to slip away when Emma continued to insist they attend so many social functions.

Lily was still behaving oddly, but as far as Portia knew, her sister had not sneaked from the house again as she had the other night.

Could Lily really have taken a lover?

The idea was astonishing.

But it was not entirely out of the realm of possibility. Lily was not quite the innocent she portrayed to the world. Growing up as close as any two sisters could be, Portia was familiar with Lily's most secret of secrets, which was why it was so frustrating and hurtful that Lily felt a need to keep this from her now.

Still, Portia was reluctant to press Lily for information directly. What if Lily refused to tell her anything?

Portia wasn't sure she was ready to acknowledge that she may no longer be Lily's unconditional confidante.

Portia hated having to consider the possibility that their relationship had changed. Since the abduction, they had already discontinued their nightly bedtime talks. What other changes were on the horizon?

On the other hand, Portia was astute enough to realize that if Lily truly had taken a lover, maybe she had every right to keep such a thing all to herself. Portia detested being excluded, but she had to respect her sister's desire for secrecy.

Unless she proved to be in some sort of danger.

Lily may have a much deeper inner life than anyone would suspect, but she was also frighteningly trustful. She could easily find herself caught up in something dangerous.

It was for Lily's own good that Portia had hired Turner to keep an eye on her. Someone needed to ensure that Lily was not putting herself at risk. Portia was simply doing her sisterly duty.

That is what she kept telling herself anyway, as she waited for Turner's reply.

It arrived after only a few hours in the form of a brief message written in strong, upright penmanship.

> *My investigation has revealed no apparent danger.*
> *You may send the remainder of my fee along with*
> *my messenger, who has been instructed to wait.*

Portia bounded up from her favorite chair in the corner of the library where she had been reading.

*A messenger.*

Perhaps it was Turner himself in disguise.

Just the thought of seeing the man again had Portia's heart racing. In an instant, she was almost as breathless as she had been that night in the lane. She had never felt anything so exhilarating as being held tight against Turner's strong frame for those moments as they listened to Angelique moving about beyond the wall. The heat of his body, the secure band of his arm around her waist, and the sensation of his low breath fanning against her neck had been a singular experience.

One she wouldn't mind repeating, to be honest, though she'd prefer to try it under different circumstances.

A blush warmed her cheeks as she rushed along the narrow hall toward the back servants' door via the kitchen. Proper young ladies were not supposed to have such lusty thoughts. But since they were in her own mind, they weren't likely to bother anyone but herself.

Though in all truth, they *had* been bothering her.

From the very first night she had met Turner, she hadn't been able to get out of her head the image of his bared torso, or the sound of his rough voice. If she closed her eyes, she could feel the intensity of his gaze. Even though he somehow managed to change the appearance of his eyes with each character incarnation, it never changed the way he made her feel when he looked at her.

Portia suspected what that feeling might be, but she needed more opportunities to explore the idea further.

As she entered the kitchen, her heart sank at realizing the messenger was too small to be Turner.

Her disappointment was followed swiftly by delight as she saw that it was the same boy who had directed

Portia and Angelique to Honeycutt's address the night of Lily's abduction. Looking up from his glass of warm milk as Portia entered, the boy's eyes flashed with recognition. He jumped up from his seat at the long table and swept his red cap off his head as he gave her a broad wink.

"'Ello, miss. What a plummy surprise to run into you again. Me luck might be changing after all. And might I say you're looking fine this day."

Portia laughed at his blatant flattery, though she had to admit he pulled it off with more sincerity than most of the gentlemen of the *ton*. "Thank you. You may call me Portia if you'd like. Are you hungry?"

"No. I ate this morning. The milk is enough."

"Are you sure?" Morning was several hours ago, and she had heard something about growing boys having very healthy appetites. "It won't take a minute to prepare something for you."

He paused to wrinkle up his nose then gave her a winning smile. "Since you put it that way, I s'pose I'd enjoy a bite or two."

"Excellent."

Portia nodded to a young maid, who was prepping the kitchen for the cook to start the midday meal. The girl immediately went about fixing up some cold meat left over from the prior evening's dinner, a crust of bread, and some jam.

"And what shall I call you?" Portia asked, taking a seat at the table.

"Me name's Thomas."

"Lovely to meet you officially then, Thomas. Please enjoy your meal."

"Thank you, miss." He plopped back down on the bench with a grateful grin. "It's not every day I get to enjoy such grand company. And the food's nice too."

Portia smiled. He was a delightful charmer.

Thomas practically attacked his plate while Portia sat at the table with her chin propped in her hand, grinning at the gusto with which he enjoyed the cold lunch.

Once he slowed down enough to allow for some effective chewing between bites rather than wolfish inhalations, she asked conversationally, "Nightshade has you running messages for him now?"

Thomas shrugged. "I do lots of things for 'im. Anything he asks, to be honest. He's a good sort. Pays me well."

"Have you worked for him a long time?"

"I'd guess five years or so."

That shocked her. "But you must have been so young when you started."

"About six, I think. Not too sure 'bout that. He caught me picking his pocket. No one had ever caught me before." Thomas laughed at that. "I thought I was a goner for sure."

"He did not turn you over to the authorities?"

"Naw. He told me he'd let me go if I did a small task for him. He needed someone to sidle up near where some blokes were chatting and report back what I heard. It wasn't nothing. A few days later he came looking for me and offered me a real job. Then he found a place for me to live, away from the gangs. It was better than I'd had up till then."

Portia could hear everything the boy didn't say. His respect for his employer ran even deeper than his loyalty, which as far as Portia could tell, only wavered under the promise of a kiss.

As soon as he finished his meal, Thomas stood and gave Portia a look that was all business.

"Now, I'll be having Nightshade's payment, miss, if you don't mind. Then I must be on me way."

Portia smiled. "I am afraid I must extend your employer's assignment for a bit longer. His work to date has not satisfactorily eased my mind."

She gave Thomas the note she had prepared before leaving the library, which requested that Nightshade continue his investigation for another week at least with the promise of an additional fee.

Though Lily had not met with her mysterious gentleman since the other night, Portia sensed her sister's dubious adventure was not over yet. It was something she saw in Lily's eyes, a subtle light of daring that had never been there before.

After Thomas's visit, Portia waited in vain for a response from Turner. Eventually, she decided to assume he'd accepted her request, since he hadn't sent another demand for his fee.

Of course, he may also have just accepted the loss of his fee so he could wash his hands of her. It was certainly a possibility. The man did seem quite annoyed with her most of the time.

Since she had no true confirmation from Turner, Portia considered the possibility of having to continue the investigation on her own. Though she relished the thought of having something to do beyond the endless parties and balls, the idea of no longer having a reason to meet with Mr. Turner left her decidedly disgruntled.

# *Thirteen*

MASON HALE STALKED WITH HEAVY STRIDES DOWN the dark alley to the side door of the brothel. His steps were weighted, not only with the mass of his impressive physique, but more prevalently with an emotion he was helpless to contain.

For a week, he had been suffering under the inescapable burden of fear, desperation, and loss.

Hale was not accustomed to wishing for anything. He accepted what was.

When he had discovered a talent for bare-knuckle fighting, he'd developed his skills and won his bouts. When he'd reached the age of twenty-six and realized he couldn't stay in the ring for the rest of his life, he'd shifted his focus to running the stakes.

He had never expected to be rich. Most of the time he'd made enough blunt to live comfortably. Certainly more comfortably than he'd ever dreamed possible when he'd been a lad.

He had never been one to harbor hope for any reason.

But hope was something he clung to now. It was the only thing giving his life any direction since he'd discovered Claire was gone. Five days ago he had woken from a two-day drunk with a phrase locked in his head.

*Under my protection.*

He vaguely remembered a gentleman visiting him at the start of his drunken oblivion. The man had used those words, and at the time they had meant nothing to Hale. The bloke's visit had just been an unwelcome interruption from his mission to reach oblivion. But the words had clung like a spider's web to the inside of his brain. Hale hadn't been able to shake the phrase through two more bottles of gin, a bottle of whisky, and the twelve-hour sleep that followed.

*Under my protection.*

His daughter was his to protect and care for. He should have taken that responsibility seriously from the start. He hadn't, and now Molly had taken Claire away to God knows where.

What a fucking arse he had been to think the child would be better off with that woman. Molly no longer possessed any semblance of the fresh-faced girl he had met nearly five years ago. She had become less fit to care for Claire than Hale was himself. But it had taken him too long to see it.

Hale was by no means ideal father material, but if he was lucky enough to get his daughter back, he would do whatever he could to keep her safe and happy.

First, he had to find her. And he needed all the help he could get.

He walked into Pendragon's Pleasure House with the confidence of a man who had been to the elite brothel many times before. The burly footman standing just inside the narrow back hall gave him a short nod.

"Where is my sister?"

"She's having one of her grand parties tonight. She's sure to be occupied for several more hours."

"Find her now and tell her I'm waiting in the library," Hale said in a tone that left no room for further argument before he continued down the hall.

A few turns brought him to his half sister's library. Liquor was set up in the corner, but Hale turned away from the bottles with a queasy lurch to his stomach. He hadn't been able to think about the stuff since he had woken up with the most vicious hangover of his life—made all the more crippling by the deepest sense of guilt Hale had ever known.

Because he hadn't been there when his baby girl had needed him.

And now she was gone.

Too anxiety-ridden to sit, Hale stalked around the room, moving the bric-a-brac about, partially to distract himself and partially because he knew it annoyed his half sister, and it was a long-standing habit to torment her in small ways.

"Mason."

He turned to see the high-class brothel's madam sweep elegantly into the room. Hale had to admit Callista had done well for herself. From gin-shop girl to madam of an elite pleasure house.

"Any news of Molly?" Hale asked without preamble, his hands balled into hard fists.

His half sister continued toward him. The dark look in her eyes answered his question before she did. "No.

The twit has not returned to London as far as I know. I take it you did not find her in Bath?"

"Not a single sign of her. I doubt she went there at all. The damn woman could be anywhere."

Hale stalked to the liquor service, but when he got there, he just stared at the various bottles without really seeing them. In his mind's eye, he saw only his baby girl. "I don't know what the hell to do, Lissy." His voice sounded raw coming through his tight throat. He fought the emotion rising from his chest and pressing against the backs of his eyes.

"I am so sorry, Mason."

Callista, who was twelve years older than he and had been more like a mother than his own had been, stepped up behind him to place her hand on his back. It was the closest thing to an embrace he had received from her since he was a small child who used to climb into her lap when their father would start one of his drunken rages.

"I had no idea how important Claire had become to me until she was taken away. If I ever get her back in my arms again, I will never repeat that mistake."

"You will get her back, Mason. There is always a way." There was a brief pause, then she asked, "Have you heard of a man called Nightshade?"

Mason turned, that damnable hope flitting delicately through his veins. "I have."

"His services do not come cheap, but if you want me to, I can send a message through his man. If anyone can find Claire, it will be he."

"Do it now."

Hale stayed at his half sister's until they received

a reply. It said only that the man who interviewed clients for Nightshade was away from London for a few days, but that he would arrange a meeting with Hale immediately upon his return.

Hale hated having to wait. It had already been more than a week since Molly had taken off to parts unknown. Every day his daughter was away allowed her to get farther and farther from his grasp. But he knew Callista was right. Nightshade was his final option. The mysterious man was known far and wide for being able to accomplish impossible deeds by whatever means necessary.

Hale had to believe he could track down the location of one small girl.

# Fourteen

LORD GRIFFITH WAS ONLY A FEW YEARS OLDER THAN Portia. He and his set of four like gentlemen, who called themselves the Merry Friars, were as wild and reckless as any young men their age. At Portia's very first ball, she happened to dance with the young Lord Griffith and quite unintentionally "charmed the pants off" him, as he had declared jovially at the time. Such a suggestive and improper phrase, if uttered to any other debutante, would have shocked the poor girl into a faint. Portia, however, apologized in a dry tone, saying it had not been her goal to cause him such an embarrassment. Griffith had laughed heartily at how smoothly she'd turned the tables on him, and from that moment, the Friars took her under their collective wing.

She was well aware they saw her as a novelty, a young lady of good breeding who caught all of their cleverly dropped innuendos and responded with unexpected wit and sarcasm. And Portia, for her part, had found the Friars to be a welcome distraction from Emma's enforced husband hunting. Here was a group of young men who took nothing seriously, least of all themselves or the society in which they existed. Their irreverence resonated with Portia's dissatisfaction with the circumstances in which she found herself.

Though the Friars were all a bit young to be considering marriage, Lord Griffith still made an effort to call on Portia quite frequently, occasionally convincing one of his mates to join him as a lark, and he made a point to ask her to dance at almost every ball. Though Portia knew there was no serious intention behind his actions, Emma was of a different mind. So when the Chadwicks and the dowager countess received an invitation to a weekend party at the Griffiths' country estate in the Cotswolds of Warwickshire, they accepted, even though it took them all out of London for several days.

Knowing the party would provide a variety of diversions not typically found in town, Portia was initially thrilled by the prospect. She had always wanted to try her hand at archery and had been doing her best to improve her horsemanship skills over the last weeks. The limited bit of riding she was able to accomplish atop Angelique's aged gelding on jaunts to Hyde Park was not likely to compare to the possibilities at such a grand estate.

But Portia's excitement was tempered by her annoyance. Yesterday, after several days of silence, Portia finally received another message from Turner.

*The subject has proven to be in no specific danger. I expect the full fee for my services at your earliest convenience.*

There had been no time for her to send a reply, and

she couldn't help stewing about the matter the entire drive to the Cotswolds.

She wasn't even exactly sure why the matter bothered her so much. If Lily was in no danger, then there was nothing for Portia to do but keep her nose out of her sister's personal business. She should be relieved. Pleased. So why did she feel irritated and disappointed?

The more she thought about it, the closer she got to the uncomfortable realization that she was possibly a bit jealous.

It was all so bloody frustrating.

At the very least, she wanted to get a more detailed accounting of Turner's investigation to ensure herself there was no further avenue to explore. She needed a bit more than *all is well* to leave the matter alone.

Being stuck in the country for days, when all she wanted to do was get back to London to speak with Turner, left her in a foul temper. Even the diversions she had anticipated enjoying did not improve Portia's wretched mood.

Saturday evening, Lily had made her excuses to retire early. Since Emma had firmly planted herself among the chaperones and old maids, Portia was left to represent the Chadwicks in the various games planned by their hostess that evening. It was some time before Portia managed to escape and head up to the guest bedroom she shared with Lily.

As she suspected, Lily was still awake. And not just awake, but pacing.

Lily never paced.

Seeing her sister's obvious and uncharacteristic distress diffused much, if not all, of Portia's persistent annoyance. Something was going on with Lily. Even if it wasn't dangerous *per se*, if it could put her sister into this sort of turmoil, Portia was compelled to try to help.

It was time to be more direct.

"I knew you would still be awake," Portia stated as she closed the door behind her. "You could have at least found a way to include me in your excuse to retire. Once you were gone, Emma insisted I stay until the charades had finished. It was dreadful."

Lily's expression was only slightly guilty. "I am sorry, Portia. I was not feeling well."

"Hmm," Portia replied as she began readying herself for bed. If Lily didn't feel well, it was not due to some physical ailment. "Are you going to tell me what is going on with you, or shall I have to pry it out of you?"

Portia continued undressing as she spoke, and when she glanced up after a few minutes, she noticed Lily had not moved from where she stood.

Portia added with a heavy sigh, "I hate this sense that we have been growing apart since our debuts. We used to be inseparable, Lily. I miss that."

She pulled her nightgown over her head then crossed to sit in front of the vanity mirror and start pulling the pins from her hair. Lily came forward to assist by brushing through any tangles left behind.

After a few moments of silence as they both settled into the familiar routine, Lily replied, "We are not growing apart, Portia, we are growing up. It is inevitable that we begin to lead more independent lives."

That was not what Portia wanted to hear.

"Independence is one thing, but you seem to be keeping secrets lately when such a thing never used to exist between us. I wish you could trust me, Lily."

She studied her sister's face in the reflection as Lily continued to draw the brush through her hair. Very little was revealed in Lily's serene expression, which told Portia that a wealth of thoughts and emotions were swirling beneath the tranquil surface.

Something finally flickered across Lily's features as she said, "I do trust you, but there are some things too private to talk about."

"Nonsense," Portia argued. "I tell you everything. Always have."

Lily lifted her gaze to meet Portia's in the mirror. Her expression was clearly dubious and a bit amused. "Everything, Portia?"

Lily had caught her there. Portia would have loved to argue, but she certainly had no intention of admitting to her subsequent meetings with Turner and the fact that she had hired the man to essentially spy on her sister. Lily probably wouldn't like that very much.

"Fine," she admitted with exasperation. "Not everything. I suppose everyone has a few secrets." She turned around to meet her sister's gentle gaze. "But, Lily, I know when you are upset. I can see something is disturbing you, and I feel I should be given an opportunity to help."

Lily's reply was a smile that told Portia nothing. She wanted to growl in frustration but knew it would get her nowhere.

She tried something else. "Is it Fallbrook again?"

Though Lord Fallbrook had proven to be a rather

tedious challenge for Lily over the Season—to the point of trying to get her sister alone in a dark garden—Portia also knew he was not likely to be the one causing her sister's current distress. But sometimes it was more effective to take the long way around in a conversation to ultimately end up where you wanted to be.

As expected, Lily gave a negative shake of her head as she urged Portia to turn back to face the mirror so she could start braiding her hair.

"I saw you dancing with him earlier tonight," Portia prodded. "What did he say to make you go so pale?"

Lily took her time finishing Portia's braid before she looked up at the mirror to reply, "Fallbrook is no gentleman. Promise me you will avoid the man at all costs."

"Oh, that is not necessary," Portia assured her with no small dose of humor. "The man already avoids *me* like the plague. I danced with him only once after the time he tried to lure you into the garden. I made it clear in no uncertain terms what I thought of his behavior. He was rather annoyed and took me back to Angelique before the dance was even halfway through."

"I so admire your audacity, Portia."

An important realization finally hit Portia. How hadn't she seen such a basic truth sooner? She had been resisting the dictates of polite society in regard to her own desires so intently and for so long, she hadn't even considered how others might experience those limitations. Lily in particular. Even Emma.

She stood to face her sister as she declared urgently, "You could do the same, Lily."

"No, I cannot."

Portia watched as Lily walked away to blow out the candles. No one should be forced to limit their true nature because of society's expectations. And Lily had spent her entire life trying to mold herself into what others needed her to be: dutiful daughter, modest and helpful sister, gentlewoman. And though Lily was certainly all of those things, Portia knew she was also much more.

"That is a terrible lie, Lily Imogene Chadwick. You have a deeply hidden vein of wickedness in your soul, and someday you will have to explore it. If you haven't already."

"You know I have never had your courage or Emma's confidence to do anything other than exactly what is expected of me." Lily's tone was self-deprecating and dismissive.

Portia was not having it. "Bollocks."

"Portia!"

"Oh yes, how silly of me," Portia noted with no small dose of sarcasm. "I forgot that all of the young ladies I know keep a collection of sinful, erotic novels and daydream of being ravished."

Portia's bluntness got at least a bit of reaction out of Lily as the other girl's expression slid into shock before she said quietly, "Not ravished, exactly."

Portia was not finished.

"Then what? What do you dream of? And do not dare tell me it is to marry one of those dull suitors who have latched onto you. Not one of those gentlemen would know how to make you happy if it were spelled out in an instruction manual."

Turning away from Portia's impassioned speech,

Lily went to pull back the bedcovers. "What would you have me do, Portia?"

The question was quiet and small, making Portia feel instantly guilty for being so brash when Lily was so obviously struggling. She answered honestly, "I want you to be happy. Are you happy?"

Lily sat on the bed, looking so forlorn it make Portia's heart ache. She went to her sister immediately and lowered to her knees in front of her.

"All I am trying to say is that we all deserve to seek our happiness, wherever that leads us. And we should support each other in that endeavor." She continued defiantly, "You should know I have decided I may never marry. I am not willing to sacrifice the kind of life I want for myself in order to satisfy some man's idea of what behavior is or is not appropriate." She could see that Lily wished to argue, but she felt compelled to express the full truth. "I cannot be what these people or Emma want me to be."

"What?" Lily replied with mock disbelief. "You mean obedient, reverent, contented?"

"Exactly."

Lily smiled. "I know, Portia. You were always meant for other things, and I promise I will support your endeavors to find happiness along whatever path you choose."

"Even if it causes scandal?" Portia asked leadingly.

"Why?" Lily asked with a hint of suspicion. "Are you contemplating causing a scandal?"

Portia rose up to sit beside Lily on the bed. Now to get across the true intention of this conversation. "One doesn't always plan such things. Sometimes they simply happen, and I want you to know that I would stand by you in the same circumstances."

Lily tensed sharply beside her. "Have you heard any whispers about…that night?"

"No, I was speaking hypothetically," Portia assured her, "in case you wished to engage in some outrageous behavior."

Lily's response was telling: the blush on her cheeks, the soft little secretive laugh. "I cannot imagine what that might be."

Portia did not believe that for a second, and she couldn't help but push a little bit more. "Oh, I don't know. Considering your reading habits, I would think you could imagine far more than I could."

"Portia!"

Portia laughed at Lily's shock. Surely, if her sister had taken a lover, she could find it in herself to accept a little blunt talk. Lily certainly did not seem to have any trouble with the explicitness in her secret stash of forbidden novels.

"I just think it is far past time for *you* to be a little daring. Take a risk," Portia insisted. "Explore a bit of that wickedness buried within you before Emma has you settled down with a perfectly boring old country gentleman."

Lily turned her gaze toward the window, but Portia could still see a bit of her profile, and there was no mistaking the mischievous smile that slowly transformed the other woman's features before she did her best to hold it back.

Portia was not about to let her get away with that. "What? What is so amusing?"

"I am sorry," Lily said as she met Portia's questioning gaze, "but this is one secret I cannot share. Even with you. Not yet."

Portia got the strong sense they had finally ventured into the area of the conversation she had been so intent upon reaching. She knew instinctively Lily was talking about her midnight rendezvous with the gentleman. Now was the moment to demand some answers.

But she couldn't.

It was the secretive curl in Lily's lips and the light of adventure that flared in her eyes that convinced Portia to leave off.

*Bloody hell.* It seemed she was going to allow Lily her secrets after all.

Lowering her chin, she spoke in an earnest tone. "Just promise me something, Lily."

"Of course."

"I swear I cannot withstand the sight of another sister descending into self-inflicted misery. If you have the opportunity to be happy—truly happy—promise me you will take it. No matter the consequences."

Lily did not hesitate. "I promise, if you do the same."

"I never had any intention otherwise," Portia answered readily. Both girls got into bed and snuggled beneath the covers as they used to do when they were children. "Now, how the hell do we get Emma to make such a vow?" Portia asked, shifting the conversation to their eldest sister.

"An excellent question," Lily replied with a heavy sigh.

Apparently, Portia was not the only one bothered by Emma's odd behavior since she had stopped working at Bentley's gambling hell. She had not been herself at all, not only in the fact that she had relaxed a bit in her constant vigilance to see Portia and Lily betrothed, but also in other ways. The changes in Emma were deep. Considering Emma's natural ability to remain composed despite any inner turmoil, her distress likely ran far deeper than even they were able to see.

"I do not know whether it is our business to pry," Lily said after a moment.

"Nonsense. You know as well as I what has her out of sorts, just as you know what is holding her back. If we do nothing, she will continue to martyr herself for our sake."

Emma had always taken care of Lily and Portia, and even more so after their mother had died and their father had taken up gambling. But they were not young girls anymore, and it was time Emma started putting herself first and allowed Portia and Lily to make a few mistakes.

Lily rolled to face her. Her expression was determined. "What do you propose we do?"

"We will have to wait for the right opportunity. Emma is not going to get away with dooming herself to a life of loneliness on our account. If it requires drastic measures to make that happen, that is what we shall do."

Lily's naughty smile warmed Portia's heart. "More scandal, Sister?"

"Emma may need the excitement as much as you do," Portia declared.

For a moment, her sister looked as though she might take offense at the statement, but then a light flashed in her eyes, and both girls stated in unison, "*More.*"

The laughter that followed served to convince Portia that Lily was likely going to be just fine. Emma might prove to be the more difficult case. It was going to take quite a bit to convince their obsessively practical sister that some risks were worth taking.

# Fifteen

AFTER BARELY ANY SLEEP, AND IN COMPLETE contradiction to her nature, Portia rose early the next morning to make use of the Griffiths' extensive stables and go for a ride.

She had spent the night thinking about Lily and Emma and her own personal aspirations. It seemed the Chadwicks were poised on the cusp of something, and though Portia couldn't begin to fully grasp the scope of all of the changes she sensed occurring with her sisters, she did understand that after this Season, many things were likely never to be the same again.

Portia was not typically one for such deep and profound pondering, and it left her feeling weighted and drawn in the hazy light of morning. She had woken with an almost desperate need to get away for a while and breathe. The idea of racing across the countryside on horseback was a perfect fit for her mood.

She wished she could bypass the required company of a groom, but even she was not so reckless as to ride alone across a landscape with which she was entirely unfamiliar. As long as the servant kept himself far enough behind her, she could at least imagine herself free and unfettered.

For the most part, the grand country manor was quiet at such an early hour of the day, with only a few others in the party making their way to the breakfast that was laid out in the dining room. Portia bypassed the meal and left the house to head toward the stables located down a short hill behind the house. The morning was overcast and not overly warm, though it felt as though the sun may soon make an attempt at an appearance.

The Griffith estate really was quite lovely, with ancient oaks lining the path that led from the house to the stables. Portia, however, was still distracted by her thoughts and barely noted her surroundings except to lift her gaze every now and then to be sure she was still heading in the right direction. So it was that she came around a curve in the path and collided quite unexpectedly with Lord Fallbrook.

They both took a moment to right themselves. The handsome lord recovered first.

"Ah, Miss Chadwick," Fallbrook stated with a smooth and practiced smile. "What a delightful surprise to run into you this morning. Quite literally," he quipped.

Portia stepped back from the man's reach, instinctively putting more distance between them. Despite Fallbrook's handsomeness and abundance of charm, he was a cad of the first order who seemed intent upon tormenting Lily. Portia had not missed her sister's discomfort in their conversation last night.

And today, Portia was in just the right state of mind to address the matter.

She smiled, her manner coated with false sweetness. "Lord Fallbrook. I was going to seek you out today. Now it seems I won't have to."

The man's smile remained perfectly in place, but Portia saw the flicker of peevishness in his eyes. It pleased her to know that she irritated him. "Indeed?" he replied smoothly enough. "I am at your service, Miss Chadwick."

Portia held back an unladylike snort with another false smile. "I just wanted to inform you that if you do not keep your wandering hands and inappropriate comments away from my sister, I will find some way to make you."

Fallbrook never lost his smile, though as she spoke, the expression on his handsome features slowly twisted into something more resembling a sneer.

He took a step closer.

In her stubbornness, she refused to step back, though the hair on her arms stood on end in rejection of his proximity.

"My dear Miss Chadwick," he began in a slippery tone, "your affront is admirable but misplaced. I happen to know your sister would not object to my or anyone else's hands wandering about her person."

"How dare you," Portia gasped, astounded by the man's insulting audacity.

He took another stalking step closer and lifted a hand to brush his fingers down the length of her arm. She had never been so grateful as she was in that moment to be wearing her long-sleeved riding habit so she did not have to feel his touch on her bare skin.

"Oh, I dare," he stated darkly. "Perhaps you would like to find out just how much I dare?"

He suddenly grasped both of Portia's shoulders in his large hands and hauled her up against him. Within less than a second, he had his mouth on hers, his tongue shoving past her lips. The sensation was altogether disgusting.

But Portia was prepared for it, having expected just this sort of behavior from the wretched excuse for a gentleman. In less time than it took for her to register the sour taste of his mouth, she brought her knee up swiftly between them at the same time she bit down hard on his offending tongue.

Fallbrook doubled over with a shriek then a groan.

During one of their ribald conversations, Lord Griffith and his mates had openly discussed the sensitivity of that particular piece of male anatomy and how debilitating it was to get struck there. She was pleased to see that at least in that, the Merry Friars had not been exaggerating.

Portia barely spared Fallbrook another glance as he rolled about on the ground, holding his privates in both hands. There was no telling how long he would be down, and she was not so stupid as to wait around to find out. Quickly stepping around him, she rushed on to the stables. Thank God they were not far away.

The atmosphere inside the stables was dark and damp. She thought in a moment of panic that there was no one else about. Then seeing a groom up ahead, she sped in his direction.

Glancing back over her shoulder, she still saw no sign of Fallbrook.

Good. Let him squirm on the ground like the snake he was.

The groom was saddling a couple of horses in an open area between the stalls. Since she had sent word via a footman that she wished to ride, she hoped one of those horses was being saddled for her. She had no idea if Fallbrook would be so bold as to chase after her to exact retribution, but she really did not want to be there if he did.

"Excuse me," she said as she stepped up to where the man was bent over at the waist, checking the hooves of a handsome roan gelding. "Would that horse be for me, perhaps?"

The groom glanced up at her from beneath a wide-brimmed felt hat and gave a sharp nod before he straightened and moved around to check the hooves on the other side of the horse.

Portia's breath caught and held at the brief glance she had gotten of the man's face. He was unexpectedly handsome. In a rugged, rough, and sweaty sort of way.

Worry about Fallbrook fell away as Portia's interest shifted to the groom. There was something wonderfully familiar about him…

Sidestepping to catch a better view of him around the horse, she noted a lean and well-muscled form beneath the woolen trousers tucked into muddied boots, cotton shirt, and beige-colored jacket. The man's skin was tanned, and a short but dark beard covered his lower face. When his dark eyes flicked again in her direction, their intensity struck Portia intimately, making her stomach tighten in a way that was not unpleasant.

She had experienced that reaction to only one man. A man who tended to present himself in a variety of incarnations; this particular version of Turner had her mouth going dry.

"Um…" She struggled to remember what she had been saying. She shook her head to clear the cobwebs. "I, uh…"

"You bloody bitch!"

At the sound of Lord Fallbrook's harshly shouted words, Portia swung around to see the man partially limping into the stable. His face was red as a beet, and a small bit of blood smeared across his bottom lip.

It seemed she had managed to inflict some real damage.

Refusing to be cowed, though she was not unaware that a man in such a temper might actually be intent on physical harm, Portia stiffened her spine and glared back at the cad. "Do not come another step, my lord."

He did not stop, and Portia glanced swiftly to either side of her, looking for anything within reach she might use as a weapon. With some relief, she reached out to wrap her fingers around the wooden handle of a pitchfork leaning against the wall beside her.

"You need to be taught a lesson," Fallbrook growled as he continued toward her.

"I believe you have that backward, my lord," she scoffed. "You have obviously never learned how to treat a lady."

Fallbrook's eyes narrowed.

Every muscle in Portia's body tensed as she realized he might actually attack her. Again.

However, before he could reach her, the disturbingly

attractive groom walked out of the stall, leading the two horses forward to stand directly between Portia and Fallbrook.

The groom kept his chin lowered as he looked at her from the shadows under the brim of his hat. "Your mount, miss," he said in a low voice, seeming entirely unconcerned with the lord huffing and puffing behind him.

Portia gave him a small smile of gratitude, not for a second believing his timing was coincidental. "Thank you," she said as she stepped forward to place her boot in his large, linked hands.

She practically flew up into the saddle and had barely a moment to find her proper seat before the reins were handed up to her and the groom strode around to swing up onto the other horse.

Portia took a moment to glance down at Fallbrook. He had stepped back at the appearance of the horses and now glared at her from the doorway of an empty stall.

"Do have a lovely day, my lord. Just be sure it is far away from my sister," she said with a sweet smile before urging her horse down the center aisle of the stables and out into the breaking sunshine. It did not pass her notice that the groom kept himself between her and Fallbrook until they were free of the stables.

She wanted to be annoyed by his unsolicited protection, but she could not deny her gratitude. It was lucky for her Fallbrook was so easily put off by the presence of another man. How typical that the cad who preyed upon innocent women would become a coward when faced by someone of equal strength and physicality.

As soon as they turned off the gravel drive and onto

a riding path that ran along the edge of the forest, Portia kicked her mount into a reckless gallop, suddenly desperate to leave Fallbrook and everything else far behind her.

Even if it was only for the morning.

# Sixteen

DELL WAS FUMING.

The idiot woman had absolutely no regard for her own life.

First, she faced down a furious lord—who was clearly intent upon doing her harm—with nothing more than a sarcastic tone and a rusty pitchfork. Then she took off over unfamiliar ground at a speed no novice rider should attempt.

That she was a novice was obvious. The woman was barely keeping her seat.

And still showed no sign of slowing down.

Dell rode up swiftly behind her. He did not want to spook her mount, but he needed to get close enough to take control. A slight bend in the path afforded him the perfect opportunity, and he urged his mount forward in a burst of speed. Drawing up alongside her, he stood in his stirrups and grasped her reins.

He could hear her heavy breath even over the sound of hooves pounding earth and the jingle and creak of the tack as he drew them both to a harsh stop.

"What in hell are you doing?"

Of course she would shout at him when she should be thanking him for saving her stubborn hide.

"Preventing you from breaking your neck, miss," he forced through gritted teeth, keeping his head bowed enough to shade his features with the brim of his hat.

If he had known the Chadwicks were going to be in Warwickshire this week, he never would have taken the job that brought him here. And hadn't he told himself he wanted nothing to do with Portia Chadwick's reckless impulses?

Yet here he was.

Dammit. When he had heard her distinctive voice in the stables, he had looked up without thinking, and his eyes had slammed into her sharp silver gaze. She looked damn fine in her fitted, gray riding habit. Thank God he was able to put the horses between them when he did, or she may have noticed the evidence of his wayward attraction.

He certainly didn't miss the slight widening of her eyes or the way her lips parted with her breath when she got a look at his face.

He was not going to speculate on what that might have meant.

Double dammit.

"I was hardly going to break my neck," she argued. "I simply wanted a little freedom. I wanted to feel the wind, the sun…so what if I take a bit of a risk now and then? That is life, is it not? A series of risks and chances? You either take them or you don't."

"Seems to me, you should take a few less."

She gave a frustrated huff. "Oh, for God's sake, Turner, I am in no mood for a lecture today." In a graceful, though shockingly unladylike move, she leaned back and swung both her legs over the side-saddle to the other side of the horse and dropped to the ground.

Damn. She knew it was him.

Why in hell was he surprised anymore?

Dell sat for a moment. Indecision rooted him to his saddle.

He should stay where he was, let her have her pout or tantrum or whatever it was she needed, then escort her back to the house. He lifted the brim of his felt hat just enough to watch her compact form striding purposefully along a path into the forest.

He should let her go.

But he still did not have any answers on the mischief he had been hired to investigate. There could be more danger in those woods than the basic risk of getting lost.

When she disappeared around a curve in the path, Dell swore beneath his breath. He secured their mounts and started after her. After only a few minutes, the narrow forest path opened to an idyllic sunlit clearing possessing a small pond nestled against a border of willow trees.

Portia stood at the edge of the water, holding her gloves and her pert little riding hat in her hand as she tapped them rhythmically against her thigh. A brief wind picked up the loosened strands of her hair and pressed her skirts against her legs. Turning her head, she tipped her face into the wind with closed eyes and a lifted chin.

Dell knew he shouldn't be admiring the way her figure was revealed by the press of her clothing to her body. He shouldn't be wondering what thoughts were traveling through her quick and restless mind. He did not want to be curious about this woman. And he certainly didn't care for the sexual attraction she inspired in him.

Dell frowned, feeling a distinct tightening in his gut.

She was trouble. From the top of her head to the tips of her toes.

With an unintentional grunt of acceptance, he lowered himself to sit in the long grass. Bracing his feet on the earth, he rested his elbows on his widely spread knees. The sun had been clearing away the morning haze and now blazed full and strong on the little clearing. Sweat trickled down his back and made his head itch beneath the felt hat.

Removing his gloves, hat, and then his coat, he knew the exact moment she turned to watch him. His nerves sparked to attention, and the heat he felt came from inside rather than from the sun's rays.

To keep from looking at her, he pulled a few long blades of grass and started to weave them together, as though he were simply passing the time until she was ready to go back. He felt her approach and still refused to glance up from his meaningless little task.

With a deep feminine sigh, she lowered herself beside him. Rather than curling her legs beneath her as a proper young lady should, she stretched them out in front of her, crossing her booted ankles and leaning back on her hands to tip her face up to the sun.

"Now, this is how I prefer to spend a weekend in the country," she said.

He grunted, twisting the blades of grass in his fingers.

"Not stuffed into rooms already overflowing with

bodies or being forced to engage in ridiculous games of charades." She stopped and sat up straight to look at him. "Do you have any idea how difficult it is to act out the phrase 'apples falling from a tree,' or just how stupid one can feel while attempting it?"

When he didn't answer, she gave a little huff then lay back in the grass.

"Very stupid, I assure you," she muttered.

Dell drew his bottom lip between his teeth to keep his smile from showing. He did not want to encourage the girl. Unfortunately, his weaving was nearly completed. He slowed the movement of his fingers, needing to prolong the distraction.

"And what brought the illustrious Nightshade to the Cotswolds?" she mused.

Dell stiffened. "I'll thank you not to say that name so freely."

Her soft laugh twisted his insides. "Relax, Turner, there is no one about."

"Jordie."

"What?"

Dell risked a glance at her. She lay far closer to him than she should be, her petite form stretched out less than a foot from his right hip. Her hat and gloves had been dropped to the grass on her other side, and she had released the top buttons of her riding jacket. A light sheen of sweat coated her skin, and her gray eyes sparkled silver in the sunlight.

"Call me Jordie," he said finally.

She wrinkled her nose. Her slim black brows dipped down over her eyes as she rose up on one elbow and looked him over with a critical gaze.

"You darkened your hair, didn't you? And there is the beard, of course. But it does not seem like much of a disguise."

"People rarely look very intently at servants," he explained. "The hat helps."

"Well, Jordie does not suit you at all. You need a name with more significance. I would say you look more like a...Rufus or a Henry."

"I am a groom," he stated blandly. "The point is to be insignificant."

She chuckled, the sound rolling carelessly over his taut nerves. "Now that is something I doubt you could ever be."

He glanced away from her smile. It did dangerous things to him.

"What is your real name, anyway?"

There was not a single reason to tell her and a hundred reasons not to.

"Dell."

"Dell Turner," she repeated, her voice going all sultry and soft as she tried his name out on her tongue. "Tell me about him. Who is Dell Turner?"

"No one."

She laughed at that. "Very untrue. He is a man of many faces and infinite talents."

He gritted his teeth and tossed aside the woven grass and trained his gaze forward toward the pond. There was no distraction strong enough to avert his awareness from her.

"Was it your work for me that brought you here, or something else?"

He didn't answer.

"Since you insisted my sister is no longer in danger, and you cannot very well watch Lily's movements throughout the party while in your current guise, I am going to guess some other task has you in Warwickshire."

Dell slid her a glance out of the corner of his eye. She was annoyingly intelligent.

"What could you possibly be investigating in a bucolic setting like this?"

"Setting has nothing to do with nefarious activity, Miss Chadwick. Not all evil is perpetrated in dark alleys and criminal warrens."

She perked up at that and pushed back to a seated position. "What sort of nefarious activity?"

Bloody hell. He should have known better than to say something so provocative in this woman's company.

"Nothing," he said as he shifted his weight to rise.

She stopped him with a hand on his arm. Her touch burned through the fabric of his shirt. His stomach tightened and his heart—the traitor—began to race.

"Oh, come on, you must tell me."

If it would get her to remove her hand, he would have said anything. "I am following up on suspicions surrounding a group of young lords. It may be nothing, or it could be they are involved in criminal activities."

She was silent for a moment, during which she thankfully dropped her hand back to her lap. Dell took a slow, steadying breath.

"You don't mean the Merry Friars, do you?"

He brought his gaze swiftly to her face. His gut tensed. "What do you know of them?"

She laughed and waved her hand in dismissal. "Oh, they are harmless. Just a bunch of bored, entitled young men trying to prove their courage and masculine prowess by committing reckless pranks."

Dell lifted his brows at her assessment.

"If those boys are engaged in anything nefarious, it is likely by accident," she insisted. "They are reckless and wild, to be sure, but I can hardly believe they are doing anything intentionally criminal."

It did not sit well with Dell that she was so confident in the nature of the young men in question. That she called them *boys* when they were all at least a few years older than her indicated her challenged perspective. What kind of dealings had she had with them? From what his new client had insisted in her interview with Honeycutt, her son was most assuredly involved with some gang of dastardly intent. Dell thought it just as likely that Lady Epping was simply an overbearing and nosy mother who had a hard time imagining her grown son leading a life of his own, mistakes and all.

Still, his investigations had led him to unexpected results before. This could be a similar situation.

Portia curled her legs beneath her and turned to face him. Her scent wafted toward him, that same subtle evocation of vanilla and moonlight. He eyed her askance, the eager look on her face making him instantly wary.

"Maybe I can help."

"No." Good God, he did not need her sneaking about the estate and coming upon the men in question while they were engaged in some dangerous plot.

"Come on, Turner. I know them. They will talk to me. They enjoy bragging about their various exploits. I am certain I can get them to admit if they are doing anything truly wicked." Her eyes were bright, and anticipation lit her pert features.

"You will keep yourself out of it."

She narrowed her gaze before glancing away. "Perhaps."

Frustration made his voice gruff. "I mean it, Portia. I saved you from one angry lord. I may not be available to save you from a whole group of them."

"Oh, tosh," she countered with a wave of her hand. "The Friars are hardly comparable to Fallbrook, and I handled him just fine. My knee to his groin managed to halt his nasty intentions quite well, in fact."

"Until he caught up to you," Dell pointed out. "What do you think would have happened if I had not been in the stables?"

She gave an annoyed harrumph but did not reply.

She was not one to stay silent for long, however, and after briefly staring him down, she noted stubbornly, "I still insist the Friars are harmless."

"I will be the judge of that."

"Fine. Since you refuse my assistance, I suppose I shall have to resign myself to dying of boredom."

Damn, but she was a difficult wench.

"Do what all the other young ladies do at these sorts of parties," he grumbled to hide his reluctant amusement.

"You mean flirt and play coy and pretend to have little in my head beyond concerns with what gown I shall wear to the next ball while smiling admiringly at gentlemen who talk of nothing more substantial than horses, wine, and the weather?"

Dell tried to imagine her as she described and simply couldn't. No. Such social diversions would not satisfy a woman like Portia Chadwick.

But that was her life.

Dell did not reply. He shifted his attention back to the pond as silence fell heavily between them.

"Dell?" she said after a few minutes.

Her voice was quiet and low. He wanted to ignore it but figured she would only keep pestering him if he did.

"What?"

"Would you kiss me?"

"Bloody hell," he muttered. His gaze swung back to her in shock. "Absolutely not."

She set her chin stubbornly, and her silver gaze probed his. "Why not?"

He replied through clenched teeth. "If you want to rebel against your circumstances, do it with someone else."

At first, it looked like his comment might have angered her, but then she gave a small shake of her head. "I can understand why you would think rebellion motivates my request, but that is not why I want you to kiss me."

Dell didn't say anything. After a minute, a faint blush colored her cheeks, but she refused to shift her gaze. "When Fallbrook forced his tongue into my mouth, all I felt was disgust." She paused, then offered a little half smile. "I want to be sure it doesn't always feel like that."

Dell shoved down the rush of fury at her mention of the lord's assault. But once he had his anger checked, he could not help but experience his wayward lust more acutely.

He swallowed hard before answering through a tight jaw. "I am not going to kiss you, Portia."

A frown creased her brow at his continued refusal. She straightened her spine and drew a deep, fortifying breath. "The truth is, I am very drawn to you, Turner."

Dell choked in surprise at her brazen forwardness and had to slam his fist against his chest to cough it out.

"And not just in a physical manner, though there certainly is that," she insisted, rushing along while he was momentarily incapable of speech. "I find you stimulating in so many ways. Your work is fascinating. Talking with you challenges my mind in ways I have never experienced. I cannot seem to dredge up the slightest bit of amorous interest in any of the men I have met since my debut. But when I'm with you"—her words grew hesitant—"as I am now, all I can think about is how badly I want you to kiss me."

A shaft of intense desire shot straight through Dell's chest at the thought of kissing her, making him hold his breath. Her honesty—her innocent curiosity—roused him and endeared her to him in a way he couldn't have predicted and he found himself ill-equipped to resist. This woman was going to be the death of him.

As though she could sense his weakness, she leaned forward the smallest degree. "Just a kiss. It's nothing really." Her gaze fell briefly to his mouth. "Please."

That did it.

With a sound of deep annoyance liberally laced with rising desire, Dell angled his shoulders toward her and lifted his hand to slide it around the back of her neck. Her skin was warm and damp. The tendrils of hair at her nape slid like silk against his fingers.

As he drew her toward him—knowing it was a mistake all the while—her eyelashes swept down over her gaze, and her lips parted on a drawn breath. With a hard clench of his jaw, he leaned forward and pressed his mouth to hers.

Blast and damn, she felt good. Every bit of her.

Too good.

The soft brush of her breath against his cheek in that second before their lips met. The intent press of her hands when she lifted them to rest on his shoulders. And her mouth—warm, lush, sweet, and determined.

But Dell did not dare take even a moment to enjoy it.

He wrapped his arm around her narrow waist with the noble intention of lifting her away from him.

As if suspecting his purpose, she curled her fingers into the material of his shirt in a silent plea not to end it just yet.

He might have found it in himself to resist, if not for the faint sound she made in the back of her throat just before she softened her jaw in an instinctive effort to deepen the kiss.

That was it for him.

With a growl of annoyance, Dell gave up the ragged shreds of nobility he struggled to maintain. Against every ounce of self-preservation and whatever bit of intelligence he possessed, he tightened his arm around her. Tilting his head, he parted his lips to kiss her properly, common sense be damned.

# Seventeen

NOW THIS WAS WHAT A KISS SHOULD BE.

Portia wanted to sigh in relief at the rush of pleasure that claimed her when he started to kiss her in full.

His arm came around her more purposefully, hauling her closer into his chest, and he tilted his head to better fit their mouths together. All the world whooshed away, leaving only him and the frantic beat of her heart.

She didn't understand how his kiss could feel like everything she had ever wanted in the world. But it did.

At the first touch of his tongue along her bottom lip, a swift and poignant arc of pleasure speared through her center, making her moan.

Seeming to be galvanized by her involuntary sound, Dell tightened his hold and rose up to turn them both. In a moment, she was lying back on the grass while he bent over her. Portia slid her hands around his neck, twining her fingers in the locks of hair at his nape, tugging in a desire to get more of him.

Thank God he obliged.

Deepening the kiss, he slipped his tongue past her lips and teeth until it slid erotically along hers. The brush of his beard against her chin and cheeks—soft and rough at the same time—was another tantalizing sensation to add to the rest. He shifted to press his knee between hers until she parted her legs to make room for him. Propping himself up on elbows braced on either side of her head, he settled the full weight of his hips between her thighs.

Feeling him there, in such an intimate place, sent a tingling rush of heat to that low spot in her body.

*This* was what everyone made such a fuss about. This rush of power and consuming weakness.

She arched her back, trying to flatten her breasts to his chest. She tugged at his hair and darted her tongue against his, seeking more of his taste, more sensations, more of this overwhelming experience.

He gave her what she wanted with a raw thrust of his hips that pressed his hardness to the exact place she craved it. The pressure was dulled by their clothing. She wanted to feel him more acutely. A soft whimper sounded from the back of her throat as she bent one leg up along his side.

He immediately hooked his hand beneath the bend of her knee, drawing her leg higher to hook over his hip as he rocked his pelvis again.

He shifted his kiss to the heavy pulse that beat at the side of her throat. His beard was rough against her sensitive skin as he trailed a shiver-inducing path with his tongue up to her ear. At the same time, he slid his hand beneath the skirts of her raised leg, easing his callused palm up the back of her thigh.

A flood of sensations claimed her, and Portia gasped for air. She was flying. Over treetops and clouds. Through a field of stars. She couldn't imagine anything more exciting, more delicious, than what Dell Turner was doing to her with his mouth and his body.

Her stomach muscles clenched with a wonderful sort of anticipation. Her body undulated beneath him. She was desperate to feel every bit of him at once and fought to figure out just how to accomplish that impossible task. Especially when her mind became a swirling haze of nonsense at the first touch of his tongue along the outer curve of her ear.

Who knew that was such a sensitive spot?

Apparently, he did.

Portia clutched at him as his fingers teased the skin of her inner thigh and his teeth scraped delicately over her earlobe. And then his voice murmured wickedly in her ear. "Is this what you want?"

He rocked his hips roughly against her core.

*Yes.*

Portia thought she heard a low grunt issue from his throat, but couldn't be sure past the sound of her own breathy gasp.

"Do you want me to take you right here in the grass?"

Another deliberate thrust of his hips.

Portia melted beneath him. Her insides were lit up with tingling heat, spreading through every inch of her. What delectable torture it was to be at the sensual mercy of this man. She pressed her foot into the ground and rolled her hips against him, catching them both off guard as the hard ridge of his arousal pressed intimately to her heated core.

His whole body stiffened. He growled a curse word Portia had never dared to use.

"You are not even trying to stop me." He made another wonderfully animalistic sound, which had Portia's insides drawing taut like a bow string.

Then he suddenly removed himself from her, pushing to his feet in a single, swift motion. By the time Portia managed to blink away the fog of desire and rise up to her elbows, he had walked several paces away and stood with his back to her as he stared out over the pond.

Tension rode through every inch of his lean-muscled frame. He remained still, with his feet braced apart and his hands propped on his hips. Portia could see the measured expansion of his rib cage as he brought his breath back to a slow and steady rhythm.

It was not nearly so easy for her to regain control.

She still felt as though she were swept up in a whirlwind, except now she was there alone.

A frown pulled down on her brows as she started to suspect something that did not please her in the least. In fact, it threatened to make her outright furious.

Portia took a few deep breaths to calm her rising temper. She would not allow her suspicious nature to send her into a rage before she knew whether or not it was warranted.

She carefully rose to her feet, a task more challenging than it should have been, due to her shaking legs and tremulous breath. Once standing, she took another moment to brush out her skirts and pull a few pieces of grass from her hair. Feeling a bit more collected—though not much—she set her hands on her hips in an exact replica of Turner's stance. Her gaze bored into his back.

"Would you mind explaining what that was all about?"

His spine tensed at the sound of her voice. Without shifting his feet, he looked back at her over his shoulder. His eyes were dark and angry, his brows nearly as low as her own, and his lips, which had been so wonderfully attentive moments ago, were drawn into a firm line.

"Your reckless nature will lead you to disaster."

Portia narrowed her eyes. "Excuse me?"

"Have you any idea what almost happened just now?" he asked through a clenched jaw.

Portia lifted her chin. She hadn't actually been thinking much past the immediate moment, but she took a minute to do so now and realized they might not have been very far from making love.

The thought of it did not exactly frighten her, as she knew he'd intended.

"And so what if it had?"

"Bloody hell," he growled as he shoved his hand back through his tousled hair. "You cannot be that foolish."

"I wanted only to know what it felt like to be kissed by you. Is it so wrong for me to admit that I enjoyed it? That I might want more?" Her body stiffened with growing frustration. "I was honest about my intention from the start. What about you? Did you think that by kissing me like you did, you would teach me a lesson? Maybe frighten me with the consequences of my boldness?"

She could see by his glowering look that she had gotten it right. Her smile then was more challenging than pleasant. "Sorry to disappoint you. You did not frighten me at all. In fact, I enjoyed every bit of your little lesson. And I suspect you did too, whether you willed it or not. Now who is the fool?"

Before she allowed her temper to take her to a point where she said something she would regret, Portia bent to swipe up her hat and gloves then turned to stalk back toward their horses. She stuffed her gloves in her pocket and plopped the hat on her head without a care for how it looked. Jamming the pins in to hold it in place gave her a tiny bit of relief from her wrath, but not nearly enough. Rather than wait for Turner to assist her into her saddle, she led her horse to an outcropping of rocks and mounted by herself.

She urged her horse into a steady trot, not wanting to give the insufferable man behind her even the slightest satisfaction of thinking he might have to save her again.

Not much later, she heard the sound of his horse, though he stayed behind her the entire ride back to the stables. Still, Portia felt his gaze on her back like a constant blast of heat. Though she knew it was the fire of his wrath he directed at her, the heat she felt beneath her skin was due to something entirely different.

Because even though she knew he had kissed her only to prove some chauvinistic point about her being unladylike or dangerous simply because she saw nothing wrong with being honest in her desires, she still wished he hadn't stopped.

She must be a total glutton for punishment.

The man obviously didn't like her. He had been trying to get rid of her from the moment she and Angelique had burst through Honeycutt's front door. She detested how that internal acknowledgment made her chest tighten with something akin to the pain of disappointment. Finally, she had found a man who fascinated her in every way. Not to mention that his kisses and the feel of his body rubbing against hers sent her into a hot and blissful haze.

And the arrogant ass thought it his *duty* to point out to her how reckless she was.

And so what if she was?

Didn't she have a right to seek adventure? Didn't she deserve to live a life of excitement? Men did it all the time. Turner himself did it, and no one thought it necessary to save him from himself.

Reaching the stable yard, Portia smiled pleasantly at the young stable hand who ran up to grasp her reins. Then she slipped to the ground unaided. Knowing he could say nothing more to her now that they were back among possible witnesses to a break in his character, she intentionally turned to stare him down as she strode across the yard.

He watched her from the seat of his horse. His brimmed hat once again shaded his intent gaze. Of course, that did not prevent her from feeling every bit of his focus. It made her skin tingle anew while her stomach erupted in wild little flutters she now understood to be a symptom of her desire for him.

Before shifting her gaze away, she curled the corner of her mouth in a suggestive little smile. His hands tightened on the reins, causing his horse to sidestep awkwardly. Satisfied, she looked away, laughing lightly as she merged onto the path leading back to the house.

*He thinks me too bold and reckless?*

*He has no bloody idea.*

# *Eighteen*

IN THE END, IT WAS DEPLORABLY EASY TO GET WHAT she wanted. Not risky or dangerous at all. Entirely disappointing.

She simply asked the young Lord Griffith what mischief he and his mates had been up to lately, and the braggart spilled every detail. Unfortunately, the ease with which she solved Turner's investigation did nothing to fulfill her hope of proving she was capable of more than he or anyone else seemed willing to give her credit for. It only proved what a ridiculous lack of discretion the pampered lords possessed and just how innocent the Friars' pranks truly were.

And Dell accused *her* of being foolish.

She did not have a chance to confront Dell with the evidence of the solved mystery. In fact, she did not catch another glimpse of him the rest of their stay in the Cotswolds—though she certainly tried—which meant she would have to bring her information to his place in London.

Monday afternoon, while her sisters were planning to accompany Angelique on various social errands,

Portia claimed a need to catch up on her rest after the long country party. Since Portia's love of sleeping was well known, no one questioned her desire to take a nap before their excursion to the theater later that night.

As soon as they were gone, she hailed a hack and headed to the East End.

By the time she reached Honeycutt's address, her anticipation at seeing Turner again had risen to epic proportions. His little lesson by the pond still irked her when she thought about it, but the man made her feel so many things, most of them quite exciting, she decided to forgive that one offense in the hopes there might be more of the good to experience.

As the hack turned the corner near Honeycutt's address, Portia happened to be peering out the window and saw Honeycutt stepping from his front door. On impulse, she knocked on the roof of the cab, signaling the driver to stop. She was far enough away not to draw Turner's notice, yet close enough to observe him as he strolled down the street in the opposite direction, his hands stuffed deeply into the pockets of Honeycutt's brown coat. It amazed her how completely he could transform himself by subtle and simple shifts in his posture, his mannerisms, his way of physically interacting with the world around him.

Fascinating.

He continued for another block before raising his hand to a passing cab.

Portia did not hesitate as she ordered her driver to follow the other hack, at a discreet distance, of course.

Here might be another opportunity to prove some of her investigative prowess.

They did not go far. Another fifteen minutes, and Turner's conveyance drew to a stop in front of a narrow, two-story building. Nothing about the place revealed its purpose, and everything in the vicinity appeared quiet.

From a crack in the carriage window curtain, Portia noted Honeycutt's distinctive form ambling its way toward the front door of the nondescript building, confirming it was his destination.

Gratefully, Portia's driver must have had some previous experience in covert undertakings as he casually passed the other hack and continued down the road another two blocks before turning the corner. He then circled around and doubled back until he drew them to a halt within a short distance of the rear of the building.

Portia grinned. She may have to consider hiring the man if she decided to continue with such activities.

Portia remained in the vehicle for a few minutes, watching the building for anything unusual.

But all remained quiet.

And Portia became impatient.

She stepped from the hack and offered some coin to the driver—a man who had to be near sixty in age, with a great bushy beard, weathered hands, and eyes of the kindest blue she had ever seen.

"You have earned an extra fare today, good sir," she said with a ready smile.

The grizzled older man tipped his hat and returned the smile. "I've been around a few times, I have, miss.

And if you don't mind, I'll be waiting right here for you to finish yer business. I'm not so far away I won't hear a good shout if you need me help."

Portia almost kissed the man.

As she made her way to the rear entrance of the building, her gaze darted into every shadow and place of possible cover. It may have been the middle of the afternoon, but it was still not the safest part of town for a young woman to be traipsing about alone.

She was grateful she had at least thought to throw a cloak over her pale-green day dress when she'd left Angelique's.

A door was tucked in at the corner of the building. Once she reached it, she stood for a bit, scanning her surroundings and listening for any movement or voices from inside. There was nothing, not even a peep to reveal Turner's purpose in visiting this place.

Portia considered her next move carefully. She would be crossing a line. The risk in sneaking into an unfamiliar structure, knowing nothing of what she would find once inside, was not one to scoff at. Not to mention she would be committing a criminal act.

Yet, she knew for a fact that Turner had gone inside.

And Portia was determined to show him she was not the helpless debutante he wanted to see her as. Why she cared so much about what Turner thought of her would need to be examined more thoroughly at another time.

With a deep breath, she tried the handle of the door and found it locked.

She grimaced. Of course this wouldn't be so easy.

When Portia was fourteen, she taught herself

how to pick various types of locks. The practice had been inspired by a particularly delicious gothic novel she had read in which a young lady escaped from a wretched orphanage by picking the lock on the door to her dismal tower bedroom. Portia decided then that if she never wanted to be at the mercy of someone who might dare attempt to detain her, she had better develop such a skill.

She had never had a practical application for the acquired talent until now.

A small thrill ran through her from top to toe as she withdrew a couple of hair pins from her coiffure. It took her only a few minutes of patient, silent work to release the lock and let herself in.

Closing the door behind her, she stood for a minute, stuffing the pins back into her hair as her eyes adjusted to the dim lighting. The door was positioned at the end of a short hallway. Up ahead, she saw evidence of a kitchen. An empty and silent kitchen.

Still, Portia remained vigilant as she crept forward. Past the kitchen was another narrow hall possessing two closed doors directly across from each other.

Portia stopped to listen before going on. If someone were to come out and find her there, she still had a clear path to the back door.

She stood still and silent for several minutes, but heard absolutely no movement sounding from beyond either door. The place was eerily still. She continued forward, her ears perked and her heart thumping a hard but steady rhythm against her ribs. At the end of the hall was a larger front room with a clerk's desk and not much else.

The place appeared to be set up for some type of business, though the exact sort of business was unclear. Perhaps it was no longer active. In truth, the whole building possessed an odd feeling of stagnancy. As if everything had unexpectedly ground to a halt and now sat waiting with bated breath.

She had just reached the bottom of the stairs leading to the upper floor when the sound of voices drew her focus.

There was definitely someone up there.

She detected Honeycutt's modulated tones and then another, deeper voice replying, but she could not make out their words.

She needed to get closer.

Peering up the narrow staircase, she saw a closed door at the top. As long as it remained closed…

Rolling her lips in between her teeth, she ascended the steps one by one, testing each one with her weight for any creaks or sighs before moving on to the next. Heavy footsteps echoed from the upper level as someone strode swiftly across a wooden floor.

She froze.

If she had to guess, the steps were not Turner's. Not only did they fall in an almost desperate rhythm, when she had only ever known Turner to move with very deliberate and measured paces, these steps also carried with them a more aggressive energy than what Turner would display while portraying the conservative Honeycutt.

She listened outside the door, her breath already slowed to a deep but silent cadence. Pressing her back to the wall just as she had done that first night at Honeycutt's, she kept her eyes focused down the stairway so as not to be surprised from that direction, while the rest of her attention stretched into the room beyond the door.

The stranger released a heavy, emotional sigh. There was a wealth of heartache and exhaustion in that expulsion of breath, and Portia tensed in sudden empathy. Whatever this man needed from Nightshade, it dealt with a very personal matter. She felt a sharp twinge of guilt for so willfully planning to eavesdrop on the man's business. Then she told herself that Turner likely never felt such compunction for the things he had to do in his line of work.

"I've had people scouring town for nearly two weeks." Anger made the man's words harsh and raw. "There's been no sign of the damn woman anywhere."

"Perhaps you should start your explanation over again," Honeycutt suggested in his annoyingly detached tone, "from the beginning this time."

"I met Molly three years ago. She was a dancing girl at a tavern I liked to frequent. She was blond and pretty. Bright blue eyes and fresh from her father's vicarage in Devonshire. I thought she might need a little protection, but I found out the woman was not as green as she looked. As soon as a bloke with more blunt—more style, as she claimed—came sniffing 'round, she moved on quick enough. I didn't know about my daughter until almost a year later, when Molly came to my door, demanding money, with the infant in her arms."

There was a pause. Portia heard more heavy steps, the scrape of a chair, a low grunt of emotional distress.

"The babe was tiny." The man's voice lowered. "Blue

eyes like her mother. Dainty. I was sure these big hands would break her. I gave what I had so Molly could care for her properly. She came back for money every now and then. It took a while for me to figure out she was using it to buy opium. It only got worse when she started selling more than a dance to her gentlemen admirers."

A loud crash startled Portia. It sounded like a cannon ball blasting through a brick wall.

"*Dammit.*" The stranger's tone was loaded with the torture of regret. "I should have taken Claire then. I didn't know... I still thought Molly cared enough..."

"Your daughter's name is Claire?" Honeycutt interrupted, his tone even and impersonal. "And how old is she now?"

"Two this last March."

She was just a baby. Portia's heart clenched.

Everything grew quiet for a few moments. Honeycutt, of course, said nothing, though she imagined him watching the other man intently with his sharp eyes masquerading behind Honeycutt's spectacles.

After a bit, the stranger continued his explanation. Though the tension was still evident in his tone, the pent-up fury had once again been contained.

"A couple of weeks ago, she said she'd be willing to start fresh, working for a milliner or something, if I could get the blunt to set her up in a new place. I needed time to get enough funds together," the man continued. "I was expecting repayment on a loan, but Molly couldn't wait. She demanded it all immediately and threatened to take Claire away. By the time I brought her the money, they were already gone."

The man paused.

Honeycutt also fell silent. Portia could picture him standing innocuously with his hands stuffed into his pockets, his gaze steady and assessing.

"A maid at the inn where she'd been staying—"

"What inn?" Honeycutt interrupted.

"The Green Hen, over near Wapping. A barmaid there said she heard Molly talking to some flashy gents about going to Bath. I walked every street of that damn town for more than a week. No one had seen Molly or my Claire. I have connections. People around London watching for any sign of Molly's return, but I'm afraid—" He cut himself off abruptly. "What if they never come back?"

The man's voice became so raw and low that Portia had to strain to hear his next words.

"I gotta get her back. I've done a piss-poor job as a father, but I can't be any worse than Molly, in the state she's in. She has not done well by Claire. Being with a clod like me can't be any worse, can it?"

"Mr. Hale, I can make no promises. Missing children are notoriously hard to track, especially if they are taken out of London. I assure you, my employer will do everything he can. Now, tell me of everyone you know whom Molly has been in touch with over the last couple of years. I need names and addresses."

There was the shuffle of papers, and Portia imagined Honeycutt taking notes as his new client began to rattle off names and places that meant nothing to Portia.

In fact, only one name spoken in the last few minutes struck any kind of chord with her. It was a deep and poignant chord that twisted her gut and squeezed her lungs tight.

Honeycutt had called the man *Mr. Hale*.

Surely, it could not be Mason Hale, the man who had loaned her father an obscene amount of money prior to Edgar Chadwick's death. The man who had sent threatening letters to Emma for months before abducting Lily off the street and selling her to a brothel.

It couldn't be.

Turner couldn't *possibly* be entertaining the idea of helping the very man who had tormented her family.

But she recalled the stranger's words very clearly.

*I was expecting repayment on a loan*, he had said.

And his daughter had been missing for almost two weeks. The timeline matched up to Lily's abduction. Had the man sold her sister to obtain the money this Molly was demanding?

Portia felt sick.

The more she thought about it, the more it made sense.

Fury churned inside her. But it was finely tempered by fear for the well-being of an innocent child. While she stood there, struggling to digest her suspicions, she realized the interview between the two would likely not go on much longer. She could not still be outside the door when it concluded.

Gliding swiftly but silently back down the stairs, she slid through the building and out the way she had come in.

# *Nineteen*

Dell's mind was circling through the information Hale had given him. There was not much to work with. The woman, Molly Andrews, could have gone anywhere after leaving London, especially if she had found a man with some wealth to latch onto. From what Hale had said, she could be quite charming when she wanted to be.

As he stepped from the front door of Hale's place, Dell noted a hack waiting on the street. He had dismissed his own when he had arrived. This one was obviously different.

Glancing at the driver, an older man with wiry gray hair sprouting from beneath his cap and a beard that extended to midchest, Dell saw the man watching him with a smile. Then the driver gave a jerk of his chin.

Dell paused for only a moment.

Honeycutt was sometimes approached in unlikely places. As Nightshade's contact man, he had become recognizable to some.

Dell accepted the driver's unspoken invitation, approaching the hack at an unhurried pace while making note of every detail as he went. The carriage sat high enough over the wheels to suggest that if anyone were already inside, it was only one person and likely someone small.

Dell had no concern for his safety. He knew how to manage himself against any type of adversary, even in a confined space, but it helped to have some idea of what he might encounter.

He opened the door of the hack and cast a casual glance over the interior to get an impression of the single occupant. "Bloody everlasting hell," he muttered before climbing in with a few more muffled curses, slamming the door behind him.

"So happy to see you as well, Mr. Honeycutt," Portia Chadwick replied with a winning smile that he really wished didn't make his gut clench and his cock stir.

Damn the woman.

Dell settled back in the seat across from her as the hack started off. He didn't bother to alter his voice to Honeycutt's, nor did he hide his glare of annoyance.

"What in hell are you doing here?"

Portia Chadwick's eyes narrowed, the silvery gray becoming sharp and direct. "I planned to ask the same of you. Is your new client the same Mason Hale who abducted my sister?"

Dell tensed. The woman had an unbelievable knack for knowing things she should not.

"He is," he replied simply, though he knew it was unnecessary.

Then he waited for the blast of her temper. He could already imagine the flash of fire in her eyes as she rained down on him a litany of reasons he should not help the man she would surely consider her enemy. The thought caused a pleasant anticipatory tightening in his muscles, as though he were looking forward to such a confrontation.

But she did not fly off into an indignant rage.

She took a moment to glance down at her gloved hands as she smoothed them over her skirts. Then she looked up at him again from beneath her thick lashes. "I am going to help you find Hale's daughter."

Dell stared in disbelief. "How do you know so much?"

"I followed you and snuck inside to listen to your interview." Her smile then was self-satisfied. "You never knew I was there."

Unbelievable.

"You are lucky no one else did either. You could have gotten yourself into serious trouble."

"But I didn't. Sometimes it is entirely necessary to take a few risks in order to get what you want. Surely, you can appreciate that."

He did not respond. She was right, but that did not mean he agreed with her actions.

He took risks. It was part of his job.

She was a young lady of gentility. Her greatest risk should be what invitation to accept. That was simply how the world worked.

"Now, I insist you hear me out before you refuse my assistance out of hand due to some pigheaded insistence that I stay out of trouble," she continued sternly. "I can help you. I know I can."

Dell set his jaw against the swift denials he wished to utter. Instead, he crossed his arms over his chest and stared back at her with a closed expression. She could argue all she wanted. It wouldn't change his mind.

She leaned forward, bracing her hands flat on the seat as she angled her shoulders toward him, her eyes intent.

"I believe I have proven I can move about as stealthily as anyone. I take direction extremely well"—she shrugged—"when I agree with it." The woman wasn't the slightest bit apologetic about that caveat. "And you cannot tell me there haven't been times when a woman would have come in handy in your work," she insisted.

It was true. One character he had never been able to pull off with success had been that of a female. But to consider having this impulsive creature participate in his investigation was ludicrous.

"Why would you want to help the man who caused such trouble for your family?"

She appeared honestly surprised by the question as she tipped her head, and her brows drew down. "His little girl is missing. Even now, she might be enduring neglect or worse. You would have to possess a heart of stone to be unmoved by the situation."

When Dell did not reply, she eyed him curiously. "You are unmoved?"

He met her gaze but revealed nothing. Of course he had felt the man's pain. He considered Hale the closest thing he had to a friend, beyond Morley, but that did not change the fact that bad things happened and often could not be undone. It helped no one to become emotionally attached.

"Such devastation is everywhere," he replied. "All you have to do is look."

"What a terribly jaded thing to say. There is beauty everywhere, as well," she argued, "if you look for it."

Dell wondered at her statement for a moment. He supposed she was right, but he hadn't seen anything of true beauty since he was a scamp trailing behind his mother's skirts. For so many years, his life had consisted of doing whatever it took to complete a job. Life was a series of tasks and accomplishments.

Beauty had no place in the dangerous world in which he lived.

"What kind of mother uses her child as a means of extorting money?" She shook her head.

"I have seen addicts do far worse," Dell answered solemnly.

She met his gaze with a challenging look. Stubbornness set her jaw. "That little girl needs to be found and her future well-being assured. Despite what Hale has done to my family, he obviously cares about his daughter." She paused, eyes dark with emotion. "Now that Lily is home safe, it helps to think something good could come from her ordeal. If the money Hale received in selling my sister to the brothel can save this child, then it is as if Lily's experience is somehow justified."

Dell stared at her. It astounded him that she could so fiercely take up Hale's cause.

"I am going to help you," she added with calm insistence.

"No. You are not."

"I have finally discovered something worthwhile for me to do, something that actually means something. I can be valuable to you, Turner, if you would just use me."

What was that in her voice? A heaviness and an unyielding intention. She was a bold one, to be sure. Fearless. Intelligent and motivated. She could be an asset, he acknowledged, *if* she did as he instructed.

Dell released a sigh and closed his eyes, tipping his head back against the wall of the hackney carriage.

"I managed to discover what the Merry Friars have been up to, if that means anything."

Since Dell already knew their exploits were harmless to everyone but themselves, it only meant she followed through on her hunches and she loved to prove him wrong.

He had to suppress the smile that threatened at that thought.

The job for Hale would take them deep into the world of addiction and prostitution. Where people were ruthless and desperate. Dell could keep her safe, but only if she did as she was told. The likelihood of that was small.

She was also much safer with him than on her own.

Dammit. He had changed his mind.

He said nothing more, and a few minutes later, the hack came to a stop. He glanced out the window and noted they were down near the docks. Leaning forward, he caught sight of a wooden sign hanging over the door of a relatively neat establishment that boasted the name *The Green Hen*. She had brought them to the last place in London Molly Andrews had been seen.

If he weren't so irritated, he might have acknowledged the logic in Portia's choice to start the investigation here.

"Will you agree to let me help you?"

Turner glanced at her where she sat at the edge of her seat, full of anticipation and energy. He still couldn't believe she had convinced him. "Very well."

Her smile was blinding, hitting him squarely in the chest. He was an idiot.

"So, what is the plan, Mr. Honeycutt?"

The woman was incorrigible.

Dell sat back again and studied her appearance. She looked as she was, a lady of quality with no business at a dockside inn.

"You will stay here," he said.

"No, I will not," she replied. Then she smiled.

They stared at each other.

But the woman would not remain quiet, and after a minute, she shifted forward in her seat. Her excitement was palpable.

"I can say I have just arrived in London. You are my uncle or guardian or something, and we are looking for my friend who was supposed to meet me at the inn a couple of weeks ago. Unfortunately, I was delayed in my travels and now believe she may have moved on, though I do not know to where."

Dell shook his head. "Such an explanation leaves room for far too many questions. It is best to keep things simple and only provide backstory if absolutely necessary. Which is why you will stay here. We are here to obtain information, not spout off some half-conceived personal history."

Her expression immediately turned mutinous, and Dell raised an eyebrow. "Are you resisting my directives already?"

He almost laughed at the way her features tightened and then relaxed again as she came to acceptance.

"Of course not," she said finally, slumping back in her seat. "Your reasoning makes sense. I will wait here."

Dell gave her a sideways look as he got out of the hack, not quite certain he could trust her acquiescence. When he was assured that she intended to remain safely in the carriage, he made his way to the inn. It was not as rough as some of the places in this area of London. It was large, likely holding several rooms, and boasted a full kitchen to provide hearty meals. He wondered how Molly had had the funds to stay at such a place while she blackmailed Hale.

Then again, she had not stayed long.

What had caused her to run off before receiving the money she had demanded? A better offer, perhaps?

Dell strolled into the public room of the inn. The noon meal had just finished, and two serving girls were moving about the unoccupied tables, gathering up dirty dishes. One of the women, the older one, glanced toward Honeycutt. Her eyes were tired and her manner dismissive as she lifted several flagons in her arms and turned away to head back into the kitchen.

The other girl was younger. As she straightened from wiping down a tabletop, she caught sight of him standing awkwardly near the door. She gave him a smile.

"'Allo, sir. We're all out of today's special, but if you're hungry, we can fix something up for ya."

Honeycutt cleared his throat. "Ah, no, thank you, miss. I am not here as a patron, exactly. I wonder if I might talk to someone who would have worked the night of two Wednesdays past."

The woman cocked her head and eyed him warily. "I been working here every night for two years now. I would've been here."

Dell walked forward slowly, hands in his pockets.

"On that night, there was a young woman, who may or may not have purchased a room. It is also possible she just made use of the public area. Pretty, with pale-blond hair, blue eyes. She would have had with her a girl-child, also fair."

The serving girl started shaking her head before Honeycutt finished his explanation. "I know who you're askin' about. There was a big, handsome fellow who came 'round asking for the same woman soon after she took off. But she never had no babe with her."

A frisson of awareness passed through Dell. He lowered his gaze to peer at the serving girl intently. "You did not see a small child, approximately two years old?"

"No, sir. I would've remembered. That blond lady was all over a pair of gents who came in for the night. Fawning over them and flirting. I would've known if she had a babe with her. And I know she didn't have no room, 'cause we were all filled up that night."

Dell's mind was whirling through the possibilities of what that meant.

"Do you know where the woman went from here?"

"I heard her and those gents talking about Bath, and then shortly after, they all left together."

"They were gentlemen, you say? Describe them for me."

"Young. Handsome. Very fancy. They wore silk

and velvet and had gold watch fobs, and they spoke all proper-like."

"And you never saw a child," Dell confirmed with a hard stare through Honeycutt's spectacles. "Did you ever hear the young woman mention a daughter?"

The serving girl snorted. "No, sir. Their conversation wasn't exactly about children. That woman was dressed near enough like a lady, but she sure didn't act like one, I tell you that. Never heard such bawdy talk, but the gents seemed to like her well enough."

"Nell!" The call came from back in the kitchen.

The serving girl tensed and rushed to another table to swipe up an armful of dirty plates. "Sorry. That's all I know. That big, handsome one who came asking questions, he seemed awful upset. Fair broke me heart, but I honestly don't know any more."

Dell walked toward her, extending a few coins in his hand. She eyed the payment with a hint of caution but set the dishes back on the table before she stepped forward to take the coins and slip them into the deep pocket of her apron.

"Thank you for your assistance, Nell. I wonder..." He paused as he tapped his finger to his chin. "If you happen to see the young woman or either of the two gentlemen again, would you send me a note?"

The girl slid a wary glance toward the kitchen before looking back to him. "I suppose I could."

"A man named John Riley is going to start coming in for lunch every day. If you see the young woman or the gentlemen, you tell Riley you need to speak with Mr. Honeycutt."

The girl eyed him with a new curiosity. Her name

was shouted again from the back room, and she gave a short nod before grabbing the dirty dishes and turning to rush into the kitchen.

Dell strolled out to the waiting hack and Portia Chadwick. After instructing the driver on their next destination, he climbed into the vehicle, where Portia practically pounced on him for information.

"What did you discover?" she asked eagerly. "Did they travel to Bath, or somewhere else? Will we have to leave London to follow them?"

Dell thought about what the maid had said and tried to fit it with Hale's information.

It was likely Hale had simply assumed Claire would be with Molly and never thought to confirm it. He had rushed to Bath in vain. Not only because Molly apparently hadn't gone there after all, but also it would seem very possible that Claire had never left town.

He met Portia's probing stare. "I believe the child is still in London."

"What? But didn't Hale say he had people looking all over town for the woman?"

"Yes," Dell concurred, "but it would appear that wherever Molly Andrews has gone, Hale's daughter did not accompany her."

Portia flinched, her expression becoming incredulous. "You mean she left the girl behind?"

Dell nodded, his lips pressed firmly together as he crossed his arms over his chest. He hated the ugly, weighted feeling that had settled in his gut the moment Nell said she had not seen little Claire. Searching for one woman through London and beyond was a challenge. But locating a small child…

"Dell, tell me what you are thinking," Portia demanded softly.

He remained silent, his gaze turned toward the window. It was far easier to think in silence rather than force ideas through conversation. He needed a few moments to sort through the possibilities and challenges this had opened up.

Unfortunately for him, Portia Chadwick did not seem to have the same affinity for lengthy internal pondering.

With a sound of impatience he was reluctantly becoming familiar with, she suddenly left her seat to kneel before him, placing both hands on his folded forearms. Her expression was stern as she leaned toward him.

"You are going to find Hale's daughter, aren't you?" she asked in a low and focused tone.

The tension in Dell's body took a swift turn toward something exceedingly inappropriate. Thank goodness the girl was too green to realize what her position and proximity did to him. Then again, it was her greenness that had her kneeling between his legs in the first place.

He drew his shoulders back and held his jaw firm as he looked down at her with a hooded gaze.

"You have to find her," she insisted again.

He thought about how many children went missing on the streets of London every day. "It may not be possible."

"It has to be," Portia replied stubbornly, her eyes flashing. "Nightshade has to find her."

Dell shook his head. "The information Hale gave me was limited and vague. It is not much to go on."

"But it is something," she insisted.

Dell studied the mutinous set of her chin, the way her eyes darkened with determination. The heat of her passionate conviction emanated from her compact form and soaked into his skin.

A job like this—one with such a slim chance of success—was something he'd think twice about taking on. Nightshade had a reputation for accomplishing the impossible, but that was only because no one talked about the jobs he refused, the ones that would have been a waste of time from the start.

But as he met Portia's intent and hopeful gaze, that uncomfortable sensation that had caught in his chest the moment he first laid eyes on this woman pulled tight again, and he realized he was going to exhaust every tool in his arsenal to try to find the girl.

He searched back through the list Hale had given him for Molly Andrews's friends and associates, her recent residences.

"All I can do is follow her trail back through the last known places she frequented and the people she last encountered. Hope they have some clues they can be convinced to share."

"Excellent," she exclaimed. "Hale said she had been…selling herself. Did he mean she was a prostitute?"

Dell nodded. "She was last known to be working at a brothel down in Covent Garden."

She gave a short nod. "To Covent Garden, then."

Dell shifted in his seat as he unfolded his arms, forcing her to drop her hands away. As soon as he did it, he wished he hadn't. The damn woman moved to rest her gloved hands on the surface of his thighs instead.

Could she really be so bloody unaware?

His muscles tensed as he fought to hold his place between physically shoving her back into her seat and hauling her up into his lap to claim her mouth. Even the topic at hand did not manage to douse the rush of desire she ignited in him.

"You think I can just swagger into a bawdy house and get information from women who have spent years being exploited and abused?" His sexual tension made his tone sharper and angrier than he intended. "Their experience with men does not lend itself to the development of very trusting natures."

Her gray eyes sparkled as a smile—a very dangerous smile—widened her mouth.

"Don't you see?" she replied. "This is where you need me. They won't trust you, but they might talk to me."

As much as Dell hated to admit it, she had a point.

There was a chance, albeit a slim one, that the women of Molly's acquaintance might take more kindly to speaking with another woman than a strange man.

But for that to happen, he would need to take this reckless, impulsive creature to a brothel. For all her boldness and cheek, she was a gently bred lady of quality. A damned debutante.

While they stared at each other, the hackney carriage came to a stop. Dell lifted Honeycutt's bushy brows, eyeing her expectantly until she heaved an annoyed sigh and pushed herself back up and onto her seat across from him. Dell wasted no further time in exiting the close confines of the vehicle. He felt her gaze following him as he stepped down to the street, yet she held her tongue.

Dell turned back to the hack and braced his hands on either side of the carriage door. He leaned forward and stared hard at her for a few long moments.

She was perched on the edge of her seat, in a state of readiness and barely contained energy. Her expression was tense, and her slate-colored eyes were focused on his face as she waited for him to speak.

Dell frowned. He could practically feel how badly she wanted this.

As he stared at her, coming to terms with what he was about to allow, she rolled her lips in between her teeth, as though it was the only way she could keep herself from speaking.

Dell could think of a couple of other ways.

"Come back after midnight tonight," he said, his tone gruffer than he intended. "And prepare yourself. This will not be a lark."

"I understand." Her tone matched his in seriousness, but he saw the silver flare of excitement in her gaze. "You will not regret this, Turner."

Dell noted the tension along his spine, the ache in his jaw, and the steady pulse of desire in his blood.

"Yes, I will," he replied before he stepped back and closed the carriage door.

He tossed some coins up to the driver and grumbled, "Take the lady back to Mayfair. No detours."

The bushy-bearded driver smiled. "Right-o, guv." He gave a nod before flicking the reins and driving off.

Dell strode swiftly into the brownstone, forgetting for a moment that Honeycutt should have conducted himself at a more leisurely pace, in case anyone was around to watch him.

The woman was messing with his methods already.

# Twenty

Could Turner have already left?

Portia stood at Honeycutt's door with the hood of her cloak drawn up to shadow her face. It was after midnight, as Turner had instructed. Though to be accurate, it was closer to two o'clock in the morning.

The Chadwick sisters and the Dowager Countess of Chelmsworth had attended a theater performance earlier in the night, followed by a dinner party. Portia had been unable to get away any earlier, having to wait until after Lily snuck from the house first.

She lifted her hand to knock again. She waited. Still no answer.

Surely, Turner hadn't gone off without her.

She had been in a state of excitement and disbelief from the moment he had accepted her help, but she supposed it could all be too good to be true.

The cad better not have changed his mind. Her hack had already driven off.

Out of patience—and frankly, becoming wary of two hunched-over shadows that were sitting across the street watching her as she waited in Honeycutt's stoop—Portia tried the door. It was unlocked. Without further hesitation, she quietly slipped inside.

The first floor of the narrow building was silent and dark.

She stood for several minutes listening. There was not even the subtle creak of floorboards above her to suggest someone was moving about on the upper level.

Of course, she would have to check to be certain.

She kept her steps light as she made her way up the stairs. When she saw light coming from the elaborate dressing room, she smiled. An exhilarating flood of warmth swept through her insides. Perhaps she would be lucky enough to catch Turner half-undressed again.

The room was as she remembered, though regrettably unoccupied. There was the large bureau and wardrobe shoved up against one wall, a table set up much like a vanity, with a mirror propped against another wall, and various pots and jars scattered across the surface. A couple of chairs sat haphazardly in the center of the room, and all around were racks full of one-piece costumes, random pieces of clothing, and an array of accessories tossed here and there and everywhere.

But no Turner.

Portia rather liked this room, with its clutter and chaos. It was the antithesis of Dell, who was nothing if not methodical and regulated in his every move and slightest behavior. Deciding she would like to meet the side of him who took off his hat and tossed it aside without thought, she smiled.

All of a sudden, two strong hands gripped her around the waist and propelled her forward into the room.

To her credit, Portia did not release the shriek that

pushed up from her chest. It was not a cry of fear, since she knew instinctively who had grabbed her. Instead, it was the delightful awareness of Dell's hands being placed intimately and forcefully on her person that caused a sudden and thrilling burst of sensation within her.

He shifted his hold to wrap one lean-muscled arm around her throat while she felt the distinct prick of a knife at her side.

A gasp caught in her chest. She knew it was he, but it hadn't occurred to her that he might not realize it was she.

"Has no one ever told you it is dangerous to sneak into a man's home?"

He growled the words at her ear. The low threat in his voice made her shiver as her nerves lit up in reaction. The man sounded quite menacing when he put forth the proper effort. Even when issuing another lecture on her ignorance.

She guessed he knew exactly who she was.

"You invited me," she whispered.

With a muttered curse, he pulled the tip of the knife away from her side but did not loosen his arm from where it crossed beneath her chin. "Your carelessness will get you killed."

Portia tried not to be insulted. "And what else was I to do? No one heard my knock, and there were some dubious characters watching me from across the street. It seemed the more prudent option to come inside."

"The men across the street are mine. You were supposed to be here over an hour ago."

"I couldn't get away," Portia replied as she shifted

her stance, testing his hold. "You have men watching your front door?"

As if just realizing he was still holding her against his chest, he made a low sound in the back of his throat—a sound that vibrated deliciously down her spine—and stepped away. "I must be mad to have agreed to this."

Portia turned around and suddenly wished she had something to brace against as she got her first full look at the real, unadulterated Dell Turner.

Of course, she had seen him in only a minimal disguise as the groom at the Griffith's estate, and before that under the moonlight in the alley behind Angelique's house after he had removed much of Lord Seymour's accoutrements. But there was nothing she could have done to prepare herself for her reaction to the true Dell Turner in full light with no distractions.

The man was attractive in a way that stopped her breath.

She realized she was staring, was likely wide-eyed with astonishment, but she couldn't stop herself.

He wore a linen shirt loosely tucked into the waistband of dark-brown trousers. The shirt was rolled up at the sleeves and opened at the throat, showing the masculine shadow of his collarbone. Portia's mouth went dry as she recalled the finely muscled planes of his bare chest. His hair—a thick, rich blend of chocolate and caramel tones—was wonderfully tousled and fell wildly over his forehead.

And his expression as he stared back at her, with his muscled forearms crossed over his chest, was forbidding. His chin was lowered, and he gazed at her with piercing hazel eyes from beneath heavy eyebrows drawn low in a scowl. He had a straight and strong nose, his jaw was shadowed by a day's growth of whiskers, throwing the angles into sharp contrast, and his mouth was held in an angry line.

He was fiercely handsome in the same way a stormy sky was beautiful. Full of raw nature and carefully contained power. Strong, sensual, and enigmatic.

The glare he sent her way should have made her nervous. But Portia was not easily intimidated. In fact, the hostility in his stare just made her more determined to prove herself unperturbed.

"You must be Dell Turner," she said with an impish grin. "A pleasure to finally meet you."

His stunning hazel eyes flashed brightly at her words, and she could have sworn she saw his lips twitch, but he did not reply.

"You *are* still going to allow me to help you," she insisted.

He did not answer right away, and Portia found herself holding her breath.

"It seems I must," he replied with obvious annoyance and reluctance.

Portia smiled brightly. "Brilliant. Where do we start?"

⁂

Dell narrowed his gaze to focus on the details of Portia's appearance. She returned his studied stare with an arrogant tilt to her head.

Her hair would need to be changed. Her gown, obviously. She would need to rough up her manner a bit, which probably wouldn't take much, considering her penchant for plain speaking and her obstinate attitude.

The type of people they would be encountering tonight would not appreciate a lady's fine intonations or polite demeanor.

Could she pull it off?

Deep down he knew if anyone could, it was this woman. But he'd never worked with anyone besides Morley, who had been with him for many years.

"You must do everything I say," he said. "Without question or hesitation."

"Of course," she replied far too readily.

Dell gave her a hard stare. "I am damned serious. This can be dangerous work. Most people do not take well to being tricked."

She did her best to school her expression into one of solemn consideration, but Dell could see the light of excitement in her eyes and the press of a smile at the corner of her mouth.

"I promise, I shall not take a step or breathe a word without your explicit instruction. Now, please, can we get on with it?"

Foreboding rippled through his entire body, and the odd tug in his center drew exceptionally taut. But his decision had been made.

"Remove your cloak."

Without hesitation, she released the tie beneath her chin and swept the voluminous garment off her shoulders to toss it onto an empty chair.

His body tightened in instant response.

If he expected to be able to do his job, he would need to get his reactions to the chit under control.

Sexual attraction, especially an attraction as compelling as what he felt for the sable-haired Miss Chadwick, had no place in an investigation. No place in his life.

Such things only complicated matters. And Dell preferred things to be simple.

The sooner he convinced his body of that, the better.

Stepping up to her, he unfolded his arms and reached out his hands to encircle her waist, noting how his fingers nearly touched all the way around except for a gap of just a couple of inches between the tips of his thumbs.

"Do you wear a corset?" he asked.

"Does it feel like I have a corset on?" she countered.

He ignored the husky humor that enriched her tone as he slid his hands down to measure the width of her hips.

He had sent Morley out to find some female garb a few hours ago. The man was astoundingly skillful in obtaining a range of costumes to suit any need. Still, they would need to fit perfectly. The devil was in the details, and ill-fitting clothes immediately set an off impression.

Keeping his chin lowered and his gaze on her person, he noticed the deep inhale she took as he slid his hands up around her rib cage. He stopped just beneath the swell of her breasts. The warmth of her skin burned his palms through her fine gown.

"Exhale," he instructed, feeling an unexpected rawness in his throat.

She exhaled on a puff, as though she hadn't realized she was holding her breath. Her rib cage constricted to normal. He would have loved to smooth his hands up over her lovely breasts to feel how they would fit in his palms. But as lust dared to take over his focus yet again, he decided he would be better off taking a guess on that particular measurement.

Finally, placing his hands on her shoulders, he took a step toward her until the toes of his boots kissed the tips of her evening slippers. "Stand straight. Look forward," he muttered and was surprised by how thick his voice had become.

The woman did things to him.

Her breath fanned hot against his collarbone; the hair piled atop her crown smelled of a summer night sky and brushed like silk against his lips. The top of her head fit perfectly beneath his chin.

Having what he needed, he quickly stepped back and turned to leave the room. He made damn sure not to look into her face. He had no doubt she would be staring at him, and he did not want to see if that little experience had affected her as it did him.

"Well, that was…interesting," she breathed heavily behind him.

Dell closed his eyes.

That answered that question.

"I need to see about your clothes," he said in explanation for his swift departure. "While I am gone, fashion your hair in a way that is a little less…elegant. You need to resemble the type of woman who would visit a brothel."

Taking long strides down the hallway, Dell drew some deep breaths. This night was already proving to be more difficult than he'd expected, and it had barely even begun.

# *Twenty-one*

PORTIA STARED AT THE DOORWAY FOR SEVERAL SECONDS after he left.

Her body still hummed from the sensation of having his large, capable hands moving over her. She could have told him her measurements if he had asked, but she was infinitely glad he hadn't. She'd rather enjoyed the experience.

No. That was a dreadful understatement.

She was *stunned* by it.

It felt as if her body had been warmed and softened from the inside out, as though preparing itself to be molded by his hands. And then he had stepped close to her. Close enough that she could see the pulse beating heavily at the base of his throat and detect the enticing scent of amber emanating from his skin and mingling with the hint of coffee on his breath.

Her knees had gone instantly weak and wobbly.

And he had just walked away.

If he had kissed her then, she would have melted into a puddle right there at his feet. But of course, he hadn't. The insufferable man had kissed her in Warwickshire only to teach her a lesson.

It was probably a good thing he had no amorous interest in her.

If he had, she would so easily become distracted by it. That one kiss had shown her there was so much she didn't know—and wanted to—when it came to that subject in combination with this man. Right now, it was far more important she prove her earnest intention to join this investigation.

Anticipation and excitement had her turning in place as she looked around the makeshift dressing room. Spying herself in the mirror above the vanity, she walked toward the reflection and gazed critically at her appearance.

He wanted her to look more like a woman who would visit a brothel.

What did that mean?

Portia could imagine, but she had never been to a brothel, had never seen what type of woman would go to such a place—at least not that she was aware of. She supposed she could start at least by removing her hairpins and disassembling her hair's elegant coiffure.

Lifting her arms, she went to work. She was still stunned by his discovery that Claire had never been at the Green Hen with her mother. Portia hoped Dell was right and the child was still somewhere in London.

Her stomach twisted queasily.

London was an enormous city, and despite what Dell thought of her, she was not so naive she did not understand the dangers that lurked in the dark for vulnerable creatures.

The more she thought about it, the more desperate she was to find the child and ensure her safety. Regardless of Hale's crimes against her family, Portia was compelled to do what she could to help find his child, and she knew Lily would do the same thing, had she known what was at stake.

Portia gave a short laugh.

Well, she couldn't exactly see Lily going to a brothel—at least not willingly. Despite the strong likelihood that her gentle sister had taken a lover, Portia could not see Lily being quite that bold. But Lily would certainly agree with helping a lost little girl in any way she could.

As she removed the final pins and her hair tumbled down her back, Portia looked about for a hairbrush.

The tabletop was covered with various creams and hair tonics and bottles filled with what appeared to be some sort of glue. There was more makeup than even Angelique used to rouge her cheeks and darken her lips. But no hairbrush.

Portia was fascinated.

No stranger to snooping, she walked to the wardrobe and took a look inside. Almost all of the clothing was fashioned similarly to what she had seen Turner change in and out of before. Pieces were sewn together for quick changes and ease of dressing. Some outfits had padding sewn in to give Turner a thicker middle, heftier shoulders, or a curved spine. There were clothes that denoted more than a dozen different characters, ranging from a gentleman of the upper class to a British soldier to clothing worn by lower classes and labor men. Silk waistcoats hung alongside rough-hewn wool and raw linen.

In the bureau drawers, she found a vast assortment of accessories. Among certain items she could not identify, there were also cravats, watch fobs, several pairs of spectacles, every style of hat imaginable, and a wonderful collection of wigs, mustaches, and full beards.

Lifting a piece she recalled as belonging to Honeycutt, Portia gave it a speculative glance.

What a life Turner led, stepping in and out of the trappings for so many disparate characters.

After a thorough exploration of the room, Portia took a seat in one of the chairs to await Turner's return. As the minutes ticked by on the clock set on top of the bureau, she grew restless. Her feet began to tap on the floor, and then her fingers started drumming on the wooden arm.

How long could it take to find a change of clothes for her? Just where would one go for an outfit suited for such a venture?

Unable to remain seated for more than five minutes, Portia rose back to her feet and decided she may as well begin undressing. No point in wasting time just sitting about. Having gotten used to dressing and undressing without a maid after her mother had died and their father had started squandering their money at the gambling tables, Portia was familiar with the contortions required to release the buttons running down the back of her evening gown.

Stepping free of the pale-blue muslin, she gently shook it out before hanging it in the wardrobe where it would remain free of wrinkles so she could wear it home again.

She figured she had until at least a little past dawn to get back to the town house. Any longer than that, and she risked encountering Angelique's minimal staff as they began their daily chores.

And so it was that when Turner returned, she happened to be standing without cover, practically in the middle of the room, wearing nothing but her shift, a light petticoat, her stockings and shoes, with her hair falling free down her back.

She assumed that accounted for Turner's muttered curse as he came to an abrupt halt. Portia had planned to throw on one of the robes that hung from a hook near the vanity but was rather pleased she hadn't had the opportunity when she turned to see the stunned look on his handsome face.

He had stopped a few paces into the room, various bits of feminine clothing draped over one arm. With a repeat of his muttered curse, he lifted a hand to shove it back through his thick, caramel-streaked hair.

Portia noticed he had taken some time to shave. The cleaner look did not in any way detract from his dangerous appeal. It just brought more attention to his mouth and his eyes.

Her stomach gave an acrobatic flip, and her skin sizzled with heat.

"Have you no modesty?" he said with a heavy scowl as he shifted his gaze away from her barely covered body and took the clothing to one of the chairs.

Portia's stomach tightened, and not in that delicious way it had when he had kissed her.

She hated that he was always scowling at her. He did not approve of her, and his distaste sparked enough of her ire to overcome any awkwardness she'd initially felt in standing before him half-undressed.

She planted her hands on her hips. "This is a dressing room, is it not? And I assume I am to change into those clothes you just brought in. What would you have me do, exactly?"

He kept his attention focused on the gown as he lifted it to shake out the wrinkles. The dress was in a simple-enough design, fashioned of lavender muslin and black lace. Not nearly as exotic as Portia had been imagining.

When he didn't answer, Portia turned to the mirror and drew the length of her hair over her shoulder to comb her fingers through it. There was silence as the tension in the room continued to seethe.

Portia wasn't even sure why she was so angry. She gritted her teeth against the painful tug on her scalp when her fingers tangled in a snarl.

Muttering under her breath, she said, "It is not as though I have to worry about you having inappropriate thoughts about me."

"You are a bloody idiot," she heard him grumble.

She shifted her gaze to view his reflection in the mirror. His entire body was taut with tension as he stared hard and intensely at her back.

A thrill ran through her blood, and a lovely swirling sensation claimed her low belly.

"You *do* have inappropriate thoughts," she breathed.

His eyes lifted to meet her wide-eyed gaze in the mirror. "Bloody hell," he muttered.

Portia whipped around to face him. "Admit it," she said. "You find me attractive. I knew there was more to that kiss than you let on."

He stared back at her, and the heat in her body spiked.

Portia smiled. "It is all right, you know. I find you very attractive as well."

His expression was hard as he strode toward her with the lavender gown. "It does not matter."

He lifted the gown over her head, and she automatically slid her bare arms into the sleeves, which were nothing more than swaths of black lace designed to drape off her shoulders.

She tried to meet his gaze again, but he immediately turned her around so he could begin doing up the buttons on the back of the gown.

The man was attracted to her.

What a heady feeling that caused.

Her stomach fluttered, her breath was short, her thoughts became scattered, and her palms itched with the urge to touch him.

She studied his image in the reflection of the mirror as he bent to his task behind her.

His mouth was breathtaking. His lips were sensual and masculine in a way that had Portia wishing she could trace the curved lines with her tongue. All she could think about was kissing him again. And that idea was terribly exciting.

Just as she finished that thought, Dell looked up.

Their gazes locked in the mirror, and neither of them moved.

Then his brows tugged low over his eyes, which had grown darkly mottled, mysterious and deep. "What do you think?" he asked.

With extreme reluctance, Portia shifted her attention to her own reflection. The sight caused an instant rush of heat to her cheeks.

The gown, which had looked common enough while draped over Dell's arm, was far from modest once wrapped around Portia's figure. She'd had no idea her body could appear so lush and sensual. Of course, she had the added assistance of an indecently low neckline that showed nearly the whole top half of her breasts. The thin muslin skirts clung to the swell of her hips and caressed the length of her thighs. With her hair loose and still gathered over her shoulder, she appeared to be readying herself for a lover.

"Is the gown perhaps a bit too small?" she asked.

"It's perfect." His reply was a low murmur.

Seeking his gaze again in the mirror, she noted his attention had also fallen to her body. The fire in his eyes and the tension in his handsome features ignited a delicate ache low in her belly. The sensation was sweet and unexpected. She bit her lower lip to keep a soft gasp from escaping.

He may have sensed her reaction, or perhaps it was something else that had him lifting his gaze. But this time, when their eyes locked in the reflection, something intense and wonderful bloomed between them.

Portia felt it, at least.

If Dell did, it only seemed to make him angry.

"Stop it, Portia," he said in a tone that was dangerously close to a growl. "We have work to do tonight."

His words immediately tempered the fire within her. A little girl needed their help, and she still needed to prove herself valuable to him.

She shook herself free of the lustful haze, though she couldn't eliminate it altogether. The tingling sense of anticipation never fully left her blood, and a sort of breathlessness had settled into her being.

It remained with her even when Dell told her to sit on the stool in front of the mirror and he dragged another chair forward to face her. He sat there with his legs spread around her knees and wordlessly began to organize cosmetics on the table beside them.

By his insistence on avoiding her gaze, Portia suspected he was still feeling it too—the connection and the heat. She was desperate to explore it further, but he was right. She turned her attention to the purpose of their evening.

"What shall be my name for tonight?"

He didn't hesitate in answering. "You will be Jenny, the illegitimate daughter of an unknown nobleman and a barmaid. The parentage explains your air of entitlement, though you were a serving wench yourself until a gentleman of means took you as mistress."

Portia considered the history. "I suppose I grew bored with the gent and sought more exciting company?"

Dell quirked a bit of a smile. "That would be me."

"And who will you be tonight?" she asked as he held her chin in one hand while he carefully applied black kohl around her eyes with the other.

"I will be myself."

"Really?" She was surprised, having assumed he always worked under an alias.

"There is a chance I will encounter people I know in Covent Garden. I may be able to garner some information if they recognize me."

Portia was infinitely intrigued. "How do you know people in Covent Garden?"

"I grew up in that neighborhood. My mother was an actress."

"Of course," Portia whispered. He had finished with the kohl and was applying rouge across her cheeks. "That explains a great deal. I imagine your mother is very accomplished. What is her name? Perhaps I have heard of her."

There was a pause while he set aside the rouge and reached for a small tin box that contained tiny black beauty patches, like those worn by ladies in the last century.

When she lifted one brow in question, he explained, "You have a penchant for the dramatic."

"How fun," Portia murmured.

He selected one shaped like a heart and used a dab of glue to apply it just above the corner of her mouth.

After a moment she realized he hadn't answered her prior question. "Your mother?"

"She died when I was eight," he replied. Though his tone was neutral, Portia sensed something beneath his words.

"I am sorry," she said quietly.

Dell shrugged. "She dreamed of getting a lead role but was mostly cast in smaller, nonspeaking parts. I'd go with her to the theater and sit in the corner while she helped the others with their costume changes or ran through their lines with them. She spoke in thick Cockney naturally, but she had a talent for dialects and could mimic just about anyone."

He paused, then continued in a lower tone of remembrance. "We'd often play a game where we would talk to each other in a different accent or as particular characters for days on end."

Portia smiled. "She sounds lovely."

He met her gaze for a moment before glancing away again.

He reached for a small pot of lip rouge and dabbed his middle finger into the pot. Then he held her chin still again with one hand while he pressed his finger to her bottom lip, spreading the color across the surface.

Was that ever a delicious feeling!

The flat of his fingertip spread warmth across the fullness of her bottom lip. Back and forth, until her lip was coated. And all the while he watched her mouth intently, his gaze half-shadowed by his lowered eyelids. When he applied the color to her upper lip, Portia had the insane thought of darting her tongue out to taste him.

She didn't, but she grew hot and breathless all over again.

And when he lifted his gaze to meet hers, her lungs caught in midexhale as flutters exploded in her belly. She realized with some surprise that the blue ring around the edge of his hazel eyes had expanded inward, leaving just a few subtle flecks of green and a burst of gold around the black center. And he was looking at her with something intense and undefinable.

Undefinable, yet it resonated with everything Portia was feeling.

He took a long breath, then averted his gaze and stood.

Portia watched his lean-muscled form as he strode toward a midsize chest in the corner. He crouched down and opened the lid to reach inside.

"Do you know how to shoot a pistol?"

Catching her breath and quickly reorganizing her scattered thoughts, Portia replied regrettably, "No."

Dell rose to his feet and came back to the chair he had just vacated. He rested something in his lap and caught her gaze. "I didn't think so. I will be well-armed, but you must have some protection of your own. How do you feel about wielding a knife?"

"I know which end to hold."

His lips quirked into a reluctant smile. "Are you right- or left-handed?"

"Right."

"Give me your right foot."

She lifted her foot to his large hands, and he removed her shoe, saying, "You will have to change these. I have some options to try. But first…" He grasped her skirts and lifted them up past her knee. Then he rested her foot on the surface of his thigh.

More breathless flutters had to be contained as Portia forced herself to ignore how wonderful the hard-muscled heat of his thigh felt against the arch of her foot.

"Your stockings are rather fine for Jenny, but there is no helping that," he muttered as he lifted the object he had brought from the chest and rested it along the outside of her calf, just below her knee. It was a slim knife in a soft leather sheath with straps that tied around her leg to secure it in place.

His hands were deft and strong as he continued in a tone of instruction. "If we encounter any threat, your first choice is to run. Always. If that is not an option, you have this knife, but it will only be effective if you are close to your opponent." He finished affixing the blade to her leg and lifted his attention back to her face. "You cannot be afraid to use it."

"I won't be," Portia answered.

He removed the knife from its sheath and held it by the blade to set the handle in her palm.

"Feel the weight, the balance. Curl your fingers around the handle and make the blade an extension of your arm. Do not grip too tightly. It is not a bludgeon. It must be fluid and swift to be effective."

Portia slowly moved the knife about in the air between them, getting a sense of how it felt in her hand. It was an elegant weapon. Slim and sleek. Would she have the gumption to use it against someone? She hoped she wouldn't have to, but she believed she could if necessary.

He slid his palm down the back of her calf to wrap his fingers gently around her ankle, then lifted her foot off his thigh to place it back on the floor. Rising to his feet, he stepped back from the vanity.

"Come here."

Portia stood, kicking off her other shoe, and walked toward him in her stockings with the knife in her hand. The sheath felt strange against her calf, but it was secure and did not move as she walked.

"You are small. Your reach will be limited. If you use the knife at all, it must be for the purpose of stalling any attack long enough to escape, you understand." He paused for her nod. Then he placed his hands on her shoulders and turned her around.

"If someone grabs you from behind…" He wrapped his arms tight around her waist, and Portia's breath *whooshed* from her lungs. His breath was warm against the side of her neck as his shoulders completely surrounded hers. She focused on listening to his instruction, forcing herself to ignore the way her body reacted to the heady feeling of his strong arms around her. "...drop your upper body and grasp the knife. You can slice at an attacker's arms." He grasped her wrist to demonstrate where to cut over his arms. "Or stab at legs or throat, depending on your degree of mobility. If your arms are pinned"—he shifted his hold to secure her arms along her body—"lift your knee to bring the knife within reach."

Once she finished demonstrating his instructions, he released her and stepped back again. She turned to face him.

He lowered his chin to say sternly, "Never aim for the chest. Ribs can misdirect the blade and send a numbing response up your arm. Go for the softer areas of the belly and groin. Your goal is simply to disable your opponent long enough for you to get away." He nodded back toward the chair. "Sit."

Portia did as he said, still without a word. She was trying to soak it all in, show him that she was taking him seriously, despite the constant distraction that was *he*.

He crouched in front of her and lifted her skirts again, then held his hand out for the knife. Portia handed it to him, and he secured it back in the sheath.

"I want you to practice removing and replacing the knife in the sheath while I go find you some proper shoes."

"Why can I not just wear my own?"

"Disguises come down to the details. The fine quality of your stockings may not be noticed without the benefit of touch." He slid his hand over the warm curve of her calf. "But shoes will not be overlooked, and yours are far too rich for Jenny."

Portia nodded her understanding, still feeling the tingling effects of his caress all the way up her leg.

"While we are out, you must shed all of a lady's practiced manners and niceties," he continued, his tone low and even, almost soothing, while his eyes remained locked with hers. "You must look about you with a jaded eye. The world holds no surprises for you, nothing shocks you. You are young and wild and reckless."

His lips curled into a smile at that, silently acknowledging the irony in his little speech as he encouraged her to be exactly what he had lectured her against in the past.

"You and I are an amorous couple in the mood for some fun," he continued as he drew her skirts back down to cover her legs. "We enjoy inviting others to join in our intimate play and are out tonight looking for someone new. You understand?"

Trying not to appear as shocked as she was, Portia asked, "Is that a common practice?"

He shrugged. "Common enough."

Portia felt her cheeks burning, but she could not resist saying out loud the thought that entered her head.

"You know…if you and I were truly lovers," she murmured, "I would not be willing to share you with anyone."

She was expecting a scowl of reprimand to chase away the sensual look on his face. He lowered his chin instead, never breaking eye contact as he rose up partway from his crouch and braced his hands on her chair to lean forward a few breathless inches. Her heart thudded heavily, and warmth bloomed between her thighs.

"I wouldn't share you either," he whispered.

Portia's heart came to a dead stop.

Then he stood the rest of the way and left the room.

# Twenty-two

"ARE YOU READY?" DELL ASKED.

They sat in the hackney carriage on a narrow street in Covent Garden.

Portia smiled. Nervous excitement rushed through every vein. This was what she had been craving for so long. This sense of purpose. Finally, she had something to do that mattered. A little girl was somewhere in this grand city, and she and Turner were going to find her.

The hint of danger in trying to infiltrate a world so completely foreign to her simply added a necessary degree of alertness.

"I am quite ready," she replied.

Dell reached across the carriage to rest his large hand on her knee, which happened to be bouncing to a staccato rhythm just then. Her nervous movement stilled beneath the warmth and weight of his touch.

"If you don't think you can alter your perfect intonation and ladylike inflection, you would be best served to keep your mouth shut." He cocked an eyebrow. "At the very least, limit your responses to a giggle or a salacious glance."

Portia cleared her throat and lowered her chin. Dropping her eyelids to half-mast with a subtle flutter of her lashes, she parted her lips on a quiet breath before she swept her gaze down the length of his body.

"That'll do," he replied with a short cough as he leaned back again on the seat.

Reaching into his coat pocket, he withdrew a small flask and offered it to her.

"Something to calm the nerves and loosen the limbs," he explained "Remember, we are lovers out looking for a good time. This is something we have done before."

Portia took the flask and tipped some of its contents down her throat. The unknown liquor burned a wicked path to her belly, and she breathed hard to quell the cough pushing up from her lungs. Dell watched her with a subtle smirk then held out his hand for the flask. Rather than hand it back to him, she took another healthy swig.

This time, it didn't burn quite so badly, and a slow wave of warmth rose up from her belly, making her arms feel a touch heavy and awkward.

Dell scowled. "I want you to *appear* a little tipsy, not actually *be* tipsy. You must keep a clear head."

She tossed the flask back to him, and he caught it deftly in one hand before tucking it back into his pocket.

"I will be fine," Portia insisted. She had no intention of making a mess of things. Casting a glance toward the carriage door, she asked, "Shall we?"

Dell gave her a thoughtful look but exited the carriage with a light step before turning back to offer her his hand. He met her gaze with an easy smile and an intimate warmth in his eyes. Portia's stomach gave a delightful little flip as she put her hand in his and stepped from the hack.

With a playful tug, he drew her in against his side and threw his arm over her shoulders. Portia gave a husky laugh that was not entirely an act as she looped her arm around his taut and narrow waist. The muscles along his side tensed and shifted beneath her hand, giving her a boost of confidence from his capable presence. Together, they strolled to the door of the shabby-looking building.

Portia did her best not to look about in curiosity, which was difficult, considering there was so much to see as they passed into the darkened halls of the low-class brothel. It was a busy night. Half-dressed women and men in various states of inebriation passed back and forth from the public rooms on the first floor to the stairs that led up to where Portia assumed more private activities ensued.

She was so focused on making sure she did not appear the green lass that she barely took note as Dell walked them into one of the common rooms, a barely lit parlor containing various couches and chairs, along with two card tables and a long bar serving up ale and whiskey. The smell of stale tobacco and alcohol permeated the space.

Dell guided them toward a settee in the corner. He dropped to the seat in a relaxed sprawl, drawing her down along with him. Portia's body, loosened by her swigs from his flask, tumbled to the cushions beside him. With a lusty laugh that tickled every nerve in her body, Dell curved his arm around her, cupping her hip in his hand as he pulled her snug against his chest.

Turning his head, he murmured against her ear, "Relax, love. We are here to enjoy ourselves."

Portia slid him a coy glance from beneath her lashes while curving her lips into what she hoped was a knowing sort of smile. The smile he gave her in return as he gazed down at her from heavy-lidded eyes made her insides twist deliciously.

Pretending to be Dell's lover was going to be a delightful experience.

Before leaving the dressing room, Portia had paused to get a good look at herself in the mirror. Dell's work with the cosmetics had done wonders. She had barely looked like herself at all, or rather, she had appeared like an exotic version of herself. Ringed with kohl, her gray eyes had become strikingly brilliant, and her lips had been reddened just enough to give them a fuller, more lush appearance. The beauty mark above the corner of her mouth had added a playful element.

When she had asked Turner what she should do with her hair, he had turned to look at her from where he stood across the room, knotting a neckcloth beneath his chin. His gaze had been dark. "Leave it."

Casting brief glances at the other women in the room, Portia acknowledged the insight in his direction. With her made-up face, her hair flowing in disheveled waves down her back, and a gown that showed an indecent amount of cleavage, her appearance was not terribly far removed from the girls working the room.

As they sat, her body practically sprawled against his

lounging form, he played with a long lock of her hair, twirling it around his fingers.

"Look out over the room," he murmured intimately in a tone only she could hear, "as though seeking a woman you'd like us to bed."

Containing the threads of excitement running through her, Portia turned her head where it rested against his shoulder. It was vital she played this right. From beneath lowered lashes, she lazily perused the women moving about. They were all scantily dressed, their feminine charms on display for the men who moved about with drinks in hand or sat at the tables playing cards. Some women had obviously already been claimed, as they allowed their companions to grope their bodies unchallenged. Those who hadn't, employed various tactics to garner attention. Sensual smiles, caressing hands, and teasing glances.

Heat flooded Portia's body, due in part to shock and in part to a rising awareness of how Dell's body felt as she pressed along his side. Her belly was flush against his hip as she curled beside him, her bent knee rested on his hard thigh, and her hand braced on the surface of his chest. The beat of his heart beneath her palm was a grounding sensation, as was the heat of his hand where it cupped the curve of her hip and upper buttock.

Despite his casual posture, there was a readiness in his muscles and an alert confidence in his deceptively careless demeanor. But his sensuality and the heat that seeped from his body to hers was more powerful than anything else. Portia knew he was playing a part. They were lovers, and he was certainly acting as though he had intimate knowledge of her as his hand at her hip smoothed intently up over the bend in her waist to wrap around her shoulders. Portia could not forget that he had basically admitted to desiring her.

His arm around her shoulders tightened, curving her further into his embrace. Tucking her face into the bend of his throat, he lowered his head beside hers. Then he traced his lips up along the side of her neck, causing shivers to course wildly over her skin before he murmured low in her ear.

"We need to find someone young enough that she has not grown bitter and jaded. A girl who is timid, but eager and not too meek. We cannot have someone too afraid to speak."

Portia slid her hand up the surface of his chest to stroke her fingertips against the back of his neck. She loved the feel of his hair curling between her fingers. Then she turned her head to press her lips softly to his ear.

His body tensed, and his breath caught in midexhale. Her move had apparently surprised him.

Portia smiled wickedly and knew he likely felt the movement of her lips. She really loved being Jenny.

"What about the girl standing near the tables," she whispered. "The tall one with brassy orange hair in the scarlet-colored gown."

Dell lifted his head to gaze curiously across the room. Portia tipped her head back to watch his expression. His features appeared intensely handsome to her in that moment. His eyes were dark in the candlelight; his jaw was strong though his lips were curved in a carnal sort of half smile as he assessed the

woman she had noticed glancing their way more than
once since they had arrived, a distinct look of longing
in her gaze.

Dell's lips quirked at the corners.

After a moment, he looked down at her, his eyes
hooded and sensual as his long fingers caressed the skin
of her bared shoulder in lazy, drifting circles. "I am
afraid the woman you indicated is already claimed."

Portia turned to look. Her eyes widened at the sight
of the redhead being tossed over a man's shoulder and
laughing as she was carried from the room. Portia hadn't
realized she was openly staring at the scene until Dell
got her attention with a sharp smack on her bottom.

Portia gasped at the unexpected assault and noted
how Dell's eyes darkened and his mouth fought
against a true smile. The wickedness in that look went
straight to Portia's center.

"Keep your head, love," he murmured thickly.

Feeling the shift that had taken place in his body
after the warning smack, and noting that his hand now
rubbed the spot on her rear where he had struck her,
Portia couldn't help but whisper, "I could say the same
to you, darling."

His expression grew so subtly tense that Portia's
breath actually stopped as she waited to see what he
would do next. But he was ever the professional, and
he gathered himself quickly enough, much to Portia's
momentary disappointment.

Glancing back out over the room, he swept his gaze
casually about then gave a short nod toward the bar.

"The small blond, over there. Why don't you get
her attention?"

The velvety sound of his voice went straight to Portia's center, but she turned to gaze at the woman he had indicated. She was small, as he had said, close to Portia's own size, with stringy blond hair and a sultry expression. As soon as the girl glanced their way, Portia caught her gaze and tilted her chin coyly in an exaggeration of what she had seen multiple debutantes do in the ballroom.

The woman smiled back. Then she turned and grasped a bottle of wine and two glasses from the bar beside her before starting in their direction.

That was easy.

"Follow my lead," Dell whispered.

Portia tried her best not to tense as the woman came to stand before them with a wide grin and an assessing glance of her own. She took in the sight of Portia and Dell sprawled together, her gaze slowing as it passed along Dell's muscled form and then again over the curve of Portia's hip and the swell of her bosom. Then she met Portia's eyes with a flash of curiosity.

She was younger than Portia had at first thought. Her makeup, which had given her a dramatic appearance at a distance, now made her look gaunt and tired close up.

"Can I offer ye both a bit o' wine?"

"We'd adore some wine, wouldn't we, love?" Dell answered, giving Portia's buttocks a gentle pat.

As the woman poured the two glasses, she said with a flick of her gaze, "My name is Anne. I haven't seen ye 'fore. Is there something particular ye're lookin' for tonight?"

"You might say that." Dell's voice was low and

inviting as he took the offered wine. Taking a drink, he slid a swift glance at Portia, encouraging her to do the same.

However, Anne did not hand off the glass to Portia as she had to Dell. Instead, she lowered herself to her knees before them, setting the bottle on the floor. Then she leaned toward Portia, lifting the glass to her lips in offering.

Portia felt a flash of surprise at the hopeful expression on the girl's face. Reminding herself who she was and why she was supposed to be there, she held the prostitute's gaze as she set her lips to the rim of the glass and took a long drink. The wine was bitter and so dry it sucked every bit of moisture from Portia's throat.

Anne watched her with deep and quiet interest.

"Is there somewhere more private where we can retire to continue this little party?" Dell asked, interrupting the moment and drawing Anne's attention back to him.

The prostitute smiled. "Of course."

She swept up the bottle of wine as she stood and led them from the parlor. Portia was grateful for Dell's arm locked around her waist as they ascended the narrow stairs to the second floor.

The woman's attentions had thrown Portia off. She glanced up at Dell's profile and saw him watching her from the corner of his eye. He gave her waist a squeeze. No longer under direct observation, he had allowed the sensual expression to slide from his face. She noted the tightness in his jaw and the hard glint in his eye. He was tense. And worried.

She could not let him regret his decision to bring

her along. Taking some deep breaths, Portia shored up her confidence. She was not a ninny. The prostitute's obvious interest in her had flustered her a bit, that's all. She had to remember that she and Dell were here for a reason.

In between taking deep swigs of wine right from the bottle, Anne cast sweet, enticing little glances at them over her shoulder as she led them past other patrons coming and going from the rooms on the upper floor.

Portia made sure to smile back, trying to insert an element of coy mystery into her gaze. She felt a twinge of guilt for the manipulation, but told herself it was not so different from what many debutantes did in the ballrooms of the beau monde, when they flirted with their beaus just enough to keep them on the line until they could be assured of the biggest catch.

It was not a good feeling to know she was behaving in a manner so similar to what she abhorred, but at least it was for the purpose of saving an innocent child.

Besides, concentrating on the flirtation helped to distract her from the general griminess of the hall and the sounds of groans and breathless laughter that came from behind the closed doors they passed.

Finally, Anne directed them into an unoccupied room. It was narrow and dark, perhaps to hide the dinginess of the sheets covering the bed. The only other bit of furniture was a narrow table on rickety legs.

Anne closed the door behind them and came forward. She handed Portia the wine glass she still held before turning to add more to Dell's glass. Her smile was warm and eager. Her gaze was soft and questioning.

"Why don't you tell me what you like, so we can get started."

Dell drew Portia in tight to his side, his warm hand strong at the bend of her waist before he released her to stroll across the room.

Portia sensed his intention, that he wanted to position himself between Anne and the door, and realized she may have to add a bit of distraction to keep from spooking the girl before they had a chance to question her. Recalling how important this interview was motivated Portia to continue the deception a bit longer.

She met the prostitute's gaze as she lifted the glass to her lips. Again, the woman watched intently. Portia closed her eyes, as though savoring the taste of the bitter wine, as she licked her lips to claim every drop. When she opened her eyes, she was surprised to see her ploy had worked, as Dell had crossed behind the prostitute without her notice and now stood leaning casually against the door.

Both he and Anne were staring at her intently.

Portia fought the blush that rose to her cheeks, but suspected she did not succeed.

Anne laughed breathlessly. "Ye're a fine one, aren't ye?" she asked in a husky whisper.

"I am afraid, dear Anne, we are not here tonight for the reasons you suspect."

Anne blinked at Dell's voice and twisted to look at him. At the sight of his position blocking the exit, she swung back around to Portia, wary accusation in her gaze. "What's this?"

Portia stepped forward, wishing to ease the other

woman's rising anxiety. "We mean you no harm. We simply have some questions."

"Aw, hell," the prostitute muttered before taking another drink from the bottle then wiping the back of her hand across her mouth. "I shoulda known you two were too good to be true. Poor Anne would never get so lucky as to have such a"—she sighed—"promising evening."

She dropped herself to sit on the edge of the bed, all thoughts of seduction cast aside as she eyed Portia and Dell with suspicion.

"We can still make this worth your time," Dell replied in a flat tone, "if you provide us with the information we seek."

"Oh yeah?" Anne asked skeptically. "And what's it you seek?"

Portia set her wine glass on the table and came forward to sit beside Anne. She ignored the slight awkwardness in knowing what Anne had intended for them to be doing on that bed and told herself she was simply having a heart-to-heart with one of her sisters. She and Lily had engaged in hundreds of conversations while snuggled up beneath bedcovers. This was not so different.

Bending her knee, she turned toward Anne, making sure her skirts still concealed the knife on her calf. She met Anne's suspicious gaze with one of compassion and leaned forward in confidence.

"We are seeking information about a child, the daughter of a woman who worked here not long ago." Seeing she had Anne's attention, though the wariness had not dissipated from the girl's eyes, she asked, "Do you know the name Molly Andrews?"

Anne stiffened, and the muscles around her mouth tensed, drawing her lips into a subtle snarl.

"Oh yes. Miss Molly," she sneered. "Ain't no one here sad to've seen her move along."

"Why is that?" Portia asked.

"That one was always puttin' on airs, though she weren't no better than any other opium addict. At least I never touch that nasty stuff," Anne scoffed before lifting the bottle of wine back to her lips.

"Did she say anything about why she left her employment here?"

"Only that she was moving on to better things. I didn't care much to listen beyond that. Good riddance, I say."

Portia took a breath before asking the most important question. "And did you ever see Molly's daughter? Did she ever speak of her child?"

Anne's expression narrowed at that, an obvious look of confusion crossing her gaze. "Not that I ever heard."

Portia's heart sank, and she sent a glance toward Dell as he remained quietly standing against the door. His expression was unreadable, but he gave her a short nod to continue.

"Did Molly reside here at the brothel? Do you know if there was someplace she went on a regular basis?"

"That was one of the things she held over the rest of us—that she had a place of her own. Though from what I know, it wasn't really hers. She just stayed with another moll named Suzanne, in a place owned by the other one's pimp."

"The pimp's name?" Dell asked, interrupting for the first time.

Anne glanced at him, her eyes full of distrust.

Portia rested her hand on Anne's thin arm, bringing her attention back to her.

"Please, Anne," she pleaded, allowing her heartfelt concern for Claire to come through in her voice and expression. "A young girl's fate is at stake."

Anne stared back at her for a long moment before answering. Then she lowered her eyes and said, "Gregor Dune. But don't you dare be saying I told you that." Her eyes swept up again, and there was definite fear present. "He's a nasty one. Likes to cut his girls to keep 'em in line. I may not belong to 'im, but that don't mean he won't come after me if he thinks he has cause. Not sure how Molly managed to live in his building while working here, but that's what I heard."

Dell nodded at the man's name, apparently recognizing it. He cast Portia a look, saying they had what they needed.

Portia leaned toward the other woman. "Thank you for this, Anne. It is greatly appreciated."

The young prostitute's smile was sad and weighted. She lifted the bottle once again in a mock toast. "My good deed for the year." Then she tipped it back and finished off what was left of the wine.

Portia rose to her feet at the same time Dell came away from the door.

"You two sure you don't want to stay a bit longer?" Anne asked. "I'd give you all I got. I promise it'd be worth it."

"I don't doubt it at all, love," Dell said with a smile as he approached to set his glass on the table beside

Portia's before turning to give Anne a few coins. "For your trouble."

Anne gasped as she looked at the wealth in her hand.

Dell once again swept his arm around Portia's waist to take her out into the hall. He closed the door behind them, leaving Anne alone with her earnings.

# Twenty-three

"ARE WE NOT GOING TO SPEAK WITH SUZANNE?" Portia asked when Dell gave Honeycutt's address to the hack driver before helping her into the carriage.

"Not tonight," Dell answered, taking the seat opposite.

"Why not? Surely, this woman would know something of the girl. We have to speak with her."

"Agreed. Just not tonight. Gregor Dune likes to keep his women as biddable as possible, and opium accomplishes that job well enough. Right now, she will be deep in the smoke and heavily guarded by Dune's men as she plies her trade. Best to seek her out in the stark light of day, when it will be more difficult for her to evade questioning."

Portia thought of her family's plans for the next day.

"I should be able to get away for a while, but I will need to be back in time to get ready for our dinner plans." Seeing his tense expression and guessing what he was thinking, she quickly added, "You are stuck with me, Turner. It is best to accept it sooner rather than later."

He was silent for a long moment. Then he sighed

and lowered his chin. "You did well tonight. Perhaps a bit too well for poor Anne." His lips tilted into a teasing grin. "She was quite taken with you."

Portia met his gaze with more boldness than she felt. His smile did odd things to her insides. "It was a singular experience to be so blatantly desired."

His eyebrows arched over the intent focus of his eyes, dark in the intimate confines of the carriage. "You do not receive lustful glances from your gentlemen suitors?"

Typically, Portia would snort in derision at the idea. Just now, however, she did not feel so flippant.

"No," she replied earnestly. "The men of my acquaintance either see me as an impertinent pest or a novel amusement. I knew nothing of desire…until I met you."

The look he gave her caused a riot of tingling in her center. He stared hard at her, his eyes glittering in the darkness, and the curve of his mouth now decidedly sensual. Even his posture emanated an innate masculine allure.

Portia melted in her seat.

"I do desire you," he said, his voice a low, husky murmur, "but nothing will come of it."

"Why?" Portia demanded in a whisper, the tightness of her chest making it impossible to speak with any more force.

"We are of different worlds. Our paths should never have crossed."

"But they have crossed. Should our origins define us? We are not so different, you and I."

His laugh was harsh. "We are very different. I grew

up running the streets of London. You grew up cozy in a gentleman's home."

"Yet, here we both are," Portia argued pertly, "sharing a common goal."

"For me, this is a livelihood. For you, it is a lark."

Indignant anger flared in her heart. "You have no idea what motivates me."

"Of course I do. You are bored with your fancy parties and insipid companions. You came to me seeking an adventure. A little risk to send your blood racing, a bit of danger to make you feel alive."

Portia frowned, but not because he was wrong. The reasons he gave were exactly what had initially kept her coming back to him. But it had become more than that. Deep down, she knew she belonged in this world. His world. With him, she believed she could accomplish important things. Things that mattered.

But he did not believe in her.

A chill cooled her skin, and she glanced away from his intent gaze just as they reached Honeycutt's. She did not wait for his assistance but opened the carriage door to leap to the ground as soon as she could safely do so.

She didn't even acknowledge the little serving man, Morley, and his pinched expression when she swept into the front hall and continued up the stairs to the dressing room.

Turner thought her useless and shallow.

Was she?

The idea made her entire body tense in revolt.

No. She was capable of so much more.

Perhaps she was stupid in thinking Turner might accept her as an equal, or an apprentice at the very least.

She swept her borrowed cloak from about her shoulders and tossed it angrily aside as she strode toward the mirror. She looked at herself, dressed as the merry young lover. Suddenly annoyed by the image of such an exotic and sensual creature, she swept up a cloth from the table and roughly wiped the cosmetics from her face. Then she twisted her arms around her back to release the buttons of the revealing gown.

With a sharp tug, she pushed the gown past her hips and kicked it into a corner. She stood there with her hands on her hips, staring at the small heap of lavender muslin and black lace, her breath short and her temper still hot.

"Are you finished?"

She spun around at the sound of Dell's voice, prepared to unleash some of her present pique on him. But her irritation dissolved the instant she spotted him leaning negligently against the door frame. He had removed his coat and stood in his wonderfully fitted breeches, which revealed the toned strength of his thighs and narrow hips. Her mind's eye recalled the perfect, hard curve of his buttocks, and she suddenly wished to smooth her hands over that particular part of his anatomy. His arms were crossed over his chest, accenting the muscles of his shoulders and arms, reminding her of the lean planes of his abdomen. Locks of his brown-gold hair looped over his forehead, giving him a rough and rakish air.

All thought fled from her brain. All self-awareness, doubt, and anger disappeared on a swift exhale. Within the span of a moment, she became pure instinct, unable to do anything but act on the overwhelming impulse that possessed her.

In long strides, she crossed to him. Lifting both hands to frame his jaw, she rose up on her tiptoes, leaned her body into his, and pulled his mouth down to meet hers.

It was the second time she had kissed him.

And the second time her insides burst with a million tingling, rushing sensations.

His arms came around her, doubling around her back, hauling her higher against him as he tipped his head to take her mouth more fully. Her breasts flattened against his hard chest, her low belly pressed firmly to his arousal. The heat of him, the life and sensuality inherent in his person, flowed into her, spreading through her blood in a wonderful wave of yearning.

She curled her fingers into the hair at his nape, tugging, as she squirmed in his hold, desperate to get closer. She wanted to sink into him, meld with him.

He slid one of his hands up into her hair to grasp the back of her head, holding her steady as he kissed her with passion and promise. Her breath came fast and harsh as his mouth moved over hers. The thrust of his tongue was demanding, the taste of him so primal. This was what she had been craving from him. This total confession of desire, this savoring of their mutual need for each other.

She stretched against him, willfully allowing every bit of what she was feeling to translate into the movement of her body. She wanted to feel his skin against hers, wanted to smooth her hands over the muscled ridges of his chest and abdomen. Grasping his shirt, she pulled it free of his breeches and shoved it up until she could flatten her hands on either side of his ribs. His lungs expanded and contracted with every labored breath as he kissed her.

Portia couldn't get enough.

Smoothing her hands over his warm, bare skin, she continued down the inward curve of his low back, then farther to grasp the hard curve of his buttocks.

He broke the kiss with a swift indrawn breath as he brought his hands up to frame her face. Leaning back, he looked down at her. His features were fraught with a beautiful sort of tension, and wickedness shone deep in his gaze.

"I shouldn't want this," he murmured, his voice husky and deep.

Breathless with her need for him, Portia tilted her chin up and tried to lean into him again, wanting his mouth back on hers. "But you do," she countered.

His smile was a subtle curving at the corners of his mouth. Still holding her face gently between his large hands, he brushed his thumb across the crest of her cheek before lowering his head. He swept his lips across hers with velvet softness, allowed his tongue to explore languidly then with rising passion. Yet, he would not take it further.

He devoted all attention to the pleasure of their mouths, with lush strokes and teasing nips. With an occasional scrape of his teeth that sent shockwaves of delight rippling through her system.

The man kissed with amazing skill, as he did everything else.

Portia tingled from head to toe. Her fingers clutched at his buttocks before sliding up beneath his shirt to smooth over the muscled surface of his back. She was infinitely grateful when he lowered one of his hands to press at the center of her lower back, bringing her body into full contact with his.

His strength, his heat, his pure, raw maleness appealed to her in a way the pampered lords of her previous acquaintance never had. Dell Turner, for all his talent in deception and concealment, was entirely without pretext at his core. He knew who he was and what he wanted and made no apologies for any of it.

And right now, he wanted her.

Portia felt his desire in every flick of his tongue and puff of his breath. The tight groan that caught in his throat when she sucked his tongue deep into her mouth told her more than words ever could and thrilled her beyond compare.

Still, she wanted more. She wanted everything.

She wanted Dell Turner to make love to her.

There was no shame with the realization, not an ounce of doubt. The rules of society that said she must remain pure, the expectations of her sister that she make a good match—they didn't matter. Here, now, in this moment, the only thing that mattered was her need for this man. And his need for her.

But within the swirl of rising passion inside her there was a seed of panic, a fear that he would draw away before she could know the full extent of what he was making her feel.

Finally, she could take no more and voiced her rising concern in a murmur against his lips.

"This cannot end with a kiss," she insisted. "You do strange things to me, Dell Turner. Exciting and wonderful things. Tell me I am not alone in what I feel."

He pressed his lips to the corner of her mouth before he drew back to stare down at her in silence. One hand splayed wide against her lower back as he brushed a lock of her hair away from her face with a gentle sweep of his fingers.

He stared intently into her eyes. His jaw was tense, but his lips were parted to allow the swiftness of his breath.

Then, brushing the backs of his knuckles down the side of her throat, he replied, "You are not alone. Come with me."

Taking her hand, he pushed off from the door frame and led her out into the hall and to the room next door. A rush of anticipation claimed her.

Once in the room, he released her hand. Portia continued forward into the dimly lit place. It was modestly furnished, but certainly in possession of the only piece of furniture she cared about at the moment—a bed.

"This is your bedroom?"

There was the sound of the door shutting behind her, enclosing them together in the intimate space.

"When I stay here," he replied.

His answer implied he at least occasionally stayed somewhere else. Tension slid down her spine, and she recognized it for what it was. Jealousy.

"When you are not with a lover?" she clarified.

There was a long pause, during which Portia refused to turn around. It was a prying question, but she needed to know.

"I have no lover," he answered.

He did not belong to someone else. Her relief was boundless. There was so much she didn't know about him, but she intended to discover every detail and nuance of his existence…if he would let her.

She turned to look at him in time to see him dragging his shirt off over his head. She stood stunned as the breath-stealing sight of his body was revealed. God, but she could stare at him for hours. He did not seem to notice her preoccupation as he kicked off his shoes and stripped off his stockings, leaving him in soft, worn breeches that did nothing to conceal the intoxicating evidence of his arousal.

Heat pooled between Portia's thighs, and her breath came short and swift.

When he did finally look up to see her standing there, surely appearing as dumbfounded as she felt, he quirked his lips in a playful smile, and Portia's heart melted. As did her knees, and her spine, and the hot core at her center.

He approached her and slid his hand into her hair to palm the back of her skull as he took her mouth in a burning kiss, setting fire to her blood. The masterful way he held her, the passionate demand of his tongue, even the subtle tug of his hand in her hair, combined to steal all thoughts from her head.

She hadn't even realized she had lifted her hands to grasp tightly to his forearms in a desperate attempt to anchor herself to him until he drew back. Her eyelashes fluttered open to see him smiling at her.

"Relax, I am not going anywhere."

"Promise?" she asked in a whisper.

Dell hooked the strap of her shift with his finger and drew it off her shoulder. Then he pressed a light kiss to the bare skin.

"I promise," he murmured before he trailed his lips up the side of her throat.

Chills raced across her skin, and a deep pulse heated her center. A wealth of sensations lit across every nerve, but his assurance had soothed her. There was no need to rush and every reason to enjoy each moment to its fullest.

She was finally getting what she wanted. *Him*. And she intended to revel in every moment of this experience.

She tingled from head to toe while he teased the sensitive spot below her ear with nibbling kisses. He still cupped her head in his large palm, and she tilted her head to the side, allowing him more access to the sweep of her neck. With his other hand, he began a slow caress down the length of her spine and over the rounded swell of her buttocks. He paused there, kneading the curve of her rear, sending delicious little aching pulses through her center.

How could he know exactly how to touch her?

She sighed deeply when he reached for the tapes of her petticoat, releasing the skirt and letting it fall to the floor in a billowing flounce. Portia kicked her shoes off as she stepped free of the garment, only then remembering the knife still strapped to her leg.

Also seeing the weapon beneath the shorter hem of her shift, Dell lowered himself to a knee before her. "You won't need this anymore."

With deft fingers, he untied the straps and set the knife aside. Then he reached for the fastenings of her garters, releasing those as well. Keeping his head bowed, he rolled down each of her stockings. Portia stood still, her breath shallow and her gaze locked on the sight of such a strong and capable man on bent knee as he removed the most delicate of her underthings.

For some reason, the action tightened her throat.

She had a hard time imagining an oh-so-elegant lord doing the same. Dell's innate lack of arrogance fascinated her. As did his humble strength and unpolished masculinity.

Finishing his task, Dell finally glanced up at her. A thick lock of hair had fallen over his brow, and his eyes were profoundly focused as he met her gaze.

Portia's lips parted, but no words came out. She had never been one to hold in her thoughts, but some intuition warned her to keep quiet. And then she forgot everything she was about to say as he slid his warm hands around the backs of her calves.

His palms were slightly callused, but she loved the rough texture contrasting with the gentleness of his exploration as he smoothed his hands higher by tantalizing degrees. His fingers tickled the backs of her knees, and she jumped.

He never broke eye contact with her, and his smile turned decidedly naughty, triggering a dance of intricate thrills over every nerve in her body.

Portia smiled back. Lifting her hand, she brushed aside the wayward lock of his hair.

He slid his hands up the backs of her thighs, reaching higher beneath the hem of her shift. Portia held her breath and braced her hand on his broad shoulder as her legs grew weak. Then he rose to his feet, bringing his hands up to grasp her buttocks.

They stood like that for a moment. Staring into each other's eyes while their swift and heavy breaths passed between them. She felt wickedly erotic with her shift drooped low over her breasts, held up by only one strap, and the rest bunched up around her hips while his large hands gripped her bare bottom.

She felt bold and free. Sensual and strong.

His fingers curled into her flesh, and Portia's lower belly tensed.

Then he released her to grasp her shift and sweep it up over her head before tossing it aside.

And Portia stood naked before him.

She would have given anything to have his hands on her body just then. But rather than reaching for her, Dell took a step back and lowered his chin to gaze at her with heavy-lidded eyes.

Portia had always felt comfortable and confident in her own skin. She had never gone through an awkward stage as an adolescent and had never worried about the details of her appearance, putting more stock in her intelligence and forthright attitude than anything else. But in that moment, she was immensely grateful to see the flare of appreciation and desire in his gaze as it traveled across the span of her shoulders then down over her peaked breasts and flat belly.

She swept a thick lock of hair back over her shoulder and stepped toward him, lifting her hands to the hard curve of his pectoral muscles. She could feel the taut expectation running through him as clearly as she felt the hard nubs of his nipples under her palms.

She couldn't resist the urge to lightly rake her finger-nails over the flat disks and was rewarded by Dell's swift, hissing inhale. The harsh breath tightened the muscles of his abdomen, drawing her attention lower. With heady excitement, she trailed her fingertips over the beautiful ridges of muscle until her fingers curled into the top edge of his breeches where they rested low on his hips.

Looking up at the handsome angles of his face, she smiled and gave a little tug on his waistband, telling him what she wanted.

He smiled back but shook his head. "Patience."

Portia narrowed her gaze. "You do not know me very well."

Dell laughed, and the sound of it rolled through her insides like a lightning storm. His hands, which had remained at his sides while she explored the surface of his chest and stomach, came up to grasp her hips and pull her against him until she could feel the hard and hot length of his arousal pressing into her belly. "Not yet," he murmured and lowered his head until his lips barely brushed hers. "But I will."

Then he took her mouth in a deep and luscious kiss before cupping her rear again in both hands and lifting her high against him.

Portia instinctively parted her legs to wrap them around his lean waist as she grabbed his shoulders to steady herself. He looked up at her with a gaze so deep and delicious that Portia's heart stopped.

In a few long strides, he tumbled her back onto the bed, following her down to settle heavily between her spread thighs. She gasped at the feel of his hard length pressing against her core. Arching her spine, she tightened her legs around his waist and rolled her hips to feel more of him.

Instead of giving her what she craved—more of his weight, more of the wonderful pressure between her legs—he pulled away, sitting back on his heels.

Portia lay splayed and vulnerable before him as he studied her body.

Placing one hand low on her belly, he spread his fingers wide before gently sliding his hand up to the space between her breasts. Then he lifted his gaze to hers.

"From the moment I first met you, I imagined you like this."

His voice was rough with desire. It flowed through Portia's blood, heating her beyond belief, shortening her breath and making her ache in a wonderful way.

With a gentle quirk of his lips, he cupped one of her breasts in his hand and brushed his thumb across the peaked nipple.

Portia gasped. It was a soft, breathy sound.

"You are unlike any woman I have ever known," he added in a low murmur while his gaze focused intently on the movement of his fingers caressing her soft breast.

Portia tried to press herself more fully into his hand, and though her eyelids felt heavy, she could not bring herself to stop watching his face as he touched her.

"I hope that is a good thing," she replied.

His chuckle was sensual and intimate. Portia tried to think of something else to say that might amuse him so she could hear it again. Before she could, he rose up over her. Still kneeling between her legs, he planted his fists to the mattress on either side of her shoulders. His arms were straight and strong, his shoulders intimidating in their width and power, but Portia was not wary.

She ran her hands along the corded muscles in his arms and up over his shoulders, reveling in the evidence of his superior strength. Finally, here was a man she felt equal to her in mind, determination, and self-assurance. Bending his arms, he slowly lowered his mouth to hers. Portia tipped up her chin to meet him with an insistent brush of her tongue across his lips.

With a sound somewhere between a harsh laugh and a groan, he delved into the heat of her mouth. Ravaging her of breath and thought.

She slid her hands down along his sides, giving a grumble of frustration when she encountered the material of his breeches.

"Won't you take these off now?" she urged, craving the sensation of his nakedness against her, especially in that place that ached so poignantly.

Dell made a low sound of dissent as he shifted his mouth to the side of her throat.

"Once I do, there will be nothing to keep me from plunging into your body. There is more of you I wish to explore before then."

The raw nature of his voice and explicit image his words created sent tremors of need through Portia. Restlessness claimed her in a wave. She shifted urgently beneath him.

In response, he lowered himself to his elbows before sliding deliciously down her body. His firm chest dragged over the sensitive peaks of her breasts, causing a deep moan to roll from her throat. And then his mouth covered one peak in luscious heat. His tongue swirled around the tip in a velvet dance of pleasure.

Portia lost herself to the sensations.

# Twenty-four

DELL REALIZED HE SHOULD HAVE EXPECTED THIS, should have known from the moment he met her that they would end up here.

His resistance to this inevitability had been futile and foolish. What sane man would turn away from such passion? He had been stupid to fight it. With every breath he possessed, every second he lived, he wanted her. So badly, he was desperate to prolong it as long as possible.

Having her stunning body in his arms, the tantalizing taste of her skin on his tongue, the scent of her in his nostrils, was as close to perfection as he was ever likely to get. He slid his hands beneath her shoulder blades and buried his face between her breasts, inhaling deeply.

She bowed her back and fisted her hands in his hair.

He knew what she wanted, and he had every intention of giving it to her, but only if he could savor every moment. Because even though he had her in his bed, he would never be fooled into believing she was anything but desperately out of his reach. He was not going to take a single second of this for granted.

Shifting his head, he suckled her other breast, drawing the peak harshly into his mouth, triumphing in the sound of her swift gasp. He flicked his tongue over her pebbled nipple before drawing it deep.

Her low moan flowed through him like molten honey.

He had never known anyone with such a deep and natural sensuality. Had never held a woman so intent upon the experience of lovemaking. She was impulsive, passionate, and demanding.

She fired him up to a savage heat, but he resisted the temptation to give in to her urging. He was determined to go slow with her, explore every inch, soak in every response. His cock ached with need, but Dell gritted his teeth and slid lower along her body. He pressed soft kisses around the curves of her ribs and down the center of her abdomen while her slim hands gripped his shoulders, her fingers curling tightly into his muscles.

He thought he heard his name escape on a harsh sigh, but he couldn't be sure. Her petite form made subtle twisting, rolling motions beneath his mouth and hands. He doubted she was even aware she was doing it, but it was effective in pushing his control to the limit.

He could take a little more. But first, he needed a taste of her.

Continuing lower, he hooked his arms under her knees, spreading her thighs around his shoulders. Then he grasped her perfect rear in his hands as he lifted her to his mouth.

She jolted and gasped. Her legs squeezed around him. Dell looked up the length of her sprawled body as he gave a long lick of his tongue along her heated female flesh. A heady moan slid from her throat, and her eyes flew open to meet his.

"Bloody hell," she whispered, her voice sultry with shock and desire.

Dell chuckled at her reaction and flicked his tongue teasingly against her swollen bud.

Her lashes fluttered and her head fell back while her body tensed in a sensual curve.

He flicked his tongue again then swirled it in soothing circles over her folds. The way she moaned was intensely erotic and triggered a sharp tightening in his loins, but he was not nearly finished with his exploration.

He continued to enjoy her with his mouth. Gently suckling and nipping at her flesh. Easing his tongue along every fold and secret valley until she softened against his mouth. Yet even then, he did not retreat. He covered her clitoris with his mouth, laving it with his tongue as he eased one finger into her slick passage.

Her entire body tensed. On a gasp, she reached out to grasp his head in her hands.

"Dell?"

The sound of his name in her breathy, sultry voice sent shockwaves of pleasure through his body.

He had reached his limit.

Rising up over her again, he settled heavily between her thighs. Then he took her mouth in a lush, erotic kiss as he rocked his erection against her core. She gasped and moaned into his mouth. Her fingers fisted urgently in his hair.

With a muttered curse, he leaned to the side just enough to reach down and release his breeches. He made short work of shoving them down his legs before settling over her once again. He was helpless against the groan of pure pleasure that rolled from his throat when he felt the slick heat of her flesh caress his hard length. He rocked his hips once, twice, sliding his erection along her opening.

Propping himself on one elbow, he reached between their bodies to position himself. Then he pressed forward.

Her passage was tight and resistant.

Dell gritted his teeth.

Her body squeezed his with such luscious heat, he wondered how he would manage a minute more of the intense pleasure rising within him. She was going to draw a climax from him in the first long thrust. He could not allow that to happen.

He stopped the progress of his possession and held himself where he was. Sweat rolled down his temples and along his spine. Dropping his head, he allowed his forehead to rest against hers. He kept his eyes tightly closed as he tried to distract his thoughts away from the million licks of pleasure running rampant through his body.

After a couple of seconds, she shifted beneath him, moving her hips in a way that allowed him to sink a tiny bit deeper.

Dell tensed against the urge to plunge to full depth and claim the release that was so readily available.

Instead, he lifted his head again to look into her face, needing to see what she was feeling, hoping the experience was at least half as pleasurable for her as it was for him.

His chest seized at the sight she made.

Her eyes shone bright silver. Her sable hair was a tangled mess beneath her, and a fine sheen of sweat coated her flushed skin. And her lips, so lush and swollen from his kisses, were parted for the passage of her rapid breath.

Dell could not resist those lips.

He lowered his mouth to hers and slid his tongue past her teeth as he rolled his hips, pressing further, going deeper. The way was slow and so damn intense he nearly missed noticing the barrier he encountered deep within her. But when he did, he jolted in surprise and lifted his head to stare at her in harsh accusation.

Burning lust was a demanding presence through his blood, but this revelation managed to hold it at bay. He realized his massive error. Somewhere along the way, he had convinced himself that with her bold manner and passionate nature, she could not possibly be the innocent he had first believed her to be. It was the only way he had allowed himself to go this far.

"You are a virgin," he muttered roughly.

She slid her hands over his shoulders in an impatient caress as she undulated beneath him, silently urging him to continue. When he did not, she opened her eyes to meet his tense gaze.

"You are a virgin," he repeated. His voice was steadier this time.

There was a flicker of awareness in her eyes, and her brow creased with confusion. "I am, though I expect very soon not to be. Does that matter?"

"Of course it matters."

How could it not matter? Anger at her recklessness

started to snake through the lustful haze in his brain. "Do you have any idea what we are doing right now?"

Her frown deepened. "Of course I do," she retorted, and her voice was strained. "Do you? Because right now you don't seem to be doing much of anything."

Dell said nothing, just stared down at her as he tried to keep his hardened flesh from pulsing within her body.

As he watched, her expression changed from defensive and irritated to something else. Something that made his gut clench. She suddenly looked vulnerable in a way he had never witnessed in her before. Her eyes swept closed for a moment before opening again. She licked her lips before she spoke.

"Please, Dell." Her voice had lowered to a soft murmur. "You cannot leave me now. I could not bear it. You must know how badly I want this. How badly I have wanted you. This has been everything I dreamed it could be, but"—she paused, and her gaze slid to the side as a blush rose on her cheeks—"there must be more. My body aches for more. Inside…I feel a craving that is overwhelming and urgent and beautiful. I am certain I will go mad if you do not continue. You said I was not alone. Do not leave me now."

Her tone grew harsh by the end, and her hands gripped painfully at his biceps as though she would try to hold him to her by any means possible.

A nobler man would retreat, leave the last vestige of her innocence unbreached.

But no one had ever accused Dell of being noble. Though a part of him might wish he could be that man, it just wasn't possible when her urgent plea rippled through him like wildfire. Heating his blood, firing his loins.

He withdrew from her sheath in a slow glide.

Her fingernails dug into his skin, and she tensed beneath him while a strangled sob caught in her throat.

Then Dell pushed forward into her heat, but no farther than he had been before. Her gasp of relief and pleasure filled his awareness.

He withdrew again, in the same slow, torturous slide. Then another careful thrust forward.

He had never taken a virgin before. He knew it was a painful experience for women, but he hoped he might ease the experience if he could overwhelm her with pleasure before the inevitable shock of pain.

He made several more languid thrusts, patiently getting her body accustomed to the invasion of his. At the same time, he kissed her with all of the skill he possessed.

His body shook with his efforts as he reaped the benefits of the prolonged yet limited thrusts into her heat. Leaning to one side, he reached down between them and found her clitoris with his middle finger. Circling her flesh in time to his thrusts, he finally felt her stiffening beneath him as her breath became stilted and fast.

Then all of a sudden, her inner flesh fluttered in deep spasms. At the same time, her body bowed and a moan caught hard in her throat as her climax stole her breath.

With a harsh grunt, Del braced himself over her and plunged hard into her body, breaking through the thin membrane and seating himself fully. She cried out his name, nails raking down his back.

That was all it took.

His release came hard and fast, wiping away all further thought, all sense of self and separation from the woman with whom he was joined. The pleasure drowned him in a welcome wave, completely sapping his strength, while filling him with a pervading sense of contentment unlike anything he'd ever experienced.

# Twenty-five

PORTIA WAS STUNNED. AND DELIGHTED.

And stunned.

She lay beneath Dell's sprawled body, running her hands in light trails up and down his sweat-slicked back while his thudding heart slowly returned to a normal pace.

She smiled.

She had done that to him. Reduced him to a weighted mass of muscle and sweat and heavy breath.

She knew how he felt. She never wanted to move again. She could die in that moment, beneath his sprawled body, and would have ended her life perfectly happy.

But after a few moments, her legs began to cramp in their position around his hips. She had no idea when exactly she had linked her ankles behind his buttocks, but the position was starting to feel awkward. With measured movements, she shifted her legs, lowering them one at a time to rest on the mattress.

Dell lifted his head from where he had dropped it beside hers. Propping himself on his elbows, he looked down into her face. His golden gaze was closed and quiet as he brushed her hair away from her damp temples. Then he dipped his head and pressed a soft kiss across her lips.

Portia's belly tightened.

"You all right?" he asked.

"Quite," she replied with a smile.

"You should have told me you were a virgin."

Portia had to lift a brow at that as she said, "It did not occur to me that you would assume otherwise."

Dell shook his head, causing thick locks of his hair to fall over his forehead. Portia almost got annoyed by the line that formed between his brows. But she was too languid and satisfied to feel much more than mildly bothered.

Lifting himself away from her, he dropped onto his back at her side then reached to draw the bedsheet up over them both.

Portia turned toward him and propped her head in her hand. She couldn't help but admire the sight of his masculine physique stretched in repose. The sheet only covered him from his narrow hips down. Reaching out, she ran her hand over the naked surface of his chest and taut abdomen. She was fascinated by him.

Even after what they had just done together, she hungered for him. Deep in her center, she craved him.

It was rather odd, really. But she didn't mind it in the least.

"How did you start doing the work you do?" she asked.

He lay with his eyes closed, and when he didn't answer her right away, she wondered if he had fallen asleep. But then he cracked open one eye to peek askance at her before closing it again and propping his hands beneath his head.

"When my mum died, I was sent to an orphanage. I lasted about a day and a half before I ran away and found my way back to Covent Garden. I did odd jobs around the theater, mostly fetching and running messages between the actresses and their protectors. It took me all over town and into neighborhoods filled with mansions and fancy carriages. Everywhere I went, I observed the people. Their mannerisms, the way they walked and dressed. The different ways they talked. I practiced mimicking them and created characters for myself, depending on who I was running for. It was a game."

"How old were you?"

"I was eight when mum died. I did that for about six years." He paused. "Then one night a fancy lord I had been delivering messages for asked me to do a special task for him for more gold than I had seen in my life. When I accomplished that, he asked me to do another. Word got around that I was good for more than delivering lovers' notes. I realized it was easier to move through certain areas of town when I looked like I belonged. I made costumes from scraps left over at the theater. Next thing I knew, I had a business of sorts."

"Have you ever been hired to kill someone?"

He turned his head to look at her. His expression was stiff, but not harsh. "I've been asked. And I refused. But that doesn't mean my hands are clean. I've had to take a life to save my own."

Portia looked at him, trying to imagine him killing someone. It didn't fit.

"I am certain it was something you would have avoided if at all possible," she said quietly.

"There is not much I won't do for the asking, Portia. Nightshade fulfills a need in this city, and he gets paid handsomely for it."

"I think your work is more than that. You have so much potential to really help people when no one else can. It is a noble endeavor."

Dell snorted. "I assure you, there is nothing noble about what I do. It is a job."

"It doesn't have to be. It could be more," Portia said quietly.

He stared at her for a while in the easy darkness. She could tell that he still disagreed with her, but it seemed neither of them felt much like arguing just then.

Portia was more comfortable lying beside him in that bed, both of them naked beneath the thin sheet, than she had ever been in her life.

She smiled.

After a moment, he smiled back.

It was a slow, reluctant curving of his wonderfully shaped lips.

Then he rolled to his side to face her. He slid his hand around the back of her neck and leaned forward to take her mouth.

How she loved his kisses.

Deep, earthy, real. They made her feel things from the back of her scalp to the soles of her feet, into every fingertip, and through the depth of her belly.

She scooted closer to him, slipping her hand over

his waist to glide her fingers up and down his back. The heat of his skin warmed her. The press of his hard chest and the muscled length of his leg slipping between hers thrilled her. The strength of his hand as it held her for his ravishing mouth made her feel cherished. She melted into him and knew his hardness to be a perfect balance to every bit of softness she felt when in his arms.

She was light-headed and stupid from his kiss, but not so unaware she didn't notice the hardening length of his erection against her belly.

Rubbing against him, sliding her leg higher over his until she could hook her knee over his hip, she flicked her tongue insistently at his. She was throbbing again, inside. She wanted to feel the stretch and burning pressure of his possession.

He drew back, but he did not roll way. His hand slid down to cup her buttock, holding her still as he gave a lovely roll of his hips, which sent his erection sliding intimately along her aching flesh.

Portia gasped and tipped her head to press her open mouth to his throat where his skin held a salty tang. She swirled her tongue over the heavy pulse and was rewarded by the sound of a deep growl rumbling from his chest.

But then he gave her rear a sharp smack.

Portia yelped and tipped her head back to stare at him in shock. Not so much because he had struck her, but because even though the act had left a stinging trace behind, it had also ignited a strange sort of pleasure beneath her skin.

"You do realize dawn has come," he noted in amusement.

"What?" Portia sat up abruptly, looking for a window to prove his statement. "Damn," she muttered as she rolled swiftly to the edge of the bed and rose to her feet. She stood there a moment, looking about for her clothes.

"You have deplorable language for a lady," he commented from the bed.

Portia saw her shift flung to a far corner of the room and strode quickly to retrieve it.

"Yes, I know," she replied as she drew the undergarment over her head. "A foolish little rebellion that gives me infinite delight."

She tried to run her fingers through her hair, but encountered more tangles than she had the patience for, and she winced as she struggled to work them out.

"There is a brush in the dressing room," Dell offered.

Portia glanced his way to see him stretched out on his side, his head propped in one hand, the sheet draped so low over his hips she swore she could see the shadowed tip of his still-erect penis.

She froze. Her mouth went dry, and she completely forgot why she had been in such a blasted hurry to leave that bed.

With a quiet chuckle, he turned away and swung his feet to the floor on the other side of the bed. "I assume you need to get home. There is a wash bowl there, if you want to clean up. Then I will help you get ready."

Portia stared as he rose to standing and reached for his breeches. She did not look away until he had them fastened low around his hips. He continued to dress while she used a wet cloth to wash the evidence of her lost virginity and their lovemaking from between her thighs.

They walked together to his dressing room, where he gestured for her to take a seat in front of the mirror. He had to rummage around a bit for the hairbrush she hadn't been able to find earlier, then he began to work through the mass of tangles.

The silence was comfortable, but after a bit, Portia realized they hadn't yet confirmed their plans for the next day.

"You know where this Suzanne woman lives?"

"I know the building where Gregor Dune keeps his women. I will confirm more exact information before we arrive. There are likely to be rough and dangerous characters lurking about, even during the day. Best we find her quickly before anyone can be alerted to our presence."

Portia's heart warmed at his automatic use of the word *we*. He intended to take her along.

"Will you go as yourself?" she asked, then caught her breath as the brush pulled sharply at a rather intricate knot.

He set the brush down to work through the tangle with his fingers.

"No. Not this time." He paused to eye her critically in the mirror. "Do you think you can pull off a lad?"

Portia's eyes widened. "I believe so."

"I will give you some clothes before you leave. You will have to tuck your hair securely away and minimize the beauty of your features somehow..." His voice trailed off, and a skeptical scowl marred his expression.

Portia, on the other hand, smiled brightly. "You think me beautiful?"

His gaze found hers in the reflection. "You know I do."

"I know now," she answered in a low whisper.

He cleared his throat and turned away. "No distractions, Portia. We must return our focus to the job."

Claire needed to be found. Thinking of the girl was effectively sobering.

"Right. Sorry," she answered earnestly as she finished brushing out her hair.

"Where is your gown?"

"I hung it in the wardrobe," she answered.

A few moments later, he held the gown out to slip it over her head. She stood to allow him access to the buttons running down the back.

"Are you sure you will be able to get away this afternoon?" he asked.

"Do not worry. I will find a way."

"Be waiting for a message. The carriage will be two blocks north of your aunt's house."

Portia nodded, envisioning the area he referenced. It contained an oak tree with spreading limbs that would provide shadow and concealment.

When he finished with her gown, Dell began tugging and twisting Portia's hair until he had it pinned securely atop her head in a simple but attractive style.

"You are truly a man of varied and exceptional talents, Dell Turner," she said with warm appreciation.

"There is something I forgot to show you." He reached for Honeycutt's coat and withdrew a folded piece of paper from the pocket and handed it to her.

"It is a rendering of Claire, so you will know her if you see her."

Portia unfolded the paper carefully until she could spread it out on the surface of the dressing table. She stared in surprise at a delicate charcoal drawing of a cherubic face. The child was lovely, with light curls dancing about her curved cheeks and wide eyes. Her smile was sweet and serene, her gaze a bit shy. She looked like an angel.

"Who sketched this?"

"Hale."

Portia felt an instant clenching in her stomach. Mason Hale, for all his faults and threats and evil actions against her family, loved his daughter very much.

She turned to look intently into Dell's eyes. "We have to find her."

# Twenty-six

HALE FIGURED HE'D FINALLY LOST HIS BLEEDIN' MIND.

All those blows he'd taken to the head during his fighting career had decided to take their toll.

He'd gotten a tip from one of the men he had watching the city for Molly's return. Apparently, her last place of residence had been Gregor Dune's place, though how she had gotten mixed up with Dune was beyond Hale. That she would risk having Claire in the vicinity of the violent madman made Hale's blood boil.

He had been hanging around outside the tenant house for two days. He had never been a spiritual man, but prayers had been falling steadily from his lips as he watched for some sign of Molly's return. His eyes burned from staring intently across the street, and his chest ached from intermittently forgetting to breathe whenever someone new approached the pimp house. Each day that passed with no sign of his former lover left him more and more certain she was gone from London for good. And with her, his baby girl.

At the moment, however, it was not someone

arriving, but someone leaving—or trying to leave—that drew his attention and his disbelief.

The ruckus across the street was not unusual in itself. Conflict broke out regularly in this part of town. When the man dressed as a dandy in faded velvets and dingy lace exited the tenant house with his young companion, he had been looking around with the cautious eye of a man accustomed to the potential dangers of such an area. And the lad seemed intent upon keeping his head hunched between his shoulders as though the weight of his oversize wool hat was too much for him, though his pace was quickened by the dandy's firm hand on his narrow shoulder.

They had almost reached the street, when some of Gregor Dune's hired thugs strolled out to greet them. It was terrible odds, with three rangy brutes against the dandy and his boy.

To Hale's surprise, the dandy immediately wrapped his hand around the boy's wrist and stepped forward to face Dune's hirelings with a casual, arrogant attitude. Hale snorted at the man's stupidity. The bloke's fancy clothes were about to be ruined beyond repair. Hale didn't doubt the outcome of the scuffle one bit, and the scene didn't much interest him at first.

But when the first thug made a lunging dive, the dandy stepped easily aside, giving the other man a swift shove that sent him stumbling past him with misdirected momentum. All the while he kept up a steady stream of chatter. As the one thug went stumbling, the other two circled around to come at the man and boy from opposite sides. The dandy gave the lad a shove a bare second before the thugs closed in, forcing the child to the ground as he spun on the ball of one foot to sweep his other leg in a high arc, connecting hard to one man's temple. Finishing his spin, he brought a swift uppercut to the chin of the other bloke.

Hale stepped away from the tree he had been leaning against. He had seen that combination of moves before. He knew it intimately. The next few punches, kicks, and evasive maneuvers solidified his impression. He had seen this man fight before. But it had not been *this* man.

"What in damnation?" Hale muttered beneath his breath.

Hale had a gift for recalling the specific techniques, impulses, and styles of every man he had ever fought. The dandy across the street was not who he appeared to be. Hale knew Dell Turner's fighting style when he saw it. He had trained the man for years, not only in bareknuckle boxing, but also in the French street fighting style for which Hale had never had much of an affinity. Hale was better with his fists—his size did not lend itself to the agility required for savate. But Dell Turner had taken to the French methods easily and, over time, had developed a sort of hybrid style of his own that combined the kickboxing with bare-knuckle brawling.

In fact, Dell Turner had surpassed Hale in the very variety and inspiration of his skill, yet he still came around Hale's place to spar on occasion. Hale suspected the man enjoyed the friendly competition as much as he did.

If he wasn't so confused by Turner's presence at Molly's former residence while disguised, he may have enjoyed the fight, especially considering Turner had his work cut out for him as he fought the three men while trying to keep the boy out of it as much as possible.

In the end, however, the boy proved useful as he jumped on one brute's back just as he was about to take Turner down from behind. The interference managed to buy Turner the time he needed to knock out the other two then finish the third. Then he grabbed his companion by the scruff and dragged the poor mite away from the scene. Turner appeared to be blistering the lad's ears as they went, though to Hale's eyes, the young'un did not look the least bit cowed.

A short way down the road, they jumped into a carriage and took off. There was only a moment of indecision as Hale glanced back at the tenant house before he strode to hail a hack of his own and took off after them.

❧

Portia struggled to catch her breath. She looked to where Dell sat slouched on the opposite seat of the carriage. He was glaring at her with a fierce scowl beneath Robert French's makeup.

"I told you to stay down, dammit."

"The man would have struck you from behind. You needed me, and I helped," she snapped back, not particularly in the mood for his guff. "Admit it. Despite your obvious fighting skills—very impressive, by the way—you would have ended up losing that one if I hadn't interfered."

"Those men could have broken you in two," he growled stubbornly.

"But they didn't. I keep telling you we make a wonderful partnership. Didn't we get some useful information from Suzanne? I would say that is the important thing."

He snorted and turned to look out the carriage window. As if ignoring her would have some effect.

Portia would have smiled if she wasn't so disheartened by what they had discovered.

Molly Andrews had indeed left her young daughter in Suzanne's keeping. Apparently, she had promised to return after a couple of days. Those days turned to a week and more while Suzanne shuffled the child between the various whores under Gregor Dune's keeping, so they could all keep working while concealing the child's presence.

Though Suzanne had a liking for the little girl, the others she called on to watch the child did not, and soon enough she had no one willing to share responsibility.

When Gregor Dune learned the child's presence was keeping one of his molls off the street, he beat Suzanne bloody. The evidence of that was still clear in the woman's swollen, split lip and the purple bruises turning to green that graced her face and encircled her throat. The man had clearly not pulled any of his punches.

And then he had taken Claire away.

That had been four days ago.

Portia's stomach had been twisted in knots since learning that the pimp had taken possession of the girl. When Suzanne admitted tearfully that he intended to sell the child on the docks, Dell had questioned her for more detail, but she had nothing more to offer.

Then, to their supreme luck, Gregor Dune himself arrived to interrupt their interview.

Dell wasted no time in using some violent and clever ways of getting the man to talk. It seemed the bully pimp did not have much tolerance for pain, and Portia could not bring herself to feel sorry for him after seeing what he had done to Suzanne. It took only a few blows from Dell and the press of a knife to his throat for the man to spit out the information.

One more swift punch to the face knocked the pimp out, but apparently not long enough, considering his goons had caught up to them so quickly.

Still, they had gotten away, and marvelously as far as Portia was concerned, though she did worry for Suzanne's fate. Dune was likely to turn his fists back on her. She needed to find a way to help the woman as soon as possible.

But she couldn't think long on that right now. Claire was her most pressing priority.

"Do you know this man Gregor Dune named? Bricken?" she asked as she pulled her woolen cap off and released her long braid from where it was coiled tight atop her head. The pins holding the braid in place had been jabbing into her skull for hours. It was a relief to let her hair fall in the single plait down her back.

"I do," Dell answered gruffly.

She did not like the tone of his voice, and she met his gaze. "And?"

"Not much is known about him other than he is deeply involved in the international black market."

"What on earth could someone like that want with a small child?"

The change in Dell's expression sent a flash of dread through her. "It's possible he extended his business to child labor rings."

Portia was afraid to ask, but had to know. "And what exactly does that entail?"

"Sometimes stray children—orphans, runaways, those unfortunate enough to be vulnerable for picking—are collected and sold to factories or worse. Here and overseas."

"That is horrific," Portia exclaimed. "Those poor children."

Dell said nothing, but she read his feelings in his eyes. She saw anger there and fear, but also a sad resignation.

"How can such a thing happen in this day and age?"

"There will always be monsters willing to prey upon the weak and unprotected. That is why most children who run the streets become part of a gang. For security. Most learn quickly that the violence and danger inherent in gang life is generally preferable to being alone and vulnerable."

Portia thought of Thomas. She wondered if he had been alone when Turner had found him a home *away from the gangs*, he had said.

But what of Claire?

Portia pictured the image of the little girl as Hale had drawn her. So small and pretty. Practically still a baby.

"Molly never had any intention of coming back for her daughter, did she?" She asked the question quietly, disgusted by the thought of a mother abandoning her child in such a way.

Dell gave her an unreadable look, but replied, "I doubt it."

"We are going after her," she said with conviction, suddenly worried that Dell's jaded perspective may decide it was a lost cause.

His gaze narrowed.

"Yes," he said finally. "We are."

The carriage had reached Honeycutt's. Neither of them said anything as they made their way into the narrow brownstone. Once in the hall, Dell gave a shout. "Morley."

The little man came running from the back of the house. After casting an unreadable glance toward Portia, he asked, "What is it, Mr. Turner?"

"I need to get urgent messages to everyone we know on the docks. We need detailed information on Troy Bricken's activities over the last week. Where are his headquarters these days? Whom has he been talking to? What ships, if any, has he shown interest in? Then we need those ships' manifests, their planned routes and scheduled departures. Everything. And we need it now."

"Yes, sir." Morley turned without even acknowledging Portia and rushed back into the shadows.

At some point, that small man was going to have to accept her presence, but not today, it would seem.

For several breaths, she and Dell stood in the hall, staring at each other. She felt her chest constrict with pride and admiration for him. He would do absolutely everything in his power to save Claire.

"What plans do you have this evening?" Dell asked her.

And he was still willing to have her as part of it.

"A dinner party, but I can—"

"No," he interrupted with a gruff expression. "Go to your party. This may take some time."

"There may not be much time," Portia whispered sadly.

"We have to hope Bricken has not shipped her off yet, but four days…"

"Even if he has, we may still be able to track her, right?"

"We will do our best."

Portia fought against the lump in her throat. "She must be so scared."

"Do not think of that," he muttered. "It serves no purpose."

Before she could respond, the front door smashed against the wall with a thunderous bang. Dell swept her around behind him before she even had a chance to glance at what had caused the explosive intrusion.

A man rushed inside, roaring, "You've got thirty seconds to explain what interest you have in Gregor Dune's place and why the fuck you are dressed in that damned costume."

# *Twenty-seven*

PORTIA'S HAND WAS PRESSED TO THE CENTER OF DELL'S back, and she could feel every ripple of tension through him as he stared down the intruder.

She had recognized the voice instantly. As soon as the initial burst of alarm swept through her, she realized they were not likely in danger, though Hale sounded fiercely angry.

When Dell did not respond right away, she peeked around his shoulder to get her first look at Lily's ruthless abductor and the man who had sketched the image of his daughter with such loving, ethereal lines.

Mason Hale was furious. And huge. And undeniably intimidating.

It was impossible to dismiss his towering form, the thick breadth of his shoulders, or the roped and bulging muscles in his arms. He was all height and breadth and physical strength. He was younger than she had expected. Barely thirty, she would guess, perhaps even younger. He had long blond hair tied back at his nape. Some strands had worked their way from his queue to fall rakishly against his bold, squarish features, currently forced into a fearsome scowl.

If not for the violence in his expression and his unsavory history with her family, she may have considered him handsome. In a rough, brutish sort of way.

"I am waiting, Turner, and my patience has worn frightfully thin in the last weeks," Hale threatened between clenched teeth.

Finally, she felt the tension slide down Dell's spine until he shook his head. "Fine. This way, Hale."

He gestured to his study, and Hale turned to lead the way with floor-eating strides. Portia followed along behind Dell, though after that first protective action, his focus had remained steady upon his unexpected guest.

Once they were all in the study, Hale swept his gaze in her direction. His eyes were hard and angry.

"Leave your wench outside. This can be of no interest to her."

Dell glanced aside at Portia as she continued forward into the room. She forgot she still held her woolen cap in her hand, and though she wore boys' clothing, the long braid falling over her shoulder gave her away. She looked back at Dell with a mulish expression, telling him she would not be chased away without a fight.

Dell swung his gaze back to Hale. "She stays."

Hale turned to look at her less dismissively, his intent gaze taking in her appearance from head to toe. His eyes narrowed, and his brows lowered darkly.

"Do I know you?"

Portia lifted her chin and gave a falsely bright smile. "Not personally. But you know my family, and you have had the unique pleasure of my sister's unwilling company. People say we do look similar, though she is by far the more genteel and forgiving. You choose your victims well, Hale."

His eyes flickered. "You are one of the Chadwick chits," he stated.

Portia executed a saucy little curtsy, made all the more mocking by her boys' togs. "I'd say it is a pleasure," she replied with smooth charm, "but...you understand."

Hale stared at her a long moment. She could see the muscles along his jaw working as though he was struggling with words. Rather than saying any more to her directly, the former prizefighter glanced again at Dell. "An explanation, Turner," he demanded, but his tone was not nearly so ferocious as when he had arrived.

"We were at Gregor Dune's today following up on some information about your daughter."

Hale's entire body stiffened, and his large hands curled into imposing fists at his sides. "What do you know of my daughter?"

There was a long pause. "You hired me to find her," Dell replied in a carefully modulated voice, as though he were not quite certain of Hale's reaction.

Hale's wary gaze swung between Dell, dressed as Robert French, and Portia, dressed as a boy. Then he heaved a deep and torturous sigh as the tension in his body fled him in a rush and he dropped down into a chair, doubling over until his elbows propped on his knees and his face fell into his hands.

With a gruff sound, he rubbed his hands over his face and then sat up straight again, having collected himself. He looked to Dell. "You are Nightshade?"

Dell nodded. "I am."

There was a pause of silence, during which Portia wisely held her tongue. She sensed the moment was vital to Hale's trust in Turner.

"What of her?" Hale asked, jerking his chin toward Portia though his gaze remained trained on Dell.

Dell took a breath before answering. "Miss Chadwick has insisted upon helping with this task."

"Why?" Suspicion was evident in Hale's tone.

"Because I did not want my sister's misadventure to be for naught," Portia answered as she crossed her arms over her chest. "I know why you needed the money. If you *truly* had no other options, I may even understand why you chose to kidnap Lily in order to get it. But my sister was an innocent victim, Mr. Hale. I would not see another innocent injured in this wretched plot if I can assist in preventing it."

Another long stare from Hale then a short nod. "Fair enough." Turning back to Dell, he asked, "And what have you learned of Molly's whereabouts? Is she back in town, then? Is that why you were at Dune's?"

The hope in his voice was unmistakable and heartbreaking, considering what they had just learned of Claire's possible fate.

Dell tugged off his wig and removed the prosthetic nose that transformed him into French. Portia held back, watching Hale. Watching Dell. This was not going to be an easy conversation.

"There has been nothing to suggest that Molly Andrews has returned to London," Dell began as he set the pieces of his disguise on a side table. "The truth is, Claire is not in her company and has not been for these last two weeks."

Hale's glower would have made anyone tremble. But Dell met his gaze squarely.

Portia realized then the mutual respect between the two men went beyond that of mere acquaintances. The realization was a bit of a shock. Why hadn't Dell told her Hale was his friend?

"That doesn't make any sense."

"Molly left Claire in the keeping of her former roommate, Suzanne."

"What?" Hale rose to his feet in a rush of muscled intention. "She has been in that bloody hovel this whole time? Dammit. I could have gone in there and gotten her myself."

Dell held up his hand when it appeared Hale intended to go back to Dune's that very second to do just that. Hale's entire body was primed to fight. His shoulders squared off, and the muscles in his arms bulged beneath his coat as his hands formed into block-like fists.

"She is not there."

Hale stopped. His expression was heavy as he stared hard at Dell, perhaps finally sensing the reluctance in Dell's tone. "Tell me, Turner. Where is she?"

"I hope to have that exact information within the next several hours, but right now we do not know."

The sound of grief that emanated from Hale's chest hit Portia like a blast, making her heart ache.

"Have you ever heard the name Troy Bricken?" Dell asked.

"No," Hale growled. "Should I have?"

"An extremely elusive criminal, he manages his business from an ever-changing location, hiring new employees, constantly altering methods of conducting his dealings."

"What is his business?" Hale asked tightly, growing impatient and tense with Dell's lead-in.

Portia understood Dell's decision to slowly reveal the circumstances they were facing. He had once told her that sometimes there simply was no hope for a happy ending despite all he may do. He was trying to prepare Hale for the worst-possible potential, should they be unable to track down Bricken's current operation. Or if once they did, it was too late.

"He sells children into the labor market, most often overseas."

"And this man has Claire?" Hale's voice had lowered to a deathly whisper.

The tone sent chills across Portia's nape. She had seen people furious before—her father when he lost big at the tables, Lord Fallbrook after she kneed him in the groin—but she had never seen anyone with unmistakable murderous intent until that moment. Hale was clearly as dangerous as she and her sisters had always feared.

Dell met Hale's fierce gaze. "I hope so. If he does, we will get her back."

They all knew what was left unsaid. If Bricken no longer had Claire, they would likely have little chance of finding her.

"I will find the bastard, and then I will kill him," Hale grumbled under his breath as he took a couple of lunging steps toward the door.

Portia swiftly stepped around to place herself directly in his path, lifting her hand to press her palm flat to his expansive chest.

In another second, Dell was there as well, standing just to the side, his expression a dark glower, his body tensed to intervene.

Hale stopped to look down at her with an expression so full of violence and anguish it nearly took her breath and her courage. But she held fast to both, even finding it in herself to give him a fierce little scowl in return.

"Remove yourself, woman. I am in no fucking mood." He spoke in a tight growl, the words barely sliding past his clenched teeth. His solid chest heaved beneath her hand.

"Hale." A single, low-spoken word from Dell. An unmistakable warning.

"You are going nowhere," Portia said. "You will turn around and sit yourself back down in that chair."

His lips twisted into a sneer, and his hands came up as if to grasp her and bodily remove her from his path. Dell shifted beside them, and Portia cast him a swift glance that begged he leave off for another moment. Then she continued in the tone Emma had used so often to brook no argument. "If you do not," she stated sharply, pressing harder into his chest, "if you rush down to the docks as you wish to do, and go blasting through every tavern and warehouse and dark alley with those massive fists of yours, Bricken will panic and take off. He will hide Claire away until he can be rid of her for good. You know this is true." She paused, seeing a wavering in Hale's gaze. Then she added gently, "Put your faith in Nightshade. Trust

Dell to do his work, and you have a chance of seeing your daughter again."

She narrowed her gaze. "Do you understand me, Mr. Hale?"

The large man stood still for a moment, staring at her while his breath remained tight and difficult. She could feel his resistance, his instinct—his need—to fight. But then his bullish head swung to where Dell stood watching the scene intently.

"Do you deal with this kind of bossiness on the regular?" Hale grumbled.

Dell quirked a half smile. "She is right, you know."

Hale dropped his chin in a brief show of defeat before he lifted his gaze again to pin Dell with as fierce a look as any Portia had ever seen.

"You will find her, Turner, and when you do, nothing will stop me from coming with you to retrieve her."

Dell stared back at him for a long moment, convincing Portia even more that these two men shared a particular bond of friendship.

Hale did not move until Dell gave a short nod of agreement, then he finally stepped back and returned himself to the chair. "How long will it take for your informants to gather the necessary information?"

"Could take hours," Dell replied. "Would you like a drink?"

"No," Hale said with unnecessary force. "I drank more than enough when I learned of Molly's deceit. The indulgence wasted nearly two days I could have been looking for Claire. I intend to hold on to my wits going forward."

"There are preparations to be made before we raid Bricken's lair," Dell said as he started toward the door, catching Portia's eye in a silent request that she follow him. "You will stay?" he asked Hale just before leaving the room.

The large brute of a man heaved a sigh and lifted his hands to rub them over his blunt features. Then he tipped his head to rest it against the high back of the chair and closed his eyes.

"I'm not going anywhere until you do, Turner," he muttered. "Still can't believe you're that one they call Nightshade." He opened his eyes just enough to look at Dell through thin slits. "Deceitful bastard."

Dell gave a low chuckle as he strode from the room.

Portia followed, knowing she needed to get home, though she hated to leave right then.

After only a few hours of sleep that morning, she had left in her boys' clothes before anyone could be expected to venture from their bedrooms. She had left a message for Emma, stating she had gone to the park to practice her riding. She could only hope that no one would have thought it necessary to actually check for any missing horses or grooms to corroborate her story.

It was a risk to lie so blatantly when she could so easily have been found out. But Portia had counted on the fact that her sisters were both rather distracted these days. Still, it wouldn't be easy to sneak back into the house without being seen in her boys' clothes.

It was exhausting—all of the sneaking out, sneaking in, staying up all night only to catch a few brief hours of sleep in the late morning. Portia naturally enjoyed later hours, but trying to keep up with two lives was more complex than she had anticipated.

Still, it was entirely worth it, except for those moments when she had to leave Dell.

"I am not going to be able to keep you from joining us, am I?"

Dell had stopped with her in the front hall and turned to look at her with a dark, unreadable expression. She could see he was still upset by the altercation outside Dune's building.

Portia shook her head, but had to ask, "Do you really want to?"

He lifted his hand to brush a few stray wisps of her hair from her brow, then continued his caress down the length of her braid, brushing his knuckles along the curve of her spine, until he grasped the end of the long plait in his fist. He pulled gently downward until her head tipped back even farther, exposing the length of her throat above the high-button collar of the boys' shirt, lifting her lips toward his until she parted them on an expectant breath.

"I like having you with me, though I am sure I must be mad to confess such a thing," he murmured, his tone husky and deep. "It is a dangerous mission we face tonight, love. There is no way to fully prepare for what we will encounter. No way to know how many men Bricken will have, where they will be housed, or how many children might be in his custody. We find Claire and get out of there as quickly as possible. We cannot save them all," he warned.

Portia disagreed. They would save every last child they discovered.

But now was not the time to argue that point.

"I am coming with you, Turner. Do not dare to even try to keep me away."

"And what of your dinner party?"

His question was uttered with light curiosity, but Portia sensed something weightier beneath his tone. She wondered at it, but answered him with confidence. "I shall return home for a bit, make a quick appearance to convince my family I am unfit for socializing tonight, and then I will return here. I shall be gone for barely more than a couple of hours. Obviously, if you receive your information before then, you must not wait for me. You must save Claire." She rose up to her toes, pulling away from his still-secure grip on her braid until she could press her lips lightly to his. "I will be here when you return," she whispered softly before claiming a kiss.

His arms encircled her slim form. One hand palmed her rear as he lifted her against him to deepen the connection.

A moment later, he set her back on her feet and forcefully turned her toward the door. "Off with you then," he said as he gave a sharp smack to her bottom.

Portia tossed him a teasing scowl, then sauntered away with a deliberate swing in her hips. Just before she stepped through his front door, she took a moment to coil her braid back atop her head and cover it with the wool cap. Then she sent one last glance toward Dell to see that he watched her every move with a wonderfully proprietary light in his eyes.

With a soft smile, she strode swiftly out to the street and the hack waiting to take her back to Mayfair.

# Twenty-eight

Dell stood in the open doorway until the hack was out of sight. Then he closed the door with deliberate care, doing his best to ignore the disturbing emotions seething through him. He took the stairs at a controlled pace, though his pulse thundered heavily in his ears.

Once in his dressing room, he removed what remained of French's accoutrements. He scrubbed his face and washed his hair before dressing again in dark but comfortable clothing. Then he proceeded to load his person with as many weapons as he could reasonably carry. It was far more than he ever would have taken on a previous mission, but he could not shake the thought that Portia would be with him this time. He had no doubt she would rush through her responsibilities to come back in time for their mission.

He had to admit her presence on this job had been more beneficial than he had expected. Her instincts were spot-on, and her approach to difficult situations was often the opposite of his own, but worked out well enough in their favor. She had more courage than most men he knew, acute observation skills, and a constantly questioning intelligence that was well-suited to the work.

But letting her work with him was a huge mistake.

*Because of this*, he thought in disgust as he tried to stuff yet one more small pistol into a pocket already occupied by a firearm. Everything was more dangerous with her around. Not because she made it so, but because with her by his side, Dell had something to lose.

He shook his head and closed his eyes.

His success to date had been based on the simple fact that he never allowed his feelings to become involved in any aspect of his work. He was methodical, logical, and entirely objective in every decision he made.

That was simply how he did things.

But from the moment Portia Chadwick had nearly stormed right through Honeycutt as he stood in the parlor doorway, she had been a distraction. A liability. She added a degree of emotion and passion to the work that shouldn't be there.

She did not belong in his world any more than he belonged in hers.

In truth, he didn't belong anywhere.

The theater had been his mother's world. And though Dell had learned how to blend into any environment, that did not mean he belonged in any of the places he visited as Nightshade's *associates*. He was always a visitor, an intruder, a false member of the crowds he infiltrated.

But Portia was so very different, despite her argument to the contrary.

She had a place where she belonged, and it was not with him, sneaking through gin alleys and bawdy houses.

He would allow her to see this job through to the end because she had invested her time and heart in it. But after this, she was done.

He stalked about the dressing room, swiping up things he thought Hale might need. He had no doubt Portia would still have the knife strapped to her leg when she returned. Perhaps he would let her keep the slim weapon. As a memento.

As soon as the thought finished in his head, Dell snorted in self-derision.

How the hell had he become so blasted sentimental?

Portia had gotten under his skin in more ways than one. It was not good for Nightshade. Not good for his work. And certainly not good for the woman herself.

Leaving the dressing room, he headed down to the study.

Perhaps some male company would help to clear his head. Hale, certainly, would not be distracted from their purpose tonight. The man was unwaveringly determined to retrieve his daughter at any cost. That he'd abducted a young lady to sell her to a brothel was a testament to that fact. Hale was not naive. He had to be well aware of the fate Lily Chadwick could have faced due to his actions. Dell would never have believed his friend capable of perpetrating such a crime. Apparently, the drive to protect his daughter outweighed any moral reluctance Hale may have had.

Dell walked into the study to see his old friend sitting on the edge of his chair. His elbows rested on his widespread knees, and his head was held between his large hands.

At Dell's return, Hale lifted his head with a heavy sigh and leaned back.

"Thank God, man. I am starting to go mad sitting here alone with my thoughts." The larger man eyed Dell curiously. "I can't believe I've been training the infamous Nightshade for years and had no idea."

Dell shrugged and walked to his desk, where he set the small cache of weapons. Hale would have time to make his choices later. "I am good at what I do."

"I'm counting on that, mate," Hale replied, tension still evident in his voice.

The waiting was difficult for Dell, who preferred the more active aspects of his work, but he couldn't imagine what it must be like for Hale, who had an emotional and personal investment in every minute that ticked by.

Hale quirked a dangerous grin as he leaned back and propped his hands behind his head.

"So tell me, Turner. How the hell did one of those lovely Chadwick doves come to be your partner?"

Dell angled a sideways glance at his friend. "I have you to thank for that," he said, his tone harsh and accusing.

Hale's expression tensed until it looked almost sheepish. "I never would have nabbed her sister if Molly hadn't forced my hand."

Dell stared hard at him. "Miss Chadwick was innocent, and you set her up for a future of ruin and potential abuse or worse."

Hale was already shaking his head before Dell

finished speaking, a heavy frown darkening his features. "No, I didn't. My sister promised me the girl would go to someone who would take proper care of her."

"Against her will."

Hale rose to his feet. "And what of Claire?" he roared. "Was it her will to be abandoned to strangers and this Bricken character?"

"Trading one innocent for another is not justice."

Hale's chest heaved; his eyes darkened. "I was desperate. I wasn't thinking straight."

Dell did not reply. He could not condone what Hale had done, even if he had believed Pendragon could assure Lily's placement with a worthy and honorable protector. But he understood desperation. Though he had never been driven to such a limit himself, he had seen it so many times in his life.

"It may mean nothing," Hale said stiffly. "But if I could go back, I'd have found another way."

Dell wanted to believe him, but he couldn't help but think of how different Lily's fate might have been.

"I'll tell your woman the same, next I see her," Hale added.

Dell narrowed his gaze and lowered his chin to send Hale a hard look. "She is not my woman."

The other man cocked a brow in obvious disbelief. "My mistake."

❦

Portia slipped into Angelique's town house through the back garden, hoping her sisters and great-aunt were busy and would not catch her returning in her boys' clothes.

She still had to figure out how she was going to
get out of attending the dinner that night so she could
accompany Dell in the rescue. She had no intention of
being excluded from that endeavor. Saving Claire had
become personal to Portia. She simply had to be there
when they found her.

Still trying to come up with the most effective
excuse to cry off from the evening's plans, Portia
turned the corner at the top of the back servants' stairs
to head down the hall to her bedroom. With a start,
she saw Angelique coming straight toward her. The
elderly lady saw Portia immediately, making it impossible for her to turn around and hide.

"There you are, darling," Angelique exclaimed.
"Just the one I wanted to see."

Portia continued forward, acutely aware of her disguise and general grubby appearance. Surely Angelique
had noticed, though the lady did not seem the slightest
bit surprised. Perhaps she was not experiencing one of
her more lucid moments.

Deciding to behave as though nothing were out
of the ordinary, Portia replied, "You were looking
for me?"

"Not at all, but now that I see you, I realize I
wanted to," Angelique answered with a smile as she
linked her arm through Portia's and turned her about
to lead her back toward the stairway. "Come, I have
something you need."

Portia was thoroughly confused. Not a lucid
moment, then. Since she did not have the heart
to refuse her great-aunt anything and had become
rather curious to find out where they were heading

once they started up the stairs instead of going back down to the main level, Portia accepted the aging lady's lead.

As they continued up and up at a pace suited to the dowager countess's advanced age, Angelique kept up a one-sided conversation in her characteristic French accent.

"You know, I have truly been blessed to have you three girls come stay with me. I had become complacent in my later years, forgetting what it is to live to the fullest. I had forgotten how much I love to be a part of this magnificent world. I really was not very good at playing the retiring widow, and I am indebted to you and your sisters for reviving me, so to speak."

Portia smiled. "It makes me happy to know we have not caused you unnecessary stress. Emma's letter requesting your patronage and chaperonage must have been a bit of a surprise."

Angelique chuckled.

"Indeed it was. It is a good thing I happen to enjoy surprises. And you especially, *ma petite*, have a way of keeping me *en pointe*. You remind me of myself when I was young." The old lady paused to lean toward Portia conspiratorially.

"*Bien sûr*, your sisters could use a little more assistance when it comes to having fun, no? One so serious, the other so quiet. At least you are not so afraid to show your spirit and take a few risks."

She patted Portia's hand in a comforting gesture as they reached the hall on the third floor. "Though you need a little help from me as well, it would seem," Angelique added with a smile.

Portia lifted a brow. This was likely to be entertaining. "I do?"

"*Certainement*," the lady exclaimed as she came to a stop and withdrew her trusty opera glasses from the pocket of her skirt to give a sweeping glance along Portia's frame. "Look at you. You are most certainly in need of my help. And I have just the thing. *Viens avec moi.*"

Portia should have known her appearance would not go completely unnoticed. She could not imagine how Angelique thought she would help her, especially as the older lady turned to usher her into a small room. As far as Portia knew, the extra guest rooms on this level were empty, since the dowager countess had not done any formal entertaining for many years.

"Come, *ma petite*," Angelique urged as she released Portia's arm and flitted forward into the room, her steps lighter now that they had reached her intended destination.

The room was not exactly empty as Portia had expected.

It held no less than three large wardrobes, an enormous bureau with more than a dozen drawers, and several trunks and chests in various sizes. An extra long sofa was set right in the center of the room, facing an elegant vanity topped by an oval mirror. And in the corner, three full-length mirrors stood at an angle to one another, so someone standing before them could see themselves from multiple directions at the same time.

Portia was distracted enough by the unexpected sight that she did not at first realize Angelique was twittering with a youthful excitement as she threw open the doors of each wardrobe to reveal within a plethora of gowns, cloaks, skirts, and shirts in every color imaginable. Silks, satins, velvets, muslin, linen, lace, wool. Items so rich and luxurious they appeared fit for royalty, all the way through to pieces that were more likely to be seen on the backs of vagrants and tramps.

"Bloody hell," Portia breathed in surprise. "What is all this?" she finally asked, bringing her gaze back to Angelique, who stood at the last wardrobe, sorting through the contents as though looking for something.

"My collection, darling."

"Collection?" Portia repeated.

Angelique tipped forward into the wardrobe, her upper body disappearing for a moment as she reached for something tucked into the back. Her response came back muffled but audible. "I was not always a countess, you know."

Portia thought of her aunt's innumerable tales of being a dancer in Paris, an actress in a traveling troupe, a spy for the French revolution, and a dozen other stories Portia had never believed to hold any truth.

Angelique reemerged from the wardrobe still empty-handed and turned to the trunks lined along a wall beneath the windows and started to flip open the lids. She kept up a steady mumbling litany that Portia could not begin to make out. Finally, she came to one in which the contents prompted a sound of approval. She started to sift through the items with enthusiasm.

Infinitely curious and still a bit confused, Portia strode toward her to get a look at what she was digging through.

"Of course, much depends on the purpose of your outing. You may need to be more incognito, *oui*? And

I do have much to assist with that as well. But, darling, there are times"—Angelique slid Portia a sly glance laden with coy mystery—"when a lady does not need to sacrifice fashion for the ruse. If you are going to go about town dressed *en déguisé*, you need as many options as possible."

Portia leaned over the old lady's shoulder to see that the trunk was filled to the top with more masculine clothing and accessories than even Turner had in his possession. And again, they ranged from the finest materials to the most common.

Portia turned to meet the sparkling gaze of the Dowager Countess of Chelmsworth.

"Are all of these filled with costumes?"

"*Oui.* I could not bring myself to throw out so many lovely memories."

"Memories involving all of these?" Portia breathed in awe. "What adventures you must have had."

The lady smirked. "More even than your impertinent mind can imagine, *ma petite*."

"And you are giving me access?"

Angelique shook her head. "Not access. My entire collection is now yours, darling. As long as you promise me you will put it all to good use. I was once your size, so the fit should be right." She sighed and glanced back at a wardrobe stuffed with brightly colored gowns. "Much of it is dated, but with a clever sewing hand, it can all be altered for your purpose."

"And what exactly do you believe my purpose to be?" Portia asked in curiosity.

Angelique blinked at her. "*Mais bien sûr*, I have no idea."

# *Twenty-nine*

IN THE END, IT WAS QUITE EASY TO BACK OUT OF THE dinner party. Portia claimed to have twisted her ankle while dismounting from her horse after the ride she purportedly took earlier that day.

Her sisters did not doubt the story in the slightest. There was a moment when Emma nearly insisted upon viewing the appendage to ascertain the degree of injury, but Portia managed to wave her off, claiming the sprain needed nothing more than a bit of rest.

Angelique, to her credit and Portia's astonishment, gave absolutely no indication to suggest that she doubted Portia's claim, and no hint that the two of them had encountered each other earlier in the day.

In the past, Portia would have taken that as evidence of her great-aunt's slipping mind, but now...she was not so willing to discount the lady's apparent flightiness. She suspected Angelique was much sharper, and perhaps wilier, than any of them considered.

As soon as everyone else left for the evening, Portia returned to Angelique's room of costumes and began to re-dress in boys' clothing, more so this time for the ease of use than for the purpose of disguise. She tucked her braid down inside the back of her coat and pulled a knit cap on her head before heading out to Honeycutt's. The knife strapped tight to her calf beneath the baggy leg of her woolen trousers gave her some small sense of confidence in the midst of her raging anxiety.

*What if Turner's sources cannot find Bricken's location?*

*What if Claire has already been moved?*

*What if we are far too late?*

Reaching Honeycutt's, Portia entered without knocking. There was a murmur of men's voices coming from the study. They hadn't left yet, it seemed.

Dell's study was a modest size, containing a few bookcases, a side table with two chairs set before the fire, and his desk in front of the window. Turner, Hale, and Morley stood in a half circle around the desk, bent over some large sketches spread out over the surface. A gas lamp set to the side illuminated the group, casting them into sharp definition against the shadows filling the rest of the room.

Portia paused in the doorway before interrupting. There was something intense and poignant in the scene. These men—the sour-faced Morley standing attentive and patient, the muscle-bound Hale, with his heavy fists and even heavier expression, and Dell, who stood with his back to Portia as he spoke to the others in a low tone of command—had gathered for a noble purpose.

She could feel it the moment she entered the room.

Portia had never felt so compelled to be a part of anything as she did in that moment. This was where she belonged. Not waltzing through ballrooms or flirting across a dinner table.

It was here.

"Your man came through?" she asked as she entered the room.

Dell glanced over his shoulder. His mouth was drawn into a firm line, and his eyes were dark beneath a heavy brow. A hardness dulled the light in the depths of his gaze as he acknowledged her return with only a slight nod of his head.

As far as greetings went, it certainly centered her in on what was important.

Lowering his gaze back to the materials spread out before him, he said, "We haven't much time to prepare. Bricken has secured space on a ship headed for the Carolinas at first light. The captain of the vessel is known for frequently dealing in questionable transports, and the manifest lists Bricken's cargo as *unstable*."

"You believe it might be children?" Portia asked with a tight chest as she came up to stand beside Dell, taking comfort in the solid strength of his shoulder against hers.

"Bricken deals in nothing else, I assure you."

"Why the fuck are we all still standing around here?" Hale growled like a man willing to tear apart the whole city of London. "Let's go."

"Soon," Dell stated firmly. "We must be sure we understand the layout of this warehouse and how we plan to enter. There are only the four of us," he said, flicking a glance toward Portia, "and we cannot risk bungling this. We will not get another chance."

"How can we be sure the children have not already been moved to the ship's hold?" Portia asked, looking down at the makeshift sketch of a building's layout from above.

"They will want to move them as close to departure as they dare, to limit the risk of them being discovered before they are out of port."

"There be two ways in," Morley stated as he jabbed a blunt finger at the sketch. "This one here is tucked in along a narrow, twisted alley. Two will sneak in quiet-like there while the other two go in through the front, in hopes that if they are discovered, it will draw attention and leave the two in back free to move through undetected."

"What sort of resistance do you expect?" Portia asked. "How many men?"

"Six at least, but there is no way to be certain," Dell answered. "One or two will be guarding the children, depending on how many they have, which I suspect will be quite a few if they are willing to pay the rate for passage to America. Unless they have the children secured another way. We will have to consider the possibility of restraints."

Hale jerked violently beside her. The sound that issued from his throat sounded more animal than human as he lifted his hands to shove them forcefully back through his hair. "If they have done any bit of harm to Claire..." he muttered through his teeth, allowing the thought to drift unfinished, but clear enough nonetheless.

Portia met Hale's fierce gaze. "First, we have to get her out of there."

"I need to know you will stick with the plan," Dell added. His tone slid to a low note of command. "Deviations create weak spots in our assault. We each have a role to play and must play it to the end. If I cannot trust you to do that, you will not accompany us."

Hale stared mutinously back at him for a moment. "You think you could stop me?"

"I know I can," Dell replied.

After a very tense moment, Hale's mouth quirked in a strange sort of half smile that made Portia wonder if he hadn't just been testing Dell. Then the large man gave a short nod of his head. "You're in charge."

The tension eased, and Morley cleared his throat with a bit more than a hint of impatience. "Now, as I was sayin', two sneak in back and make their way up this way. There's not much for enclosed spaces inside, so there's only a few options for where they could be keeping the babes. Here, here, and here."

Dell interjected. "Hale, you and I will enter through the front. Once inside, we will need to take care of as many of Bricken's men as possible. If we can manage them one at a time, it would be best. If it turns into a war of gunfire, we risk the children. This is a covert mission. Do you understand?"

Hale gave a grunt and a nod, crossing his huge, muscled arms over his chest.

"Portia and Morley will go in through the back. It is your job to locate Claire and do what you must to free her." He looked down at Portia. His gaze was as hard as flint, in possession of none of the tenderness or passion she had been privy to just that morning. "You will stay at Morley's side. Keep the children calm and manageable. We cannot have them getting in the way or becoming pawns for Bricken's men."

Portia thought of the children in Bricken's hold. How many were frightened and confused? The image of Claire as Hale had sketched her rose to her mind, and her heart gave a painful lurch.

She would do everything in her power to get to those children and see them safe again.

Dell looked toward the clock on the mantel. "We leave in forty minutes. Let's go through this again. We must imagine every contingency and aberration that might occur, from the moment we leave this building until we return again."

# Thirty

DELL'S SOURCES REVEALED BRICKEN'S CURRENT LOCATION to be in a small warehouse not far from the old Howland docks. It was an ancient building of crumbling brick and soot-stained glass that would have appeared abandoned to anyone in passing.

The lanes and alleyways were dark and shadowed with very little sign of movement beyond the scuttle of rats and the occasional hiss and growl of feral cats. The air smelled briny and sour with the decay of refuse.

Dell had been in areas like this a hundred times, but this night he felt an uncomfortable pricking along the back of his neck, and his stomach was twisted into a hard, heavy knot.

Portia shouldn't be here.

What the hell was wrong with him to allow her to come along?

If this thing went bad, he couldn't even be at her side to ensure her safety. In entering with Hale, he hoped to draw as much attention and danger away from Portia and Morley as possible, freeing them up to find Claire.

He would have preferred pulling her aside and telling her to stay behind, wait it out at the house. But when he got a good look at her face as they had prepared to leave, he couldn't do it. Portia's beautiful features were trained into a look of fierce determination. Her gray eyes shimmered with intent and courage. Her lush mouth was pressed into a stubborn line. Everything about her was in total readiness. The woman had absolutely no training, but she made up for it in intelligence and grit.

He hoped it was enough.

A man Dell sometimes used when Morley was needed for other purposes had driven the carriage and would stay with it just around the corner from the rear of the warehouse, prepared for a quick escape if needed.

The group of four moved silently along the tangled lane toward the building. Each of them were fully aware of the individual tasks they had been assigned. Dell had made sure of that. If he was worried about Portia, he was equally worried about Hale. Here was another person who should not be along on this job. The man was far too emotionally invested. But again, Dell hadn't the heart to keep him away.

He was getting damned soft.

Approaching the point where their two groups would separate, Dell struggled to keep from giving Portia more than a passing glance. He nodded silently toward her and Morley then watched as they turned to run swiftly down the alley. A second before their matched forms disappeared into the black shadows, Dell noted how difficult it was to pick out one from the other. If not for the coil of rope slung over Morley's shoulder, Dell may not have been able to differentiate his woman from the small man.

*His woman.*

Damn.

He refused to allow his mind to envision the path she would take this night. He had his own part to play. As long as he did his job, hers would be easier. And safer.

Swinging his gaze past Hale, he noted his friend's intense posture and rigid expression. The man was a bloody Viking ready for battle. Dell was counting on Hale's mind to be as swift as his fists tonight. Raiding a criminal's den was nothing like facing a fair fight in the ring. But Hale had grown up on the streets, just as Dell had. He had to trust him to do what needed to be done.

He gave another nod, and they headed for the front entrance. The warehouse had once possessed a door large enough for a wagon to pass through, but as Dell's informant had described, that entry had long been boarded and blocked, leaving just a narrow walk-through door.

The entrance was their first problem, allowing only one of them in at a time. Even if they managed to get in covertly, there was still no telling where Bricken and his men might be positioned in the building. According to his informant, Bricken was often seen with at least three other men, and it could be well assumed that on a night when they intended to move their cargo, that number may double or more depending on how many children they needed to transport.

He hoped Hale's daughter was still in Bricken's possession. If Suzanne's timeline was to be trusted, Claire had been with the man for more than four days. The possibility that he had already sold her to someone else stabbed at the back of Dell's mind. He held fast to the understanding that Bricken preferred to work in bulk when moving his wares out of England.

They both carried pistols and knives, but Dell had instructed Hale to use their weapons only as a last resort. Dell had learned long ago that weapons could provide a false sense of security. He preferred to rely on his fighting skills. They were quieter and more accurate than the blast from a gun. And could take out an opponent without having to kill him.

They reached the door, and as planned, Hale entered first. If anyone was in the immediate vicinity, the former prizefighter's large, muscled form may create an element of immediate intimidation that could allow Dell to enter swiftly behind him and gain the upper hand.

Their entry met with no shout of warning or interference at all. The interior of the building was quiet and dark and smelled of damp lumber.

As expected from their study of the building's layout, they had stepped into a large, open area. Their eyes were already adjusted to the lack of light from the dank streets outside, and Dell noted stacks of rotting lumber filling the spaces between old, rusting machines designed for some unidentifiable and likely outdated purpose.

Dell's concern was on anything that moved in the shadows between.

They crept forward. Silent and listening. Alert and cautious, they moved through the space as swiftly as they could.

The faster they got in and found Claire, the sooner they could get out.

The floor plan of the building was clear and crisp in Dell's mind, and they had almost reached the first room likely to be holding the children when there was a soft, scuffing step behind them, then a swift intake of breath.

Dell whirled around. A man had just come from behind one of the stacks of lumber and was staring in shock at the intruders. This gave Dell a moment's advantage. He took two long, running steps toward the man, then leapt into the air while lashing out with his leg to bring his foot solidly against the side of the man's head. The other man fell back against the lumber, dislodging several large pieces with a crash that echoed through the silent building, before slumping to the ground.

And the covert nature of their invasion was lost, which meant it was now time to make the most of the distraction they had caused to draw attention away from Portia and Morley, who were moving through the back of the warehouse.

Almost instantly, another man rushed out from where the first had come. Two others appeared swiftly after from other directions.

Dell saw no weapons in hand, but that did not mean Bricken's men were not armed. He dove for the man nearest to him, catching the rotund figure around the waist and driving him back against the wall. Although the move managed to force the breath from both of them, the other man was far too massive to be disabled by the move. He brought his fists down hard on Dell's back, further stealing his breath.

Dell got in a couple of swift punches to the other man's midsection and kidneys, to little effect.

Changing his strategy, Dell stepped back, allowing his opponent to come at him. And he did, with lumbering steps and wide, swinging arms. The man was a troll, with no speed and little skill, but he made up for it in sheer mass and an apparent imperviousness to injury. As Dell lured the man farther out into an open space, he glanced aside to see Hale standing at the ready with the other two men circling him like wary predators.

The expression on Hale's face was pure, bloodthirsty violence as he shook his long hair back from his face and gave the two men a scathing glance, then a wide grin, before he said, "Come on, then, enough with the dancing lesson. Let's see whatcha got."

The men rushed him together, and Hale gave a wicked laugh as his mighty fists started swinging.

Dell would have loved to watch Hale in action. The man's skills had been unmatched when he'd left the ring a few years ago.

But there were other things to do just now.

Focusing on his own opponent, he realized he was not likely to knock the man to the ground without significant effort, but he could certainly tire the ox out. He gave a few more jabs—hits intended to annoy more than anything—before circling away, forcing the other man to twist and turn in his efforts to keep Dell in view.

Behind him, someone hit the ground with a heavy thud and muffled groan. The sound of another body meeting the dirt quickly followed. Hale's snort of derision said exactly what he thought of the quick fight.

"Continue on. I'll finish up here," Dell ordered.

"I don't think either of you'll be goin' any farther, mates." This came from a newcomer flanked by two more men.

By all the descriptions he'd had of Bricken, Dell realized it was the man himself who faced them now with a pistol in his hand.

The hearty ox Dell was fighting turned at the words, giving Dell the opening he needed as he delivered a well-aimed hit to the side of the man's head, felling him instantly.

His action drew the attention of the newcomers, allowing Hale to rush the three of them like a raging bull. A shot rang out as they crashed back into a pile of stacked crates.

As he sprinted forward to join the fray, his gaze seeking the hard glint of gunmetal, Dell forced himself not to think of Portia somewhere in the shadows at the far end of the building. He sent a swift prayer that their diversionary tactics would work to draw the attention of anyone else who posed a threat, allowing the other two to make their way undetected and unchallenged.

⤙⤚

Portia crept along behind Morley. Her heart beat like a bass drum in her ears, nearly drowning out all other sound—except for that gunshot still ringing through her brain.

Dell had *not* been shot. He was far too skilled, too clever, too *important* to be hurt.

She swallowed down her fear.

As badly as she wanted to rush through the haphazard maze of stacked lumber and makeshift walls, she held fast to his earlier instructions.

*No matter what, stay focused on what you need to be doing. Complete your task and trust the others to do the same.*

She trusted Dell, with all her heart. And oddly, she trusted Hale and Morley. She could not let them—or Claire, or any of the other children who had to be cowering somewhere in this building—down by losing her focus now.

So far, Dell's plan was working as she and Morley made their way through the deep shadows without interruption. She found herself impressed by her companion's silent movements despite the fact that he carried a hefty coil of rope over his shoulder. Clearly, he was more than just a pseudo butler and ofttimes driver. He had done work like this with Dell before.

Finally, past the small man's shoulder she saw the shadowed outline of a door, indicating their first point of search. Relief at having made it this far crowded her awareness, along with the intense surge of crackling energy through her system. She hoped the children were beyond that door, hoped they were safe and unharmed, hoped she and Morley would get to them without incident and that she would find a way to release them all before they left.

Their job was to find and rescue Claire, but Portia was not leaving this warehouse until all of Bricken's captives were freed.

As they crept closer to the room, a sound infiltrated Portia's awareness. It broke through the heavy thudding of her heart and the scuffling sounds of fighting that came from the front of the warehouse. It was someone's steady breath. Someone who had no need to slow their exhalations to avoid detection. Someone who made a disgusting, snorting sound every couple of seconds.

The room had a guard, still concealed from their view.

Which likely indicated that there was something in that room worthy of guarding.

Three more creeping steps and they saw him, standing only a few paces from the door they intended to go through. Luckily, his attention was focused in the opposite direction, toward the sound of the fighting.

Morley gave a signal to stop. Then he looked back at her with his tight face, made even sharper by the night shadows. He gestured for her to go to the door; then without any other communication, he slid toward the man.

Portia did not wait to see how he managed with the guard, who topped him by at least a foot. Regulating her breath to an even thread, she approached the door on swift feet. It was unlocked and opened readily to reveal a tiny room, possibly an office at one time or a small storage closet.

And there, huddled in groups or cowering alone on the dank and filthy floor, were the children. Perhaps a dozen or so. It was difficult to know for sure, when some of them clung so tightly to each other. Her stomach knotted with an odd mixture of anxiety and relief. They had reached the children, but they were still far from safe. Her heart rising up through her throat, she scanned the group for a pale, cherubic face, the image of Claire as Hale had sketched her.

The children stared at her with wary eyes, and some of them attempted a defiant tilt of their chins but failed to manage it. They ranged in age from perhaps seven to twelve. But there was no small girl-child with fair curls about her face.

Portia felt sick. She shoved down her nausea and shored her determination. They would keep looking for Claire, but right now, these children needed help.

She stepped toward them. "Shh," she whispered when a few of them flinched and shrank back. "I am here to help you. You must come with me."

They stared back at her in silence, but they did not move. Not at first. But then a girl, perhaps nine years old, rose carefully to her feet and stepped forward. "You'll take us home?"

Portia nodded. "I will. Please, all of you, don't be afraid. There are others with me. We came to get you out of here."

Finally, her words seemed to have an effect. A few of them glanced at each other in silent communication. Others slowly stood and shuffled forward.

"There's one problem," a larger boy declared gruffly, as though trying to conceal his fear. "Some of us be shackled."

The children shifted as a group. Those who could do so moved to the other side of the room nearer Portia, leaving behind four boys, all of them older, tougher. Likely their captors saw them as the most liable to rebel and attempt escape.

Portia wasted no time, but swept forward to the child nearest her and dropped to her knees, pulling out some tiny tools from the pocket of her woolen trousers. She had thought these might come in handy. She bent over the first iron manacle latched around a slim ankle and started to work at the lock.

The manacles were old and cumbersome. While Portia attempted to figure out the sensitivity of the rusted mechanism, the children grew restless.

"Where are these mates o' yers?" one of them asked in a desperate whisper.

Portia didn't answer, keeping her head bowed and her focus on the lock.

"Leave us," one of the shackled boys positioned at the back of the room said in a gentle voice. "Take the others and leave us."

Portia didn't stop her work on the lock to look up and see who had uttered the self-sacrificing statement, though her heart squeezed painfully. She heard the thin thread of fear in the brave words, and she refused to consider that option.

She would get them all.

Just then the lock clicked free. Releasing a breath she didn't know she held, Portia turned to the next boy. "I will get you out of here," she muttered.

The next locks released much more quickly, and finally, she came to the last. Not looking up from her task until the final manacle dropped away, she lifted her gaze to meet that of this last boy. His eyes were dark and haunted in a way she had never seen before. He looked back at her with no expression, and Portia felt her stomach clench with sadness as she knew for certain this had been the boy willing to sacrifice himself to save the others.

"Please come with me."

The boy shifted from his place on the ground, and Portia noticed something moving behind him.

A whisper of white cotton.

As the boy stood, more of what he had been shielding was revealed. A small girl dressed in a dingy nightgown—pale curls dulled by dirt and soot—clung to the back of his coat, hiding her face against him.

The boy, who couldn't have been any more than twelve years old, turned to wrap his arm carefully around his ward. "No worries. See, you'll stay with me," he whispered to her.

Finally, the girl peeked up and around him toward Portia.

Though she had already suspected the child's identity, her heart stopped at the sight of the beautiful face Hale had so lovingly drawn.

Claire.

# Thirty-one

"YOU WERE TO STICK TO THE PLAN, MISS," MORLEY suddenly hissed from behind her.

Portia lifted her chin and gave him a fierce stare. "This *was* my plan. Now let's get them out of here."

Gratefully, the man chose not to waste another moment in argument as he began ushering the children through the door and back the way they had come, some of them clutching each other's hands, others forging ahead independently.

Portia waited until the last of them was free of the room. As she followed behind them, she glanced to where the guard had been and saw a body slumped to the floor. Two steps to the left, another unconscious form lay quietly groaning. New respect bloomed for Morley. As they rushed as silently as possible through the shadows with the shuffling children between them, she strained to hear what may be occurring with Hale and Dell.

There was only silence.

Pain squeezed at her heart, and she refused to consider what the silence indicated.

The children were her current concern.

Their exit was up ahead, and relief swept through her in a tingling rush. They were going to make it.

Just as the thought completed in her mind, she found herself grasped tightly from behind. So tightly her breath expelled on a choked gasp as her lungs were painfully constricted by arms holding her in a fierce grip.

The children in front of her yelped in fear as they rushed after the others to get away. She could not see Morley up ahead, but she sent a swift prayer that he would get the children to safety.

"Ye bastards think ye can raid me place, take me treasures, and leave none o' yer blood spilled?"

The man shifted his hold to lift the edge of a blade to Portia's throat. As he did so, his arm passed over her breasts, and he gave a sick sound of pleasure.

"Ah, yer no bastard, are ye, lovie? Mayhap I'll take a little something else from ya."

He lowered his knife to press it under the swell of her breast.

The disgusting threat spurred Portia into action. Guided purely by an intense instinct for self-preservation, she lifted her right knee in a swift movement that brought her knife within reach. She had been practicing the move, and a flick of her thumb released the blade into her palm.

The knife felt like an extension of her fury as she drove the tip back and up into the side of the man behind her, feeling the sickening scrape of metal against bone as the blade slid beneath his lowest rib, then a wash of hot, sticky blood flowing over her hand.

With a grunt, the man stumbled behind her. The knife he still held tightly beneath her breast slid to the side as he moved, searing her with a burning pain.

Withdrawing her blade from his side, she felt another wash of blood. She twisted enough to give a sharp jab of her elbow into his midsection.

With a rush of air from his lungs and another groan, he fell back, flailing his arms as if trying to grasp something to keep himself upright. His hand still clutching the knife flew past Portia's head, the hilt connecting hard with her temple.

Bright pain burst inside her skull. She took a few staggering steps and turned to see the man hitting the floor, a red stain spreading across his side.

Then the floor beneath her feet tipped wildly, and a strange fuzziness invaded her vision as a sound like the rush of a waterfall filled her ears.

*Bloody hell*, she thought with no small bit of shock and dismay a second before the world went black.

❧

Dell rushed toward the back of the warehouse, Hale following close behind him.

As they neared the back, Hale split toward the right, heading to where the last room was located, while Dell raced toward the soft, scuffling sound up ahead.

Dell gritted his teeth against the desire to shout Portia's name as he moved swiftly along the dark, twisting pathways between the stacks of lumber.

He and Hale had finally taken care of Bricken's two additional guards. Using the length of rope Dell had brought along, they tied them securely with the other men in case they came to and decided to fight a little more. Bricken, however, had managed to slink away in the melee. They ran into no one else as they searched and found the first two rooms empty, which meant the children had either been in the last room at the back of the warehouse, or they were not here at all.

Turning a corner, he saw several small shadows rushing along the back wall of the warehouse toward the open rear exit. Dell continued forward carefully, glancing in every direction to be sure the children were not being moved by more of Bricken's men. When he finally caught sight of Morley at the front of the group, directing the children into the alley beyond, he approached the other man quickly and whispered, "Where is she?"

Morley peered back over the heads of the last of the children rushing silently past. Then he glanced back to Dell. "She should be there."

Icy fear squeezed Dell's chest. "Get the children loaded into the carriage."

Morley nodded.

"Hale's daughter?" Dell asked.

"Aye."

*Thank God.*

Dell's relief was intense at the confirmation that they had Claire, but it was not enough to temper his fear at not seeing Portia. He had no doubt it had been her decision to rescue all of the children. He should have expected no less. He also knew she would not have let the children out of her sight unless it was for a good reason.

He turned away as Morley swept through the door into the alley after the last child.

On swift feet, he slid through the darkness.

When he saw the two bodies lying on the floor, his fear and every other emotion left him in a violent whoosh. Everything—his world, his self—suddenly ceased to exist.

He dropped to the floor at Portia's side where she lay facedown with a violent red stain covering her side and back.

His lungs closed off, causing a wave of fire to spread through his insides. He experienced a rush of emotion unlike anything he'd ever felt, an internal pressure that threatened to crush him from the inside. It was a mixture of pure fury and unadulterated fear. If he lost her now…

He couldn't complete the thought. He refused to.

But his hands shook as he carefully eased her onto her back. The groan that slid from her lips made his heart grind to a stop. It was evidence that she lived. An angry, swollen discoloration was forming at her temple, but otherwise, her skin was deathly pale. Leaning over her, Dell placed his hand against the side of her face to feel the warmth of her skin.

She lived, but he still had no idea what injuries she'd sustained.

Scooping his arms beneath her, he lifted her against his chest as he stood, hoping he did not cause further injury and bleeding by moving her, but he had no choice other than to get her out of there and to safety.

Just then, Hale came from the opposite direction, stumbling to a stop in front of the other body.

He met Dell's gaze briefly before his glance flickered to Portia and then the still, prone body.

"Bricken."

Dell nodded, desperate to get Portia out of there and to a doctor.

"There was no one in the back," Hale added. His words were choked with grief and tension.

Portia stirred and tried to lift her head from Dell's shoulder. "The children," she muttered.

"We have them," Dell replied and heard Hale's heavy exhale at the confirmation. "Where are you injured?"

"I'm not." She tried to shift in Dell's hold, and he tightened his grip.

"You are covered in blood."

"Not mine. I fainted. That is all. I am fine."

The relief that washed through Dell's body made him weak, allowing her to shift in his hold until she could place her feet on the ground. She looked down at the body lying at Hale's feet.

"Is he dead? Did I kill him?"

Needing something to distract him from everything he was feeling, Dell crouched at Bricken's side. The man's breath was thready and shallow. Blood still seeped from his side, adding to the pool spreading out beneath him. He lived, but wouldn't for long without attention.

"Tie him up," he instructed Hale as he rose to his feet. "Any others?"

"Two more, already trussed up," Hale grunted as he uncoiled a length of rope from where it draped over his shoulder. He secured it expertly around Bricken's ankles and wrists then rose to his full height to pin Portia with a frightful stare. "My girl?"

Portia nodded quickly. "Yes. She is with the others."

Without another word, Hale swept past them in ground-eating strides. Dell wrapped his arm around Portia's back, holding her to his side as they swiftly followed him into the alley.

At the far end, Morley was loading the children into Dell's carriage. Hale hesitated as he drew close to the last of the children. Ahead of him, Dell saw a tiny girl in a white nightgown, fair curls in disarray about her head, clutching desperately to the hand of an older boy.

The boy, Dell noticed, had the girl's hand secure in his and his other arm crossed in front of her small body as he glared hard at Hale's approach. It was clear the boy would have protected the girl against the former prizefighter with everything in him. More than the child's bravery, there was something else about him that stood out.

He was not dressed in the clothing of a street urchin. Though filthy and worn, his clothes were of high quality. The boy's manner and his near-lordly bearing were not suited to a boy of the streets.

Hale took another tentative step toward his daughter. His large boxer's hands were open in supplication.

The girl hid her face in her companion's side.

Hale crouched down before her. "Sweet pea," he said quietly. "It's me. Papa."

At the sound of his voice, the girl looked up sharply. She stared at Hale for a long, hard second while Dell held his breath.

"Papa!"

She launched herself into Hale's arms then, wrapping her tiny arms around his thick neck. Her body became swallowed by his heavy arms as he held her silently for a long moment.

At Dell's side, Portia slid her hand into his and leaned against him with a sigh.

Dell clenched his teeth as the scent of stale blood—Bricken's blood—wafted to his nostrils.

"We need to get out of here," he said sternly to the group. "It's not safe."

"That's all that'll fit in this carriage with me as well," Morley stated, having gotten all but Claire and her protector into the vehicle.

Dell nodded. "Take them to the safe house. Frances can help you to figure out where to return them. I imagine most are orphans, but some may have been snatched from homes they'd like to go back to."

Before climbing into the carriage, Morley sent Portia a curious glance. "It was mighty clever of you to pick those locks, miss. These chits have much to thank ye for," he said.

Portia nodded and glanced at Claire held tightly in Hale's arms.

*More than a job.*

Against Dell's will, this had become just that.

"Let's be away from this place," Hale stated in a gruff command that didn't quite disguise the emotion in his tone.

Dell agreed wholeheartedly, anxious to get home to verify that Portia had not been hurt.

It took them a while of walking before they reached an area where they could hail a hackney carriage. Dell didn't even want to guess what the driver must have been thinking of their ragtag group.

Everyone was silent as they drove away. The boy especially was rather somber for having just been rescued. Though the child had certainly gone through a horrendous ordeal at Bricken's hands, Dell suspected he had a far greater tale than what was contained within that warehouse. With his rich clothes, he surely had someone aware of his absence, someone searching for him, yet he said nothing of his people.

The boy did not trust them.

Claire had been quiet in her father's arms through most of the ride home, but at one point she peeked at the boy over Hale's shoulder and immediately began to squirm until her father released her so she could slide down onto the seat between him and her protector. The boy immediately put his arm around her shoulders and murmured something incoherent. The girl-child settled against him and closed her eyes.

Dell glanced at Hale, who watched the whole thing with an intent and serious gaze. It was difficult to detect what thoughts and emotions churned behind the man's eyes, but Dell suspected they were anything but quiet.

# Thirty-two

PORTIA SLID DOWN FARTHER INTO THE ONCE-STEAMING bathtub until the tepid water lapped at her chin. She tipped her head back to soak her scalp, rinsing away the last of the soap from her hair.

As soon as they had arrived back at Honeycutt's, Dell had insisted she bathe and change. Though she would have liked to stay below to see Claire and the boy settled, she was anxious to rid herself of the blood-soaked clothing that stuck uncomfortably to her back and side. The boy had glanced at the stain more than once with a wary, haunted gaze.

Portia had no wish to be the cause of further trauma to him or Hale's bashful daughter.

The bump at her temple throbbed insistently, and the laceration from Bricken's knife sliding beneath the curve of her breast had stung at first contact with the hot water, but certainly not enough to deter a thorough scrubbing. After three consecutive washings, she finally felt cleaned of Bricken's blood. It had taken a bit longer for the involuntary tremors to leave her limbs.

Dell had returned downstairs once he'd had the bathtub filled. Portia would have liked him to stay but knew he had some issues to wrap up regarding the gang of criminals still detained in the abandoned warehouse.

In the end, she was glad he had left her and had not witnessed further evidence of her weakness. Having been found in a heap on the floor was one thing, but the shaking that later claimed her was inexcusable. As soon as she was alone, her entire body began to shiver uncontrollably as if she were freezing, though the room was well heated. The warm bath had eventually helped to soothe her nerves, as did thinking of anything other than the moment when her knife had gone into Bricken's side.

She was certain she would never forget the sick feeling of another's blood washing over her hand.

Now, more than an hour later, aside from a little shakiness that remained in her hands, she finally felt like herself again.

And she was anxious to rejoin Dell and find out how everything had gone with the children. Just as she shifted in the tub, preparing to rise, the bedroom door opened and Dell entered.

He had also taken the time to clean up and change into a fresh pair of trousers and a white shirt still open at the throat and untucked at the waist. He was barefoot, and a shadowed growth of beard covered his jaw, making him look delightfully rugged and handsome.

Seeing her there, her arms propped on either side of the tub, the edge of the water lapping just below her breasts, he stopped abruptly. His gaze slid over her exposed shoulders and bared breasts with a studied focus, as though he had never seen anything quite like her before.

Portia did not move. Not to cover herself with her arms or to continue rising. She remained sitting tall and proud while her skin flushed with heat, despite the cooling water, and the beat of her heart skipped into a frantic rhythm.

"You did not tell me he cut you," he noted in a low tone as his gaze fixed upon the thin red line Bricken had made with his knife beneath Portia's left breast.

"It is nothing," she replied.

When Dell gave her a look that said otherwise, she responded with a challenging lift of one brow. She thought for a moment that he would argue. But then his expression shifted and his gaze slid to the side.

"I brought you a change of clothes."

He crossed the room to carefully drape a pale-pink gown and underthings over the back of a chair. She loved the way his body moved, with so much strength and grace and efficiency. She loved that he bothered to take such care of details, not only with her, but with everything he did.

He set a small purse on the table beside her clothes. "And your cut of Nightshade's fee."

Portia looked at the purse in surprise. "I did not do it for payment."

He glanced over his shoulder, his expression closed, unreadable. "I know, but you earned it."

His simple acknowledgment warmed her significantly. She couldn't help the impish smile that curved her lips. "You should probably keep it, since I believe I still owe you for a prior job."

He shook his head and glanced away from her. "You don't owe me anything."

There was something in his tone that worried her, but before she could explore it, he turned to face her fully.

"I have a towel here if you are finished with your bath?"

A rippling wave of awareness swept through her body. "I am."

He approached at an unhurried pace and opened the towel in his hands.

With heat igniting her blood, Portia stood from the water. His golden eyes darkened, and the muscles of his jaw tightened, though he did not shift his gaze any lower than her chin. He seemed intent upon remaining unmoved and casually imperturbable. His expression was annoyingly passive.

She mutinously stared back at him, daring him to view her naked body as she lifted her arms and he wrapped the soft cotton towel around her. As soon as she grasped the ends of the towel over her breasts, he stepped back and turned away.

If Portia were the betting sort, she would have put a fortune on his feeling the same rush of sensations she felt whenever in his proximity. She would have bet even more that he was avoiding them.

A frown pulled harshly between her brows.

She thought they had gotten past his reluctance to accept the attraction between them.

Tucking in the end of the towel to secure it around her body, she pulled the length of her hair over her shoulder and wrung out the excess water into the tub.

When Dell started toward the door, she spoke up, desperate to keep him near. "Don't leave."

He paused and glanced back over his shoulder. His chin was lowered, and though his expression had not changed, his eyes confirmed her suspicions. Their focus was glittering and direct. Intense and…hot.

Portia clung to that.

"Has Hale gone?" she asked and was pleased by the flicker of surprise in his expression at her unexpected query.

"He has."

"And what of the boy?" Trying to act casual and unconcerned, though every nerve in her body was drawn tight with desire, Portia crossed to the mirror that hung over a washstand in the corner.

There was more than one way to break past his resistance.

Focusing on her reflection, she began to finger comb through her wet hair. She kept her tone light and inquisitive as she continued. "There is something unusual about little Claire's champion. There is a story there, I think. Did he tell you where he comes from? Who his people are?"

There was a long pause, during which she could hear his breath slowly entering and leaving his lungs while she held hers.

Finally, he replied. "He has claimed to have no people. For the time being, the boy has accompanied Hale back to his home."

"Really?" That surprised her. Portia gathered her hair and began to plait the length into a single braid as she turned away from the mirror.

Dell had made his way to a chaise that extended from the far corner of the room. He reclined against the angled end with one foot still on the floor and the other propped on the chaise. One arm was lifted and bent beneath his head as he directed his gaze toward the corner where the far wall met the ceiling. His other hand rested on his abdomen.

Portia had never seen a sight more enticing than Dell in repose. Because even though his reclined form should have made him appear relaxed, instead he gave her the impression of being primed for action. The contradiction was stimulating.

Her heart actually stopped and skipped a beat, while wonderful, sensual heat flowed through her, making her legs momentarily weak.

But he was doing everything in his power to avoid the sight of her.

She was not going to allow it for long.

"The boy claims to have no family," he continued, "no one searching for him, no one awaiting his return."

"That seems...odd," she said as she wandered over to the chair holding the clothing he had brought for her.

He gave a low grunt of agreement.

Turning her back to Dell, Portia oh-so-casually dropped her towel to the floor.

His sharp intake of breath told her he was not as oblivious to her as he would have her think.

Flames of desire licked along her skin, and naughtiness claimed her. She pushed it a bit further as she leaned forward to reach for the shift.

He made a raw sound.

Portia bit her lip as pulsing heat flooded her core.

It seemed seduction affected the seducer as well as the one seduced.

*Interesting.*

Lifting the shift over her head, she stretched her body and lengthened her arms, allowing the light garment to drift down over her skin. It was a short piece, and the hem barely brushed her knees.

She turned back to face him and felt the full force of the desire she had willfully roused in him. He still lounged back against the chaise and had just turned his head to watch her, but the change in him was intensely obvious. His piercing gaze was hot and stabbing. Sexual need radiated from him.

It amazed her that the room did not burst into flames around them.

"You do not believe him," she stated, bringing the focus back to their conversation.

He swallowed hard before answering.

"No, and neither does Hale," he said. His voice had lowered to a richer, gravelly sound. "But the girl would not allow herself to be separated from him— threw quite the tantrum—so Hale agreed to take the boy in until we could figure out what to do with him."

"And the boy was agreeable to that?"

"Reluctantly, but yes."

Portia thought about that for a moment. Hale was not only father to a small and timid child, but now also makeshift guardian for a half-grown boy. The man was turning out to be nothing like she had expected. He displayed so many contradictions of character. From his threats against her family and Lily's ultimate abduction to the tenderness he had revealed regarding his daughter. He was unmistakably ruthless, and violence seemed to seethe just beneath his surface, but he had somehow earned Dell's friendship and now had taken on the responsibility of two young children.

She would always hate the man for his crimes against Lily, but she had to consider the possibility that he was not the complete monster she had once believed him to be.

"What will happen to the other children?" she asked.

"I received a message from Morley not long ago. Of the nine other children, four will be taken to an orphanage, two will be returned to their families, and three wished to be released back onto the streets from which they came."

Not one of those children who had been huddled together in that tiny room could have been over the age of ten or eleven at the most. The idea of any one of them being on their own in the city made her heart ache.

"But, surely—"

"They will be watched as best I can manage," Dell added quietly.

Portia should have known he would not simply send them to the streets. Her heart warmed. Of course he would have people keeping an eye on them.

"And Bricken?" she asked as she approached Dell with unhurried steps, allowing him plenty of time and incentive to watch the movement of her body beneath the transparent shift.

His gaze flickered over her breasts and swept down the length of her legs before leaping back up to meet hers.

"Bricken?" she prompted with a quirk of her lips.

"An anonymous message has been sent to the magistrate, advising where to find a gang of criminals tied up and injured. The list of his crimes is long. They will be dealt with."

She was near enough now to see the tension in his thighs and in the corded muscles of his neck as he strained to hold himself in the passive pose.

She continued forward, her bare feet padding silently on the carpeted floor until her knees came up against the side of the chaise. She looked down at him.

"Dell."

She spoke his name in a low whisper, knowing he would detect all the things she wasn't saying just then, trusting he would know what she wanted.

His eyes stared fiercely into hers. After a moment, he reached for her. His fingers touched first at the sensitive skin of her inner thigh, just above her knee. Then with tantalizing patience, he slid his hand higher.

Portia's lips parted on a breathy gasp. Her eyelids grew heavy as her body tensed for his touch where she ached with a delicate pulse of yearning.

He held her gaze, forcing her to stay focused on him. The golden light in his eyes pierced steady and strong, inciting her breath to a shallow rhythm. It seemed as though in watching her, he could feel her. Feel the changes in her body, feel the pleasure and anticipation flickering through her blood as his hand inched ever higher.

She lowered her chin, and a damp tendril of hair slid from her braid to brush against her collarbone, inciting tingles and chills. She knew what he was doing. Tantalizing her. Making her want it even more than she did already. Driving her to the edge of her limited patience.

Lifting her gaze to meet his again, she curled just one corner of her mouth in a knowing smile.

He smiled back, sending a frisson of heat through Portia from head to toe. She parted her lips on a shaky inhale. He chose that moment to gently slide his middle finger along her slick crease.

Portia's knees nearly gave out, and a soft moan issued from her throat as tingling flames spread throughout her body. He immediately repeated the torment, pressing between her folds for a more intimate caress.

Portia's knees wobbled in truth then, and she bit her lip at the wrenching pleasure.

He wrapped his hand around the inner curve of her upper thigh, as though to steady her, as her name slid from his lips on a ragged sigh. The sound of it was like a catalyst in her blood, heating it to a dangerous level, sending shockwaves of desire and need through her very soul.

She moved to lift her knee onto the chaise beside his hip, opening herself to him.

His fingers tightened on her flesh. His gaze was so dark and deep, like molten fire. Igniting more need when she already felt consumed by her craving for him.

"I want to be with you, Dell," she murmured gently. "More than anything in the world, I want to be with you."

Portia caught herself from saying more. She realized the words could be interpreted in more than one way, and though she meant them in all the ways possible, something held her back from issuing a full declaration.

Moving slowly, she lifted her leg over him until she straddled his strong thighs. But she did not lower her weight. She knelt straight and proud, looking at him with an expression of expectancy and desire, demanding without words that he take what she offered.

For a heart-stealing moment, she did not know what he would do. Then he lifted his upper body away from the reclined edge of the chaise, sitting upright. He curved his hands around the backs of her thighs to slide up beneath the hem of her shift and cup her bare buttocks in a firm grip. A sigh rose up from deep inside and escaped on a shaky exhale. Her breasts were even with his face and close enough that the warmth of his breath bathed her nipples, bringing them to hard peaks beneath her shift.

A not-so-subtle arch of her spine thrust her breasts forward in blatant offering.

The look he gave her from beneath his brows as he leaned forward to take one aching peak deep into his mouth was as wicked as anything she had ever seen. That, combined with the lush feel of his mouth closing over her sensitive nipple, saturating the thin material, sent spears of intense pleasure through her center, causing a sweet and heady pulse of heat between her thighs.

Her head fell back, and she lifted her hands to his shoulders.

Shifting his hold to her hips, he urged her down onto his lap, drawing her forward until she could feel the length of his erection where she craved it most. A moan caught in her throat. Reveling in the sensation, Portia arched her lower back and rolled her hips.

He wrapped his arms around her, bringing her belly flush against his as her breasts flattened against his chest.

Lifting her hands to his face, she paused to enjoy the texture of his beard against her palms, then swept her thumb over his bottom lip until she could wait no longer to taste him, and she put her mouth on his in a burning kiss.

She tilted her head and parted her lips, sweeping her tongue insistently past his teeth. When the velvet texture of his tongue slid along hers, she lost herself. Her eyes closed, and a heady moan slid from her throat.

That was when Dell took over, plundering her mouth while his hands, his wonderful hands, stroked over her back and hips and thighs.

Portia's body went up in flames.

# Thirty-three

DELL CURSED THE UNIVERSE FOR CREATING A WOMAN like Portia Chadwick. His life had been ordered and focused. He earned a hefty purse for his work because he was very good at what he did. He had been content.

Then Portia happened, and his life had been upside-down ever since.

And the devil help him, he was enjoying it far too much. No, he craved it. In her contrary and stubborn refusal to do as she should, she challenged him to meet her halfway.

He enjoyed not knowing what she was going to do or say.

She was clever, brave, incorrigible, and beautiful. In matters of passion and desire, she gave all of herself without reservation.

He clenched his teeth as she undulated in his lap again. The heat at her core soaked through the material of his trousers where he ached with need for her.

He lured her tongue into his mouth. She tasted of recklessness, purity, and passion. Gripping her buttocks in his hands, he moved her against him, rocking her back and forth along his erection. The gasp and moan she released into his mouth fired his blood, and the squeeze of her thighs around his hips sent a sharp twist of need through his insides.

She was stunning.

He had thought it before and could not help thinking it again.

Dell swept his hand up along her narrow rib cage to cover her breast with his hand. Her heart pounded beneath his palm, matching the rhythm within his chest. He trailed his fingers up past her collarbone until his fingers curled around to press against her nape.

Sweeping his tongue over her lips, he memorized their lush shape, their silken texture. He sipped from her mouth and breathed her breath until, with an incoherent sound in the back of her throat like something between a plea and a cat's contented purr, she drew back. Her gaze was direct, needful, and bright with desire.

"You are an exceptional man," she murmured in a husky tone.

His breath caught at the hard squeeze his chest gave in reaction to her words. "Don't," he said, not knowing what else to say.

With a sultry smile, she fitted her small hand against the side of his face. "It is the truth."

His hand still cupped around her nape, Dell drew her forward and ran a path of kisses down the side of her throat. He didn't want words right now. Words—especially her words—were far too convincing. They made him want to believe in things that couldn't be. He touched his tongue to her pulse and tested the sensitivity of her skin with his teeth.

She gasped and shivered delicately in his arms. Then, because Portia would never be a passive participant in anything, she slid her arms around his neck and turned her head to claim his mouth with hers again.

Dell's gut tightened.

He understood that she likely needed this as badly as he did after her experience tonight. This affirmation of life. This total release of self to another. To a moment.

Suddenly impatient, Dell broke from the kiss to reposition her farther back on his thighs, putting necessary space between them.

She gave a brief sound of protest, but quieted as he lifted his shirt over his head and tossed it aside. She instantly reached out to smooth her palms over the surface of his chest and dance her fingertips across his stomach. Her touch sent thrills through every inch of him.

While she explored his bared skin, a private little smile curving her lips and lust brightening her gaze, Dell made quick work of opening the fastening of his trousers as he leaned back again on the angled rest of the chaise. She lifted herself just enough to allow him to shove the trousers down past his hips to free his erection.

He barely had time to take a breath before she grasped him in her hand. His head pressed back, and he released an involuntary groan as her fingers tightened and slid along his length from root to tip.

She explored him, seeming to delight in discovering all the different ways she could touch him to elicit a reaction. It quickly became too much.

With a harsh growl, he finally gripped her hips in

his hands and brought her forward against him. Her bare, heated flesh slid wet along his aching length.

Her moan matched his then, and she leaned forward onto his chest, her mouth seeking his.

Kissing her deeply, he lifted her over him, intentionally taunting her with just the tip of his erection at the hot entrance to her body. Then he began to lower her, slowly claiming his bit of paradise.

By the time he was fully sheathed in her heat, his heart was beating so hard and fast, he thought it might burst. He would have stayed there a few moments to fully appreciate the exquisite experience of being so deep inside her. But she rolled her hips, forcing him to move, drawing a tight breath from his throat. The sensation was torturous and divine. She flicked her tongue along his as she moved again.

He should have known Portia would not hesitate to claim the advantage of this position and the power it gave her.

Dell wanted nothing more than to see what she would do with it.

Releasing his grip on her hips, he raised his arms over his head to grasp the upper edge of the raised chaise behind him.

She looked at him with a brow arched in question.

Her lips were soft and glistening from their kisses. Her breath was short and sweet against his face. And there, in the heart-stopping mystery of her gaze, was a flash of sudden knowledge.

And then her smile.

Dell's chest hitched painfully at the beauty and delight in that smile.

She gave one more delicious roll of her hips before pushing away from his chest. Holding his gaze, she sat proud and beautiful as she swept the shift up over her head and tossed it aside.

Dell eagerly feasted his gaze upon her body, the pert breasts still begging for his mouth, the lovely curve of her waist and the flare of her hips. He throbbed insistently within her, and her eyelids fluttered.

Then she placed her hands flat on his stomach. Her expression was wicked as she watched her hands slide up over his chest, then along the backs of his arms still bent up over his head. She paused to brush her nipples back and forth across his, teasing him. She was playful and bold, unabashed in her desires.

Holding his gaze, she reached over his head until she could curve her hands over his, sliding her fingers in the spaces between his own, her elbows pressed inside his. Then she lifted her hips, slowly easing along his length until just the tip of him remained in tantalizing contact.

She looked hard into his eyes and spoke in a husky murmur. "You are mine, Dell Turner. And I am yours."

He did not disagree. He couldn't. Because in that moment, she lowered, taking him into her heat once again. For the first time in his life, Dell understood what it meant to truly give himself to someone else.

This small, dark-haired, silver-eyed woman had dug deep into his soul with barely any effort at all. She had become an indelible part of him.

They moved together in a rolling, balanced rhythm. Taking from each other and giving in equal measure. Though her eyes fell closed as she gave herself over to the sensations slowly building between them, Dell kept his gaze fastened upon her. He didn't want to miss the rise of tension in her features, or the beautiful flush that spread across her body. The thousand wonderful ways she expressed her passion was dazzling to behold. With pleasure pulsing steadily along every nerve and searing his blood, he wished they could stay like this always. Forever on the verge of magic. No separate history, no uncertain future. Just the now.

She gave a deep and luxurious roll of her hips that had Dell clenching his teeth and arching his neck.

Her fingers tightened in his, and she leaned forward, her lips seeking his once more. Dell could have lost himself in that kiss, but he fought to retain his self-control, needing her to take her pleasure first.

Her movements became faster and more demanding. She broke from the kiss with a ragged gasp before her breath caught in her throat then shifted into a low moan. As her climax overtook her, her body stiffened, her thighs squeezed his hips, and her teeth bit sharply into the flesh of his shoulder. She was unapologetic in her passion. So totally honest and unfettered that it made his heart ache. The raw nature of her response kicked him over the edge. The pressure that had built within him broke free, and his climax tore through him in a rush, leaving him shaken in more ways than one.

After an indefinite period of time, her body slowly softened atop him and her breath eased to a soothing rhythm, but Dell had been forever altered.

"What happens next?"

Though her tone was soft, Portia's question filtered

harshly through the receding cloud of pleasure that encompassed them both. It was the question itself that jarred him.

He could try to assume she was still asking about Hale and the children, but he knew—after what had just transpired between them—that her inquiry was much more personal in nature.

He gathered his resolve.

"I must leave town for a few days," he said.

She did not reply at first. For a moment, he thought she might have drifted off, but then she released a long sigh and slid to his side, leaving one leg draped across his body as she gave a languorous stretch. The chaise was narrow, and without thought, he lowered his arm around her back to keep her snug to his side.

Tipping her head back, she looked at him. "Can I come with you?"

"No."

She stiffened, and her fingers, which had started drawing lazy circles across his belly, stilled. The fluidity was suddenly gone from her movements. With deliberate care, she lifted herself to an elbow. Her eyes were direct and questioning.

"Why?"

"You are a lady, and I am a bachelor. We cannot travel together without a proper chaperone."

"We could if we were married," she replied smoothly.

His heart lurched violently. God's teeth! The woman had just proposed to him.

And heaven help him, it was harder than he could have imagined to resist the urgent desire to say *yes*.

He slid away from her warmth and turned to sit

facing away from her. "Do not be ridiculous, Portia. I cannot marry you."

There was a pause before she answered, and Dell stood, needing more distance.

"Of course, I meant we could pretend to be married," she qualified, but the strain that had entered her voice belied her true feelings.

He pulled his trousers back up to his hips and secured the fastening before he turned back to face her. What he saw made his heart stop.

Portia reclined on the chaise. Her gorgeous bare legs were long in repose; her sable braid fell in a heavy rope over one shoulder. Her eyes possessed incredible depth, while her lips and her breasts were rosy from his kisses. Dell had never seen anything so beautiful. And so out of reach.

Though he had assured himself that Bricken's mark beneath her breast was nothing more than a scratch, it stood out as a bright-red reminder of the danger she had been in, as did the dark bruise at her temple. She would have a hard time explaining such a mark to her family. He hardened his resolve. "This trip is personal."

"Oh. I see." She took a long breath and lowered her chin, suddenly looking vulnerable and young.

Dell clenched his teeth against the guilt growing within him.

After a moment, she looked up again and flashed him a smile. "I understand. I suppose we can discuss the rest when you return."

"There is nothing else to discuss."

"Of course there is," she declared with a wide gesture of her hand. "Have you another job already lined up? Where do you plan to start? What can I do?" As she continued along this new train of thought, she rose up onto her knees and sat back on her heels. "Oh, I nearly forgot. You won't believe what my great-aunt has given me. It is simply fantas—"

"Portia. Stop."

To his amazement, she did. Her rising excitement ceased at once. She tipped her head to the side and placed her hands calmly on the tops of her thighs as she looked at him with a questioning gaze.

"You have gotten ahead of yourself," he added.

"You must know I wish to continue working with you."

"That was never an option," Dell countered immediately.

Her gaze narrowed. "Why not?"

"You are not suited to this work—"

"Bollocks."

Her vulgar interruption stopped his argument, and he stared hard at her. He could see it in her flintlike gaze and the jut of her chin. She would fight this to the death.

So would he.

Seeing her on the ground with Bricken's blood soaking her clothes had been the most wretchedly painful thing Dell had ever experienced. Even after she assured him that she was unhurt, he had not been able to catch his breath.

His line of work was not for her. Her life was too precious. Her future too dear.

When he spoke again, it was in a quiet tone, intensely controlled.

"You have no skill. No training. No experience with what can be encountered. You have no business with any part of this."

"I have plenty of skills. More than you are aware of, I would wager. You can train me in whatever I am lacking. And experience comes with the job. More than anything, I am motivated. This *is* what I am meant to be doing." Her expression was frightfully earnest. "I can be of help to you. I know I can."

"You are wrong. Look at you," he stated baldly as he raked his gaze down her slim, petite form currently bristling with affronted pride, possessing a core of determination the likes of which he'd never seen before. Her guileless sensuality called to him even now as she fervently argued with him naked, the scent of their lovemaking still clinging to the air. "You have no idea what it takes to do this work every day. This job for Hale was simple and straightforward. What about when you have to do something that disgusts you, something that goes against your moral fiber, something you know is wrong? What then?"

Portia narrowed her gaze until the silver of her eyes shone like shards of steel. "I know what you are doing, Turner, and it will not work. I am more than capable of coming to terms with what may be required. Just as I know we can also be more discerning in the jobs we take on. We can *help* people."

Dell laughed roughly. That statement proved as much as anything how naive she was. How utterly unfit she was for the role she wished to fill. "I do what people pay me to do. It certainly helps them." He allowed his jaded attitude to reflect in his tone. "But rarely anyone else."

"It doesn't have to be that way," she argued.

He lowered his chin. "That is how I like it."

"There is so much good you could do in this world."

"I am no do-gooder. If that is what you desire, go start a ladies charitable society or something. Isn't that what your sort typically does?"

"My *sort*?" Her tone arced to a dangerous level.

Dell tensed. He had crossed a line, but he would not take it back.

"I think I finally understand what you are saying," she said dramatically as she started to rise. "How stupid of me. Not only am I a woman, which of course is an immediate strike against me, but I also have the audacity to be young, and worst of all, I possess an elite social status."

She laughed as she strode proud and naked—her tangled braid swinging against her backside—to where her shift had been flung to the floor.

"Obviously, *my sort* cannot possibly aspire to be anything other than what I am: a simple adornment. Lovely and accomplished in needlepoint and the pianoforte, but certainly not a creature with ambition, original thoughts, or"—she stopped in the act of lifting the shift over her head to pin Dell with a striking glance—"desires. Heaven forbid."

Dell's chest tightened, but he said nothing. Instead, he clenched his teeth and held fierce to his frown. He could not fault her her ire. He understood how fiercely Portia hated such limitations.

But the anger and self-assurance in her tone made

him realize something else. He could not stop at refusing to allow her to work with him. She would never accept such dictates, and eventually, she would wear him down.

Dell was suddenly overwhelmed by the weight of what he must do.

She didn't seem to notice his silence. She was quite immersed in her tirade and continued in a scathing tone as she drew on the dress he had procured for her. "You are quite right indeed. It is far past time for me to return my helpless, hapless self into the care of my family and the society that believes me incapable of anything more taxing than to prance politely upon the arm of a man of wealth and prestige. Never mind his weak character or empty head," she added in a grumble as she bent forward to draw on her stockings one at a time, then slipped her feet into the shoes he had brought for her.

All the while, Dell stood in silent awe and admiration for this woman. He understood her deep-seated irritation, even as her fiery temper inspired in him an odd mixture of respect and lust and amusement, though he was careful to keep her from seeing any of it.

It would do her no good to see the true depth and complexity of his feelings for her. It wouldn't change what would come next.

Fully clothed now, though her hair was still a delightful mess, Portia crossed to the door in long strides. Before quitting the room in dramatic fashion, she stopped to glance at him. Her mouth had opened to say something, but she appeared to abruptly change her mind.

Instead, she claimed a swift inhale and deliberately captured his gaze with hers.

Dell's heart stalled. A look of longing and anger flared hot in her eyes before it was tempered by an expression of subtle consternation.

"Enjoy your trip," she said. Then she swept from the room.

# Thirty-four

PORTIA SPUN ABOUT ON THE ARM OF LORD EPPING. SHE forced a laugh at his raucous tale of another escapade conducted by the Merry Friars, though beneath it she couldn't help but recognize the irrelevance of the young lords' activities. There was no meaning behind the Friars' exploits. No purpose or greater intention beyond momentary diversion.

The group of young men, whom she counted as friends, lived a life so far removed from Dell's it was truly laughable.

Bloody hell, just thinking of him made her body heat with an unnatural flush. And it wasn't all good. Her lingering fury over his refusal to allow her assistance in his work mingled with a physical yearning that simply wouldn't go away.

It was a good thing he was gone from town for a few days. Portia needed that time to sort out her feelings. She had thought she knew exactly what she wanted: the opportunity to work with Nightshade—as assistant, apprentice, it mattered not as long as she could be with him.

And that was the crux of the issue and what had her so blasted twisted up inside. It was the work, yes. But it was also Dell.

Although it had angered her to hear him belittle her contribution and deny her capabilities, what wounded far worse was the idea that his refusal might be based on more personal reasons—or rather, a lack of the personal connection she had hoped was developing between them.

Portia silently cursed the situation. She had never been very good at introspection, and right now she truly needed some insight into her own mind. And heart.

Carefully concealing any evidence of her inner anxiety, she smiled at Lord Epping as their dance ended and he brought her back to Emma's side. He gave a jaunty bow before striding back to his friends where they gathered near the entrance to the ballroom, likely masterminding their next prank and readying themselves for a hasty retreat.

There had been a time not long ago when Portia had envied the lords their fun, knowing that as a young lady she would never have the freedom to join them. That was before Dell, before she had discovered something far more worthy of her time and attention.

She would never forget the rush of satisfaction she had experienced when she'd discovered those children and knew she would do anything to ensure their safety and freedom. Of course, the tussle with Bricken hadn't left her mind either. But with proper training, she had no doubt she'd be able to handle any similar encounter with poise and confidence.

But how to convince Dell of that? He may think

the matter finished, but she was not ready to give up just yet.

Perhaps she would ask Hale to train her. The idea had merit.

Before she could explore the idea further, she caught sight of Fallbrook skulking not far away, watching her with a menacing expression. She stared back at him, refusing to be cowed by the flash of anger in his eyes. And as the distaste deepened across his handsome features, Portia lifted a brow and smiled. Mostly because she knew it would annoy him more than anything else.

His lips moved as he muttered something beneath his breath before he turned and disappeared into the crowd.

Taunting the man was probably not the smartest thing to do, but Portia couldn't help it. She would have to continue keeping an eye on the cad, and if he tried anything else with her or either of her sisters…well, Portia had taken to wearing Dell's slim knife as part of her daily accoutrements.

"You are frightening off potential dance partners with that scowl, dear sister."

The statement drew Portia rather forcefully out of her head. She hadn't even noticed Lily stepping up beside her. Her sister's smile was almost cheeky. It had been ages since she'd seen such mischief in her sister's expression.

What was this?

"It is a very precise strategy," Portia replied with an answering grin. "Though I do not suppose you would wish to employ it."

Lily shrugged gently, and her gaze slid to the side. "It is true. I happen to enjoy society. Many people do, you know. You do not always have to be so determined to resist contentment."

Portia narrowed her focus on Lily. "Tell me, then, what among all this fluff and nonsense manages to bring you joy, Sister?"

Portia may have missed her sister's flickering glance to the far right of the ballroom if she hadn't been watching intently for just such a telltale sign. She followed that glance to a group of lords, resplendent in their finery. The gentlemen, all of the highest social echelon, stood in quiet, dignified conversation. Portia noted a duke, no less than three earls, and a marquess among them.

*Bloody hell.* Was Lily's lover a member of that distinguished assemblage?

She slid a pointed gaze back to her sister, who had already moved her attention out toward the masses shifting through the crowded room.

"It is not all nonsense, Portia." Lily's tone softened, and she continued thoughtfully. "Deeper meaning does exist behind the veil if you are willing to seek it. If you have patience."

"And an endless supply of hope," Portia added intuitively.

Lily smiled, and her gaze gravitated once more toward the group of noble lords.

This time, Portia noted that one of the group—an intensely elegant, dark-eyed gentleman with a fierce and glowering expression—was staring back. His hard glare fell on her sister for only a moment, but oh, what a moment!

Portia expected the spot where Lily stood to ignite with the force of heat in that stare.

Lily clearly felt it as well. Her cheeks had turned a flushed pink, and her lips had parted on a swift inhale as she lowered her gaze to her hands.

Apparently, her gloves needed some serious adjusting just then.

Portia held back her amusement. But only just barely.

"Hope is a powerful incentive," Lily replied after a minute.

"Indeed," Portia noted in agreement.

She hoped, for Lily's sake, that her sister's affections were not misplaced. Though if she were any judge at all of what she had just observed, there was something very significant going on between Lily and her secret lover.

And, of course, thoughts of lovers led her back to thoughts of Dell.

How on earth was she going to convince the stubborn man to give her a chance?

That was the question that followed her for the next few days as she waited to hear word of Dell's return to London.

The longer she waited, the more foolish she felt for believing he would send for her.

Finally, she could wait no longer. Late one night, she remained in her bedroom until the house was quiet, which meant waiting until Lily had also slipped out through the gardens to the carriage waiting in the lane beyond.

Portia sat by the window of her darkened room, watching as her quiet, modest, dutiful sister dashed through the night to meet her lover.

She couldn't help but give a little snorting laugh.

Emma would be shocked to her toes to know what her little sisters were up to these days.

Enveloped in her full-length cloak, Portia crept down to the street and hailed a hack. As she tipped her head back to give the driver the address, she was stunned to see a familiar face. The very same man with the bushy beard and floppy felt hat who had driven her the day she had followed Turner to Hale's.

"Well, hello," she exclaimed with a smile. "What perfect luck."

"'Ello, miss. Up to some trouble again, are you?"

"Just a little," she answered pertly.

The round-faced man gave an indulgent nod. "Right then, in you go."

The drive to Honeycutt's went quickly, though not quite fast enough to outpace her growing anxiety.

She was being ridiculous. There was no reason to think anything was amiss simply because she hadn't heard from Dell. His return must have been delayed. Surely, if he were back in London, he would have sent word to her. Despite their argument, he must know she expected some sort of communication from him.

Still, as the hack approached the familiar address, something about the location was glaringly different.

The streetlamp outside was no longer broken. It lit up the block in a way that seemed eerily inappropriate.

With a stab of trepidation, Portia asked her driver to wait as she walked up to the front door and knocked. She wasn't sure why she knocked instead of entering boldly as she had in the past, but she was grateful she had as the door was opened by a sleepy young maid.

"Can I help you, miss?"

Portia stared, then stuttered, "I...I am here to see Mr. Honeycutt."

The maid shook her head as she glanced down the street cautiously. "Ain't no Honeycutt here. The home is newly let to Mr. and Mrs. Frye."

"I see," Portia replied, and she was afraid she did see. All too clearly.

She did not doubt the maid. Did not feel in her bones this was another aspect of Dell's disguise and deception as Nightshade. He hadn't been out of town at all in the last days. He had been executing this little escape.

And now he was gone. Well and truly gone.

Her steps were heavy as she returned to the hack. A fire burned in her stomach. Anger. Injured pride. And the creeping uncertainty of a kind of heartache she tried forcefully to ignore.

It was the heartache that ignited her temper and spurred her to action.

The cad thought he could be rid of her so easily, did he?

She looked up at the driver and gave a quick instruction before climbing back into the carriage.

It took only another half hour of circling the lanes and parks of the nearby neighborhood to find whom she sought. He sauntered down the street with a sack slung over one shoulder and a red cap on his tousled head.

Portia brought the carriage to a halt and boldly called out.

As soon as Thomas saw her, his face split with a wide grin, and he came jogging quickly to her side.

"'Ello, lovely."

Portia smiled. "Hello, Thomas. How have you been faring lately?"

He shrugged and sent a sweeping glance about the square. "Well enough, I s'pose."

"I see you are still under a certain character's employ," she said, giving a pointed look at his red cap.

"Aye," he replied as his gaze narrowed. "Are ye having some more trouble?"

"No," she quickly assured, warmed by his concern, "but I do need to speak with him. Where is his new location?"

Thomas shook his head and glanced down at his feet before he looked back up to meet her gaze with obvious regret. "You know I'm not s'pose to be telling anyone that."

"I do, and I'm sorry to put you in this position, but I really must see him. It is important"—she paused and decided to be honest with the boy—"to me personally."

Thomas gave a fierce little frown. "Damn me," he muttered under his breath. Then a second later, his dirt-streaked face lifted in a half smile that was frightfully knowing for such a young boy. "I be guessin' this means I've lost me chance with ya?"

Portia laughed. "I am afraid so. But I will still give you a kiss for your trouble."

"I'll take it." He swept his hat off his head, and Portia leaned forward to press her lips to his cheek as she had done once before.

The boy stepped back again. "Yer a prize, you are," he said with a grin as he smashed his hat back down on his head. "I may lose me hide fer this, but damn if it ain't worth it."

"I am infinitely grateful, Thomas. And if you are ever in need of anything with which I have means to assist, I hope you will come to me."

The boy shrugged off her offer with a prideful lift of his chin. "I do all right, miss. Don't worry 'bout me."

Fifteen minutes later, Portia was outside Nightshade's new headquarters, a modest-size brownstone not far from St. James's Park. It was certainly a step up as far as neighborhoods went from Honeycutt's modest abode.

She wasn't sure yet what she was going to say to Dell about his essentially disappearing on her. She was furious but intended to at least give him a chance to explain before she told him what she thought of such a dastardly move.

The building was deceptively quiet, looking empty and unlived-in.

Portia was not fooled. She walked boldly to the front door and gave a pert knock.

Only a moment went by before the door swung open on a well-oiled hinge to reveal Morley's expected image. The small man did not give any indication of surprise at seeing Portia there, just executed an acknowledging lift of his chin before turning to melt into the shadows at the back of the hall.

Portia stepped inside and closed the door behind her.

The place was dimly lit and significantly larger than Honeycutt's prior residence. Portia wondered how Dell had come by such a place and at such short notice.

She glanced around. Where would he be at this time of night?

She started up the stairs on silent feet. Part of her was dreading an encounter. Another part of her knew she had to see him, watch him as he said the words she suspected he would say.

Portia knew herself well enough to know her heart would trust nothing but the bold truth. And she had no intention of pining away, never having had the courage to face the man and demand an explanation for his behavior.

Light spilled from an open door on the second floor. Portia stopped in the doorway before entering the room.

Dell lounged in an overstuffed armchair, slumped back in the corner with a leg dangling over one chair arm and a book open in his large hands. He was intent upon what he was reading and did not immediately notice her arrival. His chocolate-and-caramel-colored hair was tousled and fell in careless waves over his slightly furrowed brow. A couple of days' growth of beard darkened his face, and as she watched, with her stomach twisting and her heart beating so loudly it was all she heard, he lifted his hand and ran his knuckles along the edge of his jaw.

Then, with a slight flick of his gaze, he looked up and saw her standing there. His expression didn't change. Not to show surprise or regret or joy at the sight of her.

The only acknowledgment was a subtle darkening of the gold in his eyes.

Portia's heart gave a frightful lurch as she felt an inexplicable urge to hit him. Or kiss him. She wasn't exactly sure which. Perhaps both.

"Hello," he said. His voice was low, and Portia detected a slight gravelly edge in the very masculine tone.

Annoyance, most likely.

She had always been an irritant to him. Was that why he had left?

Strolling forward—impudently—with her chin high and her gaze sharp, Portia looked pointedly at the book. "Another job for Nightshade?"

Dell closed the small volume—a journal—and tipped his chin back to look up at her. He was not the slightest bit intimidated by her stance or the hard tone of her voice.

"Why are you here?"

His cool impatience injured her more than anything else could have. Was she so easily dismissed? She couldn't believe it. Or perhaps she just didn't want to accept it.

She gave him a look of disappointment mixed with exaggerated disbelief.

"Come now, Turner, you know why I am here." She swept her cloak back over her shoulders. Her hurt sparked fear, and that gave swift rise to her temper. Crossing her arms tight beneath her breasts, she pinned him with a narrow-eyed stare. "Did you think you could just slink away, like a thief in the night? Did you think I could not find you? Or that I wouldn't look?"

He quirked a brow but didn't answer.

Portia sighed, feeling suddenly weighed down by everything she was feeling. She did not like this sense of uncertainty, this feeling of rejection. But there it was, heavy and dark inside her.

Why was she here?

She met Dell's shadowed gaze and felt it down to her

toes despite the distance he had forced between them. She saw the tension in his jaw, the deceptively relaxed sprawl of his lean, muscled body, the way he held the small book in his hands as though protecting it from her.

He didn't trust her.

And that hurt.

Portia took a deep breath. She straightened her spine and set her hands firmly on her hips. "Tell me the truth, Dell."

His frown darkened, and he shifted in his chair, setting both feet firmly on the ground. He appeared to be squaring off for battle.

But Portia also knew how to fight. In a way, she had been fighting all her life.

She tipped her head and smiled. There was no warmth in the smile, just a tight widening of her lips. "You have claimed more than once that my involvement with you, with Nightshade and his work, was just a lark, a temporary diversion to distract me from my boredom. Is that all I was to you, then?"

Her question inspired no reaction at all. Nothing, save a minute deepening in the crease of his brow. For some reason, that infinitesimal physical response made Portia's stomach flutter, and something—Lily's damnable hope—sparked in her heart.

With a gruff sound, Dell rose to his feet. He looked so strong and masculine. So confident and...cold.

The delicate light flickered inside her.

Dell took a step toward her—just one—and she nearly crumpled at his feet. The overpowering yearning to be taken up in his arms was disconcerting. Was she so weak, then?

But she didn't fall. She held her ground and held his gaze, as dark as it had become.

"What would you have me say, love?" he asked, his voice low and rough. "We've both had our fun. Now it is over. I have work to do, and you have"—he gave a dismissive wave of his hand—"your silks and suitors and soirées to attend to."

Her hands fisted. "You know I detest such trappings."

"It is your life. Go back to being a lady."

Portia wanted to scream her frustration, her disbelief, her personal conflict. But she would not give Turner an opportunity to belittle her any further. He thought her naive and pampered. Useless.

"I never was much of a lady to begin with," she scoffed. "And it seems I will have to leave out *suitors* going forward," she noted with a humorless smirk. "You took care of that one for me."

"With your eager cooperation, sweetheart."

She narrowed her gaze at his irreverent quip.

As she stared at him, she noticed the racing pulse in the side of his throat. She noted the fine sheen of sweat at his temples, though the room was not overly warm. She realized just how deliberate his casual behavior and cool demeanor appeared once she managed to shift her perception past her personal emotion to look closely enough.

*Interesting*.

᪣

Dell wanted to kick himself in the arse. Perhaps he'd have to visit Hale and go a few rounds with the prizefighter. Maybe then he'd feel properly punished for this.

Despite how fiercely she tried to hide it, he could see the hurt he had caused by his callous words and what could be seen as nothing less than betrayal. Her injured pride was obvious enough, but it was what lay beneath her fierce outward attitude that worried him most. That brief shadow of uncertainty that had crossed her flintlike gaze before she shoved it aside.

His gut twisted as he waited for her to fly into a temper. Instead, she did something he hadn't expected but was suddenly desperate to avoid.

She stepped toward him.

Her potent stare shifted into a sliding assessment as it traveled down the length of his form. His blood boiled hot and fierce beneath her searing gaze. His muscles tightened, and his chest nearly closed against new breath.

Portia's sensuality, as she turned it on him in full force, was a humbling thing. She held nothing back. Her honesty, desire, and anger were there for him to read in every splendid little detail of her face and every subtle movement of her body.

"Is this how it ends, then?" she asked, her voice low and deep, like raw silk.

It was all he could do to present himself as unaffected by her nearness. Every bit of his concentration was directed toward keeping his expression entirely neutral, bored even, as she tipped her head back.

He knew what she was about. He steeled himself to deny her, to reject this last bit of defiance on her part. Dell looked down into her gorgeous face, his heart racing wildly as he replied in a slow drawl, "It is already over."

A flash of heat and fire in her gaze.

She took another step, coming to within a few inches of him. Just as she shifted in preparation to reach for him—at the exact moment when he needed to push her away—he grasped her to him instead. Wrapping his hands around her upper arms, he crushed her to his chest and swooped down to claim her mouth.

The kiss was an instant fiery mating. Passion, anger, regret, and a delicate sort of longing fueled the moment. Their tongues danced, teeth scraped, lips bruised. And then, as a deep and luscious moan slid from her throat, Dell forcefully shoved her away. Perhaps with more strength than was required, though he worried if even the strongest power in nature would be enough to enforce a proper distance.

Though a deep-seated craving ran hot through every avenue of his body, Dell managed a cool tone as he asked, "Now, have you gotten what you wanted?"

Her mouth was beautifully reddened from his kiss, and her lips were still parted to claim rapid breaths. The silver fire in her gaze shot through him, flashing with fury and pain before she tempered its heat, refining it into a sharp, cold weapon.

"Indeed, I have," she replied icily as she stepped back. "You are a coward, Dell Turner."

He was far worse than that.

She drew the hood of her cloak up over her sable tresses, then without another word or even a fleeting glance, she turned and left him.

# Thirty-five

PORTIA SAW DELL EVERYWHERE.

At a ball the night after she had tracked him down to his new address, she swore she'd seen him dressed as a soldier, standing stoic and stiff along the wall. But he had disappeared before she could make her way to him to confirm her suspicion. The next night, she thought for certain he was one of the footmen passing trays of champagne and punch.

That is, until she crept up to the poor fellow, startling him so badly he upended his tray, and she realized he wasn't quite the proper height. Then there was the plump matron on the street, the hack driver with the long, red beard who passed by their carriage, the hawker who came to Angelique's door selling various trinkets and jewelry made of paste and glass.

He was everywhere and nowhere. And Portia was seriously starting to hate the man.

Well, she wanted to hate him, but she couldn't seem to manage it. Despite everything he had said to her, she still longed for his presence.

She was in serious need of a distraction.

And that was what she was hoping for as she attended a party celebrating the engagement of Lily's friend, the attractive and ambitious Miss Farindon, to the very upright and noble Mr. Pinkman.

The evening was going along as they all did, so it came as quite the surprise when everything took a decidedly more interesting turn due to a member of her own party.

Portia was engaged in a half-hearted conversation with the Lords Griffith, Epping, and Kitson, also known as the Merry Friars. It seemed the Friars were losing their infatuation with the round of reckless pranks they had indulged in all Season. A definite ennui had claimed the group.

That is, until a strange stir seemed to shift the tone of the room. Lord Kitson glanced out over the ballroom and nearly choked on his champagne. He gave Lord Epping a sharp nudge with his shoulder. Epping's eyes bulged comically, and he, in turn, nudged Griffith, who tried his best to ignore him, since he was at that moment in the midst of trying to convince his friends that a trip to Bath was just the thing to combat their universal boredom.

Portia watched the proceedings with a spark of amusement. But then Griffith finally glanced out in the direction his friends were staring and a second later exploded with a huge guffaw. He looked at Portia with a wide grin.

"Didn't know your chaperone was such a gem."

Portia turned slowly in place and scanned the crowd for Angelique's inky-black hair and the blood-red gown she had chosen for the evening. One never really knew what to expect of Angelique. It must be something quite exceptional for the rather jaded young bucks to find such humor in it.

It took less than a moment to find her, since practically everyone in the room had stopped what they were doing to watch the elderly dowager countess.

Laughter bubbled freely from Portia's chest at the splendid sight, and without a word to her companions, she made short work of crossing the room to meet up with Lily, who was already heading back to Emma's side near a fiercely twittering group of matrons and chaperones.

Falling into step with Lily, Portia did not bother to contain her delighted smile. "Isn't it just wonderful?"

Lily turned a rather stunned glance toward her and asked in a low tone, "What on earth?"

"I have no idea, but I cannot wait to find out."

Reaching Emma, who was perhaps the most stunned of them all, Lily and Portia took up positions on either side of their eldest sister, and the three of them stood in silence for a bit as they all watched Angelique twirl brilliantly about the dance floor on the arm of the young and currently astonished Lord Nicklethwaite in a splendid exhibition of the waltz.

Portia had had no idea her great-aunt could dance, let alone execute the sweeping movements with such grace and style.

"Do you think perhaps her many tales of being a ballerina in Paris prior to her marriage may not be imagined after all?" Lily asked, voicing the exact thoughts in Portia's head.

"And if *those* fantastical stories are true, what of all the others?"

"It is amazing, isn't it?" Emma finally added.

A sneaky smile slid across Lily's face. "Poor Lord Nicklethwaite. He seems a bit dazed."

Portia laughed. "He appears to be holding on for dear life."

"What could have prompted such a fantastic display?" Lily asked.

"She wanted to show me that everyone can dance," Emma replied, her tone flat with shock. The Chadwick who was always perfectly poised and in command of herself was unable to do much beyond stare at the spectacle before them.

"I believe she proved her point," Portia replied smugly.

She knew exactly what Angelique was doing—something she and Lily had not been able to accomplish. The old lady had found a way to jolt Emma out of her self-constructed cave of imperturbability, which had only gotten denser each day their sister went without seeing her former employer, Mr. Bentley. It seemed Angelique had taken it upon herself to give Emma a few nudges in the right direction.

"So, are you?" Portia prompted.

"Am I what?" Emma looked at her, confusion in her eyes.

Portia arched a brow. "Going to dance."

"No." Emma gave a sharp shake of her head. "Of course not."

"Why not?" Lily prodded.

Emma's tone when she replied revealed more

than she realized. "Because I am a spinster. I am not seeking suitors."

Though the words had been spoken many times before, this time, Portia heard the regret buried deep in her voice. And a very fine note of anger.

Good. It was time Emma railed against the confines of society she had so long been upholding. Portia certainly had no intention of being limited by such things. And if all the evidence regarding Lily's latest exploits were true, she did not either.

"What if Mr. Bentley was here?"

Portia looked to Lily. Her sister's tone had been more leading than hypothetical. Had she seen Mr. Bentley tonight?

Emma's entire demeanor changed at the mention of his name. Her focus flipped inward, and her expression became closed again. "Why would you mention him?"

"Because it is clear you miss him," Lily answered gently.

Portia briefly met Lily's gaze. It was time to push the issue with their stubborn sister. "You are obviously in love with the man."

Emma balked immediately, as expected. "That is ridiculous. I am not in love with Mr. Bentley."

"You are a terrible liar, Emma," Portia drawled. "If you could have seen what I saw that morning after you spent the night at his club, you would not bother to deny it."

"What did you see?"

Portia grinned. They had her.

"He cares, Emma," she answered. "The whole time he stood in our parlor, he watched you. Every slight change in your expression caused him to tense. He strained at the bit in his effort not to go to you. It might have been amusing if it hadn't been so sad, since you barely acknowledged him until it was time to shoo him out the door. Do not try to deny how gloomy you have been since you stopped going to the club. Your mood has been quite depressing. It is obvious you have been heartsick over the man."

"That is ridic—"

Emma's tired argument was cut short by Lily, who blurted out rather sharply, "It is not ridiculous. Must you be so full of pride, Emma?"

Lily's frown was practically ferocious. Portia was impressed.

"The man loves you, and you love him," her sister continued. "What exactly is the problem?"

"And don't you dare say it has anything to do with us."

Portia saw the exact moment of Emma's acceptance. Her sister's face softened almost sadly, and her gray eyes deepened to a darker hue.

"You are right. About me, anyway. I do love him."

"And what are you going to do about it?" Portia pushed again.

"What can I do? You both know his position in society. He is barely accepted in most circles and downright rejected from others."

"And?" Portia asked imperiously. She took serious exception to Emma's excuse. It was snobbish and not at all something she would have expected from her sister. "Tell me that is not your reason for denying your feelings for the man."

Emma shook her head. "Of course not. I honestly could not care less about what ninety-nine percent of the people in this room think of me. But I do care what they think of the two of you. Such a thing could ruin both of your chances for a great match."

Lily put her hand on Emma's arm. "Enough, Emma," she said gently but with a firm resolve. "I know I speak for us both when I say none of that matters a whit to either of us. We will manage quite well with fewer invitations and a closer, more loyal group of friends."

"Besides, we will still have Angelique," Portia noted with cheek, "the great example of virtue and propriety that she is, as our sponsor."

Emma looked out over the ballroom while Portia and Lily shared another look, waiting in silence for Emma to sort through her thoughts. There was no rushing Emma to any decision, and certainly not one as personal as this. Yet surprisingly, it took barely any time at all before Emma lifted her chin with fierce determination. The light came back to her eyes as she declared with her characteristic confidence, "I have to go back to the club. Right now. Tonight."

"Oh, I would not do that," Lily noted.

"Why not?" Emma asked.

Portia lifted a brow toward Lily in silent question and saw the secret sort of smile her sister could not conceal.

"Mr. Bentley is not there."

Emma turned to Lily. "How on earth could you know that?"

Lily's delight was apparent. "I saw him enter the game room about an hour ago. I am quite certain he is still there."

Emma lifted her gaze to stare intently toward the gaming room set at the back of the ballroom. Portia held her breath in anticipation of the only decision her sister could make. Honestly, if Emma did not grasp this opportunity now, Portia may have to go to more drastic measures. Just what, exactly, she did not know yet. But she would come up with something.

Then finally, Emma looked back to them, and Portia released a sigh of relief.

"Would you girls mind having one more eccentric in the family?" Emma asked. "I am quite certain I am about to do something rather shocking. Scandalous even."

*It's about time.*

"Excellent," Portia declared with a nod of agreement.

"Perhaps we shall become an entire family of eccentric women," Lily added with a soft blush that pinkened her cheeks.

Emma looked at her sharply, but when Lily gestured back toward the gaming room, Emma's attention followed. Their proper sister took a calming breath, then without even another glance toward either of her sisters, Emma started out across the ballroom in strong and sure strides.

Portia had never been more proud.

Emma had made her decision. There would be no stopping her.

Just as Emma passed out of sight, another figure crossed in front of them. A much-taller, darker, more imposing figure.

Lily must have seen him at the exact same moment. Her sister's stance suddenly tightened; her breath caught then released in a whispered sigh. The atmosphere around her practically simmered.

Though the gentleman spared only a passing glance in Lily's direction as he continued across the ballroom, it was more than enough.

Portia bit her lip against the urge to declare her knowledge of Lily's relationship with this lord. Seriously, how in hell did everyone in the ballroom not feel the heated connection between these two?

The lord strode out into the hall beyond. A second later, Lily turned toward her. Though she valiantly appeared to be trying to suppress it, a very wicked gleam was present in her eyes.

"I have to, ah…" she began, then stopped. "I have to go…"

The desire to roll her eyes was enormous, but Portia overcame it gallantly to answer in a rather dry tone, "Visit the necessary?"

Lily didn't seem to notice the cheek in Portia's suggestion as she accepted the excuse readily. "Yes, the necessary."

As her other sister walked away, Portia allowed herself the pleasure of a very dramatic eye roll, though no one was there to notice it. Glancing out over the ballroom, she railed against the sudden rush of loneliness—the deep-seated need to see Dell, speak with him about the development with her sisters, share the joy of it.

"Blast," she whispered as the feeling spread in a painful, rolling wave.

She did not sleep at all that night, but sat in a chair pulled up to her bedroom window and stared out at the lights of London. Her soul yearned to be among those lights. Her heart ached to be at Dell's side through the uncertain hours of night. Her body craved his presence, his touch, his heat, and his kisses.

The silence of her room was stifling, the stillness unsettling.

The buzz along her nerves made her grit her teeth. She needed to do something, but the one thing she wanted to do, she couldn't.

He wouldn't have her.

He was finished with her.

The thought made her angry, though not because she believed he didn't want her. She knew he did. That last kiss had proved it.

What fired her blood and kept her awake was the knowledge that he did not want her badly enough to ignore the differences between them and see only what really mattered.

"Bloody idiot," she muttered to herself, and it would not be the last time the epithet slipped from her mouth before dawn arrived. Unfortunately, the next day brought with it a deeper sense of melancholy as Portia was forced to acknowledge that for the first time in her life, she hadn't the slightest idea what to do.

# *Thirty-six*

DELL DONNED HIS HAT AS HE DESCENDED THE STEPS out in front of one of the largest and wealthiest mansions in Mayfair. He carried an ebony walking stick and wore fine, tailored clothes beneath his swirling greatcoat. Tonight, he was Mr. Thomas Davies, Esq., a barrister with a much more impressive education than Mr. Black, a more discretionary clientele, and deportment equal to that of the lords he served.

Mr. Davies, Esq., was assisting Nightshade in an investigation requiring extreme discretion, since the result of their work was likely to result in a scandal with the potential to rock the entire *ton*, not to mention devastate the members of one very elite family.

The most unusual aspect of the case was that the head of that fine, pedigreed, aristocratic family was Nightshade's client. Dell had never encountered a gentleman of such elevated breeding who was committed to seeking the truth behind dark family secrets, with the purpose of bringing them to light for the world to see. There were many people whose lives would not only be touched by the investigation, but altered forever. The lord himself would feel the worst of the repercussions, and Dell wanted to ensure that the man was quite clear on the likely outcome of the investigation.

He was.

The client made it clear that he wanted to go forward. Sparing no expense. The lord gave all appearances of having thought through the issue in great detail.

Morley was waiting with the carriage, and Dell gave him a short nod as he swung up into the vehicle and closed the door. As they rolled through one of the finest neighborhoods in London, Dell thought of Portia.

He didn't want to think of her, but he couldn't help but acknowledge that she would be fascinated by the lord's tale. Dell could just imagine how her eyes would widen and her lips part in shock as she read through an old man's devious confessions.

As quickly as it formed, the vision was shattered as Dell recalled—with a heavy press against his sternum—that she would never read the journals. The reminder immediately brought back the sense of unease he'd felt since that night in his study. That parting look she'd given him had been seared into his brain, making it impossible for him to forget that he had been the one to force that icy tone to her voice as she accused him of cowardice.

And she had been right. So damned right.

He dropped his head back and closed his eyes.

He had been terrified. For her life, for her future. But that was not what she'd meant, and he knew it.

She thought him a coward for not even trying to hold on to the greatest thing he was ever likely to possess.

But his decision had been necessary. For her safety and his sanity.

In time, she would see that he had done the right thing. Perhaps in time, he would too.

Arriving at his new residence, Dell asked Morley to join him in his study after he'd taken care of the carriage and horses. Once inside, Dell began discarding the accoutrements that made him Mr. Davies. The greatcoat, hat, and gloves in the hall. Then the evening coat, waistcoat, and cravat once he reached his bedroom. A pitcher of water was waiting at his vanity to remove the reddish hair dye and the face paint that had given him an almost ruddy complexion.

Finally himself again, Dell went to his study, poured a drink, and took a seat before the fire to wait for Morley.

And as he waited, Portia once again intruded upon his thoughts. She had been doing that incessantly since he'd forced their farewell. If it wasn't her imagined comments and insights into his work, then it was the flashing image of her smile, or her stubborn scowl of determination, or the fearless light of intelligence in her gaze. The worst was when he'd hear her sighs of passion and feel the silk of her hair sliding through his fingers.

Though it irritated Dell to no end, he welcomed the invasive thoughts as much as he dreaded them. Because in some twisted, torturous way, it kept her with him.

He tipped the remaining contents of his drink down his throat.

He was damned pathetic.

"Mr. Turner?"

Dell blinked and lifted his gaze to see Morley standing in front of him, wearing an expression that suggested he had been there for a while.

He frowned. "What is it?"

"You asked me to come up, sir."

He did?

Oh, right. The journals. The job.

As he advised Morley of his strategy for the investigation and they began to pin down the logistical elements that would need to be arranged, Dell could not help thinking of what role Portia could play at each crucial moment. What she would bring to the job with her passion, excitement, and determination to do what was right.

Damn it. He was losing his mind.

She was gone. He had made sure of it. And the few times he'd broken down and placed himself in her vicinity, just to make sure she was all right, he'd seen how she'd managed to slip right back into her life as part of the beau monde. He'd done the right thing by her.

So why the hell did he regret it with every breath he took?

"Sir?" Morley again.

Dell mumbled a curse as he realized he had lost the thread of their conversation. "Sorry, Morley. I seem to be distracted tonight."

The smaller man gave him a pinched look of disapproval. "Not just tonight, Mr. Turner. You've been like this ever since—"

"Don't say it," Dell interrupted in a forbidding tone.

But Morley wasn't cowed. His expression only got more pinched and pointed, making his hawklike nose stand out in harsh contrast as he stared back at Dell.

After a few moments of tense, uncomfortable silence, the servant spoke first. "You need her."

The phrase struck Dell like a cannonball to the chest. *You need her.*

Truer words had never been spoken.

He did. He needed her. And not just because she was fiercely intelligent and brave, and brought an element to his work he hadn't realized was missing, but also because she brought something into his life he hadn't known he wanted. Needed.

Damn.

She was better off without him, without the risk and danger he lived with every day. Without the thrill and excitement of his work. Without the passion they'd only just begun to explore.

Wasn't she?

Dell imagined her once again as she'd been when he'd spied her walking down Bond Street with her sisters and her great-aunt, or the time he'd watched her in the ballroom talking with those young bucks she called friends. But this time, he heard in his mind the many times she'd declared herself destined for something beyond what that life could provide. She had always insisted that she was more than a debutante, more than a gentleman's wife.

Maybe she was right in that, as well.

She had certainly been more than that to him. Portia Chadwick had swept into his life and changed him. She had stripped him bare with her boldness and honesty, and with her courage and compassion she had carved a new pattern on his identity. She had been his partner. And he needed her.

Double damn.

Dell rose to his feet, feeling a rush of energy and purpose. "Morley, there are a few changes that must be made to the arrangements."

"Of course, Mr. Turner."

❧

"*Très intéressant.*"

Portia glanced up from the poached egg she was viciously mutilating, curious only because she had no reason not to be.

"What is interesting?" Lily asked Angelique, who had already finished her meal and was reading through some letters.

"An old and dear friend of mine is planning a trip to Scotland. She intends to take a relaxing tour of the Highlands and the Isle of Skye." Angelique looked up from her letter to blink at the Chadwicks. "Why on earth would she wish to travel through such wild country?"

Emma smiled. "I am certain it is quite civilized, Angelique."

The dowager countess glanced back to her letter. "She says she expects to have some adventure before she dies." She snorted. "Ha! She is not so old—barely seventy, if I recall. Still, what adventure could possibly be found away from town? Now, Paris…that is a place for adventure. And romance." The lady actually waggled her eyebrows at the last.

Portia shook her head with a smile as she looked back at the unappealing mess of her poached egg.

Shoving her plate forward, she noted Lily watching her. She flashed her a smile, but her sister frowned in response.

Portia could have tried harder to hide her growing state of melancholy over the last couple of weeks, but honestly, as her sisters' relationships with their gentlemen progressed, it left Portia with fewer and fewer options for proper distraction.

Lily's secret lover had become her suitor, and a proposal seemed inevitable, though he hadn't actually declared himself in so many words yet. And Emma had a future of her own to plan with Mr. Bentley. The scandal of their unusual betrothal had overtaken the city for a time, and the talk was just now starting to die down.

Portia should have been thrilled by all the time she had to herself.

Unfortunately, the only thing she wanted to do was the one thing she absolutely refused to. She had too much pride and pure stubbornness to go back to Dell's brownstone again. If he couldn't appreciate her for what she was and all she could give, then he simply did not deserve her.

*Bloody idiot.*

"At least the fool woman has decided to take along a companion. In fact, that is the purpose of her letter." Angelique glanced up again to wave the sheets of her letter toward them. "She has heard of my three lovely nieces and wishes to inquire into whether or not one of you would be interested in accompanying her."

"Now, that is an interesting prospect," Emma replied with some enthusiasm. "Do you know how long she plans to be away?"

Angelique brought the letter into her view. "Ah, here it is. It shall be a nine-week trip. *Mon dieu*, she plans to depart in only eight days."

Emma glanced between Lily and Portia. "It is not much time to prepare, but summer is approaching, and the Season will be coming to an end soon. I suppose it would be a nice change of pace. Lily, Portia? Would either of you be interested in getting out of town for a while?"

The girls exchanged a silent glance. Portia could see the brief flash of panic in Lily's gaze. No, her sister would not wish to leave town. Not while her gentleman remained.

Portia, on the other hand, had absolutely nothing to keep her in London.

"I will go," she stated. As soon as the words were free of her mouth, she felt a crushing sense of loss. But if the idea of leaving town made her feel so wretched, then it was exactly what she needed to do.

No more of this morose and melancholy existence.

She needed to shake things up again, and a jaunt through the northern country may prove to be the perfect opportunity. At least Dell would be too far away for her to be tempted to swallow her pride and go to him again.

"Yes. I will go. It will be a lovely time," she said with a tight little smile.

Two days before Portia was due to leave London with the elderly Lady Burnbrooke, she snuck from Angelique's town house one last time.

It was late afternoon, and she had claimed the need for a rest before attending the birthday party of Lady Winterdale's eldest granddaughter that evening.

She had crept up to Angelique's costume room instead, and just for fun, dressed in the clothes of a housemaid, complete with apron and mobcap. It was slightly old-fashioned, but certainly not so much it would cause any undue stir on the street.

As she slipped from the servants' entrance and started off at a leisurely stroll, she felt a breath of liberation seep through her skin and begin to flow gently through her blood. She was anonymous. Just another young working girl heading off on an errand. After a block, her steps grew lighter. After two, a smile curled the corners of her mouth.

Though she was enjoying the walk, she hailed a hack several blocks from Angelique's and gave the driver an address. Her destination was too far to walk the entire way.

In a frustratingly similar experience to when she had sought Dell the last time, she arrived to find the place empty. There was, however, a note tacked to the door, directing anyone who came by to a new address not too far away.

She soon arrived at a modest-size town house in a relatively sedate and comfortable neighborhood.

Portia worried she may have gone to the wrong place but approached the door anyway.

A maid of middle age answered her knock. The

woman's expression was harried, her cheeks flushed, and her brown hair a riot beneath a lace cap that had become slightly askew. Portia opened her mouth to speak but was interrupted by a tremendous shriek followed by a low and frightening growl as a tiny girl with pale curls in a flounced pink dress raced across the small entryway. The very serious little boy from Bricken's warehouse was close on Claire's heels, a wide smile splitting his face as he looked back over his shoulder.

Claire grasped the boy's hand and swung around behind him just as Hale entered the foyer with another thunderous growl.

Both children shivered in fright and shook with laughter as Hale bore down upon them to sweep them both up in his arms. The boy got tossed over Hale's broad shoulder, while Claire was hoisted against Hale's chest, to their mutual delight.

It was in that moment that Hale noted Portia standing in his doorway.

"Uh, hello," he said rather dumbly as he lowered the children back to the floor. Both of them responded with groans of dismay.

"Oh, please do not stop your play on my account," Portia said quickly, unable to keep from smiling at the scene. "I would never presume to interrupt such a wonderful romp."

Hale nodded toward the maid who had opened the door, and she came forward with spread arms to corral the children toward the back of the house with promises of thick cream and fresh tarts to refresh them after their play.

Portia watched the children leave, Claire's tiny hand folded securely in the boy's. They seemed quite well.

She was surprised and admitted that a part of her had hoped he may need some help. It would have been something for her to do, at least.

Glancing back to Hale, she noted that he watched her with an expression that combined a forbidding glower of annoyance with a slightly raised brow of inquiry. Then he dropped his glance to her maid's uniform and gave a short jerk of his chin.

"On another job for Nightshade?"

"No," Portia replied, standing a bit taller, "I am here on my own."

Now both of Hale's brows lifted, and his eyes flashed with open curiosity.

"All right, then. Come on into the parlor. It may as well be used for something more than gathering dust."

Portia followed Hale to the quaint little room that must have been furnished prior to Hale's acquisition of it. She just could not imagine him choosing the pale-pink, flowered wallpaper and the nearly miniature-size settee and chairs.

She took a seat on the settee and looked about the room. Noting the various chintzy bric-a-brac and lacy accents that abounded, she couldn't keep a smirk of amusement from her lips as she said, "You keep a very lovely home, Mr. Hale."

He grunted. "It was the best I could find under short notice."

"I stopped first at your offices. They appeared closed."

Hale had stalked toward the fireplace to lean an arm on the mantel. Apparently, he didn't trust the furniture with his great weight.

Portia did not blame him.

"I couldn't exactly keep the children in that one-room hovel, could I?"

"I suppose not," Portia agreed.

"I've decided to shift my business focus, turn the office into a full training space."

"Really?" She was intrigued.

The large man shrugged his great shoulders. "Turner gave me the idea. I trained him, after all, and a few others. There are places all over town that could make good use of a well-trained doorman or personal guard."

At the mention of Dell, Portia had tensed from her head to her toes and realized, in that moment, she had come here with another motive beyond wanting to assure herself of the children's care.

But there was no way in hell she was going to ask Hale about Dell Turner.

"An excellent idea. I am certain you will do quite well in such an endeavor." The tension in her limbs coalesced into a hard knot in her stomach. "The children seem well settled," she noted.

Hale's face hardened a bit, and his voice lowered. "That is why you are here? Were you worried I'd forget to feed them? Lock them in a closet?"

Portia ignored his intimidation tactic and remained seated casually with her head tipped back as she met his harsh gaze. Then she offered a sweet smile. "Something like that."

This time his grunt sounded more like a chuckle. Then he gave a shake of his head and looked down at his hands as he replied, "I'm in way over my head, that's the truth. But Claire is safe now, and I won't let anything harm her again."

"Has she exhibited any aftereffects of her ordeal?" Portia asked gently.

"Nightmares, sometimes. Otherwise, she seems all right as long as Freddie isn't far away."

"She has really attached herself to the boy, then?"

"Like a leech," Hale answered as he looked up again. "I can only hope he is worthy of her devotion."

"Have you learned anything of his true identity?"

"No. Turner is looking into things, but the boy himself is as tight-lipped as a nun." He paused to push his large hands back through the strands of hair that had fallen from the queue at his nape during his play with the children. "Whatever he's hiding, he won't give it up easily."

"Do you feel he poses any threat?" Portia asked.

Hale heaved a great sigh and met her gaze openly. "No. I don't trust many people, but oddly enough, I do trust the lad."

Portia rose to her feet, feeling some relief at what he had said. Things would end up working out all right for this odd little makeshift family. She gave him another smile. "Then I am certain all will be well in the end. If anyone can discover the truth, it is Turner."

"I'm a mite surprised you aren't a part of that anymore," Hale suggested with a leading tone.

"Yes, well…" She allowed the words to trail off. "If you see Dell Turner, please don't tell him I came by."

Hale arched a brow but said nothing.

Portia wasn't even sure why she had requested that Hale keep her visit secret. Maybe she just wanted Dell to be wondering about her as much as she wondered about him.

"I should be going," she said. "If there is anything I can do for the children, please let me know."

Hale nodded, and Portia left feeling much better on one account and infinitely worse on another. It was a good thing she was leaving England for a while. A change in scenery was exactly what she needed.

She only hoped being companion to Lady Burnbrooke would not prove to be too tedious.

# Thirty-seven

THE DAY OF PORTIA'S DEPARTURE DAWNED GRAY AND misty. A perfect match for her mood.

She tried—really, honest-to-goodness tried—to dredge up some excitement for the trip. But melancholia had a grip on her unlike any she had experienced before. Portia often got moody or fell into an emotional slump, but it never took very long for her to find the proper motivation to pull herself out again.

Not this time.

Random and frequent thoughts of Dell kept her in a constant state of feeling as though something was left unfinished. And that annoyed her to no end.

They belonged together. As lovers and partners in life and work.

But she had been right to walk away. Hadn't she?

Her pride insisted it was so, but something deeper, stronger, more insistent questioned whether or not she should have pushed him harder to accept the truth.

Ah! She hated dealing with all of this nonsense. Such things should be straightforward and simple. How on earth did other people manage affairs of the heart?

Emma had found a way with her Mr. Bentley, though it had admittedly taken some time.

Lily was also undeniably content.

Why was Portia struggling so wretchedly?

It was Dell's fault. Obviously. The man was more stubborn than she was.

Those were the thoughts still racing through her mind as she stood on Angelique's front stoop, awaiting the arrival of the elderly and adventurous Lady Burnbrooke, a woman she had never met, yet who she intended to spend the next several weeks attending. Her bags were packed and waiting beside her, and she had already made her good-byes. Emma had tried insisting she wait in the parlor, but Portia preferred the fresh air.

She was leaving town to clear her head. When she returned, if thoughts of Dell still tormented her, she would simply have to find a way past his reticence.

But what if he truly did not feel for her the way she felt for him?

Portia refused to entertain that possibility. She had seen the look in his eyes that last night in the dressing room. She had not misinterpreted what she had seen there.

A well-appointed carriage, painted a garish pink and yellow with small accents in vivid purple, drew up in front of the house. Even the driver and groom wore the unfortunate colors.

She would be touring Scotland in that gaudy conveyance?

With a roll of her eyes, Portia turned to the footman and gave a nod. He immediately swept up the first of her bags and headed down the steps to the street.

Portia hesitated. Then grew angry with herself for the strain of doubt running through her.

As she stood there staring straight forward, Lady Burnbrooke's groom hopped down from his perch and rushed forward to open the carriage door with a flourish before moving to assist Angelique's footman with securing her luggage.

Still, Portia could not bring herself to leave the top step of Angelique's front stoop.

A figure appeared in the open door of the carriage: a rather large woman, dressed in pink and yellow to match her vehicle, wearing a bonnet with more feathers and fruit than any one person should possess in a single arrangement. Lady Burnbrooke lifted her hand to wave a lacy handkerchief toward Portia as she called out in a nasally whine, "Hallooo, dear."

Oh no. The lady could not possibly sound like that all the time. Portia's ears would surely be bleeding by the end of this trip.

Unable to put it off any longer, she started toward the carriage.

Lady Burnbrooke sat back again, but as Portia approached, she saw that even though it was a rather large carriage, the lady and her many ruffled skirts took up much of the vehicle's interior. Portia would likely be relegated to riding on the opposite seat, which meant she would be traveling backward. For nine weeks.

Suppressing a groan, Portia glanced toward the horses, a lovely set of four matched grays, as they stamped their hooves in their desire to be moving again. At least they were anxious to be off.

When she flicked a glance past the driver, she stopped in surprise.

Twinkling eyes met hers above a wide grin framed by a bushy gray beard. "Hello, miss. How do ye fare this fine day?"

"It's you," Portia exclaimed with an answering smile. For some reason, seeing her helpful hack driver sparked a hope that perhaps this trip would not be so bad after all.

He tugged on his forelock. "Jem Brighton, at your service again, miss."

"You do seem to show up at the most opportune times. Do you know that, Mr. Brighton?"

His rolling chuckle was quite infectious. "Sure as the sun shines...most days," he replied with a wink and glance toward the gloomy sky.

"And a new position, it would appear."

"Indeed, miss. Moving up in the world," the driver quipped as he slid a disparaging glance toward his pink-and-yellow livery.

Portia laughed and started forward again, only to be brought up abruptly once more when she reached the groom who waited patiently by the carriage door with his hand ready to help her into the vehicle.

"Thomas!" This time her exclamation was accompanied by a short laugh and quick, impulsive hug for the young lad. "What on earth are you doing here?" she asked as she drew back again to see the boy's wide grin.

"Got meself a permanent position, I did."

"And what of your previous work?" she asked carefully.

Thomas made a comical face that combined disgust with affronted pride. "Seems my loyalty came into question."

"Because of me? Oh, Thomas, I am sorry."

"No worries, miss. This new lot suits me fine."

He grinned again, and Portia experienced a sharp twinge of suspicion. The fine hair on her nape and along her arms stood up, and a flutter of something unexpected traversed her awareness.

How interesting.

She glanced again at the hack driver, then back to Thomas, then snuck a swift peek into the carriage. All she saw was a mass of pink-and-yellow flounces.

Interesting, indeed.

With a very different sort of feeling rushing through her, she took Thomas's hand, climbed into the carriage, and took the back-facing seat.

Thomas closed the door, and within a moment, they started off.

Looking at the person who would be her companion for the next several weeks, Portia acknowledged with a delicious tightening in her low belly that Lady Burnbrooke was a very ugly lady.

But an extremely handsome man.

"You make a deplorable matron, Dell Turner," she stated in a calm and controlled voice, though her insides were rioting something fierce.

Dell grasped the bonnet with gray wig attached and tore it from his head. Opening the carriage window, he tossed the offending thing out onto the wind before closing the window again and drawing the curtains. Then he grasped the front of his gown and tore it away in one swift swipe and kicked the ugly heap to the corner of the carriage floor with a vengeance.

"Thank God I can be rid of that ridiculous getup. Remind me to never again think I can pull off a female."

Portia did not reply. His implication was that she may have some future opportunity to dissuade him from such an act.

The other reason she couldn't speak was because he had worn only breeches beneath the gown and was now naked from the waist up. Anything she might have said was entirely lost to her.

She resisted the frown of disappointment that threatened when he reached beneath his seat cushion and pulled out a neatly folded shirt and coat. He pulled the shirt over his head but left the coat on the seat beside him. Only then did he direct his gaze to her.

"Was this elaborate getup necessary?" she asked.

The look in his eyes was completely unreadable.

Portia made sure hers was as well. Though her heart was pounding thunderously, and the muscles along her spine were so tense that she was certain the slightest extra movement would snap her in two.

"Considering the possibility that you would refuse to come along once you knew it was me waiting for you, yes, it was. Anyone who bothered to look saw you entering a carriage with the elderly and eccentric Lady Burnbrooke. If you wish"—he paused, as though reluctant to say the next part—"I can drop you back at home with no damage to your reputation. You can tell your family that you and the lady did not suit."

As far as explanations went, it had not shed much

light on the current situation or his intentions, and he did not offer anything more.

After a while, the tense silence got to be too much for her. "Why am I here, Turner?" she asked in the most disaffected tone she could manage.

He tipped his head and lowered his chin. The act gave him the look of a man who was perhaps a touch uncertain. That slight change in his manner sent a thrill of curiosity and anticipation racing through her blood.

What was this?

Dell Turner was never uncertain about anything.

"I have need of your assistance in my current investigation."

Portia's brows shot up before she could stop them. "Really? You have need of *my* assistance?" Her tone was sarcastic, while everything in her was hopeful.

His gaze narrowed at her reply, and he gave a nod.

"I am untrained. My involvement in finding Claire was nothing but a lark, a momentary distraction for a pampered, useless, selfish, spoiled—"

"I never called you those things," he interrupted with a dark scowl.

"But you implied every one of them."

He did not deny it, and their argument fell back into silent staring.

Portia waited for his next move with more patience than she had ever thought herself capable of. She could make this easy for him and leap across the carriage into his lap and say all was forgiven, that she had never believed him anyway, that she would go anywhere with him as long as he accepted all of her, at his side and in his bed.

But Portia preferred to make him work for it a bit.

He had come for her, and that definitely said something.

But not enough.

She crossed her arms over her chest and forced her spine to relax enough to lean against the back of her seat. This time, she would prove to be more stubborn than he was.

Perhaps ten minutes passed before he spoke again, though to Portia it felt closer to eternity.

"This job may be of particular interest to you. It involves someone of your acquaintance."

"Is that so?" She refused to turn away from her perusal out the window, though that comment did spark her curiosity.

He grunted an affirmative response. Then a moment later added, "It will take us all around Britain, starting with this trip to the Scottish Highlands."

Portia kept her voice casual. "So, we *are* heading that way. I was wondering."

"Does that mean you agree to come with me?" he asked, his voice low, a raw note hidden in the depths.

Her heart leapt like a wild deer at the sound of it, and she finally turned to look at him.

His frown was really quite attractive. His obvious struggle with her reserved manner made her want to laugh in an absurd way. She managed to resist. "I suppose that all depends."

"On…?"

Portia took a leveling breath. Her fingers curled into tight fists, but she kept her gaze steady and direct on him. She would not waver.

"Why do you want me?"

She thought at first he intended to wave off the question. His expression tensed, and his gaze became even darker. But then he heaved a great sigh and leaned forward in the carriage. Propping his elbows on his thighs, he reached across to set his large hands on her knees as he looked up at her from beneath his brows.

"Portia Chadwick," he began in as earnest a tone as she had ever heard from him, "I want you with me because of your intuitive and inquisitive nature. Your curiosity and compassion fill the spaces where I am lacking. You are driven in your commitment to seeing things through. I admire the ferocity of your spirit and the fire of your intellect."

He paused to run his hands over the bend of her knees and up along the outer curve of her thighs.

Portia sincerely wished she hadn't worn a pelisse over her traveling gown, expecting cooler weather as they traveled north. The heat of his hands burned, but in a delicious way that she wanted to feel everywhere. She clenched her gloved hands into tight fists as she pressed them firmly into the cushioned seat on either side of her hips.

"You inspire me to do better things," he added intimately. "To be better."

Portia had become quite breathless but managed to ask in a normal tone, "Better in your work?"

The look in his eyes melted her insides, reducing everything she was to a soft, melty mess. "In everything."

A delicate shiver ran down her spine, trailing sparks of warmth in its wake.

He certainly knew just what to say. But she was not

finished with him yet. Forcing a sternness to her gaze, she gave him a questioning look.

"All right, Turner. I will agree to assist you on this undertaking on the condition that you immediately begin my training in the skills necessary for someone working alongside Nightshade."

The corner of his mouth curled upward. "Such as?"

Blast, but the man could make a common-enough phrase sound unbelievably sensual.

"I need to learn how to shoot a gun—various types, of course. And use a knife effectively. And I want to learn those defensive maneuvers you displayed with Gregor Dune's men." The excitement of actually becoming Nightshade's partner was intoxicating. There was so much to learn from Dell. "You must teach me the fighting methods Hale taught you. And I want to start practicing different accents."

Her litany was interrupted in a rather wonderful way as he slid from his seat to crouch before her at the same time that he lifted his hands to her face and brought her mouth to his.

The taste of him eliminated all thought. The scent of him, the feel of his rough hands against her cheeks, the delicious sweep of his tongue, and the suddenly overwhelming knowledge that she had him now and she was not letting him go, filled her with such deep pleasure that she feared she was going to cry.

But then he shifted the nature of the kiss, and it became so much more. He tilted his head, and the strokes of his tongue became longer and more languid and alternated with sensual sips of her lips.

Portia willingly—eagerly—gave herself up to his

direction. She ran her hands up his sides then along the taut muscles of his arms until she could slide her fingers over his where he still cradled her face.

Then she pulled back from the kiss with significant reluctance, just far enough to meet his gaze.

"You are an idiot," she whispered.

"I know."

"You will never be rid of me, you realize."

He smiled. "I hope not."

"Do you mean that?"

"With every bit of me. Come here."

Dell drew her along with him to his seat, pulling her against his side with one arm around her back, his large hand cupping her hip. Portia rested her head against his shoulder and removed her gloves to toss them across the carriage to the seat she had just vacated. Then she took his other hand in hers and brought it to her lap.

"I missed you, Portia," he said in a lovely, low-sounding murmur against her temple.

"I missed you too. You know I love you, don't you?"

She felt him stiffen and held her breath as she waited for his response.

"I had hoped," he finally replied, and that raw tone had entered his voice again, "but I feared..."

When he didn't go on, Portia lifted her head and twisted her upper body to look into his face. "What did you fear?" she asked.

"That the appeal was all in the adventure, and I was just another small part that went along with it."

"Bloody hell," she exclaimed in astonishment. She'd had no idea. "You could never be a small part of anything, Dell Turner."

Turning toward him more fully, she looked at him with the full force of everything she felt for him in her gaze. "The entire world exists in you. *You* are the adventure. The rest is just an added benefit. All I want is the chance to share it with you. All of it. Work, life, the good, the bad." She gave a rueful smile. "That sounds terribly greedy, but it's the truth of it."

A grin split his face. "Sounds perfect."

Portia grinned back at him. "I am glad you think so."

He lifted his hands to brush the backs of his knuckles across the crest of her cheekbone, then down along her jaw and beneath her chin to tip her face up to his. "I love you too, you know."

She allowed her eyelashes to sweep down over her gaze as she parted her lips on a soft sigh. "I know."

He kissed her again, for a blessedly long time. Until her fingers and toes tingled and her belly erupted in a rush of fluttering yearning. By the time he pulled back, she had drawn her legs up over his lap, and her hands had tangled in the front of his shirt. She was hot and wild with the craving in her soul. "How long until we reach our first stop?"

Dell chuckled and grasped her hips in his hands to lift her up and over him so she could straddle his thighs.

"An awfully long time, I'm afraid," he replied, already releasing the buttons of her pelisse, then peeling it down her arms before flinging the garment aside.

Portia grasped his shirt and drew it over his head and tossed it over her shoulder.

"Where exactly is this job taking us?"

"Ultimately, to the Isle of Skye," he answered as he began the work of releasing the buttons along the back of her gown, "but there is no rush. I thought we'd first stay a couple of days in a quaint little village I know of just over the border."

"Oh?" Portia asked, only half interested in what he was saying as his upper torso was bare again. She couldn't keep herself from delicately tracing her fingers over the defined lines of muscles crossing his abdomen. "Sounds lovely."

"While there, we will have to complete the first task of our trip. It isn't proper, you know, for an unmarried couple to travel alone together."

His explanation came just as he lifted her gown up over her head. Her choked exclamation at his reply got muffled in her skirts before she was free again to stare hard at him in astonishment.

"Excuse me?" she asked dumbly.

He stopped in the middle of untying her short stays and looked at her almost sheepishly.

"If you are in agreement, that is."

"Dell Turner, are you asking me—"

His fierce frown cut her off.

"Won't you let me do the proposing this time?"

Portia grinned and squirmed a bit on his lap as she sat straighter and folded her hands demurely on his lower abdomen. "I suppose it is only fair we each have a turn." She gave a sharp nod. "You may continue."

He chuckled and grabbed her buttocks in his hands to draw her forward until her groin pressed to his.

Portia caught her breath on a ragged gasp. His desire was hard and hot beneath her, and the light of love shone brightly in his eyes.

"Nothing would make me happier than to have

you for a partner and my wife. Will you marry me in Scotland?"

"Yes, yes, and yes," Portia replied enthusiastically as she wrapped her arms around his neck and kissed him soundly, then added, "Just remember I asked you first."

Dell firmed his lips against a smile and arced one brow as his hands ran up and down her back. "If I recall, you said we should just pretend marriage. If that's what you'd prefer…?"

Portia knew he was teasing her, but she grasped his face firmly in her hands and nearly growled, "Don't you dare take it back. You are mine."

He did smile then. "And you are mine," he said in a seductively low voice that made Portia's stomach flutter. He kissed her, and her whole being seemed to soar.

"Are you all right with your family not being present for the wedding?"

Portia thought about it then shook her head. "My sisters and I have been through a great deal together since our mother's death. And I love them dearly, but I am quite content to begin this new adventure with just the two of us. We can always have a grand celebration once we return to London."

She realized something and gasped as her eyes widened. "Wait a minute. How on earth did you manage to arrange this little getaway in the first place? Is there a Lady Burnbrooke? What will Angelique think when she discovers this farce?"

Dell just laughed and went back to removing her stays.

"I am serious," Portia continued, "how did you manage this whole thing?"

"I think I shall save that revelation for another time."

"You cannot keep me in this kind of suspense. You must tell me."

"I prefer to have a few secrets and surprises up my sleeve. I would not want you to get bored."

Portia eyed him suspiciously, the wheels in her mind turning at record speed as she tried to figure out how he had gotten around her great-aunt.

Then again, maybe he hadn't gotten around her.

The thought was rather intriguing.

"You may be right," she said with a secret sort of smile. "I will likely have a few surprises for you along the way too."

"I do not doubt it for a moment," he said, but then his features shifted as he gave her a regretful look. "I *was* an idiot, Portia. I tried to turn my back on this. On what we are together. I could have lost you forever."

Portia stopped him with a press of her fingertips to his lips. "Not possible. I would have gone back to you. Once I finished being furious with you for your narrow-minded stubbornness and figured out a way to convince you that we belong together." She smiled. "Though I am pleased you came to your senses on your own."

With a sigh of relief, Dell wrapped his arms around her narrow waist, enfolding her in a deep embrace as he buried his face in the curve of her neck and breathed deeply. "We are good, then, love?"

"I believe we are quite fantastic. Though we will be even more so when I can call myself Mrs. Turner."

He turned his head to press his lips to the side of her throat, sending tingles down her arms. "You are sure you want to be my wife? Marriage to me will be very different from what you would have expected with one of your society gentlemen."

"Thank God," Portia exclaimed, then shivered as he trailed his lips up to the sensitive spot behind her ear. She tipped her head to the side, allowing him more access as she ran her hands down the smooth muscles of his back. "I want nothing more than to be your wife, your lover, your partner, the mother of your children," she said in a breathless murmur.

A quiet growl sounded from deep in his throat as he nipped at her earlobe with his teeth. "I rather like the sound of all those," he said.

"So do I. Now finish removing these wretched stays."

His laughter filled her with warmth and contentment to a degree Portia had never expected to experience.

# Epilogue

PORTIA GRINNED UP AT HER HUSBAND AS THEY MADE A turn on the dance floor.

"You are a superb dancer, Mr. Turner."

Dell looked down at her, his expression dubious. "You are a shameless liar."

She laughed. "Not at all." She eased in a little closer to him—closer than propriety would deem modest—as they made another turn about the floor. She had never loved to waltz so much as she did now that she could dance with Dell. Looking up at him, with her most coy and sensual glance, she murmured in an intentionally sultry voice, "Everything you do is superb."

She loved watching how his eyes darkened with the rush of desire she could so easily inspire.

It never got old, this wife business.

His hand at the small of her back tensed, and he drew her to him until only a breath kept their bodies from touching full-length.

Heat smoldered in the space between them, infusing Portia with a wealth of love and pure, complete happiness. During these past months as man and wife, they had traveled through the rough and inspiring beauty that was northern Scotland. They had explored Wales, spent time in quaint country villages, and peeked into areas of London Portia had never known existed. Every day was something new and exciting, but the most exciting of all was being able to share it with Dell.

He knew just how to direct her focus when she became restless. He was calm when she flew into a temper, and possessed a wealth of patience when she lost hers. In return, she managed to convince him to focus on more worthy jobs. She showed him that there was good in the world, and he could contribute to that good in a phenomenal way. He had come to trust her implicitly and had even started spending full days away from his work, days filled with the simple joy of being Mr. and Mrs. Turner. And along the way, he had taught her so many things.

To her pure delight, Portia was becoming quite adept at many of the skills in which Dell had started training her. Though Nightshade's focus had a far less mercenary bent than it had in the past, the work they did was still often quite dangerous. Portia found she was a natural with a pistol. Through endless practice, she had also developed her lock-picking talent to cover just about any kind of lock one could imagine. Her skill in that area far surpassed her husband's.

Husband.

She loved that word.

Lily and Emma had certainly been shocked the first time they'd heard her say it.

Perhaps not oddly at all, Angelique hadn't seemed the slightest bit surprised.

Of course, Portia had to explain everything to her sisters, and though they were stunned by her adamant insistence that she couldn't be happier in her new role as wife and partner to a mysterious man of the night, they slowly grew more accustomed to the idea as they got to know Dell.

And Emma, bless her, was so caught up in her own plans that she didn't seem the least bit worried about the scandal Portia's elopement had caused among the *ton*. The scandal delighted Portia, but lasted only a week or so before something juicier occurred for the gossipmongers to sink their teeth into.

Lily had insisted upon an intimate discussion the night before Portia was to move her belongings over to Dell's place. Her concern was for Portia's heart. It had not taken much to convince her gentle sister that her heart couldn't possibly be in safer, more capable, tender, loving, wonderful hands.

Indeed, Portia couldn't be more pleased with her husband's hands, his heart, his exceptional mind, his endless bravery, or the quiet nobility he displayed without even knowing it. Not to mention his lean-muscled body and the way he made her feel like the most desirable creature that ever existed.

"Portia," Dell said in a low tone, heavy with warning.

She blinked innocently. "What?" she asked as she met his narrowed stare with a carefully measured smile she knew he would see through in an instant.

And he did. His jaw tensed, and his fingers flexed against her waist.

Then he lifted his gaze to scan the ballroom.

"How much longer are we expected to stay?"

A thrill coursed along every nerve in Portia's body, and she looked about for her sister. By pure habit, she scanned the outer rim of the room, looking for Emma among the matrons and chaperones, then shook her head at her own folly. Emma would not be consigned to that area again for a very long time.

She finally spotted her oldest sister standing close beside her new husband, both still looking resplendent in their wedding finery.

Portia had been tickled beyond measure to learn that her very proper, follow-the-rules sister had decided on an evening celebration for her wedding rather than the traditional breakfast. Of course, Emma had still insisted upon planning every detail to death, doing her best to trim the extravagant budget Bentley had insisted upon. In the end, Bentley's club had been turned out in spectacular fashion for the event.

The Chadwick sisters had managed to astonish the society they had been so focused on impressing. Portia perhaps least of all, since everyone had suspected from the start that she would end up doing something shocking eventually.

That Emma had caused a stir could never have been predicted. And then there was Lily's astounding *coup*. An earl, no less.

"I have something special for you tonight."

Portia glanced at her husband with open curiosity as desire flared acutely through her center. "Something special?"

He chuckled. "I knew that would gain your attention."

She gave him a sly grin. "Are you certain you wouldn't like to stay a while, drink some punch, engage in small talk?"

His answer was a low, intimate growl as his brows drew into a forbidding scowl.

Portia laughed. "Give me ten minutes to say good-bye."

It took her only five before they were heading out to their carriage, her arm slipped into the bend of Dell's elbow, a silly grin widening her lips.

As soon as the carriage door closed them in darkness, Dell drew her in against his side and started kissing her. Another thing she loved so much. Sometimes he would just kiss her. With languid, unhurried attention, holding her close. As though he simply craved the taste of her and wanted to sip from her lips forever.

Such kisses often heated Portia's blood to the point where she had to insist upon taking things further.

Tonight, however, she found herself content to sink into the lovely bliss of his kisses.

When they stopped and he helped her down to the ground, it took her a moment to realize they had not gone home. She blinked away the sensual haze from her mind and stood in confusion, looking around at the neat row of newly built and elegant town houses lining the street.

When she finally looked back at Dell, it was to see him watching her intently.

"What is this?" she asked.

"Come," he said, holding out his hand. "I will show you."

Fingers linked, they walked up the steps of the house in front of them. A tingling sort of buzz had started to spread to Portia's fingertips.

Dell opened the front door without a knock and led her into a beautiful foyer, glowing under the light of a half-lit chandelier hanging from the ceiling.

Portia stepped reverently across a shining parquet floor and swept her gaze up along a wide curved staircase to her right, then past the open French doors on her left, which revealed a lovely parlor, and ahead to what could be a breakfast room. The atmosphere was elegant but simple, with only the bare minimum in the way of furniture and decoration.

Spinning in a slow circle, Portia soaked it in until she came back around to face Dell, who stood silent, with the front door still open at his back.

He looked more uncertain than she had ever seen him, as though he had left the door open behind him to allow for a quick retreat if it became necessary.

Portia's heart welled with love for him.

"I figured you would want to put your own touch on the place, so there is not much to show yet."

"It is ours?" she asked, though she had known it to be so the moment she'd crossed the threshold.

He nodded.

"It is perfect," Portia stated earnestly. "But how did you…?"

He shrugged. "My work has been very profitable over the years. I just never had anything to spend my money on until now."

Portia walked toward her husband and slipped her arms around his waist, pressing her body to his until she could feel his heart beat against hers. His arms came around her back, and he looked down at her.

"You are amazing," she murmured.

He shook his head. "I love you and want to share a true home with you."

"What of the place near St. James's? Your work?"

"Morley will continue to reside there. Honeycutt has moved on to greater things. Nightshade has a new contact man named Mr. Rivers."

"But won't he need an assistant?"

"Morley has recruited his nephew for the position, and there is Thomas, of course. But to be clear, this really only affects Honeycutt and will not change much for Nightshade or his other *associates*."

"Oh, thank goodness," Portia exclaimed with a heavy sigh of relief. "I was hoping you weren't trying to suggest a full retirement."

Dell chuckled, drawing her tighter to place a quick kiss against her temple. "Not yet, anyway. My new partner is just getting seasoned to the job."

Portia rose up on her tiptoes and lifted her mouth to his.

This kiss was anything but languid and soft. Need burned hot between them as Dell slid his hands down to grip her buttocks and pull her roughly against him.

Portia gasped. Her low belly tightened, and heat rushed to her core, making her ache for his touch.

"You had better show me where our bedroom is," she murmured huskily against his lips, "before I insist you take me right here on the floor."

Dell kicked the front door shut behind him. Then he had her up and tossed over his shoulder as he started across the hall in long strides. "I'll never make it to the bedroom," he said in a tone that sent delicious shockwaves through Portia's center. "The parlor will have to do."

Portia laughed and braced her hands on his firm buttocks.

"An excellent place to start, dear husband."

Read on for an excerpt from Elizabeth Michels's

# The WICKED HEIR

Book 3 in the Spare Heirs series
Coming July 2017 from Sourcebooks Casablanca

MOVEMENT CAUGHT FALLON'S EYE, BUT HE DIDN'T turn toward it. If Grapling was watching, it was best to allow him to think he and his friend weren't aware of his presence until the time was right. It helped that Brice was still rambling at his side, creating the perfect cover. "We'll need to have every auxiliary parlor checked," he stated. Then he saw one heavily lashed, round blue eye peer around the tower of sweets.

A heartbeat later, the owner of the blue eye made a quick retreat behind the trays, blond ringlets dancing in midair.

Someone was indeed watching them, but it wasn't Mr. Reginald Grapling.

"You take the card room while I stroll through the garden," Fallon said to Brice, collecting his thoughts. "If Grapling's still here, we'll find him and question him."

"A stroll through the garden? You're getting soft, St. James."

"On my way to my carriage," Fallon clarified, checking his pocket watch. As much as he would like to assess the threat Grapling posed, Fallon had to be across town in an hour. "I have quite a few meetings planned for this evening. Only a handful of minutes are left for the untimely return of a former Spare Heir."

Fallon glanced once more to the tower of cakes. The watchful eyes were back, this time in a gap where he was certain two slices of cake had been only a moment ago. He followed the line of sight back to his longtime friend, Brice.

Kelton Brice, who was a known bachelor and had no plans to change that fact? What lady in her right mind would glance in his direction if she were looking for anything more than an evening's entertainment?

Fallon stepped closer to the table in an attempt to see around the display. If someone was stalking one of his men—even if it was only a light-skirted lady—he needed to know of it. After all, he knew everything.

"I'll see to the card room and instruct the other Spares to keep a wary eye," Brice said, pulling Fallon's thoughts back to their present situation. "Will you need anything further from me tonight? There's this barmaid…"

Brice might see life as a game, but for Fallon, protecting the Spares, his men, was much more than that—it meant everything in his life. He was still watching Brice leave when he heard a small feminine sigh from behind the tower of sweets.

The lady bumped into the table as she attempted to skirt it and follow after Brice. The table shifted, knocking loose a tiny pillar holding up one of the great, head-high platters of sweets.

The next moment slowed to a series of heartbeats.

Fallon watched as the display wobbled ominously. Without thought, he reached out and caught the third tier from the top in an attempt to stabilize the display before the entire contraption could fall to pieces. His quick grab shifted the series of platters and stands in the opposite direction.

He sucked in a breath of vanilla-and-strawberry-scented air as the display began to slip toward the floor. Then a small, gloved hand caught the other side, and he found himself face-to-face with the ever-watchful lady with eyes only for his friend.

"Fancy a cake?" she asked, as her eyes cut over to the tower between them.

"Or fifty of them for that matter?" he returned, his gaze trapped, not leaving her.

She bit her lower lip and shifted her hold on the display. "I must admit, I'm rather surprised at the weight of this platter. I can see now why Mother gained a stone when she hired that new cook. Cakes always look so fluffy and light."

"Until you're balancing several score of them with the palm of your hand."

"Precisely," she said with a small laugh. "Why did you send Mr. Brice to the card room?"

Was this lady not at all concerned that if either of them moved the wrong way, the whole display could come tumbling down? She should be. He certainly was. "Wouldn't a better question be how are we going to remove ourselves from this predicament?"

"I suppose that depends on one's priorities," she murmured.

"And your priority is Mr. Brice." He eyed her. She

wasn't old enough to be a widow, and the innocent sparkle in her eyes showed a decided lack of any clandestine ideas. That left only one explanation. "You must know he's a confirmed bachelor."

"That means he's available."

"How do you reason that?"

"He isn't married," she said, as if explaining something to a child. "That fact is confirmed. Therefore, he is available for the prospect of marriage. That's what *confirmed bachelor* means."

"Do you think so? Because I know Brice quite well and—"

"He showed me a kindness once, winked at me," she cut in.

"He winked at you?"

Her eyes lit up. "He did. It was magical. He was visiting my father. He swooped in quite gallantly, and he winked. At me. There was a good-natured smile as well."

"Oh. All is explained then."

"Wonderful! I'm pleased it's settled. You can see now why I wouldn't want him to leave."

"Remind me to keep my grins to myself when in your company," he murmured.

"You think me that impetuous, that I go about hanging upon every smile of every gentleman?"

"No, I..." He didn't know what his thoughts were regarding this woman besides the obvious: perplexed.

"Go ahead then." She raised her chin in challenge. "If you dare. Smile. Do your best."

"Now?" He glanced around, noticing the room was empty—where were the blasted footmen?

"Here is mine." She smiled, and dawn seemed to break in the candlelit room.

Her smile crept into every cold crevice of his mind and warmed it with its light. It wasn't until a moment later, when the edge of the platter began to cut off blood flow to his fingers, that he realized he was staring at her. "What's your name?"

"When you haven't even offered me a kind smile?"

"I've saved you from—" He broke off, knowing he'd yet to save her from anything at all. He sighed. "Very well." He exercised the muscles in his cheeks and exposed his teeth in a smile.

She sighed and gave him a pitying shake of her head. "You're safe from a leg shackle with that. I'm Isabelle Fairlyn. You don't smile often, do you? I can see why. You really should work on it a bit more."

Fairlyn… Knottsby's daughter? Her name alone should have made him see the lady back to her chaperone and leave at once, but he was too busy being offended. "What's wrong with my smile?" His teeth were straight and white. No woman had ever complained of his looks before. And he'd never found fault in the mirror.

"Your smile lacks meaning." She adjusted her grip on the display. "Smiles should come from the heart."

"I'm holding up a tower of cakes at the moment. My *heart* is elsewhere."

"If you say so."

"St. James," he supplied, wondering if she would recognize the name.

"Ah. You have a terrible lack of a heartfelt smile but a nice name, Mr. St. James."

"Thank you?" He found he was relieved that she didn't know of him yet oddly saddened at the same time.

"You're welcome," she practically sang in return. "Now, how are we to get ourselves out of this mess?"

"Carefully. Move your left hand to the right. Your right, not my right. That's your left."

"I moved to the right."

"There!" he commanded with a bit too much force in an effort to still her movements. He glanced up and saw the top layer of the contraption wobble before stabilizing again. "Now, if we lift the top off, we can set it down on the table." He nodded toward his intended destination.

"On the fruit platter? We'll squash the berries!"

"I don't see another option, other than letting this thing crash to the floor and cover us both with icing. Or would you rather stay here forever? I could entertain you with my unnaturally affection-free smile."

"What about on the cold meats?"

"Berries have feelings about such things but ham doesn't? Think of the pigs when you say such a thing." Why was he arguing about this? He should set the damned platter down and leave for his meeting. He would be late as it was.

"I didn't mean to insult the pigs," she leaned in to implore. "If you only knew my affinity for animals of all kinds—nature in general, really—you wouldn't suggest such a thing."

"Meanwhile this platter isn't getting any lighter. Let's move to that side table just there and set this contraption down where no foods will be harmed."

"All right," she agreed with another bright smile. "How should we do this? Count to three?"

Three… Yes, counting would keep him from staring at her again. "One, two, three… What are you doing? I said three."

"Was it to be on three or after three?" she asked.

"Three! Three! Just move!" He shouldn't order a lady, but she didn't appear to be capable of following his direction anyway.

"We're going to the table across the room?" She moved with him down the long table as if they were involved in some intricate new dance to which neither knew the steps.

"All to save the berries and swine," he murmured as he rounded the end of the table and walked backward across the open floor.

"It's quite far," she complained. Then with a gasp, she exclaimed, "My grip is…"

The tiered platter crashed to the floor between them, sending bits of cake flying into the air. They both jumped back just in time to avoid being completely covered in icing.

"Slipping," she finished with a grimace.

"It may be a bit too late to ask you this, Lady Isabelle, but do you have issue with *cake* being harmed?"

They both glanced down at the bits of cake littering the floor between them. The platter had landed in a large heap and splattered sugary confection across the tops of his boots and the hem of her gown. He could use a thorough cleaning now, but the sprinkling of icing on her gown would likely go unnoticed.

Looking up, her large blue eyes met his once more,

this time rimmed with laughter. "As it happens, I believe I am quite fine with cake being harmed."

"Good. That's…good." He took her arm and pulled her toward the door until she was running to keep up.

"Where are we going?"

He glanced behind them and then back at her as they rounded the corner into the hall and kept moving. "If there's one thing I know, it's that you shouldn't ever be caught at the scene of a crime."

"That's the one thing you know? I know how to weave flowers together to make a wreath for my hair. And now I know how to bring terrible harm to a platter of cakes."

He began to laugh. His chest shook with it as if his body were knocking the cobwebs off of a seldom-used piece of furniture. He paused and looked down at her after they'd rounded another corner into a narrower hall.

"There," she said, staring up at him in amazement. For a long second, his chest contracted as he waited for her to explain her comment. Why was this wood nymph in a ball gown looking at him with such awe in her eyes? Her thoughts shouldn't matter to him. He was Fallon St. James. Men across the country feared and respected him for his work—that's what was truly important.

"You *are* capable of a heartfelt smile. You may need to worry about a leg shackle yet," she said, still looking up at him before blinking and taking a step away. "Not from me, of course. I have my sights set elsewhere. Nevertheless, you will do quite well this season."

He watched her as she took slow steps away from

him. Some irrational voice inside didn't want her to leave. "I don't want to do well this season."

"That's silly. Everyone wants to do well in their endeavors."

"I'm not endeavoring," he said, forcing himself to remain still. "I never endeavor—not in what you speak of anyway."

"Is this more *confirmed bachelor* talk?"

"I have obligations, business to see to—"

"With no time for dancing?" She gasped as she searched his face for some secret held there. "You don't dance, do you?"

Fallon let out a chuckle. When was the last time he'd laughed twice in an evening? "I really should..." he began and glanced away down the hall toward a door that led outside.

"You're planning to leave now, when it's still early in the evening," she replied with a tone of disapproval.

It wasn't often that anyone dared to disapprove of his actions.

"I am thankful for your aid in my escape tonight, Mr. St. James." She glanced over her shoulder toward the ballroom and the waltz playing there.

"Of course. Is there somewhere I could escort you? To your family perhaps."

"I've already taken up enough of your time." She took a few steps away before turning back to him once more. "Practice that smile in my absence."

He caught himself before promising to do just that. What was wrong with him?

"Stay away from falling cakes," he called after her. *And gentlemen like Brice*, he finished to himself.

"I can't make any promises," she said with a laugh, and she disappeared around the corner.

Fallon stood looking at the empty hall for a moment to gain his bearings, feeling as if he'd been thrown into sudden darkness as Lady Isabelle waltzed away. But a second later he was moving toward the rear of the house. As late as he was already, he would make one more lap through the ground floor in search of Grapling and then be on his way.

The Spare Heirs required all of his attention. He had nothing remaining for other *endeavors*, as Lady Isabelle had put it. Some gentlemen might have spare time for smiles, dancing, and staring after perplexing ladies, but he had the Spare Heirs Society to see to. And that was exactly how he preferred his life to be.

# About the Author

Amy Sandas's love of romance began one summer when she stumbled across one of her mother's Barbara Cartland books. Her affinity for writing began with sappy preteen poems and led to a bachelor's degree with an emphasis on creative writing from the University of Minnesota Twin Cities. She lives with her husband and children in north central Wisconsin.